POOLBEG
GROUP SERVICES

£200 worth of
Lily O'Briens chocolates to be won

Lily O'Briens
FINEST IRISH HANDMADE CHOCOLATES

IT'S A GREAT PLEASURE . . .

TOO LITTLE, TOO LATE

by

Colette Caddle

Bittersweet & Delicious

Lily O'Briens

finest handmade

chocolates

In a word – extraordinary

AN IRRESISTIBLE COMBINATION

for

20 lucky winners!

Go on, indulge yourself!

Simply complete the following in 25 words or less: *Too Little, Too Late* and Lily O'Briens an irresistible combination because:

_____

_____

_____

_____

_____

Post your entry with your name & address clearly marked *Too Little, Too Late* competition to: Poolbeg, 123 Baldoyle Ind Est, Baldoyle, Dublin 13.

Prizes awarded for best entry. Judge's decision is final. Closing date 26/4/99

Name: _____ Address: _____

Contact no: _____

Colette
CADDLE

TOO LITTLE, TOO LATE

POOLBEG

*All characters in this publication are fictitious
and any resemblance to real persons, living or
dead, is purely coincidental.*

Published 1999 by
Poolbeg Press Ltd,
123 Baldoyle Industrial Estate,
Dublin 13, Ireland

© Colette Caddle 1999

The moral right of the author has been asserted.

A catalogue record for this book is available from the British Library.

ISBN 1 85371 693 6

Cover photography by Retna
Cover design by Slatter Anderson
Set by Poolbeg Group Services Ltd in AGaramond 10.75/12.75
Printed in Scotland by Caledonian International
Book Manufacturing Ltd, Glasgow.

Acknowledgements

My thanks to Patsy McGuirk and Derry Clarke for spilling the beans on what really goes on behind the scenes in a restaurant!

To Gaye, Philip and everyone at Poolbeg for all the hard work. It's been an education!

It's impossible to write an acknowledgement and not mention the huge part played by Kate Cruise O'Brien in getting this book off the ground. I am eternally grateful for the time I had with her and deeply saddened that she's not here to see the finished product. Without her encouragement and support I would never have got this far.

On a personal note, my thanks to Trish Keogh who insisted that I send off the manuscript in the first place. Thanks, Trish!

Thanks to my darling son Peter – for sleeping!!

My eternal gratitude to my mother for encouraging me all the way and providing wonderful dinners and baby-sitting services! Thanks Mam.

Lastly, thanks to my better half, Tony, for always being there – no matter what life has thrown at us.

About the Author

Colette Caddle works in computers and marketing in the insurance industry. She lives in Dublin with her husband, Tony and new baby son, Peter. This is her first novel.

Dedicated, with love,
to the memory of my dad,
Stephen Lynott

CHAPTER ONE

"And the barman turned to the drunk and said, 'You can't leave *that* lyin' there!' And the drunk said, '*Thas* not a lion, thas a *ghiraffe*!'"

Annie looked blankly at Stephanie.

Stephanie shrugged. "Ah, it wasn't that bad. I suppose it's the way you tell 'em. Want another coffee?" The cafe was quiet at the moment and there was no queue at the counter.

"I thought you had to be back by twelve?" Annie checked her watch. It was ten to.

"There's no rush."

Annie raised an eyebrow. Her sister-in-law was always punctual. "What's up?" she asked when Steph returned with two steaming mugs.

Steph sat down and looked at Annie, her vivid blue eyes large and mournful. "Ah, just the usual."

"Look, if you're so miserable, why don't you leave? You'd walk into another restaurant, no problem."

Steph looked doubtful. "Think so?"

"Of course. You'd be snapped up."

Stephanie didn't have Annie's confidence in the job market. "But I don't *want* to leave Chez Nous. I love my job. It's just *him*. I can deal with the others, *even* George."

Annie shivered. "That man gives me the creeps."

Stephanie laughed. "George is a bit of a lecher but he's a good chef."

Annie wasn't convinced.

Steph added sugar-lumps to her coffee. "No, I can deal with him, and the other lads are great. Well, Sam's an asshole, but," she shrugged, "you get them in every walk of life. It's just . . ."

"It's just Chris. So what are you going to do?" Annie asked.

"Probably kill him," Stephanie replied simply. She lit a cigarette.

Annie took a cigarette from Steph's pack. "Don't tell your brother," she warned as Steph looked at her in surprise.

"Chris has turned into such an awful bastard," Steph continued. "I'm not really sure when it started to happen. I think it was once I established myself. Or as *he'd* say, when I got opinionated. I started to question some of his actions. Not something you're supposed to do with a head chef. He's difficult with everyone but I seem to get the worst of it. Probably because I'm a woman."

"I'd say it's because you stand up to him," Annie said wisely. "And if you do it in front of the others . . ." She shrugged.

Steph laughed. "Yeah, you're right. That really gets him going. Maybe if we got Liz to come back it would put him on the straight and narrow."

Annie frowned. The last person who could sort Chris out was his wife. Liz was great fun, a good friend and pretty sharp when it came to sizing people up, but she had one blind spot. Chris. Annie hadn't admitted it, even to Steph, but she'd never liked Chris Connolly. There was something about him she didn't trust. He was a pompous man. Full of his own importance. From what Stephanie said, he seemed to have got even worse.

Still, Liz seemed to be happy, and her life had been complete when their daughter was born. She'd lost interest in Chez Nous, spending all of her time with her baby. She reminded anyone who'd listen that Lucy's father had to work long and unsociable hours and that it was important that one parent was always there for their daughter.

It was strange how birth affected some women, Annie thought. Liz used to be very ambitious. She'd been the driving force in the early days of Chez Nous. She was the one who pushed Chris to leave a trendy city-centre bistro and buy a restaurant in Temple Bar. She'd been working and sweating at his side when they'd got the Michelin Star, two years later. And it had been Liz who realised that they needed a good manager, namely Stephanie, to leave them free to concentrate on the food.

It was no surprise that Liz had given up work. It was difficult to leave a new baby. But Annie was surprised by how completely she'd bowed out. She'd been an accomplished chef, responsible for the impossibly delicious desserts served in Chez Nous. Now, she seemed satisfied to stay at home.

Annie tucked an auburn curl behind her ear and turned her attention back to Stephanie. "I don't think Liz is the

3

answer. Does she know what's going on between the two of you?"

Steph thought for a moment. "I doubt it. I haven't said anything and Chris doesn't seem to discuss work with her any more. I try to behave myself when she's around. On a good day I can even manage to smile at him."

"Well done," Annie replied, her green eyes twinkling. "It'll stand to your defence when you top him!"

"Oh Annie, what am I going to do?"

"Stop moaning for a start. There must be something you can do. Let's look at the options. Killing him is one. Any others?"

"I could buy him out."

"OK. Do you think he'd be interested in selling?"

Steph made a face. "That was a joke, Annie."

"Why?" Annie replied equably. "You've got the money Uncle Jack left you. I'm sure you could get a loan for the rest easily enough."

Stephanie looked at her, slightly shocked. "I'd better get back."

"OK," Annie smiled calmly.

Steph stood up, pulled on her coat and fumbled with the buttons. She looked at Annie warily. "I'll give you a ring. Oh, the bill . . ." She opened her bag, rummaging for her purse.

Annie waved her away. "I'll take care of it. You go on. Phone me."

"Yes, yes I will." Steph left, pausing at the door briefly to stare back at her friend.

Annie stubbed out her cigarette. Joe would kill her for putting such wild ideas in his little sister's head. He was very protective of her. Silly man. Steph was more than capable of looking after herself, and her problems were a lot more exciting than Annie's. Than, where was Joe's favourite tie? Would Danielle's teddy dry before she woke up? How could she disguise vegetables so that Shane would eat them? "Stop feeling sorry for yourself, woman," she muttered and gathered up her bags. She paid the bill and made her way over to Dunnes. Now what would she get for dinner? Some smoked salmon for starters. A little treat. Joe would like that.

* * *

"Where the hell were *you*?" Chris barked as a blonde head flashed past the kitchen door.

Steph walked back slowly. "Is there a problem, chef?" she said quietly. She was damned if she was going to make excuses for being less than five minutes late, in front of all the kitchen staff.

"You've to sort out the wine order and I told you I want Reilly's to take back those rotten potatoes." Chris glared at her before going back to the fish he was preparing.

"I've sent in the wine order," she replied calmly, "and Reilly's are sending over a van to pick up the potatoes and drop off replacements. They've also agreed to give us a discount on the next order."

Chris snorted and continued filleting.

Steph caught Conor's eye and winked. "Anything else I can do for anybody?"

"*There's* an offer." George sidled up and slipped an arm around her slim waist.

"Dream on," Steph said and moved out of his grasp and into the hallway.

"Stephanie?"

Steph turned and smiled at Marc, one of their newest recruits. He was very young but showed great talent. He was quiet and worked hard. The best and most unusual combination in a chef, she thought wryly. "Yes, Marc? What can I do for you?"

"I was hoping to take some time off. *Maman*, she is not well. Chef said I should get you to check the roster. He was not . . . eh . . . happy." Marc faltered, his cheeks red.

"I can imagine. Come on up to the office and we'll see what we can do. Your mother, is she back in hospital?"

"*Oui*, yes, and Papa he wants to be with her, but the business . . ." Michel Le Brun ran a small vineyard near Bordeaux and lived in constant fear of his grapes being rejected by the local co-operative.

"I understand. How much time do you need?"

"A week?"

Stephanie hung her coat up and took out the roster. This should be Chris, Conor or George's responsibility, but it had become hers. It was one of the most difficult parts of her job. If she got the balance wrong and they were understaffed, she brought the wrath of all the chefs on her unlucky head. There was open warfare between them as to whose needs were greater. But there was no problem this time. No one was on holidays, no one was off sick and two trainees had just started. "Pat has Saturday off. You can go on Sunday but could you be back by the following Saturday?"

"*Bien sur*, certainly. Thank you, Stephanie." He smiled broadly and ran back down to the kitchen.

Stephanie threw the jacket of her black wool suit carelessly over the back of a chair and turned her attention to the post. Lots of brown envelopes. Great! She was still wading through them an hour later when Chris came in.

"I've got to go out. Any problems, talk to Conor."

Stephanie looked pointedly at her watch. It was the second time this week he'd done a runner at lunch-time.

He shifted uncomfortably like a naughty schoolboy. "Everything's in hand. It's unlikely there'll be any more customers arriving at this stage. Good experience for Conor anyway."

Stephanie didn't bother to reply. When Chris had left she slipped on her jacket and took out her compact to check her hair and make-up. She added some more grey eyeshadow to the corner of her lids, touched up her foundation and renewed the coral lipstick. After flicking a comb through her short bob, she went down to the restaurant. The large room hummed with muted conversations and staff moved quietly and efficiently between the tables. The stark white table linen was a wonderful contrast to the dark green of the walls and carpet and the formal scene was softened by a cheerful fire crackling in the grate of the large fireplace. The restaurant was full and five tables were on starters, while three waited for their main course. "A great time for the head chef to walk out," Steph thought angrily. She went out to the kitchen. A rush of heat hit her as she pushed open the door. She stood for a moment taking in the scene. She never tired of watching the team at work and the intense concentration on their faces as they prepared the food. Each dish was unique, each portion a creation. Though totally different people in personality, from a variety of backgrounds, the chefs all shared one passion: food. Steph had seen Pat throw out a whole pan of sauce if he wasn't happy with the texture or seasoning. George cursed anyone and everyone near him when something went wrong, and would crack a joke or break into song five minutes later. Conor would refuse to cook beef if the meat hadn't been hung for long enough and argued vociferously with Chris over the menu if the necessary herbs weren't available. Steph found herself refereeing and calming tempers on these occasions. In stark contrast, the pastry chef, John Quigly, talked to no one and no one bothered him. He was first in each morning and the first to leave. He worked quietly, efficiently and merely blinked when Chris screamed or raged at him. Steph sometimes wondered if he was a bit deaf. Not such a bad thing when you worked for someone like Chris.

She went over to Conor, but when she saw the look of fixed concentration on his face, she moved on to Pat who was preparing a sauce to accompany the *confit* of duck.

She sniffed appreciatively. "That smells good."

He flashed her a grin. "Taste." He held a spoon to her lips.

She tasted and nodded her head, rolling her eyes in ecstasy.

That wasn't enough for Pat. "Is it too bland? Maybe a little more seasoning?"

She shook her head. "It's perfect," she assured him firmly. Pat was one of the few chefs in Chez Nous who invited comment. Most of them were dismissive of any criticism, constructive or otherwise, especially if it came from someone front of house. It amazed Steph that Liz had survived in this atmosphere. But then she'd been the pastry chef and generally left alone. Anyway, she was a bloody hard worker and an excellent chef and had earned a grudging respect from her colleagues.

Steph watched Marc tie small bunches of string beans together with strips of red and yellow peppers. She shook her head, amazed at his patience. Jim was beside him, painstakingly piping the Chez Nous version of creamed potatoes into a perfect cone. He looked up at Marc expectantly.

Marc inspected the creation. *"Bon,"* he said simply.

Jim flushed with delight. Steph smiled at the young commis. He was going to do just fine. She glanced around the room. It was noisy and hot, but there was little or no conversation. They were oblivious to her, engrossed in their work.

It was a weird business, but she loved it. And for all their idiosyncrasies, she respected the talent around her and tolerated the temperaments that went with it. How could she ever think of leaving?

CHAPTER TWO

"Yes, Paddy, I understand that but . . . well, yes, I see your point and I agree . . . well, I'm sure Chris didn't mean that *quite* the way it sounded . . . " Steph looked up to see Conor in the doorway. She waved him in.

"Paddy, I'm sorry about all this. I've sent off the cheque and I'm sure that Chris really does appreciate your point . . . yes, yes, of course, right, sure, thanks . . . bye now, thanks again." She put down the phone and banged her head on the desk.

Conor laughed. "Well, that sounded like fun. Paddy Brennan?"

Steph nodded. "Chris told him where to shove his fish and that his bill could go the same way."

Conor shook his head. "Our chef, the diplomat. You can always rely on him."

Steph frowned. "It's not funny. He can't treat people like this. We won't have any suppliers left. And what if he starts on the customers?"

She offered Conor a cigarette and he lit up and stretched his long, lanky frame in the chair in front of her.

Restaurant managers and chefs rarely got on and never

socialised but Conor and Steph were way past that now and were quite close. Conor had joined the team over two years before and initially had taken a leaf from Chris's book in his treatment of Steph and other front-of-house staff. Chris had enjoyed the hostility that built up between the two and fanned the flames on more than one occasion. Over time, though, Conor came to realise how heavily Chris relied on Stephanie and that she was actually damn good at her job. She in turn had to acknowledge that, unlike his boss, Conor worked very hard, loved food and had a quirky sense of humour when you got to know him. Gradually they came to support each other when Chris was being difficult and the initial dislike was replaced by respect and friendship. Conor was an artist, who wanted to spend all of his time and effort on the food. He hated having to deal with rosters and staff problems. The only admin work he undertook was supervising food deliveries. Routine matters he was happy to leave to Stephanie and Chris didn't care once the work was done. She was a good manager and things went smoothly when she was around.

"Ah, don't let him get to you," he advised her now. "They're all well used to him. Paddy will call him a few names, but he won't want to lose the business. You shouldn't worry so much."

"You're right," she agreed, "but he drives me nuts. He spends all his time giving out about everyone and everything, but if *he* screws up, he finds someone else to carry the can. Usually me."

"Or me," Conor pointed out.

Steph nodded. "Or you. He's been giving you a hard time lately, hasn't he?"

11

"Yeah, but then you can't have everything. *Sous-chef* at twenty-four, I can't complain. Anyway, the more Chef skives off, the more experience I get. If it weren't for George . . ." He grimaced at the thought of the older chef who made his life miserable.

"Well, George isn't good at taking orders at the best of times. Taking them from a young fella like you . . ." She shrugged.

"Got a minute, Stephanie?" Sam said from the doorway, ignoring Conor.

"I'll leave you to it." Conor glared at Sam and was out the door in a flash.

Steph didn't blame him. She'd leave too if she could! Sam was a reasonably good head waiter but his attitude had always irritated Steph. He was constantly whinging about something, yet when Chris was around he positively fawned over him. Chris wasn't really taken in, but he enjoyed the flattery and ass-licking that Sam did so well. Steph forced a smile. "Sam, come in. Have we a full house tonight?"

The head waiter gave her a long-suffering look over the rim of his book. "No, we don't. We could fit in two tables for two or one for six. The new play's opening at Andrew's Lane tonight, that may bring in some punters. We really should think about doing some kind of promotion or advertising."

Steph sighed. Not that old chestnut. She decided to ignore it. It was unlikely the new play would bring in customers. Chez Nous wasn't the kind of restaurant you dropped into on the off-chance, unless you were a tourist and didn't know any better. It was the third time in as many weeks that they'd had empty tables on a Thursday.

"Lavinia Reynold's review may be hurting us," she said at last.

Sam frowned. "Do you think so? It wasn't *that* bad."

Steph looked at him, eyebrows raised. "Not that bad? Are you kidding? *'Prices are up, standards are down.'* That's as bad as it gets. Lavinia's out for blood."

"Why not invite her back?" Sam asked. "Point out that everyone has a bad night."

"It might work," Steph admitted grudgingly, "but the invitation would have to come from Chef. Lavinia wouldn't stand for less and there's no hope of Chris agreeing to grovel to her.

Sam shrugged. "Well, pride is cold comfort when you go out of business." He turned on his heel and walked out of the room.

Steph stuck her tongue out at his receding back. Prat! Still, he was right. She'd have to have a word with Chris.

*   *   *

Stephanie drove across the East Link Bridge, tapping her finger on the wheel in time to the song on the radio. She glowered at the little old lady who attempted to cut her off on the bend.

"Not on your life, missus," she growled. She checked the time. Six thirty! She was never going to make it on time. Oh well, Seán would forgive her. He always did.

Stephanie had first met Seán Adams at a student's party fourteen years ago. He'd been at college with Ruth. Poor

Ruth . . . she shook her head. Don't think about it. Not tonight.

Within a month of meeting, Steph and Seán were inseparable. They liked the same books, the same food, finished each other's sentences. They were made for each other. After Ruth died, though, it sort of fizzled out. When Seán left to work in Apple in Cork, it never occurred to him to ask Stephanie to go with him. He already knew the answer.

He'd been back in Dublin two years now. Ten years, one failed marriage and one son later. Stephanie had bumped into him in Doheny and Nesbitt's and they quickly slipped back into an easy relationship. They rarely discussed Karen, Seán's soon-to-be-ex-wife, or Billy, his young son. Seán didn't offer any information and she didn't ask. She was happy he was back in her life. The only fly in the ointment was his insistence that they should marry as soon as he was free. Stephanie loved him. She didn't want anybody else. But marriage? The thought of publicly putting all of her trust in one man, even if that man was Seán . . . It frightened her, after all this time, that she was still reluctant to make a commitment. She shivered. What in God's name did Seán see in her? She wouldn't even let him move in. She liked waking up beside him, but there were times when she preferred to be alone.

She moved up a gear and turned up through Clontarf heading towards Malahide and her little apartment. At least they were eating nearby so she could still probably grab a quick shower before Seán arrived. It had been a while since she'd been in Bon Appetit and she was looking forward to a relaxing evening and great food.

Her thoughts turned to Annie and her comments this morning. Buy out Chris. It was a scary thought. An amazing, wonderful but ludicrous idea. What would Seán say?

The traffic-lights at McAllister's Garage were red. She tilted the rear-view mirror and inspected her image critically. God, she looked terrible. Dark circles under her eyes, pale face, dull hair. Late nights, too much wine and not enough exercise were taking their toll. She'd go to the gym in the morning. Well, she would if she got a reasonably early night. And if she didn't have a hangover. Oh, what the hell. Her health would just have to wait.

Seán Adams waited patiently as Stephanie studied the menu. He knew she wasn't choosing her meal. She was sizing up prices, studying combinations and storing them away to relay to Conor tomorrow. It was his own fault for suggesting they eat at Bon Appetit. He wondered absently what he'd be eating tonight. Steph would choose. Well no, she'd *suggest*. She never had the same dishes as he did. To her, that was a missed opportunity. When she was in a restaurant, she wanted to experience as many dishes as possible. She often charmed the head waiter into giving her half portions of two main courses.

"Are you ready to order yet, or should I send out for McDonald's to keep me going?" he asked.

"Oh, stop moaning." The dazzling flash of blue eyes took the sting out of her words and made his heart flip.

"What do you fancy?"

"You," he replied with a leer. "Oh sorry, you mean food?

Well, I was going to have the bisque and then the Sole McGuirk. Is that OK with you?"

Steph looked indignant. "Of course," she replied, "though I *thought* you might like to try the Clonakilty black pudding to start."

"I suppose I would," he agreed and was rewarded with another broad smile.

"And I'll have the scallops," she continued happily. "I suppose you *could* have the sole but then there's the duck. OK, sole it is," she said hurriedly when she saw his expression. "*I'll* have the duck. Now what about the wine?"

Seán scanned the list. "How about a half bottle of white Hermitage to start and then the Côte de Beaune?"

Steph licked her lips. "Perfect."

They gave their order and settled back with their drinks, enjoying the warmth of the fire in the cosy sitting-room. Steph studied Seán and thought, not for the first time, how handsome he was. The black-brown wavy hair that hung to his shoulders when they'd first met was now cut tight and stopped half an inch short of his shirt collar. The eyes, that were almost as dark as his hair, usually twinkled with amusement but had been known, very occasionally, to flash with temper. His style was casual but sophisticated. Tonight he wore a grey suit that was simply cut but obviously expensive. His shirt was the palest blue, and his silk tie was a blaze of colour, showing the slightly rebellious side of his nature.

She smiled at him. "So any news? How are things in the cut-throat world of software?"

"Cut-throat," Seán responded drily. "No, not bad at all, actually. I just landed myself a nice little contract. Only it's not so little."

Steph's eyes widened. "Not the American plastics company?"

Seán nodded, pleased that she'd remembered. Karen had never shown much interest in his work.

"That's fantastic!" she squealed. "Congratulations!"

Seán reddened as a couple of people turned to stare at him and his beautiful girlfriend.

"Thanks, but there's no need to tell everyone," he said, both pleased and embarrassed.

Steph laughed. "Of course there is. They should all drink to Dublin's newest entrepreneur. My God, Seán! You're only in business two years, and look at what you've accomplished. If you won't blow your own trumpet, I'll do it for you." She lifted her glass. "Seriously, love. I'm so proud of you. Well done!"

"Thanks, I must say I am pretty chuffed with myself. Their IT director was a tough nut to crack, but once we got talking, we clicked. I'm looking forward to working with him."

"Is he Irish or American?"

"American. From Phoenix, Arizona. That's where the company's based. I'll be going out there for a while," he added casually.

Steph's face clouded. "How long is 'a while'?" she asked quietly.

"A couple of months," he said, pleased to see her look of dismay. No matter how long or how intimately he'd known

17

this woman, he was never quite sure how she felt about him. When she was hurt or sad, she withdrew into a shell and wouldn't let him near her. It hurt him, and she knew it, but she couldn't seem to do anything about it. Even after all these years.

He'd once tentatively suggested that maybe she should talk to someone, get professional help, but she'd been shocked and upset at the suggestion and he hadn't brought it up again. Occasionally when they'd had a few drinks and she was relaxed, he'd tried to talk to her about Ruth, but she would clam up immediately, her face a mask of misery and anger.

"Come with me," he said before he lost the courage.

Steph looked blank. "What?"

"Come to Phoenix with me. Why not? You're miserable at work. It would be good for you, for both of us."

She stared at him, confused. "But, but what about my job, I couldn't take so much time off . . . oh . . . you want me to *leave*?"

"Why not?" he asked. "I left my job and made a new life, why shouldn't you? There comes a time when you just have to admit defeat and move on. This could be your opportunity."

Stephanie looked at him steadily, her face pale. "But you're not talking about me making a fresh start, you're saying I should throw in the towel and go on holiday. I couldn't work in the States. Are you mad?" Her voice rose. She finished her drink and lit a cigarette.

"You could get a job when we got back. You'd walk into another restaurant."

That's what Annie had said, she thought. No problem. But how could she walk away from *this* job without feeling a loser? Her dad had always said that there was no point in running away from problems. No matter what you did for a living, you were bound to come up against difficult people or situations. You just had to knuckle down and learn how to cope with them. So why couldn't she? She'd wanted to tell Seán about her conversation with Annie but now it all seemed a bit silly.

"So will you come?" he asked.

"Your table is ready, if you'd like to follow me."

Steph stood up, grateful for the interruption, and followed the waiter.

* * *

"You never answered me," Seán commented as they wandered back to the apartment, hand in hand.

"I can't go with you, Seán. You know how I feel about my job. It's the first job I felt I could do really well. I'd feel a failure if I gave up now, and I'd probably end up blaming you."

Seán said nothing. He was tired. He wanted a steady comfortable relationship. He wanted a wife and a home. The split with Karen had been tough and he missed Billy every day. He couldn't believe his luck when he'd rediscovered Steph, and now it looked as if he was going to lose her again.

"So that's that," he said sadly.

Steph looked up in surprise. "What do you mean?

You're only going for a couple of months. I'll be here when you get back, you silly sod. Nothing's changed."

"Sure about that?" He cupped her cheek with his hand.

She turned her head and kissed his palm. "I'm very sure about that," she said as she reached up to kiss him. "Let me prove it to you," she whispered and led him up the steps to the apartment.

CHAPTER THREE

"What time is your flight?" Steph fiddled with the frills on the sofa cushion.

"Ten." Seán took her hands in his and held them tightly. "Look, Steph, I don't want you to come to the airport. Let's just say goodbye now. I'll call you as soon as I get there."

Steph swallowed her protest. She knew how Seán hated emotional farewells. "Sure. Whatever you want, love. Don't you go falling for anyone though," she warned him, trying half-heartedly to inject some humour into the conversation. "I expect you to concentrate on your work and have plenty of early nights. Alone."

"Yes, ma'am." Seán saluted and then pulled her into his arms with a groan. "Oh, I'm going to miss you so much. It's going to be weird going to restaurants and eating what *I* want to eat."

Steph punched him. "You're supposed to be whispering sweet nothings in my ear, not slagging me!"

"Sweet nothings, sweet nothings, sweet nothings," Seán mumbled obediently in her ear.

Steph pulled back and looked at him intently. "Hurry back, Seán. Please."

"I will," he promised her. He looked at his watch. "I better get going."

Steph stood at the door long after Seán's car disappeared around the corner. Eventually she went back inside and huddled up on the sofa. She felt an emptiness that she hadn't expected. A chill of loneliness that hadn't been there when he'd gone to Cork all those years ago. But they'd only been kids then. And anyway, Ruth had been all she could ever think about. Ruth and how she'd let her down.

* * *

"Ask me another question, Steffi," Ruth implored, pulling distractedly at the mass of brown curls framing her small face.

Stephanie took a drag of her cigarette and blew the air out the window. "OK, OK," she agreed, scanning the book in front of her. "Why is transpiration useful to plants?"

Ruth paced the room, chewing on her pen. "Eh, I know this one . . ."

"You know every one," Stephanie replied.

"Eh, because it supplies water and minerals to the leaves and cools them down in hot weather."

"Correct. See, I told you, Ruth. You know it all."

"And do you know it all?" Catherine West said from the doorway, a tray of tea and biscuits in her hands.

"Oh Mam, you're the best." Stephanie tried frantically to stub out her cigarette behind her back. When she finally succeeded, she hopped off the bed and cleared books off the

corner of her dressing-table. Her mother set down the tray. "Of course I know it all, Mam. Oh ye of little faith!"

"Of course you do, dear. Take a break now, Ruth love. A cup of tea will do you good."

"Thanks, Mrs West. You're very good to let me study here. I wouldn't get a minute's peace at home."

Ruth was the eldest of six children and it was hard to find a quiet corner in the three-bedroom semi-detached house. Steffi was lucky. With only one brother, she had a bedroom all to herself. Ruth couldn't wait to leave home. She'd miss her mam but it was the only way if she was ever to get a bit of privacy.

"Now don't stay up too late, girls. A good night's sleep is more important at this stage. Best of luck tomorrow, Ruth. You'll be fine." Catherine paused halfway out the door. "Make sure you put that cigarette out properly, Stephanie."

Ruth burst out laughing when the door closed. "There's no foolin' your mam, Steffi."

Stephanie shook her head in wonder. "I swear she's eyes in the back of her head. Either that or she's got the place bugged. Ah, one of these days I'll have my own place. I'll get a brilliant job, buy a car and a nice little flat in Ranelagh. What about you, Ruth?"

Ruth didn't believe in day-dreaming. She had very definite plans for the future. Once she got into Trinity it would be plain sailing. She'd work like the devil himself to get the best possible marks. She'd get her degree in Computer Science and then she'd join one of the big companies. Maybe IBM. "A flat would be nice," she said finally. "But it's all very well talking, Steph. What are you going to actually do?"

This was a conversation the two girls had regularly. Ruth was amazed at Steph's casual attitude towards getting a job and Steph couldn't begin to understand Ruth's driving ambition. For all their differences though, they were best friends and while Ruth helped Stephanie with her maths homework, Stephanie helped Ruth with Shakespeare and Yeats.

"I'll apply to the banks and the insurance companies and the civil service. You know, the usual. I'm not like you, Ruth. I'm not sure what I want to do yet. I need some time to figure out what I'm good at."

Ruth nibbled on a digestive biscuit. "I can't believe the Leaving actually begins tomorrow."

Steph twirled around the bed. "Imagine. In two weeks' time we'll be finished with school forever. No more uniforms, no more homework! Oh, it's going to be a great summer."

"I'll have to get a job," Ruth pointed out. "I need to save up some pocket-money for college. Dad's paying all my fees, I can't expect him to fork out any more."

"Yeah, he'd give you his last penny if he had to," Steph agreed. "His darling daughter, brainy and beautiful."

"And modest," Ruth added. She threw her maths book to Steph. "Ask me something."

Steph groaned. "Do I have to? I'm actually beginning to look forward to tomorrow. At least I won't have to spend the day swatting with you."

Ruth was unperturbed. "Don't forget I'm coming over tomorrow night. We need to cram for the English exam."

* * *

"So will you call her?"

"What?" Chris looked blank.

Steph swallowed hard. "Lavinia Reynolds. Will you call her?" God, did the man not listen or was Alzheimer's setting in?

"Stupid oul cow. She wouldn't know good food if it jumped up and bit her."

Count to ten, Stephanie. "Maybe not, but she's still the most respected restaurant critic in Dublin. It's better to have her with you than against you. Look at Jean-Jacque. She's done him a lot of good." Reverse psychology, she thought smugly, as his face went purple. Mentioning Chris's arch-rival was sure to push his blood pressure up.

"That bastard!" Chris spluttered. "He doesn't cook. Everything comes out of a freezer and into a microwave."

"Allegedly," Stephanie replied, straight-faced.

Chris glared at her. "OK, I'll talk to her."

Steph sighed in relief. "Good. Here's the number." She handed him a card and waited.

"Now?" he asked uncomfortably.

"No time like the present," she insisted.

He dialled the number. "Lavinia, my love, how are you?"

Stephanie stood up, smiling. Sometimes she got her own way.

* * *

"Hello, Steph? It's Annie."

"Hiya, Annie." Steph leaned back in her chair, glad of the interruption. "How are things?"

"Great, no problems. I was wondering if you fancied a

night out. Get Liz to come along. Just the three of us like in the bad old days."

"Sounds good to me," Steph replied. "I could do with a few laughs. Just promise me it's not going to be your place with a bottle of Bull's Blood."

Annie laughed. "God, how did we ever drink that stuff! No, I was thinking of something a bit more up-market. When's your day off?"

"Tomorrow, but I've got an awful lot to do. How about Monday?"

"Yeah, that's fine. Why don't you come over early? We could go down to the gym, have a sauna and a beauty session." Annie and Joe were members of an elite health club in Clontarf that also housed an excellent beauty salon and hairdresser's. Steph had become a regular guest of Annie's and was planning to join.

Steph smiled. "That sounds like just what the doctor ordered. Liz probably won't go for it though. You know what she's like."

"Well, tell her to bring Lucy. I'm going to have to get a baby-sitter anyway. She could stay the night. Danielle would be chuffed to have a playmate to sleep over."

"That's a good idea. You're not just a pretty face. I'll give her a call and ring you back."

"Steph!" Liz reacted with genuine delight to the voice on the other end of the phone. "How are things? I haven't talked to you in ages. What's the problem, fed up putting up with Chris all day, every day?"

Stephanie cringed. Liz was a lot closer to the truth than she realised. "Absolutely! But then he always drove me nuts,

26

you know that." She quickly changed the subject. "How are things? How's that beautiful goddaughter of mine?"

Liz settled herself at the foot of the stairs and cradled the phone in her lap. "Taking after her father and driving me nuts. Ah no, she's great really. I seem to spend my life chauffeuring her from ballet class to parties to swimming. Her social life is better than mine but then that wouldn't be hard."

Stephanie didn't miss the sad note in her friend's voice. "Well, we'll have to do something about that then," she said cheerfully. "What you need is a girlies' night out! Annie was just on. We're organising a get-together on Monday. We'll get the glad rags on, have a few drinks, a bite to eat – *not* in Chez Nous," she added hastily, "and then on to one of those trendy clubs for a bop. How about it?"

"Oh, I don't know, Steph! I'd have to get a baby-sitter and I've nothing to wear since I put on all this damn weight and then, well, Chris doesn't really like me to go to clubs without him." She caught sight of her reflection in the hall mirror. Her mane of dark hair was dishevelled and badly in need of a good cut. She wore no make-up and there was a smudge of flour on her nose. She wiped it away with floury hands and succeeded only in spreading the damage across her cheek. She looked at herself in despair. The large brown eyes mocked her for the dowdy mum she'd become.

"Stop making excuses," Stephanie broke in on her thoughts. "It's all arranged. You bring Lucy over to Annie's and she'll organise a baby-sitter for the three of them, and she can stay the night. Come on, Lizzie, you know Lucy would love that."

Liz wavered.

"We'll go and get our hair done, have a massage, facial, the works! Then, back to my place, open a bottle while we get into something black, slinky and sexy – it'll be just like the old days."

Liz laughed. "No Bull's Blood, OK?"

"No, I'll spend at least three quid on the wine. Promise. The airs and graces of you! In the good old days you'd have drunk cider and liked it! Anyway, then we'll go on to a club and bop till we drop."

"That should take all of ten minutes," said Liz drily.

"Oh, shut up," Steph said briskly. "You're thirty-five not ninety-five."

Liz glanced back at her reflection. The sloppy jumper and leggings didn't do much to hide her bulging stomach and flabby thighs. "I don't feel it," she said gloomily,

"Oh come on, Liz, it will be fun. Lucy will have a ball." Steph was alarmed at her friend's tone. She sounded so depressed.

"I'm not sure what Chris will say."

Who gives a shit? Steph thought, but said, "I'm sure he'll be delighted. He's always saying you should get out more, that you deserve a break."

"He is?" Liz was doubtful.

Steph crossed her fingers. "He is. So, now that we've dealt with all your excuses, madam, what's it going to be?"

"Let's do it," Liz said simply.

"That's my girl! I'll pick you up. About two? I'll sort everything out with Annie, seeya then." Steph rang off before Liz could have a change of heart.

"We're all set," Steph said when Annie answered the phone.

"Great stuff? What time?"

"I'm picking them up at two, so we should be with you by three."

"Grand. I'll phone Jeanette and warn her. Seeya then."

* * *

When Liz put down the phone she was still smiling. It would be nice to have a night out. It was ages since she'd got dressed up and gone out without Chris in tow. She frowned as she thought of how her husband was likely to react. She found it hard to believe he'd told Steph she should get out more. He hardly ever took her out these days and he wasn't happy when she went out with anyone else either, especially Steph. Maybe he was jealous. She chuckled softly. That was a nice thought! If he still got jealous, surely that meant that he still cared? Maybe there was hope for them yet. If she could just get him to spend a bit more time at home. She looked at her figure critically in the mirror. It was no wonder he was losing interest in her. She'd let herself go. She couldn't really blame him if he strayed – she wasn't doing a whole lot to hold his interest. She'd never been beautiful, not like Steph. She thought of her gorgeous, confident friend. She had it all, Liz thought enviously and wandered back to the kitchen and her pastry.

She caught sight of Lucy through the kitchen window and her heart lifted. The little girl was scampering around the garden with a jamjar, chasing after unsuspecting bees. She smiled fondly at her antics. Oh, well. Maybe Steph didn't *really* have it all.

* * *

Steph sat frowning at the phone. It looked as if she wasn't the only one having problems with Chris. Liz didn't sound too happy. She wondered if Chris was playing around. George had hinted as much on more than one occasion, and he would know. They were great boozing buddies and Chris was the type who'd boast about his conquests. What in God's name would any intelligent woman see in him? And what would her guide dog think? She chuckled at her bitchiness. Still, Liz had seen something in him. She supposed Chris had been different when he was younger. He'd always been a bit of a flirt but he'd seemed happy enough to settle down with Liz and when Lucy came along he'd been as proud as punch. It was later that he started to change. Once Liz was out of the way he'd turned into a patronising bully and a lazy bugger to boot. When he was on the premises, he was usually eating and drinking the profits. The rest of the time he spent visiting other restaurants. He said he had to keep an eye on the competition.

The effects of his self-indulgence were beginning to show. A good-looking man when he was younger, he now had serious problems keeping his weight under control. His eyes were puffy and red, his jowl slack and his once-skilful hands shook slightly. He was only forty-three but moved like a man of sixty. He still had a roving eye and, unfortunately for Liz, there would always be women who were flattered by the attentions of a famous restaurateur.

Steph wondered if, when he checked up on other restaurants, he had company. She knew he rarely took Liz out these days. There had been times when Liz had said that Chris was working late when Steph knew he wasn't. She never told Liz, though, and usually tried to change the subject. Not to protect Chris – she owed him nothing and was sorely tempted to land him in deep water – but she didn't want to hurt Liz. Besides, she'd no *real* evidence and even Chris Connolly didn't deserve to be judged on the basis of gossip. She put Chris to the back of her mind. Thinking of him only annoyed and upset her. She forced her attention back to the books in front of her. Her brother would be here in an hour to go over the accounts. It wasn't going to be a pleasant afternoon.

CHAPTER FOUR

Stephanie parked her blue Toyota Corolla outside the imposing detached house in the quiet cul-de-sac off the Stillorgan Road. She blew the horn a few times and was greeted with shrieks and giggles as a little body raced down the driveway, teddy bear in one hand, pencil-case in the other.

"Hiya, Auntie Steph," Lucy said breathlessly as she tugged on the back door.

Steph reached back and swung it open for her. "Hello, princess! All set?"

Lucy nodded enthusiastically, but then frowned. "Mummy said not to bring any paper. She said Auntie Annie would have some. Do you think she will?" Lucy looked worriedly from her pencils to Stephanie.

"I know she will," Steph promised solemnly, "and I happen to know she has colouring books and there are lots of other surprises."

"What are they?" demanded Lucy excitedly, hauling herself up by Steph's headrest.

"You'll find out soon enough, young lady," Liz said as she pulled open the door and flung a couple of bags in beside Lucy. She tied the wriggling child into her seat before climbing into the passenger seat.

"Hi, Steph, sorry to keep you waiting, but this one takes so much time deciding what she's going to bring." She rolled her eyes in mock horror, but they were full of laughter and love.

"Well, Mummy, I had to show Danielle my new crayons and Ted would have been lonely if I left him here."

"Quite right, Lucy." Steph started the engine and slipped into first gear. "Let's go, folks!" She turned northward onto the Stillorgan Road heading for Joe and Annie's house.

It was a beautiful sunny morning, though still cold, and Steph took the coast road so that they could enjoy the view across to Howth Head.

"I feel very guilty." Liz leant back and watched the world go by. "I have a mountain of ironing to do, the kitchen floor needs to be washed and there are a hundred and one other things I should be doing, but I'm not." She grinned wickedly. "I'm having a day off!"

Twenty minutes later the three women sat at Annie's kitchen table sipping coffee and chatting while the sound of the children's laughter carried from the pretty little garden.

"Don't take off your coat, Lucy," Liz called out warningly. She turned back to Annie who had been talking. "Sorry, Annie, but as soon as she sees the sun, she wants to put on her shorts and T-shirt!"

"They're all the same." Annie glanced fondly out at the

three children who were unsuccessfully trying to persuade Oscar, their twenty-year-old Labrador, to perform tricks. Danielle was making a big deal of looking after her little friend and Shane was trying to act indifferent and cool with the two little girls, but failing miserably.

"I love this kitchen. It's so big and bright – you really did a great job with the re-decoration. I must do something about my place." Stephanie groaned as she thought of all the repairs her little home needed.

Liz winked at Annie. "I didn't think you'd be staying there for much longer. Isn't it time you moved into Seán's pad?"

"Yeah," chimed in Annie with a wicked grin, "when are you two going to give us a day out?"

"Oh leave me alone, will you? You know I'm not the marrying kind!"

"Maybe not, but I think Seán is. Everything OK with you two?" Annie added as the smile faded from Steph's face.

"It could be better," Steph admitted. "Seán's gone to the States."

"He's emigrated?" Liz looked at her in shock.

"*No*, of course not! He'll just be gone for a couple of months but it won't be his last trip either."

"Wow," breathed Liz, "you never said a word."

"No, you didn't," added Annie indignantly. "Two months. Give. What's the story? Are you two splitting up?"

Steph cupped her head in her hands and considered the question. "I don't think so. Things were a little frosty before he left though. He calls nearly every day but we don't have much to say. You see, he wanted me to pack everything in and go with him. He's not too impressed that I wouldn't."

"What basis, *exactly*, did he want you to go on?" asked Annie gently.

"Oh, the usual. He didn't actually mention marriage but I knew he was heading that way. But what really got to me is that he actually thought I'd just walk out on my job, just because he asked me to." She shook her head in frustration and lit a cigarette.

"Well, would that be such a bad idea? I mean, you are thirty-two," Liz said, missing Annie's warning glance and the angry flash of Steph's eyes. "Isn't it time to forget the job and start thinking about a husband and family?"

Annie gave up on subtlety. "Shut up, Liz, and have a scone before you say something that *really* gets you into trouble."

Liz looked puzzled. It made perfect sense to her. Seán was a lovely guy. Good-looking, a bit like Tom Hanks – or was it Tim Robbins? – and he was well off too. There was no doubt that he was crazy about Stephanie. Was there ever a time, she wondered, when Chris looked at her the way Seán looked at Steph?

"Anyway, Liz, don't you think Chris would have been devastated if Stephanie had left?" Annie asked innocently.

"No. Probably relieved," Liz replied without thinking. "He's thinking of selling up."

Stephanie nearly dropped her mug and Annie's mouth fell open in astonishment.

Stephanie was the first to recover. "He's selling up? It's the first I've heard of it. When, exactly, was Chris planning to tell me? Who's he selling to? When?"

Liz fidgeted uncomfortably in her seat. "Well, it's not definite. I'm sure he'll talk to you as soon as it's settled, but well . . ." She wasn't sure how much to say. Chris had warned her to keep quiet but Stephanie *was* her friend. She came to a decision. "He hasn't done anything about selling up. Honestly, Steph. But he's been offered a job. A new restaurant in Galway wants him and, frankly, I want him to accept it. If he does, we might actually manage to get our marriage back on track."

The other two women tried to look surprised.

Liz shook her head and smiled sadly. "Oh, come on. I'm not a total fool. I think Chris might be messing about. I suppose I thought if I stuck my head in the sand it would all go away. Maybe it's just a mid-life crisis, a temporary thing. Anyway, if I could get him away from Dublin, we'd have a better chance of starting over. I'm sorry, Steph. I don't want to see you left high and dry, but my marriage and Lucy come first."

Stephanie squeezed Liz's hand. "It's OK. I'll survive." She met Annie's questioning gaze and laughed.

"What is it?" Liz looked from one to the other. "What's so funny?"

"Annie thinks I should buy Chris out, don't you, Annie?"

Annie shrugged. "Seems like a good plan to me."

Liz gaped at Stephanie. "You?"

"Why *not* me?" Steph asked, nettled at Liz's reaction.

"But how?" Liz asked. "You don't have that kind of money, do you? And how could you run it without Chris? Keep up the standards. Or are you thinking more along the lines of a coffee shop?"

Stephanie took a deep breath and counted to ten. "No. I'd keep it exactly as it is. Well, not *exactly* the same," she added avoiding Annie's eye. "I'd probably give the place a face-lift, a more modern and up-beat image. And the menu definitely needs updating." She looked at Liz's crestfallen expression and immediately felt guilty. "As for money," she looked heavenward, "God bless Uncle Jack."

"I forgot about the money he left you. You must have been thinking about this for *ages*." Liz's words were an accusation.

Stephanie looked at Annie who burst out laughing again.

"Oh yes, she's been planning it for ages," Annie said, wiping a tear from her eye.

"Ages," Stephanie agreed solemnly.

Liz looked at them, bemused.

"Enough of all this." Annie cleared the dishes from the table. "Time we were making tracks. Shane," she yelled to her son, "run next door and tell Carol we'll be leaving in ten minutes."

As they drove away from the house, with the children running after the car waving and shouting, Annie stretched across the back seat and sighed contentedly.

"This is the life! I can't remember the last time I was out without the kids. I feel as if I'm playing truant from school or something. It's great! What do you say, Liz?"

"Oh yeah," Liz replied vaguely, still shell-shocked by what Stephanie had said.

Stephanie glanced over at her. "Honestly, Liz, I haven't

given any thought at all to buying Chris out. Please don't say anything to him. It's just one of Annie's mad ideas."

Liz sighed loudly. "Oh, I should have known! You've been pulling my leg. God, I'm so gullible. I actually *believed* you."

Steph looked at Annie in the rear-view mirror. Annie winked back at her cheerfully.

* * *

Stephanie leant forward and threw more water on the coals. The three women were enveloped in a cloud of steam.

Liz groaned. "Oh, for God's sake Steph! Will you stop that? I won't have the energy to tap my foot tonight, never mind dance!"

Annie mopped the sweat from her brow with a fluffy lemon towel. "Rubbish, once you've had a nice cold shower you'll be ready for anything."

Liz looked horrified. "Well, you enjoy your shower, I'll wait and have a nice bath in Steph's. Yes. A hot bath, a glass of wine and a good novel. That's what I fancy."

"It didn't take you long to get used to the good life, did it?" Steph teased. "Half an hour ago it was, 'I wonder what Lucy's doing now? I wonder if Chris will miss me?'"

"Oh, shut up and leave me alone," Liz threw her towel at Stephanie and missed. "It's all ahead of you. I know you don't think so now," she insisted as Stephanie shook her head, "but your time will come and when it does, Ms West, I'll be the first to say 'I told you so'."

Steph's laugh was forced. It seemed unlikely Liz would get her wish. Annie was right. Seán wouldn't hang around for ever. Even if she agreed to move in with him, it wouldn't be enough. He was a very old-fashioned man. He'd want the ceremony, the ring, the whole ball of wax. He'd want her to be Mrs Stephanie Adams. She sighed. That's what everyone wanted. Her mother, her father, Joe and all of her friends. They all adored Seán and they couldn't understand what was holding her back.

Her mother loved Seán like another son. Sometimes when the two of them got together, Stephanie just sat back sipping her tea and listened to them rabbitting on about a recent TV programme, the neighbourhood gossip or the latest antics of the new, and rather eccentric, parish priest. Whatever happened, Seán and her mother would always be friends.

"Seán's a lovely man," her mother said more than once, "and he thinks the world of you. He's not one of the bad sort," she'd added carefully. "He's honest and decent. You could trust *him*, love."

That was the closest Steph's mother ever came to mentioning Ruth's unhappy love affair. Catherine West was well aware of the effect Ruth's death had had on her daughter.

Stephanie knew that when she'd got back together with Seán her parents had expected, hoped for, an announcement. Joe was anxious to see her settled too. He was more than a little protective of his sister. Sometimes that irritated Stephanie but more often she enjoyed it. He wasn't your typical accountant. He was conservative and practical but his sense of humour was intact and marrying Annie and having kids had rounded him off nicely. Steph relied on him. Whenever she needed advice, she could turn to him. He'd always been there for her.

Annie prodded her with her toe. "Hey, sleepy head, we're going to be late for Jeanette if we don't get a move on."

"Yeah and we don't want to make her angry." Liz rolled her eyes dramatically. "We might come out bald!"

Laughing, the three women headed back to the changing rooms, donned their robes and set off to the beauty salon.

Jeanette eyed Liz critically as if she were sizing up a piece of meat.

"Right. Your skin is in dreadful condition and those eyebrows badly need plucking. You're not getting any younger, you know. You have to look after yourself." She grabbed handfuls of Liz's dark locks in her hand and then dropped them in disgust. "Split ends." She eyed Liz accusingly in the mirror as if she'd committed a heinous crime.

She turned away for a quick consultation and Liz looked at Steph in horror.

"I feel like I'm back in school," she hissed. "I thought I was supposed to be here to relax and enjoy myself."

Stephanie flicked through a copy of *Cosmopolitan*. "Haven't you ever heard the saying, 'suffer to be beautiful'?"

Jeanette swung back to Liz, smiling brightly. "Never mind, we can work wonders for you. First, I think you need a complete new look."

"No, I don't think so. Just a trim for me," Liz said primly.

"No, Liz, really, Jeanette's right." Annie insisted. She glanced at Jeanette. "And maybe some lowlights too?"

Jeanette nodded approvingly while Liz looked around in panic.

"Oh, I really don't think . . ."

"You relax and let me do the thinking." Jeanette signalled to one of her girls.

"Shampoo for Mrs Connolly, with conditioner." Liz was led away, like a lamb to the slaughter.

CHAPTER FIVE

"Chris is going to kill me," Liz said for the tenth time as she studied her new look in Stephanie's bathroom mirror.

"To hell with Chris." Steph came in behind her with a glass of wine in one hand and a novel in the other. "Honestly, Liz, he's going to love it. You look stunning! The haircut takes years off you and it makes your eyes look huge and somehow even browner. Now hop in that tub, drink some wine and get in the mood. We're going to paint the town red tonight, girl!"

Steph sashayed out of the bathroom and Liz turned back to look at the stranger in the mirror. It was true, she admitted, the style suited her. Jeanette hadn't taken too much off the length, but she'd given it more shape. It looked a lot more sophisticated. The eyebrow-trim emphasised her large wide-set eyes and the facial had left her skin glowing and healthy. She slipped into the tub, took a sip of her wine and settled back contentedly.

She hadn't felt like this in a long time. Young and sexy. Maybe this change of image would make Chris sit up and take notice. She thought of how sulky he'd been this morning when she'd kissed him goodbye. He didn't like it when she went out and did her own thing, especially if Stephanie West was involved. Well, she opened her eyes wide and smiled, maybe that was the answer. Maybe she was just *too* available. Maybe the way to win back his interest was to become less available. After all, men liked a little mystery, didn't they? She'd discuss it with Steph and Annie later. She slipped further down into the bubbles and reached for the novel. Within minutes she was lost in another world, all problems forgotten.

Stephanie lounged on the bed, sipped a glass of wine and watched while Annie sat applying her make-up. "Liz looks great, doesn't she?"

"Sensational," Annie agreed. "Pity it'll be wasted on that scumbag."

Steph scowled. "Oh, why did you have to mention him? You'll spoil my appetite."

"Where are we going?" Annie asked.

"L'Ecrivain."

"Oh, lovely! We'd better pay in cash or your dear brother will complain."

"Joe's not mean," Steph protested.

"Just kidding. God, blood really *is* thicker than water. So tell me. What are you going to do about Chez Nous?"

Steph shook her head. "I don't know. I can't believe Chris is actually thinking of leaving. I'm stunned. I'm not sure I could take it on, though. Do you think I could? And what about a head chef? Conor's very young but the thought of hiring someone . . . " she trailed off.

She was at once excited and terrified by the idea. The longer she was in the restaurant business, the more she was convinced that she was good at it. Not only could she maintain the restaurant at its present level, she firmly believed she could improve on it. There were plenty of successful restaurants in Dublin where the owner wasn't the head chef. So what was stopping her?

Annie read her thoughts. "You like the idea, don't you? I think you'd be great. Did you tell Seán?"

Steph shook her head. "I was going to, but then he told me about Arizona and there didn't seem to be much point after that."

"Why don't you come over at the weekend and thrash it out with Joe. There's no harm in discussing it."

Steph's face lit up. "Yeah, great, thanks. Joe will be objective. Besides, he knows the state the books are in."

"That bad?"

"Not really, but not as good as they should be. Steps need to be taken, and quickly."

Stephanie broke off as Liz arrived in, wrapped in a towel and singing "I Could Have Danced All Night".

Annie groaned. "I can feel the hangover starting already."

Stephanie insisted on applying Liz's make-up, while Annie looked on and gave advice. Annie and Liz puffed happily on Steph's cigarettes as they chatted. If their husbands could see them now, Steph thought. It was just like old times. All they needed was a bottle of Bull's Blood! The transformation in Liz was amazing. The little black number that Stephanie had lent her for the evening was going to look great on her.

With Liz's make-up complete, Steph went off to rummage in the wardrobe, wondering what she could wear to compete. She smiled at the amount of blue in her wardrobe. Seán always said that blue made her eyes look like sapphires. She leant her head against the door. She missed him more than she'd expected. She seized a red dress she rarely wore from the back of the wardrobe. It was a little risqué with a plunging neckline and a side slit which showed a fair amount of thigh. It would turn heads but that was exactly what she needed right now. Some dancing and flirting with no strings attached. Yup, she decided, this was the dress to do it.

Annie was coolly sophisticated in a black satin trouser suit. The beautifully cut jacket revealed an ample cleavage. The emerald earrings and pendant Joe had given her for her birthday complemented her startling green eyes and completed the chic image. Jeanette had trimmed her hair and soft auburn tendrils framed her heart-shaped face.

"Oh, you look lovely, Annie." Steph looked at her friend in open admiration. "We'll have to do this more often."

"We certainly will. Have you fallen down, Liz?" Annie rapped on the door of the loo.

"Coming." Liz slipped her dress over her head and smoothed it down over her hips. She turned to the mirror and was taken aback at the pretty woman looking back at her. Steph's dress covered a multitude. She almost looked slim! She took a deep breath and opened the door. "Not bad for an oul one," she said.

"Wow, girl, you look hot!" Steph twirled Liz around while Annie attempted a wolf whistle.

"You don't look so bad yourself," Liz replied eyeing the

dramatic red dress. She'd never have the guts to wear something like that. It emphasised Stephanie's fair skin, slender frame and golden hair. Gold earrings and strappy golden sandals completed the outfit.

Annie clapped her hands. "OK, enough of this mutual admiration society – finish your wine and let's get this show on the road. The taxi should be here any minute."

Liz knocked back the remains of her drink, and was slipping on her coat when the intercom buzzed.

Stephanie threw open the door with a flourish. "Come on, Cinderellas. Let's go to the ball!"

* * *

"Oh, that *Crème Brûlée* was delicious." Liz licked her lips with relish. "Why is it that everything that tastes good is bad for you?" She looked mournfully down at her stomach.

Stephanie smacked her hand. "Oh, forget about your weight for tonight. You can dance all the calories off later."

"I could quite happily sit here all evening," Annie said, looking at the bevy of efficient waiters swarming around the tables. "That duck was sheer ambrosia." She sipped on her glass of port and accepted a cigarette from Stephanie.

"Isn't that Lavinia Reynolds over there?" Liz whispered excitedly. "She is *so* sophisticated. Looks great for her age. Didn't she write something about Chez Nous recently?"

"She did," Stephanie replied grimly. "None of it good."

Liz looked horrified. "The ugly bitch."

Annie laughed. "Oops, watch out, she's coming over."

"Stephanie *darling*." The two women kissed air. "Enjoying how the other half live this evening? How's that *wonderful* boss of yours?"

Stephanie glanced at Liz uncomfortably. "He's fine, Lavinia. Have you met Liz Connolly, Chris's *wife*? And this is Annie West, my sister-in-law."

Lavinia's eyes raked Liz's appearance. "How nice to meet you both. Isn't this the most wonderful restaurant? Next to Chez Nous, of course." She gave a hard tinkling laugh. "Well, nice to meet you both. See you *quite* soon, Stephanie. *Ciao*." She moved on, leaving a cloud of heavy scent in her wake.

Steph smiled grimly after her. "*Ciao*, bitch."

"She's obnoxious, isn't she?" Annie said amiably.

Liz frowned and said nothing.

"Annie! How are you? Where's Joe? Don't tell me he let you out on your own? Stupid man."

Annie stood up to hug an extremely attractive man. "Edward! How wonderful to see you! Joe's at home, I hope! This is strictly a ladies' night out."

"And what lovely ladies," he replied, glancing admiringly from Liz to Stephanie.

Annie introduced her friends. "This is Edward McDermott. Edward, this is Liz Connolly and surely you've met Joe's sister, Stephanie."

Edward shook hands. He looked at Steph quizzically. "We must have met before, though no, I'd never have forgotten *you*."

Stephanie felt her face flush. Dammit. But he'd already turned to Liz. "Not the chef from Chez Nous?"

Liz was taken aback. Not many people associated her with the restaurant these days.

"Ex-chef," she corrected. "My husband runs the business now. I'm just a housewife."

Annie could have cheerfully kicked her for the apology in her voice.

"That's a pity," Edward replied, "I used to have offices around the corner, you see. Oh, it must be five years ago now. But your desserts were the main reason I used to go there."

Liz's face lit up. "Really? How nice that you remember."

"Well, I hope you plan to rejoin the culinary world at some stage. It's a shame to hide away that kind of talent."

Who was this guy? Stephanie wondered. He'd brought a sparkle to Liz's eyes that she hadn't seen in a long time.

"Why don't you join us for a drink, Edward?" Annie said, enjoying the effect he was having on her friends.

"Oh, I can't, I'm with someone." He looked regretfully towards a table at the back of the room. "Lovely to see you though, Annie. Kiss the kids for me and tell your lug of a husband to give me a call. I owe him a thrashing on the squash court. Lovely to meet you, Stephanie, Liz."

With a wave he was gone.

"Who was that?" breathed Liz.

Annie smiled. "Nice, isn't he? If it weren't for Joe . . ."

Stephanie looked at her in mock horror.

Annie was unperturbed. "Nothing wrong with looking at the menu," she said.

"He's so nice. Imagine him remembering my desserts," Liz said dreamily.

"*Very* romantic," Steph grinned at her friend's lovesick expression. "I hate to remind you two, but *I'm* the only one at this table who's single. So what does he do, Annie?" She tried to sound off-hand.

"He's a solicitor. Joe's known him years. They met at Trinity. I'm surprised you haven't met before."

"Is he married?" Liz asked.

Annie shook her head. "No – and I can't image why not. He's a partner in some large firm, rolling in money, drives a beautiful car and he's great with Dani and Shane."

"A positive paragon. He seems to be great with the ladies as well," Stephanie nodded towards Edward's table. A very attractive red-head was leaning towards him, smiling into his eyes.

"Hardly surprising. He's gorgeous *and* nice." Liz was definitely smitten.

"Enough drooling, ladies," Annie admonished. "Drink up. It's time to hit the clubs."

They went out to the waiting taxi and gave the driver directions to the trendiest nightclub in Dublin.

* * *

"Lord, I'm getting old." Liz pushed her way back through the swaying bodies to their table and took a long gulp from her glass.

Stephanie flopped down beside her. "Oh, I don't know. I think we can hold our own against that mob." She nodded towards the dance floor. "Would you look at Annie flirting with that fella? He doesn't look old enough to vote! What's she like? If my brother could see her now . . ." Steph's voice faltered as she saw the look on Liz's face. "Liz, what is it? What's the matter?" She followed Liz's gaze and saw Chris. He was standing at the bar. A beautiful girl, about twenty, with long blonde hair stood at his side laughing at something he was saying. As they watched, he slipped his arm around her.

"What's up?" Annie arrived up, out of breath from her efforts on the dance floor. Stephanie nodded towards Chris.

Annie blinked. "Oh my God, oh Liz, Liz? What are you going to . . . Liz?"

Steph ran after Liz as she headed determinedly across the room. "Liz, you don't know what the story is, there could be a very simple explanation."

Liz gave her a withering look without breaking stride. When she reached the bar, she tapped Chris on the shoulder.

"Liz!" Chris flushed and paled. His expression said it all. "What are you doing here? Just dropped in for one with George. He insisted. I was just leaving . . ."

Liz threw her drink in his face and then turned an icy glare on the bemused girl.

"You silly little bitch. Do you make a habit of chatting up married men?" She gave a harsh laugh, but her eyes were bright with tears. "*He's* pathetic," she continued, "but you must be desperate." She stared at Chris in disgust and walked out of the club with Annie hot on her heels.

Chris made to follow her, but Stephanie planted herself firmly in his path.

"I think you've done more than enough for one night, don't you?" she said, before following Annie and Liz out of the club.

CHAPTER SIX

"How is she?"

Steph looked up from the phone at the closed door of her spare room. "I don't know, Annie. She hardly said a word last night, and I haven't seen her this morning. I'll bring her in a cup of tea in a minute. What have you told Lucy?"

"Just that Liz was spending the night with you. She wasn't too bothered. She's having too much fun with Dani."

The bedroom door opened and Liz emerged, looking pale, her eye-sockets black with smudged mascara. "Is that Annie?" she asked.

Steph nodded and Liz took the receiver.

"Hi, Annie. Would you do me a favour? Could you keep Lucy until tomorrow?"

"Sure," Annie said, surprised at the composure in her friend's voice.

"Can I talk to her?"

"Sure," Annie said again and put her hand over the

mouthpiece. *"Luceeeee,"* she yelled, "your mum's on the phone!"

Lucy came running down the stairs and grabbed the phone. "Mummy? You'll never guess what me and Dani did last night and she has pencils just like mine and I drew you a picture and one for Daddy."

Liz raked a hand through her hair and let her daughter prattle on for a while. Finally she cut in. "Well, it sounds like you're having a great time. Would you like to stay another day?"

Lucy squealed with delight. "Oh, that would be great, Mummy."

"OK, love. I'll pick you up tomorrow afternoon. Be a good girl for Auntie Annie now, won't you?"

After a few more moments of blowing kisses, Liz handed the phone back to Stephanie and went back into the bedroom.

"Liz? Liz are you there?"

"No, Annie, it's me. She's gone back to bed."

"She seems all right. What do you think?"

Steph sighed. "Oh, I don't know, Annie. She's too bloody quiet. I'd be a lot happier if she cried or screamed or called him all the names under the sun."

"Did *he* call?" Annie couldn't even bring herself to use the man's name. God, if she got her hands on him . . .

"He hasn't stopped calling. I'm dreading going into work. Look, I'd better go and see how she is. I'll call you later." Steph rang off. After a tentative knock, she put her head around Liz's door. "Can I come in?"

Liz nodded mutely.

"Are you OK?" Steph asked inadequately. What a bloody stupid question.

Liz smiled grimly. "Nope, but I'll survive."

"What are you going to do?"

"Kick him out, of course," she replied, pulling on her jeans. "He should have left for work by now. Do me a favour. Grab the yellow pages and find me a locksmith in the Stillorgan area. Ask him to meet me at the house in two hours."

Steph stared at her. "Are you sure? That's a bit drastic, isn't it? Would you not talk to Chris first? He may not have actually *done* anything." Steph couldn't believe she was defending the bastard.

Liz scowled. "I saw something last night that confirmed my suspicions. He's playing around, has been for years. If I don't act now, I never will. Please help me," she pleaded, her voice trembling slightly.

Stephanie opened her mouth and then closed it again. She went into the living-room and began to thumb through the phone book.

* * *

Liz let herself into the hall and fell back against the door. It hadn't been easy getting rid of Stephanie. She'd wanted to come in and stay with her.

"You've got a job to get to," Liz pointed out, "and the boss isn't exactly understanding."

Stephanie had finally left. Liz started for the stairs, but paused when the doorbell went. The locksmith.

"Hello, love. You called about changing some locks?

Had a break-in then? Bloody disgraceful the thugs running around these days. Don't you worry, love, I'll sort you out. Point me towards the damage."

Liz sighed. This was all she needed. A chatty, cheerful tradesman. "I just want the front-door lock changed and a safety chain added."

The man frowned, examining the lock. "Looks fine," he remarked.

Liz bit her lip. "It is, but I lost my bag, and the keys were in it. I don't want to take any chances."

The man nodded wisely. "Oh, you're right there, love. You can't be too careful . . ."

"Yes, right," Liz interrupted. "I'll be upstairs. Call if you need anything." She went upstairs and pulled out the two new Samsonite cases from under the bed. "No, fuck him," she thought and shoved them back. She collected some black bags from the kitchen and proceeded to crumple his clothes into balls and shove them into the bags. She thought about cutting up his shirts and suits. She'd seen a woman on a talk show once who'd cut the right arm off all her husbands suits. It seemed funny at the time. Her eyes filled up. No, she wouldn't do that. It was childish and, more to the point, it wouldn't make her feel any better. Then there was the woman who'd raided her husband's very expensive wine cellar and left a bottle on all the local doorsteps, along with the morning milk. Well, Chris didn't have *that* much wine. He drank it as fast as he bought it. No. She'd keep what was left and drink it herself. She looked at her watch. Twelve noon. Was it too early to start now? She turned her attention to his tie rack. Chris was very proud of his ties. They were all of the very best silk. It was the one purchase he made himself. He didn't like her choices, they were usually too subtle for him. She looked at the variety of flamboyant and garish colours. She could cut them up, she thought idly. That would upset him. It didn't seem enough, though. What could she possibly do to him that would make him hurt the way she was hurting now? What would make him feel as if his heart was breaking in two? She slid to the floor and let the tears come. Once she started crying it was hard to stop. She sobbed uncontrollably, rocking back and forth like a child.

"Eh sorry, missus, I did shout. Eh, are you OK?" The workman stood in the doorway, shuffling from one foot to another and looking distinctly uncomfortable.

Liz scrambled to her feet, and wiped her eyes. "I'm fine. What do I owe you?" She wrote a cheque and hurried the embarrassed man out of the house. Next she phoned for a taxi. She went back upstairs and started to snip the ties into neat little pieces. Oh well, so she wasn't imaginative. She found a large brown envelope and dropped the pieces into it. She sealed it and stuck it to the side of one of the bags. She tugged the bags downstairs, pausing to blow her nose and wipe her eyes. When the taxi arrived she gave the driver the address of Chez Nous and two twenty-pound notes. "The bags are for Chris Connolly, the owner. He's waiting for them. They're very important. Make sure you deliver them to him personally."

The taxi-driver agreed readily, delighted with his fare.

Liz closed the door, slid the safety chain into place, went into the kitchen and opened a bottle of wine. "Cheers, Chris," she said and downed the contents of her glass.

* * *

Stephanie tiptoed past the kitchen and climbed the stairs to the office. She wasn't looking forward to seeing Chris. She was furious with him and didn't trust herself to keep her temper in check. But he was still her boss. She opened the office door and stopped short. Chris was in her seat. He was pale and drawn and slightly unkempt.

"Morning," he said. "Sorry if I gave you a start. I wanted to talk to you."

Stephanie's immediate reaction was to tell him to go to hell, but that wouldn't help Liz, and it certainly wouldn't help her. She nodded silently and took the seat opposite him. She stared at her hands resting in her lap and waited.

"Look, Stephanie, I know what a stupid bastard I've been, but I do love Liz. I'd never do anything to hurt her."

"You wouldn't do anything to hurt her?" Steph raised an eyebrow, her voice icy. "I must have imagined it all, so. It must have been someone else I saw in that club. Some other dirty old man who was chatting up a girl half his age."

Chris flushed angrily. "I'm not denying anything but I don't owe you an explanation." Instantly he regretted showing his anger. "Look, Steph," he continued placatingly, "I was a fool, I know that. But I'll sort it out. I'll take her away on a holiday, she'd like that." He nodded, as if his problems were solved.

Steph looked at him in disbelief. He really had no idea of the mess he was in. She almost pitied him. Almost. "I'm afraid it's going to take more than a holiday, Chris. Liz is *very* upset." She reached for her bag and pulled out her cigarettes.

"She'll get over it. I'll talk to her."

Steph shook her head. The phone rang and she picked it up. "Yes? Oh, right . . . OK Sam, I'll tell him." She put the phone down. "There's a taxi-driver downstairs with a delivery for you. He says he has to give it to you himself."

Chris looked puzzled and went downstairs followed closely by Stephanie. Four black bags were stacked in the hallway. Chris peered into one and then looked at the taxi-man in confusion. "What's all this?"

"Dunno," he replied cheerfully. "The lady said you'd understand. There's a note for you there." He pointed at the envelope. "Bye now."

Chris tore open the envelope. "Jesus Christ." He dropped it and patches of silk drifted to the floor like confetti.

Stephanie suppressed a grin. She watched Chris rummage through the bags. "It's all my stuff," he gasped. "She's thrown me out. The bitch has thrown me out." He turned to Stephanie, his face pale. "You've got to do something."

Steph nodded. "Right then. I'll get started on tonight's menus." She turned on her heel and left him standing there. "Good girl, Liz. Good girl," she muttered.

CHAPTER SEVEN

"I'd love to have seen his face," Annie said. "I can't believe Liz cut up his ties."

"Neither could he," Steph replied drily.

"Do you really think she's finished with him for good?" Joe asked as he topped up their glasses.

Steph shrugged. "Hard to say. She won't talk about it. She seems in good form, though."

Annie looked doubtful. "She can't be. She was crazy about him. You don't get over twelve years of marriage, just like that. I bet she'll take him back."

Steph took a sip of wine. "I'm not so sure. It's been four weeks. The real crunch comes when Chris moves to Galway. Which brings us back to the matter at hand. What do you think, Joe? Am I mad?"

Joe considered the question. He wasn't a man to be rushed. Typical accountant, Steph thought affectionately.

"I think the restaurant's a good investment and you know it better than anyone, but you need to do a lot of research before you commit yourself. For example. What's involved in holding on to the Michelin Star?"

"Way ahead of you," Steph said through a mouthful of bolognese. "I was talking to Conor about that, in a casual sort of way of course. The Star belongs to the restaurant, not to Chris. Once the menu remains much the same, they'll let us hold on to it and then judge us as usual for next year. Their findings are announced in February. That would suit me just fine. I'd just have to maintain standards for the remainder of this year and I'd be able to concentrate on making plans for next year."

Joe looked sceptical. "What are the chances of Chris agreeing and you taking over so quickly? It might be wiser to think in terms of next year."

Steph shook her head. "I don't agree. Chris is desperate to do something to get Liz back. He's scared to death that she's dumped him for good. The other problem is his attitude. He's been slacking off lately and it's affected the restaurant's standards. What's he going to be like now? I'm terrified he's going to really hit the bottle."

"What about a chef?" Annie asked.

"Conor," Steph replied without hesitation. "I know he's young but that works to my advantage, really. It's a wonderful opportunity for him, he'll jump at the chance. He's another reason to move quickly. If we're not going to make any immediate changes Conor will have plenty of time to develop his own ideas. He's also unknown. It's an opportunity to build the reputation of the restaurant and not the chef. That way, when he eventually moves, it won't cause too much of a stir."

"But you've raised another point," Joe said. "Chez Nous is inexorably linked with Chris Connolly. Will people keep coming if he leaves?"

"We have to use the critics to make sure they do. PR is going to be very important. If Chris plays along, then he can endorse Chez Nous and its staff. It's no skin off his nose, he's leaving the city anyway. I'll need to hold on to Conor for about two years – if I lost him any earlier than that it could be a problem. I'll have to make his terms very attractive. What?" She stopped as she saw Annie and Joe exchange looks.

Annie laughed. "When you started talking, it was 'if' and now it's 'when'. It looks like you've made up your mind."

Steph smiled slowly. "Maybe I have."

Joe frowned. "Don't rush things, Steph. Do the research. Do the figures. Talk to the bank manager. Don't be afraid to wait. It's better to hold off for a few months, even a year, and do it properly than to rush in and make a hash of it."

Annie nudged him. "Don't be such a pessimist, Joe. Have a bit of faith in your sister."

"No, he's right, Annie. Don't worry, Joe. I'll do my homework, but do me a favour? Check out my business plan before I go to the bank."

"I'll do better than that. I'll put together some notes for you on the current state of your finances. That should help. It's not too bad, but it could be better. Then again, I'm sure it's the same story for a lot of restaurants. I'll go with you to the bank manager if you like, explain things."

"Thanks, bro. Let's see how it goes." Steph was grateful for her brother's help, but she didn't want him to take over. This was her baby. "I suppose my first job is to talk to Chris. I can't say I like the idea, but it's got to be done."

"Has he talked to Liz yet?" Annie asked as she cleared away the plates.

"He's tried, but she hangs up when he phones and she won't answer the door when he comes around. He nearly had a fit when he realised she'd changed the lock."

"What about Lucy?" Joe didn't particularly like Chris, but he felt sorry for his pretty little daughter. No child should have to deal with a situation like this.

Steph thought about her godchild. "I don't think Liz has told her anything yet, but Lucy's not easily fooled. I'm sure she's picked up on the atmosphere. Liz won't be able to keep her in the dark for much longer."

"Poor kid." Annie was very fond of the little girl. She was a lively, bright child and she and Dani were fast friends. Sometimes Annie worried that Danielle was too quiet and shy, but when Lucy was around she came to life.

Steph and Annie took their drinks into the living-room while Joe washed up.

"How's Seán?" Annie asked.

"OK," Steph replied glumly. "I think he's fed up with me, though. Can't say I blame him. It's only when you think about rats like Chris, you realise how lucky you are."

"Amen to that," Annie said, raising her glass. "Do I detect a softening in Ms West?"

"Well, I realise I could do a lot worse," Steph agreed.

"Very romantic," Annie said drily.

Steph made a face. "You know what I mean. I've been very hard on Seán. He means well, and he cares a lot about me. Maybe it's time we settled down."

Annie nearly choked on her wine. "You're going to marry him?" she managed when she got her breath back.

Steph looked as if Annie had taken leave of her senses. "Of course not, don't be silly. But I think it's time we moved in together. I need to make *some* sort of commitment to him. Otherwise he might decide to move on."

"I can't pretend the thought didn't cross my mind," Annie admitted. "He's a very nice bloke but I'd say he's had enough by now."

"Thanks very much!" Steph glowered at her friend.

"Just being honest, pet," Annie smiled sweetly. "That's what friends are for."

* * *

Seán wiped his hands nervously on his jeans, lifted the gun, aimed carefully and fired. He was shocked and disoriented by the noise, despite his earplugs.

Barry laughed. "You were way off the mark, dude. Have another go."

Seán took a deep breath and turned back to the row of cans in the distance. It was five in the evening but the Arizona sun beat down relentlessly on the stark, barren desert. He aimed and fired. Again, with no success.

Barry threw him a full can from the cooler. "Have another drink, it might improve your aim."

Seán leaned back against the four-by-four and took a long swig from the can. He watched, enviously, as Barry blew away the row of cans with the semi-automatic.

"Easy when you know how," drawled Barry and he wandered off to set up a new target.

Seán sighed and looked up at the cloudless sky. He'd been away from home for over a month and was missing Stephanie like hell. He'd been out on the tiles with Barry most nights since he'd arrived, but he still couldn't banish her from his mind. He watched Barry approach. He was becoming very fond of this laid-back, funny Arizonian. Nothing seemed to faze him. He was the IT director for Senfield world-wide, and it was largely through his influence that Seán had got the business.

"You should stop thinking and start shooting," Barry observed shrewdly and shoved the semi-automatic into Seán's hand.

Seán sank under the weight of the gun. "I can't lift it, never mind shoot it. What else have you got?" He walked around to the back of the truck and inspected the arsenal. Arizona amazed him. Everyone seemed to have guns – for sport, hunting and protection. Barry had more than thirty in his collection, but he'd chosen just four for today's sport.

"Here. Try this." Barry handed him a 44 Magnum.

Seán looked in wonder at the weapon in his hand.

"Be careful. There'll be kickback," Barry warned.

Seán aimed and fired the gun. The shot forced his arms up and he felt the wrench in his shoulders.

Barry grinned at the shocked look on his face.

Seán tried again. Finally he hit his first can and, with renewed confidence, whooped as two more hit the deck. "Jeez, ten minutes with a magnum and I feel like Dirty Harry! This is fun." He aimed the gun again and thought of Chris. He hit the can square and it flipped off the rock. He thought of his bank manager and another can bit the dust. He laughed. "This is great therapy altogether!"

"Yup," agreed Barry, "and a lot cheaper than a shrink."

Two hours and many dented cans later, Seán sat in the passenger seat watching the sun set over the desert as Barry guided the truck back to the main road. He'd never seen anything more beautiful. Steph would love it. Damn it! Why couldn't he forget about her? Everything he saw, every restaurant he went to, he wondered what she'd say, what she'd think. He raked his hand through his thick, curly hair. He wished, not for the first time, that she would make a commitment. He wasn't like Ruth's boyfriend, Des Healy, for Christ's sake! He'd look after her, love her. He'd never do anything to hurt her. But it probably would never happen. Stephanie just couldn't seem to forget Ruth and wouldn't find any peace until she came to terms with what had happened. As the years past, this seemed more and more unlikely.

Seán knew he'd screwed up by asking her to leave Chez Nous, but he was sick of watching Chris treat her like a second-class citizen. She was worth so much more than that, but she was too stubborn to call it a day and move on. She cared more about that damn restaurant than she did about him. He knew that many of their dates happened purely because she wanted to check out another restaurant. He sighed and Barry shot him a sidelong glance.

"Anything you want to talk about, Bud?"

Seán shook his head. "I wouldn't know where to begin, Barry. Woman trouble."

"Oh, OK. You just need another beer." He swung the truck off the road and into the carpark of a bar and steakhouse.

Seán laughed. He was hot, sticky and stinking of gunpowder but what the hell? Who'd give a shit? "Sounds good." He could do with a few pints to wash Steph out of his mind.

CHAPTER EIGHT

Stephanie paced the office nervously. She'd asked Chris for a meeting two hours ago and he still hadn't surfaced. She knew better than to repeat the request. He'd only keep her waiting even longer.

Chris looked at his watch. Let the bitch wait another while. He wondered what she wanted to moan about this time. God, he'd love to fire her, but he couldn't if he wanted to get back with Liz. She'd never forgive him for sacking her best friend. He slammed pots around as he thought about Stephanie. Bad enough that he had to put up with her in work, but her involvement in his personal life was really annoying. He was convinced she was egging his wife on. Liz would never have had the guts to take such drastic action on her own. Stephanie had always been a bad influence. It made him sick that she was his daughter's godmother as well. Why had he ever agreed to that? But then that all happened years ago when Steph had been his friend too. When she'd come to work for him, she'd been the first person to put the computer to any good use. Chris had bought it, full of enthusiasm, but had never had the patience to sit down and figure out what to do with it. Stephanie had purchased a package that allowed him to input and update his recipes with ease. She'd stepped in every time he banged the mouse down in frustration, showing him where he'd gone wrong. Then came the costing program which had really saved him a lot of time. But Chris didn't 'remember' any of this now. Steph was merely an irritant, someone who encouraged his wife to behave disgracefully. Someone who'd got above herself and was far too opinionated for his liking. He washed his hands, donned a clean apron and headed for the office. Time to go and see what was wrong with her.

Stephanie was stubbing out her fifth cigarette of the morning when Chris walked in. She immediately lit another. "I want to talk to you about the restaurant," she said without preamble, her voice trembling.

"What's your problem *now*?"

She swallowed hard and tried to ignore the patronising tone. She wouldn't let him rattle her today. "No problem," she replied. "I just want to know if you're planning to sell or not."

Chris's head jerked up. Damn Liz. What had she said to the bitch? "What are you talking about?" he asked, keeping his face blank.

"Liz told me about the offer you got. Are you planning to take it?"

"What's it to do with you?" he said rudely.

"I think it's pretty obvious what it's to do with. Chez Nous is my livelihood. Anyway," she continued more gently, "I think it's a good idea. It may be the only way you'll get Liz back."

Chris sighed and ran his fingers through thin, greying hair. "I want her back and I'd do anything to make that happen. Going to Galway might just clinch it, but it's easier said than done. Finding a buyer, sorting out all the legalities, selling the house . . ."

Stephanie sent up a silent prayer of thanks. He still didn't have a buyer. "It may not be that difficult, Chris. I could buy the restaurant."

Chris threw back his head and laughed. "Oh, Stephanie, it's not quite that simple," he said finally.

She shrunk at his tone, but said nothing.

"You can't decide to buy a restaurant, just like that. It's a *little* bit more complicated," he explained as if he was talking to a child.

"I didn't," she replied quietly.

"You didn't what?" He was confused now. What was the woman rambling on about?

She turned to face him. "I didn't decide 'just like that'. I decided several weeks ago *and* I've most of the finance arranged."

She got some satisfaction from the startled look on his face.

Chris finally found his tongue. "Jumping the gun a bit, aren't you? What makes you think I'd sell to *you* anyway?"

She looked him in the eye, for the first time. "How many other offers do you have, Chris? Let's cut the bull. You want out and I have the cash. What do you say?"

"You've one major problem," he said ignoring the

question. "What about a chef? George couldn't handle it and Conor's too young."

"Young chefs are in. People are fed up of old chefs with old ideas. Conor will be fine once he gets some more experience under his belt. Anyway, that's my problem, not yours."

He shook his head. "That would take time. What would you do in the meantime? Close the restaurant? That could be dangerous, and you'd lose the Star." He looked at her triumphantly. The silly cow didn't have a clue! She hadn't thought any of this through. She wouldn't last a month without him.

"I've no intention of closing. I want you to stay on until he's ready."

"Stay on and work for you! You're joking! Why should I . . ."

"Do you want Liz back, or not?" she snapped.

He glared at her but said nothing.

"If you go to Galway now, she won't go with you. Even you must realise that."

He looked at her sullenly, but said nothing.

"And if you go without her, you'll be completely tied up in the job, and you won't have any time to commute to Dublin and sort things out. Then you'd never get her back."

Chris shook his head irritably. "You're telling me I *should* go and then that I shouldn't go. I don't know what you're on about."

"OK, look at it this way," Stephanie said patiently. "If you took this job you'd have to find a buyer and go through all the legal hoops, so you wouldn't be in a position to move for a few months anyway. Presumably, whoever made you this offer realises that."

"Yes," he agreed reluctantly. "I told them it would take a while to sort. They agreed to wait up to a year, provided I sign the contract soon."

"Well, there you go," Steph said triumphantly. "You could stay on here for a while, keep an eye on things. Conor could go off and get the experience he needs and you could channel all your energy into convincing Liz that she should take you back and go to Galway."

Chris thought fast. This might be the answer to his problems. If he signed the restaurant over to Steph, he'd have some money in his pocket. He could take six months or so to sort his marriage out. That should do it.

He wouldn't have to work too hard either. Pat and Marc were well up to speed, and though George was a lazy bugger, he was an excellent *chef de partie*. This could suit him very well. Very well indeed. "It might work," he said finally. It wouldn't be good to look *too* eager.

Steph looked surprised. "Are you agreeing with me? Have we got a deal here?"

Chris shrugged. "I've had enough of this bloody place. You're welcome to it. We still need to talk money, of course. But, in principle, I've no objection."

Steph wanted to dance around the room but decided to restrain herself.

"Do you think she'll take me back, Steph?" It nearly choked him to ask but she *was* Liz's closest friend.

Steph was taken aback by the question. "I-I don't know," she answered honestly. "She won't talk about you.

She hasn't really said anything. If you like, I'll try to get her to talk to you, but I can't make any promises."

"That night, Stephanie. I was only . . ."

"I don't want to know, Chris. If you're feeling guilty about anything, go to a priest. Don't unburden yourself to Liz. It might make you feel better but it'll destroy her, and I guarantee your marriage will be over. If you *do* get to talk to Liz, I suggest you lie through your teeth."

Chris scowled. Who the hell did she think she was? He smiled grimly. "Why don't you put your proposal in writing and we'll discuss it again."

CHAPTER NINE

Steph and Liz sat in a corner of the large but slightly gloomy restaurant. Liz had taken care with her appearance, but the black wool dress just accentuated her pallor and her face seemed thinner.

"So he wants me back." Liz said dully.

Steph smiled. "Yes, he does. He's very sorry and realises what a prat he's been. I think he actually means it. I told him I wanted to buy Chez Nous. Told him everything. He's interested. He's ready to do anything to get you back."

Liz said nothing.

Steph watched the blank expression on Liz's face. She tried again. "You don't have to rush into anything. But remember, he may not have done anything more than chatted up that one girl. You'll never know until you talk to him." Stephanie almost choked on the words. She looked around irritably. "We've been sitting here ten minutes and we haven't even got menus yet."

Liz looked around the restaurant absently. "Why did you want to meet here?"

"It's only been open a few weeks. I wanted to check it out. The chef was poached, excuse the pun, from The Food Factory. He was developing quite a reputation there and so there's a lot of interest in this place." Steph paused as a harassed-looking waiter hurried towards them.

"Are you ready to order, ladies?"

Steph looked at him in disbelief. "We haven't seen a menu yet," she pointed out testily.

"Oh. Right." He hurried off again and returned with the menus a few minutes later.

"Do you want something to drink?"

Steph glanced at Liz's pale, tense expression. "Some wine, I think. Can I see your list?"

The waiter sighed loudly and hurried away again.

Liz sniffed. "Helpful, isn't he?"

Steph laughed. "I suppose I should be delighted. If this is the way they treat their customers, we've nothing to worry about." She fell silent as the waiter returned with the wine list. It consisted of three pages and the variety of prices and regions was impressive. She ordered a white Bordeaux and turned her attention to the menu as the waiter departed once more. "What do you think?" She asked, ignoring the fact that Liz hadn't so much as glanced at it.

Liz forced her attention to the menu in front of her. What did she think of it? Frankly she didn't give a damn. She didn't care. She didn't want to be here. She didn't want to eat. She just wanted to curl up in bed and see no one, talk to no one. She'd agreed to come out today because Steph had nagged and nagged. In the end it was easier to give in. She looked at the selection. "It's interesting," she said. "There's a good choice in both the starters and the main courses and they're quite light. That's important in a lunch menu. Most people have to put in an afternoon's work and if the meal's too heavy and there's wine involved . . ." She finished her sentence with a shrug.

"I agree with you. It's one of the things Chris and I argued about . . . oh sorry, Liz. What a dumb thing to say."

"It's OK, Steph. You say 'one of the things' you argued about. Does that mean you argued a lot?"

Steph cursed herself for opening her big mouth. "Well, lately we did. He thinks I interfere too much. If I tried to discuss a menu, he'd tell me to concentrate on my job and leave the food to him."

Liz winced. "I can't believe he talked to you like that. Why didn't you tell me? You never let on that anything was wrong."

"Oh, how could I talk to you of all people, Liz? You're his wife, for God's sake."

"Was," Liz corrected.

Steph opened her mouth to reply but shut up as she saw the waiter approach, pen poised.

"Ready to order, ladies?" he said with a thin, watery smile. They gave their order and as he turned to leave, Steph called him back.

"Yes?" he said abruptly.

"The wine?" Steph indicated the empty glasses and gave him an icy look that usually made her staff quake in their shoes.

The waiter was unimpressed. "Oh right. What did you want?"

Steph looked at him in frustration and repeated the order.

Liz giggled at Steph's outraged expression as he disappeared again. "Maybe we should have just settled for a glass of the house wine."

Steph grinned. "The food *better* be good after all this."

The waiter brought the wine. It was the wrong year but Steph decided to hold her tongue. They'd die of thirst if she sent him away again.

"Nice wine." Liz emptied her glass.

Steph cringed. God, surely *she* wasn't going to take to the drink. "Could be colder," she replied, "and it's overpriced for the year. What do you think of the place? I think the furniture is wrong." She looked around the room. There were only two other parties in the restaurant. A table of four businessmen and a couple in a quiet corner who only had eyes for each other. She looked at the tableware. The glasses were good quality and a reasonable size but the cutlery was light and insubstantial – it wouldn't last long. Whoever had decked the place out was new to the business. It was put together on a budget and wasn't designed to last. They'd got it right with the napkins and tablecloths. They were good quality, obviously rented. Steph had strong views about table linen. The only way to maintain quality and cleanliness was by renting.

Liz looked around her half-heartedly. "I'd say it looks better at night. Anyway, forget about this place, tell me more about you and Chris."

Steph fidgeted with her fork. Damn. She'd hoped Liz had forgotten that conversation. "There's not much more to tell. He seemed to lose interest in the business. Profits have gone down in the last few months. That got me mad, then he got mad with me for pointing out his 'inadequacies' . . ."

Liz looked at her in dismay. "The quality went down? It was Chris's fault? But he seemed to be working so hard, he was never home . . . oh . . ." she trailed off, realising how Chris must have *actually* been spending his time. Her mouth set into a hard line.

Steph rummaged for her cigarettes. She'd promised Chris she'd help and instead she was damning him.

"The quality suffered a bit," she admitted, "but there's been a lot more competition this year. Three new restaurants have opened in the last six months and they're hurting us. Anyway, I didn't help. I could have handled Chris better." She hated herself for saying the words. She'd stopped blaming herself long ago for Chris's mistakes, but Liz didn't need to hear that.

She watched Liz as she fiddled nervously with her glass, lost in thought. She'd lost weight and looked drawn and tense. There was a fragile air about her. It reminded Steph of Ruth. She shivered.

Liz looked up absently as the waiter placed her salad of smoked chicken in front of her.

Steph leaned across to inspect. "That looks good." She'd opted for the soup.

Liz nodded, trying to appear interested. "Yes. The colour's good and there isn't too much dressing. There's nothing worse than a soggy salad." She popped a piece of chicken into her mouth. "It's good. Very delicate and light." She nodded appreciatively, though the food tasted like cardboard in her mouth. She chewed mechanically and pushed the plate towards Steph. "Try some."

Steph helped herself to a forkful of chicken and salad. "That's great. You know, you sounded like a chef there. I can't remember the last time I heard you talk about food like that. Would you ever think of going back into the business?"

Liz grinned wryly. Poor Steph. Trying to cheer her up. "I never really thought about it."

"You should," Steph said firmly, sniffing the aroma drifting up from her soup. "You're a damn good chef and the challenge might do you good."

"I don't know, Steph. It's not really me. I'm not like you. You know, I could never understand your ambition. I thought all women wanted what I wanted. A husband, a family, security. Security, that's a laugh. You must think I'm stupid."

Steph grinned at her friend. "Only sometimes. Anyway, you've a short memory. You were always much more ambitious than me before Lucy came along. If it wasn't for you, I'd probably be still in that bloody bank."

"I suppose," Liz agreed doubtfully. "Will you ever marry Seán?" she asked abruptly. Personal tragedy allowed you to cut through the bull and ask all kinds of intimate questions.

Steph was taken aback. "I doubt it," she said finally, carefully examining her perfectly manicured nails.

"Don't you want children?" Liz persisted.

Steph's voice was cold. "No, Liz, I don't."

Liz was shocked. "How's the soup?" she asked for want of something better to say.

"Very good." Steph frowned. "If they iron out the problems with the service, I think we've got some heavy competition here."

Liz looked at her sadly. Steph couldn't switch off long enough to discuss relationships, never mind have one. What an empty, pointless life!

Maybe she should take Chris back. Life with him, whatever his behaviour, was infinitely better than the prospect of being alone.

* * *

"Who was that?" Tom West looked up from his newspaper as his wife came back in from the phone. He was a large, heavy-set man, with steel-grey hair, tanned skin and brown eyes. He was easy-going, relaxed, but even a short conversation with him revealed a very keen mind and fine intellect. It was a year now since he'd handed over the reins of the business to Joe and his attention these days was focused on his family, his garden and his golf.

"Stephanie. Good news."

"She's marrying Seán?" he asked hopefully.

Catherine West rolled her eyes. "Don't be silly, Tom." She sat down gracefully in the chair opposite. She was a youthful sixty-four and it was obvious where Steph got her looks from. Catherine had the same incredible blue eyes, though hers had faded with the years. Her hair, once even blonder than her daughter's, was now darker and peppered with grey. She kept it in a neat bob, brushed back off her face. Her figure was slightly fuller these days, but she was still a very attractive woman.

Tom smiled at her affectionately. "Well, there's no harm hoping. So what is the news?"

"Chris has agreed to sell the restaurant to Stephanie."

"I think she's mad. What does she want to take on a responsibility like that for? She should be saving Jack's money for a rainy day."

"Don't you say that to her," she warned. "As long as she's happy, and she is." For the moment, she added silently to herself.

"I won't, I won't. When's she coming down?"

"Probably not until Monday – she's working all week."

"That Chris is a real slave-driver, though she'll be working even harder when she's her own boss." He saw his wife's expression. "Oh, Catherine, I'm proud of her, love, you know that, but I just wish she'd settle down a bit. She always seems to be on the go."

Catherine nodded. She knew it was hard for him to accept his daughter as a career woman. He'd always encouraged her in her ambitions but he'd assumed she'd marry and have a family as well. That was looking more and more unlikely. She sighed as she thought of her beautiful daughter. Not many people realised how insecure she really was. Ruth's death had had a terrible effect on her. She'd become suspicious and wary of men – she couldn't even seem to trust Seán. Catherine had been thrilled when Seán and Steph had got back together. No one understood Steph as well as he did. He *knew* her, he'd lived through that terrible time with her. Catherine had hoped that the years would have dimmed the memories, dealt with Steph's fears, that she'd be ready to settle down, but Stephanie seemed as determined as ever not to get involved.

Now Seán had gone off to Arizona. He'd asked Steph to

go with him but she'd refused. Catherine sighed. Poor Seán. Poor Stephanie. She became aware of her husband's scrutiny. "Would you like a cup of tea?" She stood up and headed for the kitchen.

"That would be nice, love." He looked after her and shook his head. She could deny it all she wanted, but he knew she worried about Stephanie just as much as he did. Maybe Seán would convince her to marry him yet. He must call him when he got back from Arizona and organise a game of golf. Have a chat, man to man. He smiled, happy with the idea, and turned his attention back to his newspaper.

* * *

Steph walked briskly down Merrion Square towards Hennessy, McDermott & Wallace. Joe had suggested Edward as the man to sort out her legal affairs. Stephanie was more than happy to use a friend of her brother's. Especially when he was as good-looking and charming as Edward. She'd taken extra care with her appearance today, discarding several outfits before finally settling on a cherry-coloured suit with a tight-fitting jacket and straight skirt that stopped just above the knee. She wanted to look smart, business-like but feminine. It was obvious from Edward's dinner companion that night in L'Ecrivain that he liked good-looking women.

"And what's that got to do with you?" said the small voice in her head. "You want a solicitor, not a boyfriend."

There's no harm in looking good though, she reasoned.

She ran up the stairs of the imposing Georgian house and buzzed.

"Coffee?" Edward asked, smiling.

Steph smiled back. "Yes, please," and looked around her with interest while Edward talked to his secretary. His office was more like a study, with a large mahogany desk that monopolised the room and green leather chairs that were both large and comfortable. To contrast the heavy furniture, the curtains were cream with a green regency stripe and a cream rug lay in the centre of a polished wooden floor. The only decorations on the stark cream walls were Edward's framed qualifications and a large map of Dublin. Edward looked completely at home in his dark double-breasted suit, pale cream shirt and burgundy tie. His dark, wiry hair was short and Steph couldn't help wondering what he'd look like in a powdered wig and gown.

Edward's secretary arrived with a tray of delicate china and a steaming pot of coffee. Edward asked about Joe and Annie while he served her. When he settled back with his own cup, he turned the conversation to the business at hand.

"Our first priority is to set out the ground rules with Chris once you've taken over. I've drawn up a draft contract, based on what you've told me. You can take it away with you, see if it's OK. Have you hammered out the figures with Chris yet?"

Steph nodded. "Yes. Amazingly enough, he's been quite

co-operative." Steph told him the figure she'd agreed with Chris and he nodded.

"Seems reasonable. And what about your loan?"

Steph's face clouded. "Ah, well, that's not going so well. My esteemed bank manager is a little on the conservative side. He's not convinced that Conor will be up to the job. He's put off by his youth. I'm afraid his idea of a good restaurant is probably an all-you-can-eat steakhouse.

Edward laughed. "You're probably right. Bank managers are the last people to actually *spend* money! Have you thought of an alternative?"

Stephanie looked at him curiously. "What do you mean?"

"Maybe a silent partner?"

Steph shook her head. "I don't know anyone with that kind of money."

Edward smiled warmly. "You do now."

Steph's eyes widened. *"You?"*

"Why not? I like to put my money into new enterprises. It's a lot more satisfying than bonds or savings accounts. It would have nothing to do with Hennessy, McDermott & Wallace. It would be a personal investment. Why don't you think about it? Give me a call in a couple of days."

Stephanie was lost for words. It would solve her problem and save her from grovelling to that small-minded bank manager. But what level of involvement would Edward want? She'd have to talk to Joe. "I will, Edward," she said finally. "It's a very interesting proposition."

An hour later she walked back across Merrion Square in a daze. Not only had she found herself a good solicitor, it seemed she might also have acquired a business partner. If it were possible, she'd prefer to run Chez Nous on her own, but there was no denying that a silent partner would make life a lot easier. And working with Edward McDermott – now that was quite a tantalising idea.

CHAPTER TEN

Liz put down the receiver, exhausted. She seemed to spend her life on the phone lying to her mother, to Annie, to Steph. Yes, she was fine. No, she couldn't make lunch she was visiting X.

X would be whoever she wasn't talking to. Her mother thought she'd spent yesterday with Steph. Annie thought she'd brought Lucy out for the day. Steph thought she was at a party in a neighbour's house tonight. That was a laugh! She hadn't mixed that much with her neighbours before but now that Chris was gone, she avoided them like the plague. She didn't need the third degree. She waved and smiled when she was coming or going, but she never stopped to talk.

Lucy peered over the banisters at her mother. Why had she told Granny that they were in Auntie Steph's yesterday? Lucy frowned. She wouldn't ask why, Mummy would just shout at her. She missed her daddy, but the amount of time she spent in Auntie Annie's with her best friend Dani made up for it. And Auntie Steph was great. She'd brought her to

83

the zoo on Monday. That was great fun. It was strange how much she got to go out now that Daddy didn't live with them. When she did see Daddy, he wasn't as grumpy as he used to be. He brought her to visit her granny last week. She loved her granny. She always had a surprise for Lucy and Granddad showed her how to plant flowers and gave her her very own little patch in his garden.

Everything would be fine if Mummy wasn't so sad. She hardly ever played games with her these days and Lucy hated the smelly cigarette smoke in the living-room. Mammy seemed to spend all day in there, sitting with the curtains drawn, watching TV.

"Lucy! Hurry up, we'll be late for school." Liz pulled a jacket over her dirty jumper, and brushed her hair half-heartedly. She felt so tired. She'd go back to bed for a couple of hours after she'd dropped Lucy.

Liz cursed her luck. There was no parking outside the school. She wouldn't be able to drop Lucy. She'd have to park up the road and walk back with her. Please God, that nosy Miss Harvey wouldn't be at the gate. That's all she needed. She took Lucy's hand and walked briskly towards the school. At the gate, she gave her a quick peck, before turning and hurrying back towards the car.

"Liz? Liz Connolly?"

Liz froze and turned slowly, pinning a smile to her face. Edward McDermott was walking towards her, a wide smile on his handsome face.

"Edward, how nice to meet you again," she lied.

"I thought it was you. Your little girl is in Carol's class."

Liz frowned. "I didn't know you had a daughter."

Edward laughed. "Oh, I don't. It's my niece, my sister's child. She works shifts, so I help out when I can. One of the perks of being the boss. I can be a little late some mornings."

Liz looked at his elegant suit, pristine white shirt and polished shoes. Why the hell did she have to meet him looking like this? She forced a smile. "Nice to see you again." She turned back towards the car.

He followed her. "How about a quick coffee?"

She looked at him in surprise. Why was this gorgeous man asking her out for coffee? God, she must look really pathetic. He felt sorry for her. He'd probably heard all about Chris. Her expression hardened. She didn't need pity. "Sorry, I've got to go. Maybe some other time."

"I'll hold you to that," he promised, holding the door for her.

She barely nodded, pulled the door shut and drove away.

Edward stood looking after the car. He wasn't quite sure why he'd suggested coffee – it was on the spur of the moment. Annie had told him about the Connolly break-up and it seemed to be taking its toll. Liz looked nothing like the beautiful woman he'd met in L'Ecrivain. She'd seemed desperate to get away from him and had taken off like a bat out of hell. He must be losing his touch.

Liz drove too fast up the Stillorgan Road. She was breathing very fast and was almost tearful. What the hell was wrong with her? A man asked her out for coffee and she'd panicked. She pulled into the driveway and ran for the door, her head down. Inside, she caught sight of herself in the hall mirror. God, she was a disgrace. Her hair was greasy and unkempt, her skin was grey and her eyes heavy. Damn it, she'd have to get rid of that bloody mirror. The phone rang and she walked past it up the stairs. When it stopped, she took it off the hook and rolled up in a ball on her bed. She wouldn't get in. She'd just lie down for half an hour. Then she'd have a shower and do the ironing.

Liz woke to the doorbell ringing persistently. Damn them, she thought. She looked at the alarm clock. Christ, it was one o'clock. Lucy! She scrambled out of bed and ran down the stairs. When she opened the door, Miss Harvey stood there with a tearful Lucy by the hand.

"Oh, Miss Harvey, I'm so sorry, you see I haven't been well and . . ."

Olive Harvey looked at the dishevelled Mrs Connolly, and the untidy kitchen in the background. "I tried to ring, but it was engaged. You really should have contacted me," she said, talking to Liz as if she was one of the four-year-olds she taught.

Liz bit back a retort. "I'm really sorry, Miss Harvey. The phone doesn't seem to be working, and like I say, I haven't been too well. I fell asleep. It must have been the tablets the doctor gave me." God, lies tripped off her tongue so easily these days. She muttered some more apologies and finally closed the door on the disapproving but slightly mollified teacher.

"Go and wash your hands, Lucy, and then we'll go to McDonald's."

Lucy looked curiously at her mother. Mummy didn't

approve of McDonald's, but they were going there an awful lot lately. "But Mummy, maybe we shouldn't go out if you're sick."

Liz hugged her daughter tightly, feeling truly sick about the worried look she'd put on her little girl's face. "But now *you're* here, love, I feel much better. Would you prefer it if I made you a *special* lunch?"

Lucy nodded in delight. Mummy's food was always great. It was ages since she'd made anything nice. Beans on toast didn't count.

"Mummy, do you hate Daddy now?" Lucy asked later through a mouthful of pasta.

Liz looked at her in shock. What was she doing to her child? "No, love, of course I don't. Me and Daddy are just angry with each other at the moment. It's nothing for you to worry about, honestly. I love you and Daddy loves you."

Lucy wasn't satisfied. "But Mummy, when is Daddy coming home?"

Liz sighed. If Lucy was like this at four, what would she be like when she was a teenager?

"I don't know, love."

"Doesn't he want to live with us anymore?"

"Yes, he does, pet, but I don't want him to live here at the moment."

Lucy stuck her lip out, a sure sign that she was ready to throw a tantrum.

"Listen, love. Grown-ups have rows sometimes. It's better that Daddy's not here right now, because we'd only fight. You wouldn't like that, would you?"

Lucy shook her head reluctantly. "But *why* would you fight?"

Liz was losing her patience. "We just would. It's nothing for you to worry about, Lucy. Now finish your lunch." Liz picked up her coffee and went into the living-room. She switched on the TV and lit a cigarette, the ironing forgotten.

* * *

Steph brought the tray of coffee over to Joe and Edward and sat down to join them. It was just gone three and there was only one other party in the restaurant. The days of long boozy lunches were long gone.

Edward flashed a warm smile at Stephanie. "That was a lovely lunch, Stephanie. Who was responsible for the rack of lamb?"

"Conor." She returned his smile. That was lucky. A brownie point for her choice of chef. "I'll give him a shout in a few minutes. Introduce you."

"Is Chris about?" Joe asked.

Steph shook her head. "No, he's headed off for the afternoon. Probably banging on Liz's door as we speak."

"She still hasn't talked to him?" Joe was surprised. He'd thought Liz would cave in much sooner than this.

"Nope. Well, not about what happened. She talks to him about Lucy, but that's it."

"How's she coping?" Edward asked.

Steph smiled. "Really well. I didn't think she could be so strong."

Edward said nothing. Either Stephanie was blind or Liz was a bloody good actress. She didn't seem to be coping at all, to him. He'd seen Lucy standing outside the school in floods because her mummy hadn't come to collect her. He'd offered to drop her home, but Miss Harvey had made it very clear that it would be inappropriate for her to hand Lucy over to a stranger. She'd made him feel like a child molester. Still, he could see her point. You couldn't be too careful these days. Poor Liz. She deserved better than a shit like Connolly. Next time he saw her, he'd insist on taking her for a coffee.

"Edward?"

He looked up to see Steph's eyes on him. "Sorry, I was miles away."

"I was just saying to Joe. We should go over the contracts together before we get Chris to sign. How are you fixed on Saturday afternoon?"

"Fine, but aren't you working?"

"Nope," she said happily. "I'm off for a full week."

"Well for some," Joe muttered.

Steph ignored him. "Come out to my place around two. We should have it all wrapped up within a couple of hours. That OK, Joe?"

Joe stood up. "No problem. I'll see you then. Can I give you a lift, Edward?"

"No, that's OK, Joe. I enjoy the walk. It's the only exercise I get these days."

Steph looked at his athletic frame and thought otherwise. Joe left and she offered Edward more coffee. He accepted, smiling into her eyes. God, he was gorgeous, Steph thought. His eyes were the strangest colour. They appeared to be grey but sometimes they looked almost brown. She wondered why he was hanging on? Maybe he was going to ask her out? Oh but she couldn't. What about Seán?

"Do you think Liz will take Chris back?" he asked stirring his coffee absently.

She looked up surprised. Was Edward worried the deal wouldn't go through if they didn't get back together?

"I don't know, but either way, I think Chris will go to Galway. Don't worry, he won't back out."

Edward smiled again. "I'm sure he won't. Why don't you introduce me to Conor. I'd love to meet him."

Stephanie went off to find Conor, feeling slightly disappointed.

Edward and Conor hit it off immediately. Edward asked intelligent questions about their lunch, and Conor answered enthusiastically, glad of the interest. Stephanie left them together and went up to the office. She was a bit nervous about how fast things were moving. Now that Edward was her partner, and Chris had agreed to stay on, there was nothing to stop the deal going through. She hadn't expected things to go quite this smoothly. She hoped it wasn't the calm before the storm. She still hadn't told Seán what was happening. Any time they'd talked, one of them had been interrupted and despite all her good intentions, she hadn't had the heart-to-heart with him she'd been promising herself. Maybe on Saturday. When Joe and Edward had gone. Yes. Saturday.

Edward poked his head around the door. "I'm off now. See you on Saturday?"

"See you then." She grinned wryly as the door closed behind him. "Big head," she muttered to herself. "He's only after you for your restaurant!"

CHAPTER ELEVEN

Stephanie brushed the hair back off her face impatiently and reached absently for her cigarettes. She was sitting cross-legged in the middle of her sitting-room floor surrounded by files and papers. In her faded denims and white cotton shirt she looked more like a teenager than a successful businesswoman. Edward and Joe were at the dining-room table in the alcove, bent over a document, muttering to each other.

Stephanie reached for her mug and took a mouthful of tepid liquid. She winced. "Are you ready for more coffee?" She stood up and stretched, massaging the crick in her neck that seemed to be permanent these days.

Edward looked up at her long slender frame appreciatively. "No. I've got a better idea. Let's go for a pint – I think we deserve one."

Joe, still lost in thought, tapped mercilessly at his calculator.

Edward gave him a dig in the ribs. "What about it, Joe? A pint?"

"What? Oh, no. You two go on. I have to get my head around this. I won't be happy until I'm finished."

"What about it, Steph?"

"Yeah, why not? Just let me get some shoes on." She hurried off to the bedroom, put on her desert boots and grabbed a sweatshirt.

"You won't be able to wear gear like that for much longer," Edward warned as she returned to the sitting-room. "You'll have to wear little designer numbers when you're a famous restaurateur and the paparazzi want to come out and photograph you at home."

Stephanie looked around ruefully. "I'll have to decorate this place first. It wouldn't do much for my image if they saw it at the moment.

"Oh, I don't know. I like it as it is." Edward looked around the airy, peaches and cream room. It was decorated with comfort in mind. The large sofa was inviting and cushions in a variety of pastel shades crowded it and the matching armchair. Apart from the suite the only furniture was a coffee table and a sleek black-ash dining-room suite. Sunshine flooded in from the balcony window, casting a warm golden glow throughout the room. The overall effect was one of comfort and space.

"I like it," Steph admitted. "Now are you buying me that drink or not? Sure you won't come, Joe?"

Joe muttered something unintelligible.

"Come on, Steph. Let's leave him to it. He won't even notice we're gone."

The phone rang just after they left.

After ignoring it for a few rings, Joe remembered he was alone and picked up the receiver.

"Hello?"

"Hello? Joe? Is that you?"

"Seán?"

"Yeah, that's right. Don't tell me I'm getting an American accent?"

"Ah, no. There's a bit of Dub there yet." They both laughed. "So how are things going in Arizona?"

"Really taking off, Joe, I'm glad to say. A few teething troubles, but I suppose that's to be expected."

"Oh sure. You're better off having them now than later."

"Yeah, you 're right. Listen, this is costing me a fortune. Can I have a word with Steph?"

"Oh, sorry, Seán. She's just gone to the pub with Edward."

"Who?"

Joe hesitated. "Edward, a mate of mine. He's a solicitor. Steph's new partner?"

"Partner?" Seán echoed.

Joe groaned inwardly. He was in way over his head here. He'd kill Steph. "Look, sorry Seán, I have to run. I'll get Steph to call you later. I'm sure she's dying to tell you everything herself. Bye now. Look after yourself." Joe rang off and sighed heavily. Why the hell hadn't Steph filled Seán in? Jesus, women.

"Hello? Hello? Joe?"

Seán took the phone from his ear and looked at it in bewilderment. What was going on? What kind of partnership was he talking about and why had Steph not

93

told him about it? And why was she down in the pub on a Saturday afternoon with a solicitor called Edward. Who the hell was he? He wandered over to the window of his apartment. A pale morning haze hung over Phoenix and the sun was making its first appearance, promising another beautiful day. He loved it here, but he couldn't wait to get back to Dublin and Stephanie.

But did she feel the same way?

Seán banged his head against the window. He'd let her down and now he had to find a way to make it up to her, make her forget all about this "Edward" guy.

* * *

Edward negotiated his way through Gibneys, zigzagging through the rugby buffs. He placed Steph's lager in front of her and settled his pint carefully beside it.

"Is it always like this?" he said looking around.

Steph grinned. "Nah. Usually it's busy."

"I must be getting old," Edward said with a wry smile.

"Come back after eight and you'll feel positively geriatric! So tell me. Are you happy with the progress we're making? Are we doing OK?"

Edward took a long gulp of his pint and nodded. "Yes, I'm very happy. What about Conor? How's he adapting to the whole idea?"

"He's chuffed. When he isn't cooking, he's studying. He's spent a fortune on all the latest cookery books. I should really reimburse him."

Edward nodded. "Absolutely. When does he head over to London?"

"Next week." Steph had been delighted and amazed when Chris had offered to phone Albert Roux and ask him to take Conor under his wing. Albert had readily agreed and Conor had been on cloud nine ever since. When he finished his stint in London, he'd be going to work in Belfast with Paul Rankin for a while.

"He's a different guy, Edward, you wouldn't believe it. He was really fed up. I was expecting him to pack his bags any day. It was very tough on him. He'd so much talent and enthusiasm but Chris just kept closing him down."

"A bit like he closed you down?" Edward asked quietly.

"Yes. I suppose so. Still, that's water under the bridge." She took a sip from her glass. "So, tell me something about Edward McDermott. We're partners now and I hardly know a thing about you, except that you're Joe's friend and you're a solicitor."

Edward leaned over and smiled into her eyes. "I tell you what – have dinner with me tonight and I'll tell you my life story."

Stephanie flushed. "You'll hold nothing back? You'll tell me *everything* I want to know?" she teased.

He put his hand to his heart. "I shall withhold nothing."

"Fair enough. Just one condition. I pick the restaurant."

He looked at her in mock horror. "You're not going to bankrupt me, are you?"

"Ummm, no, not quite."

"Then it's a date." He smiled warmly at her.

Joe raised his head as the door opened. "Seán's looking for you. He seems a bit in the dark about things."

Stephanie looked from Edward's curious face to her brother's grim one. She forced a smile. "No problem, I'll call him later. Now I want you two to get out of here. Annie will be really fed up with you, Joe. I appreciate all the work, but I don't want to be the cause of a divorce."

Joe stretched and yawned. He looked at his watch and sprang up. "Jesus, I'd no idea it was so late. Come on, Edward, she'll kill me."

"OK Joe, don't panic." Edward slipped some papers into his briefcase, closed it with a snap and followed Joe to the door. "Pick you up about eight, Steph?"

"Eh yeah, great," she looked down to avoid her brother's questioning gaze. "Thanks again, bye now." She hustled the two men out and leaned against the door with a groan. Time to face the music. She picked up the phone and put it down again. Just a little Dutch courage. She went out to the kitchen and poured a glass of wine. She checked her watch. Six thirty. It would be lunch-time over there. She took a sip from the glass and dialled.

"Hello – Seán Adams. Sorry I'm not in right now. Leave a message after the tone."

"Seán, it's me, Stephanie. Eh, sorry I missed you earlier. It's – eh – six thirty here, eh – talk to you later. Bye." She slammed down the receiver. Damn it!

Two hours later, as she walked down the steps to the car, laughing and talking with Edward, her telephone rang and the answering machine kicked in.

"Hi Stephanie, it's Seán. Sorry we keep missing each other. It's probably around eight your time so I'll try to catch you at Joe's. If not we'll talk tomorrow. I miss you."

* * *

"Ruth! Who's he?" Stephanie strained to get a good look at the man standing at the door.

Ruth looked around. "Oh, that's Seán. Seán Adams. Nice, isn't he?"

"Nice? Nice? He's gorgeous! Introduce me, but make it look casual. Bump into me or something. Well, go on!" she urged.

Ruth knew she'd get no peace if she didn't so she pushed her way through the crowd. "Hiya, Seán," she shouted over the noise of Led Zeppelin. "Thanks for coming. I think you know everyone. Follow me and I'll get you a drink."

"Howya, Ruth," Seán grinned at her and proffered a six-pack. "I brought some of my own."

"Good man, but let me get you a cold one," Ruth said as she crashed into Stephanie. "Oh sorry, Steph. Didn't see you there. Have you two met?"

Steph looked up into a pair of gorgeous twinkling brown eyes and felt weak at the knees. "I don't think so," she said, smiling up at him. She was quite tall at five foot seven, but he still seemed to tower over her.

"Believe me, we haven't," Seán murmured.

Ruth looked from one to the other and grinned. "I'll get you that drink, Seán." He didn't appear to hear her.

"I haven't seen you around the campus," Seán said.

"Oh, I'm not a student. God forbid! I'm a working woman."

"Really? What do you do?"

"I'm in the bank."

"That sounds interesting," Seán said. "Tell me all about it."

Steph had never thought of the bank as interesting before. "Well, I'm usually on the front desk. Either at the cashier's desk or in the foreign exchange."

"They must think very highly of you, to give you such responsibility at your age," he said, his eyes full of admiration.

"Oh, I don't know," Steph said, flushed with embarrassment and pleasure.

Ruth returned with Seán's drink. God, they really had it bad. Seán hardly noticed the can being shoved into his hand.

"Are you studying computer science too?" Steph thought it only polite to ask.

"Yeah. Ruth's in my year. She's a great girl. Definitely going to be top of the class. I'll probably get through by the skin of my teeth."

Steph nodded sympathetically. "That's the way I was at school. I don't know how you could go on and do another four years of studying. It would kill me."

"I'm sure you'd be great at anything you tried to do," Seán said, moving closer. "Has anyone ever told you that you have the most amazing eyes?"

Steph looked up into his face thinking his weren't so bad either. Chocolate brown, melting. They were certainly making her hot!

"It's hard to talk with all this noise, isn't it?" His mouth was almost touching her ear. "Want to go somewhere a bit quieter?"

Steph felt her heartbeat quicken. "That would be nice," she said with a stupid smile.

"Where are you off to?" Ruth asked as she saw Stephanie sling her bag over her shoulder and head for the door.

Stephanie smiled dreamily at her. "Just going somewhere a bit quieter. Where we can talk, you know?"

"Talk, huh?"

"He's OK, isn't he?" Steph asked anxiously. "Not an axe-murderer, or anything?"

"Not that I know of," Ruth said drily. "No, seriously, he's a great guy. You could do a lot worse."

Steph winked happily. "I'll call you tomorrow."

"You'd better," threatened Ruth and then went off in search of the dishy history student who answered to the name of Trev.

* * *

Steph snuggled up to Seán on the sofa. "Happy anniversary," she whispered and kissed him on the ear.

"It's our anniversary?" he asked, raising an eyebrow.

"Yup. We've been going out together two and a half months."

"Oh well, in that case we'd better do something to celebrate. Any ideas?" He swung her onto his lap and kissed her slowly.

Steph drew back. "Mmmnn. That's one idea, or we could go out."

"Where?"

"Well, the gang are meeting up in the Baggot Inn."

"The gang?" he asked suspiciously. "Would that consist of Ruth and Des Healy by any chance?"

Steph ducked her head. "Oh, Seán, I know he's a pain, but what can I do? Ruth's my best friend."

"For a clever girl, she sure has lousy taste in men. I thought Trev was bad enough. At least he was just a druggie. But Des Healy. He's such a prat. If I have to spend one more night listening to him talk about that damn car of his. And he's always going on about the commission he makes, but you never see him put his hand in his pocket." He broke off as he saw Steph's expression. "OK, Steph. But just keep him away from me."

Steph hugged him fiercely. "You are the best, Seán Adams. You know that?"

"It's true," he agreed.

"Steph, over here."

Steph and Seán pushed their way through the crowd.

"Hiya, Ruth."

"Hi. Hi, Seán."

"Howya, Ruth. Is Des getting the drinks, then?" he asked ignoring Steph's warning look.

"No, Seán. He couldn't make it."

"Ah, that's too bad." He grinned broadly.

"No, he had to go down the country. Important business."

"What else?" Seán muttered and was given a dig in the ribs from Steph.

"Why don't you go to the bar," Steph asked him pointedly.

"Right so. Harp OK? Same again for you, Ruth? Right. Back in a minute."

Steph pulled off her coat and scarf and pulled up a stool beside Ruth. "Well?"

"Well what?" Ruth asked.

"You and Des. Is everything OK?"

"Of course. I told you. He's away on business."

"He does a lot of that," Stephanie remarked grimly.

"What's that supposed to mean?" Ruth asked hotly.

"Nothing Ruth, nothing," Steph said. "Just saying."

"Well, don't say. You don't know what you're talking about."

"Fair enough," Steph muttered. "So is anybody else coming?"

"Why? Afraid I'm going to play gooseberry?" Ruth asked.

"Of course not. I was just asking."

"Robbie, Richard and Karen said they'd be here," Ruth replied.

"Great," Steph said brightly. Good. She'd get Seán to herself for a while after all.

CHAPTER TWELVE

"Stephanie. How *are* you? *Good* to see you."

"You too, Tony," Steph replied drily. Maybe it had been a mistake to bring Edward to Lorenzo's.

"Your table isn't quite ready. Why don't you – and your *friend* take a seat at the bar, have a drink and I'll get some menus."

Steph looked at Edward.

He nodded. "Yes, that's fine. What would you like to drink?"

"I think I'll have a Bloody Mary." She smiled at Edward as she climbed on to the high stool and fixed her dress. Thank God she'd decided against the mini. She'd decided that something more sophisticated was called for and she'd chosen a long blue silk sarong that reached to her ankles. The effect was breathtaking and youthful. She was glad she'd discarded the casual mini when Edward arrived in a smart navy blazer, lemon Calvin Klein shirt and beige chinos.

Edward turned to Tony. "A Bloody Mary and a gin and

tonic, please." As Tony went to get the drinks, Edward bent his head towards Steph's. "Is it my imagination or is there something going on between you two?"

"Don't mind Tony. He just likes slagging me. I told him you were a business partner, but he obviously doesn't believe me."

"Is that *all* I am?" He said, looking injured and she felt her cheeks get hot.

Damn. You weren't supposed to blush when you were in your thirties!

She fumbled in her bag for cigarettes, momentarily thrown by the warmth of his voice. "Well, like I said, Edward, I hardly know anything about you, so until you fill me in I'll have to reserve judgement."

She looked up at him through a haze of smoke, hoping she looked calmer then she felt.

"I see I'm not going to be let off the hook but at least let's order first." Edward handed her a menu.

Stephanie started to relax now she was back on solid ground, talking about the subject closest to her heart. They made their choices and turned their attention to the wine list.

They were almost finished their drinks when Tony approached them. "I'll show you to your table. One of the girls will bring up the wine." He led the way upstairs and showed them to a table in a dark corner, avoiding Steph's eyes as he held out her chair. "Enjoy your meal."

When he left, Stephanie rolled her eyes. "He doesn't give up, does he? Now, Mr McDermott, tell me all about yourself."

"Well, what's Joe told you? Or, more to the point, what has Annie said about me?"

"Why do you say that?" Steph said, curious. She thought Edward and Annie got on very well.

"Oh, I don't know. She's a lovely lady but sometimes I get the feeling that she doesn't quite approve of me."

Steph laughed. "You're probably right, but that shouldn't surprise you. You're not exactly the kind of man that a woman likes to see her husband befriending."

Edward looked wounded. "Why not? I'm a nice guy."

"A nice guy who's single, has a hectic social life and always has a beautiful woman on his arm."

He leaned forward his eyes travelling over her, "Well, the last part is certainly true tonight."

Stephanie blinked. Was he actually chatting her up? She smiled coolly. "Stop trying to change the subject. I want your full life history."

He shrugged. "OK, but it's boring. I'm an only child, born in England. We came back to Dublin when I was ten."

"Whereabouts did you live?"

"Terenure."

"A south-sider!" Stephanie said in disgust.

"You are too, surely, or do you call yourself a Wicklow woman?"

Stephanie shook her head vehemently. "Neither. Mam and Dad only moved to Greystones when Dad retired. I was born and bred in Clontarf. Just up the road from here."

"Oh. I didn't realise. Joe was in a flat by the time I met him, so I presumed . . ."

"Nope. I'm a staunch north-sider and remember to behave yourself," she gestured at the people around them, "because tonight you're surrounded."

"I'll remember," he promised solemnly. "Anyway, Dad was a solicitor, so I suppose it was taken for granted that I'd follow in his footsteps. I went to Trinity, joined his firm and here I am."

Stephanie looked at him suspiciously. "You sound like a cross between a bookworm and a choirboy. What about teenage drinking binges? Wild parties when your parents were away? Girlfriends?"

Stephanie was interrupted by the arrival of their starters. Bruscetta for him and tiger prawns in a garlic and chilli sauce for her. Steph eyed the food appreciatively. This was what she loved about Lorenzo's. Proof that it wasn't necessary to pay a king's ransom to get a good meal in Dublin. She said as much to Edward.

"That's good coming from the owner of one of the most expensive restaurants in the city!" he retorted with a laugh.

"Ah, but we're worth every penny. No, seriously, you know what I mean." She gestured at their food. "This is good, simple food for a reasonable price. No frills, no gimmicks, just good value."

Edward bit into his bruscetta. "Well, it certainly tastes good," he agreed.

Steph smiled triumphantly. "Anyway. You were about to tell me about the juicier parts of your past," she prompted.

"I was hoping you'd forgotten." He took a gulp of his wine. "Wild parties? Not really." He shrugged at her disbelieving look. "Honestly. It wasn't until I left home that I really discovered the pleasures of a bohemian life. I shared a flat in Ranelagh with three other lads. We were too broke to go to the pub, so we'd stay at home or go to other flats and have parties that involved very cheap wine, or cider when we were really desperate. That's when I met Joe. As for girlfriends, it was your typical student scene. We all hung out in a gang and changed partners on a regular basis."

Stephanie dabbed her lips with her napkin. "So then you qualified. You'd more money in your pocket. What then?"

"Oh, well, then I *did* start to live a little. I had to put in a lot of hours at the office, though. My father was a firm believer in starting at the bottom. So I worked hard. But I played hard too."

"Aahh, now we come to the sordid details! Fast women and wild parties?"

Edward grinned wickedly. "Absolutely!"

"So was there ever anyone special?" Stephanie couldn't understand how he was still unattached. He was charming with a good sense of humour and he was very good-looking. It never occurred to her that she was in a similar position.

He twirled his glass absently, his face tense and withdrawn.

"I'm sorry. Have I overstepped the mark?"

He looked up, almost surprised to see her there. "No, no, of course not. Anyone special? Only one. A very long time ago."

"And you never met anyone else? What about the red-head?" she asked curiously.

Edward looked confused.

"The woman who was with you when we met in the restaurant?" she prompted.

"Oh, Gayle. She's just a friend. Not exactly the girl-next-door type. She enjoys life. I stand in when she's between boyfriends. There have been a couple of others, but nothing serious. I'm not interested in getting involved."

"I don't blame you." Steph agreed drily.

"That sounds a bit cynical. What about this 'Seán' character?"

"Seán's the best in the world," she admitted. "I've never met anyone like him. We've known each other for years, but . . ."

"But?"

She sighed. "He wants more," she said simply.

"And you're not ready?"

She shook her head.

"The restaurant's very important to you, isn't it?"

"It's my big chance. An opportunity to turn things around and make something of my life. I can't walk away from that."

"And is that what he's asked you to do? Tell him to take a hike." He dismissed Seán as if he were swatting a fly.

Steph was amused. "Oh no. Seán's not like that. It's not quite that simple. I'd be happy for us to go on as we are, but I don't think he is. I'm not really interested in being a wife or a mother. I don't think I'll ever be." She pulled out a tissue and blew her nose noisily. "How did we get on to this? You're supposed to be telling me all about you, and instead, I'm telling you *my* troubles."

He smiled. "It's my charm. No woman can resist it."

"Modest too. You know, you're not at all what I expected."

"What did you expect?"

"I thought you'd chat me up and then try to talk me into going to bed with you."

He gave her a lascivious grin. "Well, the night's not over yet!"

She slapped his hand. "Shame on you, Mr McDermott! Seriously though, thanks for inviting me out. It's ages since I've had such a good time."

"Glad to be of service." He bowed solemnly. He leaned forward, his eyes suddenly serious. "I want this partnership to work, Stephanie. I want you to feel that you can come to me about anything. I won't interfere, but I'm there if you need me."

"Thanks, Edward. I appreciate that."

"You obviously love what you do. How did someone who started out in a bank end up running a restaurant?"

"It's a long story." Steph explained how Liz and Annie had known each other for years. They'd met in the local youth-club and become fast friends. Annie and Steph had worked together in the bank and Steph had first met Liz at a dance in Clontarf Rugby Club and the two girls had hit it off immediately.

"Liz had just finished her training and had got a job in The Burlington. She was doing very well for herself. She met Chris on a training course. They were married two years when they decided to go out on their own. A few months later, Liz asked me to come and work for them and the rest, as they say, is history. I took to it like a duck to water. I'd never really had any idea of what I wanted to do before. Joining Chez Nous was like coming home. I loved the thought of being responsible for someone's enjoyment for a couple of hours. To feed them, help them to relax and then see them come back for more." She looked up at him, slightly embarrassed. "I'm afraid I don't explain it very well."

Edward shook his head. "You explain it very well indeed. I only wish more restaurateurs felt as passionately about their job as you do."

Steph smiled. "That's the first time I've been called a restaurateur. I think I like it."

Edward raised his glass. "I look forward to working with you, partner."

She smiled happily. "Me too."

CHAPTER THIRTEEN

"Seán? Seán, hi, it's me."

"Steph? Hi, thanks for getting back to me."

Odd reply, she thought. You'd think she was a stranger. She decided to ignore it. "Sorry I missed you yesterday – things are hectic here. I've got so much to tell you."

"Oh. Right." Seán sounded slightly mollified. "I'm glad *you're* paying for the call so."

Steph was relieved to hear the lighter note in his voice. "I don't know where to begin, Seán. I haven't said anything before because, well, because I didn't know how you'd react. I thought you'd give me a hard time. Look, the fact is, I'm buying Chris out. Me and a partner, Edward McDermott. He's a solicitor. A friend of Joe's."

"You're what? How? That's great! Why did you think I'd have a go at you?"

"I don't know. You wanted me to leave and I wanted to stick with the job. Then it turned out Chris was thinking of moving on anyway, so everything has kind of fallen into place."

She told him about their progress and the plans for Conor's training in other restaurants.

"He's working his butt off already. Wait till you taste some of his new dishes," she told him. "My mouth waters just thinking about them."

"He must be over the moon. It's a great opportunity for someone so young."

"Yes, he's delighted. We're hoping that will attract some good publicity. You know the sort of thing. Young, trendy, progressive." She went on to give him a brief history of Edward's involvement and referred casually to their business dinner the previous night.

There was silence at the other end of the phone.

Finally. "So it was just the two of you?"

"Yeah, Joe wasn't in the mood," she lied – it was easier.

"Right. And this guy's come up with thirty per cent of the capital?"

"That's right."

"Where did he get that kind of money? It's not the sort of thing you'd think a solicitor would want to invest in, is it?"

Steph paused. "I don't know where he got the money. I suppose he earned it. He's very successful. He's bound to have put some money by, isn't he? Anyway, why wouldn't he want to invest in a well-known restaurant?"

Another silence. Then: "Why didn't you ask me? I could have put you in touch with a potential investor. I've plenty of contacts. Have you checked this guy out?"

Stephanie was getting impatient. "I *told* you, Seán. He's a friend of Joe's."

"I've never heard Joe mention him before," he remarked.

"Why would he? Look, they've known each other since college." She paused but he said nothing. She continued more gently. "I'm sorry I didn't tell you, but I didn't think you'd take me seriously. I thought you'd try to put me off and I couldn't handle that."

"God, I can't believe this. I can't believe you were afraid to talk to me."

There was another pause and she could almost see him raking his fingers through his hair, a habit of his when he was frustrated.

"You have to believe me, Steph. I never doubted *you*. But you were so depressed about Chris, about Chez Nous. I was just worried. You were cracking up before my eyes and I didn't know what to do or say. I should have known better, though. I should have realised you'd sort him out. I'm sorry I let you down, love."

"You didn't. It's OK," she said gently. "You're right. I was cracking up. But I just couldn't have given up and walked away."

Seán sighed. "You're something else, you know that? I'm so proud of you. You'll make a great success of this. With your strength how could you possibly fail? Steph? Steph? Are you still there?"

"Yes," she sniffed. "Why are you so nice to me? I don't deserve you. I'm always fighting with you."

Seán laughed softly. "Ah but deep, deep, down I know you really care."

Steph laughed and hiccuped at the same time. "I've missed talking to you."

"Me, too. Look, I'm going to hang up now. This is costing you a fortune. I'll call you tomorrow, say at five your time?"

"OK."

"Oh, by the way. I knew I'd something else to tell you. I'm coming home on Wednesday morning."

"Seán! That's brilliant!"

"I'm glad you think so. Any chance of you taking the night off?"

"I'm actually off all week. Are you sure you won't be too tired after the flight, though?"

"Well, if I am, we could always have an early night."

Steph smiled. "Mmmn. I suppose we could."

"OK love, look, I'm going to hang up now. I'll talk to you tomorrow."

"Bye Seán . . . and Seán?"

"Yeah?"

"I love you."

"I love you too. Take care."

* * *

The following morning, Stephanie was up early, moving quickly around the apartment tidying, polishing and scrubbing. She sang along with the radio as she worked. The windows and doors were thrown open to allow in the sunshine and sea air and washing swung on the line on the balcony.

Annie stood in the doorway, mesmerised by her sister-in-law's vitality and good humour. Steph was balancing gingerly on the windowsill, hanging on to the window

113

frame with one hand and polishing furiously with the other. Her face was flushed with the effort and she hadn't noticed Annie. In her T-shirt and cut-off jeans she looked about sixteen.

"Any chance of you coming over and starting on my place when you're done here?" Annie put a hand up to steady Steph as she swayed precariously. "Sorry. Didn't mean to startle you."

"That's OK." Stephanie climbed down and brushed her hands off on the seat of her jeans. "Coffee?" She headed for the kitchen.

Annie followed. "Just a quick one. I'm on my way round to Mam's. I was just wondering how things went with Edward on Saturday night."

Stephanie put on the coffee and took two mugs from a shelf. "Edward and I had a lovely evening."

"Oh?"

Steph looked at Annie in amusement. "Oh? Oh what? We had a nice evening, he's a nice man and I think we're going to make a good team. *Working* team," she added hastily when she saw Annie's expression.

"Any word from Seán?" Annie asked innocently.

"Yes, as it happens. I was talking to him last night. He's coming home on Wednesday."

"And what about Edward?"

Stephanie looked confused. "What about him?"

Annie looked at her blank expression. She wasn't going to get any information out of her. "Did he leave you home?" she asked.

Steph wagged a finger at her. "He dropped me off in a taxi. You've a dirty mind, Annie West!"

"Just asking."

"I told you, Annie. The only thing that interests me about Edward are his contacts and his money. Anyway, he's not interested in me either. Determined to remain footloose and fancy free and good luck to him."

Annie sighed in relief. Thank God for that. She checked her watch. "Aren't you going in to the restaurant today?"

"Nope. I've got the week off." Steph ignored Annie's look of mock horror. "Oh shut up! I've been working every hour that God sends for weeks now. I'm in a lull at the moment and I haven't seen the folks for a while so I thought I'd go down to Greystones this evening.

"I suppose it would also allow you to spend some time with Seán," Annie said innocently.

"Well, I am seeing him on Wednesday evening," Steph conceded with a grin.

"Your mam will be chuffed to see him."

Steph pulled a face. "I know. She'll be thrilled."

"Why don't you hit the road now, while you've got the light?"

Steph shook her head. "No. Liz is coming to lunch. I've been trying to get together with her for weeks, but she always seems to find an excuse. Why don't you stay? She'd love to see you."

"I can't. My mother's expecting me. I said I'd bring her to town. She needs some curtains." Annie was disappointed. She quite liked the idea of a leisurely lunch and a natter. "How is Liz?"

"A lot better, I think. She seems to be living a fairly busy life anyway. She still won't talk about Chris though, and she's showing no interest in Galway."

"And how *is* Chris?"

"Keeping out of my hair, thank God. No, he seems to be behaving himself. I hate to admit it, but he's working quite hard. He seems genuinely upset about Liz, but then, you never know with Chris."

"Well, I'd better go. Tell Liz I was asking for her and give my love to your folks. Tell them we'll be down next week."

Liz drove her Fiat 127 along the Malahide Road, lost in thought. She'd wracked her brains for excuses not to come out today, but Stephanie knew that Lucy was with Chris so there was no way out. She didn't want to get into any heavy conversations about her marriage at the moment. Mind you, Steph would probably take the hint. She hated being questioned about Seán. With Annie it was harder. She knew exactly how her mind worked and what questions to ask. Liz didn't think Annie would be too impressed with the way her mind was working lately. She was thinking of taking Chris back. What else could she do? How would she ever manage on her own? Lucy needed her daddy. The thought of resuming her life with Chris seemed almost attractive after the last couple of months.

It would be easier if he came back. He wasn't perfect, he never would be and she'd never trust him again. But he was better than nothing.

She pulled up outside Steph's apartment. As she grabbed the wine and got out of the car, Steph ran down the steps to meet her. She'd changed out of her shorts and into a lemon shift mini-dress and she looked vibrant and pretty. Liz's heart sank even further.

"Hiya, Lizzie." Steph threw her arms around Liz, then stepped back to examine her friend. Liz's dark eyes looked huge in her face and she'd lost weight. She'd taken care with her appearance, though, and wore a white shirt and flowery silk skirt. Her legs were bare and tanned. She wore some eyeshadow and lipstick but Steph's overall impression was one of a sad and fragile woman. "You look well," she lied. "How are things?"

"Pretty good, Steph. Pretty good," Liz lied back.

"Good woman. I hope you're hungry. I've cooked way too much."

"I'm starving," Liz lied again.

She followed Steph into the kitchen. "Smells good," she said, forcing a smile.

"Chicken kebabs, new potatoes and salad."

"Lovely. Want me to do anything?"

"Well, you could open the wine. I have a bottle of Macon Lugny in the fridge. It should be colder than yours."

Liz took the bottle from the fridge, replacing it with the one she'd brought. "It'll be cold enough by the time we've finished this one."

"It's going to be *that* kind of afternoon, is it?" Steph shook her head. "I don't know. You're a very bad influence on me. I wouldn't normally take a drink at this hour of the day. I'm just being sociable."

Liz pointed up at the ceiling. "Look! There goes that pig again." She puffed as she tugged on the cork. "Where are the glasses?"

"Outside. It was such a nice day, I set the table on the balcony."

"Lovely." Liz went outside with the wine. Small

117

dinghies bobbed on the water. Two little boys played chasing along the promenade and a young girl was stretched out on a rock, her blouse tucked up to expose white skin to the sun. Liz sighed. Oh, to be young again without a care in the world! She poured the wine and carried the glasses back to the kitchen. "You're lucky to have a view like that. It's beautiful."

Steph took her glass. "It is, isn't it? Right. I just have to make the salad dressing and then we're ready to eat. You go and sit down. Enjoy the sunshine. I'll be there in a minute."

Liz went back outside. It was still early in the year and the breeze was cool, but the balcony was sheltered and bathed in sunshine. She felt the heat on her face and closed her eyes, trying to shut out all the hurt and unhappiness.

"Are you all right?"

Liz looked up to see Steph standing over her with two plates of food. "Yeah, sure." She sat up and smiled at her friend's concerned expression. "This looks lovely," she said bending her head over the plate. The last thing she needed was Steph probing. She'd burst into tears, she knew it. She seemed to do that a lot lately.

Steph sensed her friend's mood and decided to change the subject. "Seán's home on Wednesday."

"Oh, that's great, Steph. Isn't it?" she added, frowning.

Steph nodded. "Yeah, I admit it, I've missed him. Annie thought I had my eye on Edward. Just because we had dinner together. "

"What's he like?" Liz asked curiously. She hadn't told Annie or Stephanie about her meeting with Edward. She wasn't sure why. He obviously hadn't mentioned it either.

"Surprisingly normal, actually. I really enjoyed myself. He's good company."

Liz was surprised by the pang of envy she felt. Trust Stephanie. She could have anyone she wanted. It was just her luck that the only time she'd run into Edward, she'd looked like a wet weekend. But then, what difference did it make? What man would show an interest in someone like her when Stephanie was around? Liz was amazed at her own feelings. Why, in God's name, was she interested in what *any* man thought of her at a time like this? Maybe it was all down to the break-up with Chris. She still felt a complete failure. She should have *made* her marriage work. Like her mother always said. You've made your bed, now lie on it. She was of the old school that believed marriage was for life no matter what you had to put up with. She probably thought Liz was lucky because Chris wasn't beating her! Liz knew that the only reason she hadn't had a go at her was because her dad wouldn't let her. He was a lot more understanding and he was furious at how Chris Connolly had treated his beloved daughter.

They finished their lunch and Steph cleared the plates away and returned moments later with strawberries and cream, and the second bottle of wine. She wasn't sure it was a good idea. Liz had drank most of the first bottle and had hardly touched her food. Stephanie was worried. If only she would open up. Talk about Chris. Get angry. There was no point in pushing her, though. Liz would just shut her down. No, at least while she was here, Steph could keep an eye on her. If she had too much to drink she could always stay the night.

They talked desultorily for a while and Liz finally dozed

off in the afternoon sun. Steph was drifting in and out of consciousness herself when the intercom buzzed. She opened one eye, debating whether or not to answer it. Probably just kids. Liz was out cold. The buzz came again. Damn it. She stood up, straightened her clothes and went to the door. She looked through the peephole. It was Edward. What the hell was he doing here? She ran her fingers through her hair and checked her reflection in the hall mirror. She was flushed from the sun and her dress was a mass of creases. Damn the man!

She fixed a smile on her face and opened the door. "Hi!"

"Hello, Stephanie. Sorry for dropping in unannounced. There's just a couple of things I need you to sign before you head off."

As usual he looked immaculate and Steph looked mournfully down at her own crumpled appearance. He was wearing a lightweight suit of pale grey and his pristine white shirt accentuated his permanently tanned skin. He looked every inch the successful, healthy and very rich young businessman.

"No problem. Come in. You caught us having a very indulgent afternoon." She led the way into the living-room.

"Us?" he asked.

She nodded towards Liz's inert body on the balcony.

Edward laughed. "Liz?"

Liz stirred as she heard her name and saw a tall dark figure standing over her. She started to sit up and then remembered that she'd unbuttoned most of her blouse. "Edward! Hi." She fumbled with the buttons and tried to straighten her skirt.

Edward smiled into her eyes and sat down in Steph's vacated seat. "Hi, Liz. I envy you taking advantage of such a beautiful day." His eyes wandered appreciatively over Liz's long tanned legs.

"Edward? The papers?" Steph interrupted, put out at the attention Liz was receiving.

"No rush, Steph," Edward said easily, not taking his eyes off Liz. "Any chance of a glass of wine?"

"Of course!" Liz smiled shyly. "Get another glass, Stephanie."

Stephanie looked indignant at the summary dismissal. She stomped into the kitchen.

"So how are you doing, Liz?"

"Getting there," she said coolly, realising that he probably knew all the gory details about the sorry mess she was in.

"That's good. He's a bloody fool, you know."

Liz looked at him, startled. "Chris? Why do you say that?"

"To risk losing such a beautiful woman. If he's not careful, you'll be snapped up," he clicked his fingers, "just like that."

Liz laughed. "Very flattering, but a little over the top."

"Not at all," he murmured.

Stephanie returned with a glass, which she filled and pushed towards him ungraciously.

"Thanks, Stephanie. That's lovely. So how's Chez Nous going to manage without you for a whole week?"

"Oh, they'll be thrilled to get rid of me, for a while. I'm driving them all nuts."

"I'm sure that's not true," he said warmly.

Steph glowed and forgave him for paying attention to Liz. He was just being polite.

They finished the wine, chatting companionably in the afternoon sunshine. The two women were disappointed when Edward finally rose to leave.

"I'd better be making tracks," he said regretfully. "I have to get back to the office, but why don't I come back in a couple of hours and take you two to dinner?"

Steph shook her head. "Sorry, Edward. No can do. I'm due in Greystones for dinner. Mam will have prepared the fatted calf, but thanks for the offer."

"That's a pity. What about you, Liz?" Edward smiled down at her.

Liz looked up startled. "Me?"

"Unless you're doing anything else?"

"No. No, I'm not. Lucy's staying with Chris tonight," she replied avoiding Steph's stare. "I'd like that."

"Edward, shall we look at those papers now?" Stephanie led the way into the living-room.

He chuckled as she bent her head over the papers. "There's no need to be ratty with me. I'm just taking her to dinner."

"I'm not ratty," she spat back, "it's just she's very vulnerable at the moment. I don't want you taking advantage of her."

"Did I take advantage of you?" he asked.

"No, no you didn't," she admitted.

"Well then. Trust me. She looks like she could do with a bit of fun."

They fell silent as Liz joined them.

"I'd better get going too, Stephanie. Shall I meet you in town, Edward?"

"No, no. I'll pick you up. Give me your address."

Liz scribbled her address down and also some directions from the school.

"Eight o'clock OK?" Edward took the piece of paper and studied it.

"Fine. I'll look forward to it." Liz smiled.

Stephanie walked Edward to the door. He bent and kissed her cheek.

"Don't worry. I'll be a good boy. Enjoy your week off."

"Thanks. Bye." Steph shut the door after him and went back to join Liz.

Liz looked at her friend's grim expression. "Now don't give out to me, Steph. Like you said to Annie, it's only dinner. I'm not going to *do* anything. He's very nice, isn't he? Easy to talk to."

There was an almost dreamy expression on her face and there was a sparkle in her eyes that wasn't entirely due to the wine.

Steph groaned inwardly. "Don't get carried away, Liz. He's just a man and he has his faults like all the others. Take off the rose-tinted glasses."

"Oh, shut up, Steph. Don't you think I deserve a night out?"

Steph was immediately remorseful. "Of course you do. I'm sorry Liz. I'm being over-protective."

"No, you're probably right," Liz said, the light leaving her eyes. "What the hell am I doing going out with another man? It's ridiculous! I should have refused. Maybe I'll call and cancel . . . "

"You'll do no such thing," Steph said firmly. "You're a

grown woman and it *is* only dinner. Go and have a good time. There's absolutely nothing to feel guilty about."

Liz hugged her. "Yeah, OK. Well, I'd better go. I have to dig out something sexy in lycra."

"Wear something very long with a very high neck," Steph retorted, wagging a finger at her.

Liz shook her head sadly. "It doesn't really matter, Steph. Edward wouldn't be interested in me even if I'd nothing on but a smile. It's you he wanted to go out with. He just feels sorry for me. He was just being kind."

"I don't know the man that well," Steph replied honestly, "but one thing's for sure. He never does *anything* he doesn't want to, I promise you that."

CHAPTER FOURTEEN

"You look lovely." Edward smiled at Liz and led her out to the car.

Liz barely replied. She'd lifted the phone several times to cancel, but she'd lost her nerve each time. Eventually she'd accepted the fact that she'd have to go through with it and she went and got dressed. She'd chosen a black silk dress with a halter top. She felt a bit bare so she slipped a gold embroidered shawl around her shoulders. A pair of gold hoop earrings was her only jewellery. She swept her hair back from her face, added the minimum amount of make-up and went downstairs to wait for Edward. Her stomach was sick and she felt guilty. She was still a married woman and here she was going out on a date! She took a deep breath. This was silly. Edward would never look on this as a date. He was just being polite. Stephanie had obviously been the target of his attention.

She shot him a quick sidelong glance. He'd mentioned where they were going, but she hadn't heard. She tried hard to concentrate on what he was saying.

"Have you eaten in Peacock Alley?" he was saying.

"Not recently. When they first opened Chris and I went to check it out."

"Of course. The competition. And what did you think?"

"Chris was very impressed."

"I asked what *you* thought," Edward said mildly.

Liz looked surprised. "Well, I thought it was good too."

"Right." Edward nodded grimly.

Liz looked at him nonplussed, conscious that she'd said something to annoy him. "Steph likes it," she added.

"Oh, Liz," Edward breathed.

"What? What?" Liz's voice was high.

"I wanted your opinion. Not Stephanie's or Chris's."

"And I gave it," Liz said defensively.

"Yes, you did. I'm sorry. Do you think Conor will be able to take over from Chris?" It was probably best to change the subject.

Liz looked at him. "Easily. He's probably been doing most of the work anyway." She closed her eyes briefly. That sounded so disloyal. "Most *sous-chefs* have had to take over completely from time to time," she added to soften her first comment. "That's what they're trained to do."

"I see," Edward said, guiding the car into a parking spot around the corner from the restaurant. "Well, he certainly seems eager. He's a nice lad, I like him."

Liz laughed. "That makes you sound very old."

Edward grinned. "Well, I *am* very old."

"What? All of thirty-nine, forty?"

"Forty," he agreed. "Almost forty-one."

"Oh, very old," Liz teased.

"Well, it feels it in Chez Nous. They're all so incredibly young."

"It's a young industry," Liz agreed.

They walked the short distance to the restaurant and before long were seated at a round table in a quiet corner.

"I like sitting with my back to the wall," Edward said. "I can see everyone and no one can creep up behind me."

"I love people watching and trying to guess who's married and who's not. It's usually fairly easy. If the woman is getting a lot of attention, she's a girlfriend. If he's totally besotted with her, she's the mistress."

"That's very cynical."

"Can you blame me?" Liz retorted before bowing her head over the menu.

Edward watched her thoughtfully. She was a total contradiction. It was obvious from the moment she'd opened the door this evening that she'd regretted agreeing to have dinner with him. She was defensive of Chris and, moments later, angry with him. All to be expected, really, given what she'd been through.

Liz, conscious of his scrutiny, tucked her hair behind her ear nervously and kept her eyes on the menu. Her eyes ran over the various dishes but her mind registered none of them. The thought of food made her feel slightly sick.

"Can I get you a drink?"

She looked up at the waiter and then at Edward. "Gin and tonic, please." To hell with it. She needed a drink.

"The same," Edward said. "Do you like lobster, Liz? It's something of a speciality here. They do it with a lemon grass vinaigrette, it's really delicious."

Liz smiled weakly. "I think I'll have the sole." It probably wouldn't make her throw up.

"And a starter?"

"Just a green salad."

Edward frowned. "No wonder you're so thin."

Liz gave a nervous laugh. Thin? Her?

Edward ordered mussels and lobster for himself and a bottle of Chablis. "So how's Lucy coping these days?" he said when the waiter had left.

Liz pleated and re-pleated her napkin. "Not bad. She seems happy enough but just when I think she's settled into the new routine she turns around and asks me when Daddy's coming home."

"And what do you say?"

"The only thing I can say. I don't know." Liz took a gulp of her drink.

"It must be very hard."

Liz swallowed hard. "It is."

"Do *you* want him back?"

"I honestly don't know," Liz admitted and then wondered why the hell was she telling this man all about her private life. He was practically a stranger. "Look, I really don't want to talk . . . "

"Of course you don't. Forgive me, I'm being much too nosey."

"Oh no . . . "

"Oh yes. Now let's talk about something else."

"Tell me about your sister. Where exactly does she live?"

"Jen is not that far away from you at all. You know the green at the top of your road? Well, her house is the corner one on the right just after that."

"Oh, I know it. Does she have other children?"

"No. Just Carol."

Liz thanked the waiter as he put her salad in front of her. "Oh. Chris wanted a son. I suppose every man does."

"Jen's husband is dead. He was killed in a car accident."

"Oh, God, that's terrible! The poor girl. When did it happen?"

"Nearly three years ago, now. Carol barely remembers him."

"That's so sad. My God. Everyone has their problems, don't they?"

"Jen's doing OK. She's a great mother and Carol's a sweetheart."

Liz watched the softening in his face when he mentioned his niece. He really was an incredibly nice man. And an extremely handsome one, too. She watched the strong tanned hands as they fiddled with the cutlery. The hands of a successful man with perfectly manicured nails. He wore a black and white check jacket, a white shirt and a paisley tie in muted grey and blue shades. She smiled. A tie that Chris wouldn't be seen dead in. Much too tame for his taste.

"What's amusing you?"

Liz reddened. "Sorry. I was just admiring your tie and thinking how much Chris would hate it."

"Why's that?"

"Too subtle."

"Oh. It's one of my more flamboyant ties, actually."

Liz giggled. "I'm glad to hear it. I always hated flashy ties."

"I'll take that as a compliment." Edward smiled at her, his dark eyes warm.

"How come you've never married?" Liz asked emboldened by the gin and the wine. "You strike me as a family man. You're obviously good with kids."

Edward said nothing while the waiter cleared away the plates and topped up their wine glasses. "It just hasn't happened," he said when they were alone once more. "And I'm probably too set in my ways now to get used to living with another person."

"I can understand that, but it's such a waste. You'd be a great father. Why is it that the men who shouldn't do?"

Edward looked blank. "You've lost me."

"Well I mean, why do some men get married and have a family and then start playing around? Why the hell do they get married in the first place?"

Edward shrugged. "Because they fall in love?"

"You're a romantic!" she exclaimed.

"Maybe. Well, when I look at the likes of Joe and Annie I have to believe in the occasional happy ending."

"Mmmn. They're perfect together, aren't they? So are Steph and Seán if only she'd realise it."

"I haven't met Seán. What's he like?"

"Gorgeous," Liz said simply. "Good-looking, very, very funny and, I know it's an old-fashioned word, but he's also very nice."

Edward frowned. "I always associate nice with boring."

Liz shook her head vehemently. "Nope. Definitely not boring."

"So you think Steph should settle down with him?"

"Absolutely! She's nuts if she lets him get away. She's already lost him once."

"Oh?"

Over the sole and the lobster, Liz told him about Seán's marriage and his son and how he'd only got back with Steph two years ago after a separation of ten years.

"And his son lives with his wife in Cork?"

"Yes. Billy comes up to stay with Seán sometimes but not often."

"That's sad."

"Yeah. It is." Liz fell silent. Lucy was in exactly the same position now. If Liz stuck to her guns, she'd be living in Dublin and her dad would be in Galway. They wouldn't see each other as often as they should. Lucy would miss out on having a full-time father. She pushed her plate away and finished her wine. Immediately a waiter appeared to refill it.

"A penny for them?" Edward said gently.

Liz shook her head.

"You're thinking that Lucy's going to be in the same boat as Seán's son, aren't you?"

She laughed. "You should become a shrink."

"Well, it wasn't that difficult to follow your line of thought. It's only natural that you should worry about that."

"I suppose. I just don't know what to do for the best."

"Whatever will make you both happiest. There's not much point in taking Chris back just for Lucy's sake. You'd probably be at each other's throats morning, noon and night and that wouldn't do her much good, would it?"

"No. no, it wouldn't. But does that mean I should just throw in the towel on my marriage?"

"Is that what you think you're doing?" Edward countered.

"No. Oh, I don't know." She tossed her hair back impatiently. "I don't know what I'm doing half the time these days." She looked at a man smoking at the next table and was tempted to bum a cigarette off him.

"You'll do the right thing," Edward said calmly.

"How can you say that? How do you know?"

"Because you're a good mother and in the end you'll do what's best for Lucy and for yourself. Just remember, if you're not happy, she won't be either."

"You make it all sound so simple," Liz complained.

"That's because it is."

Liz looked at him sadly, her eyes bright with unshed tears. "You're probably right," she whispered.

CHAPTER FIFTEEN

Stephanie paced the living-room, pausing every few minutes at the window. She knew that the woman was supposed to keep the man waiting but she didn't believe in all that. Seán wasn't due for another ten minutes, but here she was ready and waiting eagerly for his arrival.

She'd spent over an hour going through her wardrobe. If only she'd brought her Paul Costello suit! Clothes were tried on and discarded. Finally she had settled on a midnight-blue satin trouser-suit with a v-necked jacket that revealed a hint of cleavage and narrow trousers that tapered in at the ankle. She chose a pair of very high silver sandals and the sapphire earrings and pendant her parents had given her for her thirtieth birthday to complete the outfit.

She inspected her make-up in the mirror over the fireplace. She'd applied a combination of grey and blues to her eyelids, defined her pale brows with a pencil and used mascara and eyeliner to make her eyes look larger. Her foundation was light and she'd used a very pale pink lipstick. Her hair was swept back off her face. She nodded, pleased with the effect she'd created. This should stop Seán from going away for too long in future!

She turned from the mirror and walked to the window just as Seán pulled into the driveway in his black BMW. She ran to the front door and threw it open as he stepped from the car. Then she paused, suddenly shy.

He turned around and stopped in his tracks when he saw her. Christ! She looked as if she'd just stepped off the cover of a magazine. He looked at the beautifully cut suit and started to think about what lay beneath. Don't go down that road. He thought. Not yet, anyway.

"Hiya, Steph," he said casually. "You're looking as gorgeous as ever."

Steph returned his almost brotherly hug, feeling disappointed. In this gear she'd expected him to run to her, take her in his arms and kiss her passionately.

But Seán had already moved inside. "So where's that beautiful mother of yours?"

Great! Here she was dressed up like a dog's dinner and he wanted to see her mother! She walked sulkily behind him as he breezed into the dining-room where Tom and Catherine West were having dinner.

Catherine jumped to her feet and hugged him. "Seán! It's wonderful to see you." She turned to her husband. "He looks great, doesn't he Tom?"

"He certainly does," Tom reached across his wife to shake Seán's hand. "How are you, Seán? Everything go well in the States?"

"Great thanks, Tom. Sorry for interrupting your dinner." He pulled up a chair.

"Not at all," said Catherine. "Would you like some?" she added, avoiding Steph's glare.

"No, that's OK. I wouldn't say no to a drink, though."

"You don't have time, Seán," Steph said with a meaningful look.

"Do I not?" Seán looked up at her, his eyebrow raised. "Why? What time are we eating? Where are we going?"

"Eight, in The Orange Grove."

Seán checked his watch. "Sure we've plenty of time. They always keep you waiting. We'll keep them waiting for a change."

"I'll get the drinks, Mam," Steph said with a tight smile. "You sit down." She walked through the arch into the kitchen, took two glasses out of the press and banged them down on the counter.

"There's some fresh soda in the fridge, love. The one Seán likes," her mother called after her. "I only got it this morning. Don't use the stale bottle."

Stephanie grimaced. "Is there any arsenic to put in it?" she muttered. She made up a whiskey and soda for Seán, a large G & T for herself and carried them back inside. She sat quietly at the table while the three chatted noisily, their conversation punctuated with laughter and thought that she may as well not have been there.

* * *

"You're very quiet, Steph. Is everything all right?" Seán looked at Stephanie with concern as they were led to their table in the restaurant.

Stephanie looked at him in disbelief, but held her

tongue until the waiter had left. "No Seán. Everything is *not* all right!" God, he could be really dense sometimes! She'd sat in silence while he chatted away to her parents and gave monosyllabic answers when comments came her way. She'd sat beside him in the car, maintaining a frosty silence as they drove down to the restaurant, and it was only now that he was getting the message that something was wrong. The silly bugger!

"What is it, Steph?" he said gently, leaning over and taking her hand. "Is it work?"

She exploded. "No! It's not bloody work! Oh, never mind. Let's just eat."

"What is it, Steph?" Seán persisted. "What have I done?"

When she saw his confused expression she relented. "Oh, nothing, love. Don't mind me. It really doesn't matter." She turned her attention to the menu and Seán shrugged.

They chatted easily as they ate their meal. About Phoenix, Conor's progress, Liz and Chris. In fact everything except what Stephanie really wanted to talk about. Relaxed from the wine, she finally decided to come out and tell him how she felt.

"Seán, you really piss me off sometimes."

He looked totally taken-aback. As usual, the man didn't have an idea as to what he'd done to upset her.

"We haven't seen each other in a very long time," she continued, "and you hardly even said hello to me when you got in this evening. Well, not properly. Then you spent the whole evening talking to Mam and Dad and practically ignoring me. I spent all day worrying about what I should wear," she said gesturing down at her suit, "and now I feel like a bloody fool."

"Did you really?" Seán cupped his face in one hand and smiled at her.

"Did I really what?" Steph was confused.

"Did you *really* spend all day wondering what you were going to wear?"

Steph wouldn't answer him, annoyed at herself.

"Don't fight with me, Steph," he said, his voice cajoling. "I've really missed you."

"Have you?" she said softening.

"Yes and to make up for having stayed away so long, I have a surprise for you."

Stephanie's eyes lit up. "What is it?"

"Now, that's no way to ask for a surprise! Ask nicely."

"Please tell me," she said, unable to suppress a smile.

"With a cherry on top," Seán persisted.

"With a cherry on top! Now tell me before I kill you."

"I'm taking you away for the weekend," he said, triumphantly.

"But you never asked if I was free," she said irritably. "You're being a bit presumptuous, aren't you?"

Seán was unflappable. "You said you were off all week. The restaurant's closed on Sundays." He shrugged.

"Even so . . ." she countered.

"Well, I can always cancel it." He fiddled with his fork.

She sat in silence. Damn it. Why did she always have to be so bitchy? Why couldn't she learn to keep her big mouth shut.

"You haven't asked where," he pointed out.

"Well then?" she asked grudgingly.

"Well then, what?" he replied grinning at her.

"Seán!"

"OK, OK. Paris. The same hotel. The same room . . ."

"Oh, Seán. That's fantastic!" She leaned over and kissed him hard on the lips.

"Does that mean I shouldn't cancel?" he asked.

"No! No way! Oh Seán. That's so romantic. I'm sorry I've been such a cow. It's just I was afraid you were going off me."

Seán kissed her hand. "You should know by now," he said, looking deep into her eyes, "that that's never going to happen. I'm crazy about you."

"Really?" Steph murmured leaning over, affording him an excellent view down her top.

Seán groaned. "Really. Now do you want some dessert or can we get out of here?"

"Nothing that's on the menu," she replied huskily. "Let's go back to my place."

"No. Mine's nearer. Waiter!"

CHAPTER SIXTEEN

"Steph? Niall Casey phoned. He says they won't be able to deliver until Friday. Oh, and Chris said he wouldn't be in until twelve. And there was an announcement on the news. There's some problem with pipes on Dame Street and they'll be switching off the water in the whole area from two until four."

Steph groaned. "Welcome back, Steph," she muttered.

"So how was your week off? Good time?"

Steph smiled at Liam Dunne, glad that it was Sam's morning off. At least she didn't have to deal with him just yet. Liam was a total contrast. At twenty-five he was great with the customers and always cool in a crisis, something that Sam never was. In fact the only problem with Liam was the number of female staff who spent their days drooling over his dark good looks.

"I had a lovely break, Liam. But now I feel like I've never been away. Does George know about the water?"

"Yeah, but he says it's not his problem."

Steph grimaced. "Does he now? OK. I'll have a word." She went to the top of the stairs. "Jean," she called down to

139

the waitress. "Do me a favour? Make me a huge pot of coffee and don't let anyone come near me before lunch."

Jean grunted and slunk off to the kitchen. Steph looked at Liam. "She's enthusiastic, isn't she?"

"A positive dynamo," Liam agreed drily. "Seeya later."

Steph sat down in her chair and waited for the coffee to arrive. She couldn't think of starting work without some caffeine. She allowed her mind to drift back over the weekend. Paris had been wonderful, though they hadn't been outside their bedroom all that much! Their love-making had been as amazing as ever, and Seán hadn't brought up the "M" word once. She sighed happily. It was wonderful to have a love life again. She'd come home physically exhausted but mentally she'd never felt better. She could tackle anyone, anything.

Jean arrived with the coffee and Steph turned her attention to the huge pile of post. It really wasn't worth going away when there was this mess to face on her return. She'd have to get an assistant. Someone to look after the wages and the accounts and definitely the mail.

A post-it got her attention. Edward had been on, enquiring about her progress in organising the PR evening. God, she hoped he wasn't going to start interfering. The sooner he was a truly silent partner the better. Not long now.

She worked steadily through the day, drank copious amounts of coffee and smoked too many cigarettes. She tidied her desk at seven o'clock, stretched and went down to the restaurant.

"Everything OK?" she asked Jean as she looked through the reservations for the evening.

"Yeah. I think so." She was lounging against a table, inspecting her fingernails.

Steph frowned. "Haven't you anything to do?"

Jean cast an eye around the empty restaurant. "Eh, not really, no."

Steph picked up a glass from the nearest table, then a fork. "These could be cleaner. Get a cloth and check every place-setting."

Jean opened her mouth to protest but closed it again when she saw the look on Stephanie's face. She sighed loudly and went into the kitchen.

Sam came out of the kitchen. "What's the problem?"

Steph waved a hand at the tables. "This just isn't good enough. She's a lazy little bitch. Standing around doing nothing. Some of the table settings are a disgrace. I'm surprised at you, Sam."

Sam pursed his lips. "I was just coming to check on things myself."

"It's seven o'clock. Cutting it a bit fine, aren't you?"

"It's Monday, for God's sake."

Steph glared at him. "I don't care what day of the week it is. See that it's done." She turned on her heel and went back upstairs.

Sam glared after her. "Bitch," he muttered to himself.

The phone rang as Steph sat back down at her desk. "Yes?"

"Steph? What's up?"

"Liz? Oh nothing. Just one of those days. How are you?"

"Fine. Sorry I didn't call sooner."

"That's OK. I was just calling to have a gossip. I was dying to know how you got on with Edward."

"Very well. Like you say, he's a nice man."

Stephanie frowned. Right. "Where did you go?"

"Peacock Alley."

"Oh, really? Was it good? It got a great write-up in the paper last week."

Liz grinned. Steph was successfully diverted. "It was very good," she confirmed and went on to give all the minute details that she knew her friend would enjoy.

"So, I hope Edward behaved himself," Steph said lightly when she'd finished.

"Stephanie! Of course he did! Anyway, enough about me. How was Greystones? How's Seán?"

"Greystones was fine and Seán is *still* great, if you know what I mean. We went to Paris for the weekend."

"Paris. *Very* romantic. And . . . ?"

Steph laughed. "And it was very nice."

"Nice?" said Liz. "Only you could describe a romantic weekend in Paris as nice! So did he propose again?"

"No, he didn't actually."

"Hah! Good. The man's getting sense. You're probably just as well off," she added cynically. "This marriage lark isn't all it's cracked up to be. Love, honour and cherish. That's a laugh!"

Steph was taken aback at the bitterness in Liz's voice. "You sound very cynical, Liz. Promise me you won't rush into anything. Make any rash decisions."

Liz snorted. "Well, now that's good coming from you," she said sarcastically. "Stephanie West, marriage counsellor!"

"Fair point," Steph said with a small laugh. "It's just

that, while it wouldn't suit me, it certainly seemed to work for you. Well, until . . . "

"Yes, until," agreed Liz. She'd been doing a lot of thinking and she was beginning to wonder whether going back to Chris was such a good idea after all. A night out with an attractive man had made her realise just how stale her marriage had been. To be treated like an intelligent adult with opinions had been a novelty. It was a far cry from, "Where are all my bloody socks, Liz? Why can't you keep them in pairs? Surely rolling them up together isn't *too* challenging." She'd also realised that the fact that Chris fancied another woman didn't necessarily mean there was anything wrong with her. So, she'd been a few pounds over her ideal weight. So what? She'd still been able to get into Steph's clothes. With the help of lycra admittedly, but still . . .

Steph broke in on her thoughts. "Liz? Are you OK?"

"Yes. I'm very OK, Steph. That's the point. I'm better than I've been in a long time. You know, I'm only beginning to realise what a pig Chris was. Treating me like a child, patronising me, even bullying me sometimes when he didn't get his way."

Steph closed her eyes. "That sounds familiar."

"Yes, and you've solved your problem. It's time I solved mine."

"What are you going to do?" Stephanie asked, alarmed at Liz's determination. "Don't be too hasty, Liz. Walking away from a boss isn't quite the same as walking out on a marriage. And then there's Lucy to think of. Whatever your feelings, he's still her father."

Liz exploded. "Jesus! Would you listen to yourself," she almost screamed down the phone. "Who do you think you are, Miss High-and-Mighty? How the hell would you know what it's like? And as for Lucy, you think you know what's best for her? Just because you're her bloody godmother! You see her maybe once a month, if she's lucky. Why don't you just go to hell!"

Steph jumped as Liz banged down the receiver. She sat looking at the phone, shocked. How could Liz say such horrible things? And to accuse her of neglecting Lucy! The bitch! Liz *knew* how demanding the restaurant business was. She knew the pressure. How dare she talk to her like that! She lit a cigarette with trembling hands. She told herself to calm down. Liz didn't mean what she'd said. She was going through a tough time. She wasn't herself. Steph understood more than anyone how Chris could get under your skin.

She'd give Liz a little space and then she'd call her. God, they were best friends, she wasn't going to let that creep come between them.

Sam stuck his head round the door. "Ready for inspection."

Stephanie looked up, confused, her face white and tense. "What?"

Sam frowned. "Are you OK?"

She pulled herself together. "Yes, of course," she said briskly. "I presume it looks like a top-class restaurant now and not like a pigsty."

Sam bit his lip. "Of course," he replied, his face grim.

"Right." Stephanie breezed past him.

* * *

"So I was thinking, all going well, we could move your stuff in at the weekend. What do you think? Steph? Steph, are you listening to me?"

Steph turned in Seán's arms. "Sorry, love. What was that?"

"You haven't heard a word I've said, have you? And you're always saying I don't listen to you!"

Steph kissed him. "I'm sorry. I just can't stop thinking about Liz. Maybe I should call her." She sat up in bed and reached for the phone.

He took it off her and put it back on the bedside table. "Give her some time, Steph. And don't be so surprised that she's hitting out. You said yourself that it wasn't natural the way she was handling everything so well. Let her throw a wobbly. Give her time."

Steph settled back in his arms. "You're right. You're always right. I hate that."

Seán nuzzled against her ear. "So what about it? Will you move in at the weekend?"

Steph took a deep breath. "Yeah, great. Why not?"

In a moment of weakness she had finally agreed to move in with Seán. She didn't regret it, but felt slightly nervous at the prospect.

Seán smiled happily. "I'll give the estate agent a call. They could meet us at your place on Saturday and have a look around."

Stephanie stiffened. "There's no rush, is there?"

145

Seán frowned. "Well, it would be good to have the cash now you're self-employed."

Steph looked away. "True, but I could always rent the apartment and have a regular income. You know the price of property in Malahide. I think I should hang on to it."

"You're right of course," Seán replied, much to her relief.

Seán tried to ignore the uneasy feeling in the pit of his stomach. Stephanie'd lived alone for a long time. She'd need time to get used to being a proper couple. It would be disastrous if he pushed her into selling up. It would be much better if she made the decision herself. In her own time. He'd waited for her this long. He could wait a little longer.

* * *

Ruth pushed Des away and straightened her clothes. "Not here, Des." She looked around the carpark anxiously.

"Well, come back to my place then," Des said, suppressing a sigh of frustration. He'd been dating Ruth for nearly three months and she still wouldn't let him anywhere near her.

He was beginning to wonder if she was worth the effort. But, as he looked down into the dark eyes which looked back at him beseechingly from that pretty little face, he knew she was. If only she wasn't such a good girl. He'd topped up her wine glass a few times tonight in the hope that it might relax her but when he'd dropped his hand from her breast to the zip of her jeans, she froze.

"I can't come back, Des. You know I can't," she pleaded for his understanding.

"Right so," he said curtly, switched on the engine and pulled sharply out on to the road.

Ruth looked at him nervously. She knew he was annoyed. He'd been trying to get her into bed for weeks now. She was afraid she was going to lose him. He was a man of the world and he could have his pick of the sophisticated girls in his office. Ruth often wondered why he'd bothered with a poor student like her. She couldn't believe her luck when Des, easily the best-looking fella in the Baggot Inn, had approached her and bought her a drink. She'd been even more impressed when he'd insisted on dropping her home in his sporty black Capri.

He'd wined and dined her several nights a week since then, although he was often sent down the country on business. He wasn't too interested in going out with her friends. He said he wanted her all to himself, but she knew he didn't like the student scene. She couldn't really blame him. What had he got in common with them? Anyway, Seán Adams hadn't gone out of his way to make Des welcome. Jealous no doubt, Ruth decided. Still, it wasn't a problem. She got together with her friends when Des was away, and she saw Steph for lunch regularly. It all worked out quite well.

Des took a bend very fast and Ruth tightened her grip on the edge of her seat. She hated it when he was angry with her.

"I'm sorry, Des," she said, slipping into his arms when he pulled up outside her flat.

"I'm sorry too, pet. It's just I love you so much. I want to be with you."

Ruth's heart soared at his words. He loved her! He really loved her! She turned her face up to his and kissed him.

Des groaned and slid his hand down to her breast. He pulled impatiently at her shirt and dipped his head, his mouth finding her nipple.

Ruth shivered with pleasure under his mouth and hands.

"Oh Ruth, I want you so much," he said hoarsely.

"I want you too, Des," she gasped. What the hell was she saving herself for? She loved this man. She wanted to spend the rest of her life with him. And hadn't he just told her he loved her? Her flatmates would be asleep by now. And she had a bedroom all to herself . . .

"Do you really want me, Ruth?" Des asked as he planted little kisses around her neck and throat.

"Yes, Des," she said, raising his head so she could look deep into his eyes. "Please come in and make love to me."

Des kissed her hard, jumped out of the car and ran around to open her door. "I'll be gentle, Ruth," he murmured in her ear as she opened the front door with an unsteady hand. "I'll make you happy. I promise."

* * *

Ruth watched Mary nervously, as she slammed around the kitchen. Des seemed oblivious to her flatmate's mood as he sat at the kitchen table and sipped his coffee.

"I'm off to Mass," Mary announced with a pointed stare at Ruth and a glance of disgust at Des.

"Say a prayer for us," Des said cheerfully as Mary left, banging the door behind her.

"God, she's never going to let me forget this," Ruth said morosely.

"Ah, she'll get over it. She's just jealous. Frustrated."

Ruth glared at him. Mary might be a bit on the straight side, but she was a good friend. Sinéad hadn't been too impressed either. She'd bumped into Des on her way to the bathroom earlier that morning. She'd asked Ruth, rather coolly, to let her know in future if she planned on having an overnight guest. Then she retreated to her bedroom and banged the door. Ruth was beginning to wonder if it had been worth it. Des had seemed to enjoy himself, but to Ruth it had seemed much ado about nothing. It had been quick and painful. Nothing like the romantic novels led you to believe. Afterwards, Ruth had fought back tears of pain and shame and longed for Des to take her in his arms and tell her how much he loved her. But he'd just given her a peck on the cheek, rolled over and promptly fell asleep. He'd reached for her this morning for a repeat performance, but Ruth was afraid her flatmates would hear. It all seemed a bit sordid in the cold light of day and she felt ashamed and embarrassed.

"I think you'd better go, Des," she said with an apologetic smile. "Sinéad won't come out until you're gone, and I'm in the bad books as it is."

Des was happy to comply. It was a sunny Sunday morning and the golf course beckoned. "Right, love, I'll be off." He pulled her to him and kissed her soundly. "You were great," he whispered.

"You too," she replied smiling up at him shyly. She'd get used to it. It was probably just because she was so inexperienced. No doubt it would be better the next time. "Will I see you later?" she asked timidly.

"Probably not. I have to prepare for an important meeting tomorrow. I'll phone you. Bye, love."

Ruth watched from the window, as he ran down the steps, hopped into his car and drove away at speed.

Sinéad wandered into the room. "So lover boy's finally gone."

Ruth flushed. "Leave me alone, Sinéad."

Sinéad held up her hands. "Hey, nothing to do with me, but for Christ's sake be careful. I hope you made him use a condom."

Ruth's eyes widened in alarm. "I never thought . . ." It had all happened so quickly. It hadn't even occurred to her that they should have been taking precautions.

"Oh really, Ruth!" Sinéad looked at her in dismay. "Better get yourself down to the doctor," she advised grimly.

"Oh no, I couldn't. He'd tell my mother." Ruth was horrified at the thought of discussing her sex life with Dr Lynch. He'd be shocked for sure.

"Well then, go to the Well Woman Centre. They won't ask any questions. Please, Ruth. It's safer," Sinéad pleaded.

Ruth dreaded the thought of discussing something so personal with a stranger, but what choice did she have? She'd make an appointment tomorrow. Before she lost her nerve.

Sinéad thought Ruth wanted her head examined, hanging around with a creep like Des Healy. He was too smooth. Too *good to be wholesome, to use a phrase of her mother's. She could have told Ruth to make Des use condoms, but it would be a lot safer if Ruth was on the pill. Then she wouldn't have to rely on Des.*

Sinéad had met him in a club in Leeson Street recently. He'd been smooching with a well-endowed, scantily clad girl, who'd had more than enough to drink. Sinéad watched from a distance, and went over when the girl tottered off, rather unsteadily, to the ladies'.

"Having a good time, Des?" she'd said sarcastically.

Des looked up in alarm but quickly pulled himself together and gave her one of his practised smiles. "Sinéad! Hi! I didn't think a poor student could afford to socialise in a place like this."

"No chance of you bumping into Ruth, you mean," she said grimly. "Relax, Des. She's not here, more's the pity. She's safely tucked up in bed, probably dreaming about you."

"As I do about her," Des answered smoothly.

"Yeah. Sure." Sinéad glared at him and went back to her friends. She slept late the next morning, and so it was the following evening before she saw Ruth. She wasn't sure whether to mention the incident or not. Ruth probably wouldn't believe her. She knew full well that Sinéad couldn't stand Des.

Ruth solved her dilemma. "I believe you met Des in Leggs last night."

Sinéad looked at her warily. "Yeah, that's right. It was Bridget's birthday. We decided to make a night of it. What was Des's excuse?"

Ruth rolled her eyes. "Oh, business as usual. It's not enough that he puts in all those hours at the office, they expect him to entertain as well. He told me you probably thought he was up to no good," she added with a laugh. "One girl got really pissed and was all over him like a rash."

"Poor man," Sinéad muttered. One up to Des. If Ruth believed that story, there was no hope for her. Love was definitely blind.

CHAPTER SEVENTEEN

Edward was striding past the kitchen when he caught sight of Conor. He doubled back. "Conor. You're back. How did it go?"

"Fantastic, Mr McDermott. A great experience altogether. Their kitchen is amazing and the discipline of the chefs – well!" He shook his head. "Let's say I learned a lot."

"That was the idea," Edward said with a grin. "A stint up in Belfast should round you off nicely. I assume all of these guys have their own ways of doing things."

"Absolutely. And it's up to me to take the best from each of them and then add my own ideas."

Chris snorted in the background.

Edward winked at Conor. "Yeah, I think that's important. Put your own stamp on it. Modern, young, trendy. I'm sure you've got lots of ideas."

Conor grinned back at him. "I certainly do. There's lots of things I've wanted to try out for some time. I'm all for French cuisine, that's where my background is, but I do feel it can be livened up with other influences. North African, for instance."

Chris snorted again. "Well, right now, *chef*," he said sarcastically, "I think our customers would settle for bangers and mash! Would it be too much to ask that you get back to work? And you," he pointed his knife at Edward. "Out of my kitchen. We've got work to do."

Edward smiled but his eyes were steely. "Certainly, Connolly. But you'd do well to remember that this is no longer *your* kitchen." He turned on his heel and Chris attacked the pheasant on his board with a vengeance.

"Hi, Stephanie. How's it going?" Edward put down his briefcase and stretched himself out in the chair in front of her desk.

Stephanie looked up at her partner. "OK. I've put together a list of journalists I think we should invite to our first tasting." She passed an A4 sheet to him.

Edward scanned it quickly. "I don't know half these people. I'll leave it to you. This is your forte. Any buttons you need me to push?"

Stephanie thought for a moment. "I don't think so. Unless you've any contacts in television. I'd love to get Conor on an afternoon programme."

"I may be able to help there. Leave it with me. When is the big night?"

"In two or three weeks, I think."

Edward nodded "Maybe we should start spreading the word now. Work up the media so they're clamouring for an invite. What about inviting in one of the major wine buffs to advise on wines to complement the food?"

"That's a great idea," Steph looked at him in admiration. "Are you after my job?"

"No. But just because I'm a solicitor doesn't mean I don't have the occasional creative idea."

"There's something else, or rather someone else I wanted to talk to you about," Stephanie said, her face serious now.

"Oh yes? Who?"

"Sam."

"The head waiter?"

"Yeah. I want to get rid of him. He's been a constant thorn in my side. He's lazy and he's a whiner."

"You're the boss," Edward said. "I hardly know the guy. Would you want to hire someone to replace him?"

"I don't think so. I plan to spend a lot more time out front myself. I'll get in an assistant to look after the office work. Also Liam Dunne is showing great potential. I think we could promote him to take over Sam's role. He's young, enthusiastic and smart."

"Sounds perfect. What about the kitchen staff? Any trouble there?"

Stephanie shook her head. "Not really. Most of the lads are delighted that Conor's taking over. Chris wasn't the most popular of bosses. John Quigly doesn't care who's running the show. He does his own thing anyway. George is another story."

"Do you want to get rid of him too?"

"I don't, but I'm sure Conor would love to," she said laughing. "He's got a friend of his all lined up for the job! But George may decide to go himself. He's not going to like answering to Conor."

"Well, at least you've someone to step in if he does decide to leave."

Seán poked his head around the door of Steph's office. His smile faded when he saw the other man. "Sorry for interrupting."

Stephanie felt his tension immediately. She smiled brightly and waved him in. "Not at all. Seán, this is Edward Mc Dermott. Edward, this is Seán Adams."

The two men shook hands. "Glad to finally meet you, Seán. Sorry if you're not seeing too much of your girlfriend these days. There's still a lot to do before we're up and running."

"She was always a workaholic, Edward. Don't worry about it." Seán turned to Steph. "I was wondering if you were free for lunch, love?"

Steph looked at Edward. "I don't think so," she started.

"Of course you are," Edward interrupted, picking up his briefcase. "I have a lunch meeting anyway. Nice to meet you, Seán. I'll be in touch, Steph."

Seán closed the door after him. "He seems OK," he said grudgingly.

Stephanie reached up to kiss him. "He is," she replied.

"You get on well then?"

"We get on very well," she confirmed.

"That's good, I suppose," he said.

"It is," she agreed. "Let's go to lunch."

"Where would you like to go?"

"How about McDonald's?" she said.

He looked at her in mock horror. "A top restaurateur eating in a fast-food joint?"

She poked him in the ribs. "Do you want to eat or not?"

"So you get on well with this guy?" Seán asked again through a mouthful of French fries.

"I do," Steph agreed, but her patience was wearing thin. "Seán, he's my business partner. That's all."

"He fancies you," he said without looking at her.

Stephanie laughed. "You think every man fancies me. Anyway, I get the feeling Edward's involved with someone."

Seán brightened. "Really? Why don't we invite him and his significant other to dinner?"

Steph was amused. Seán wanted proof. "I'll ask him," she promised, "but he's a very private person. No matter how much I dig, I can't find out anything about him. Even Joe doesn't seem to know anything."

"Strange. Maybe he's gay," Seán said hopefully.

"*Definitely* not," Stephanie assured him.

Seán looked at her suspiciously.

* * *

Liz looked at her watch. She'd ring Steph now. It was lunchtime. She was sure to be there and it was unlikely that Chris would answer the phone.

"Chez Nous, can I help you?"

"Sam? Hi, it's Liz. Is Steph there?"

"Hello, Liz. How are you? I think Steph's up in the office. Hang on. I'll put you through."

Liz heard a couple of clicks and then the office phone rang, but there was no answer. She hung up. Stephanie had phoned several times but Liz had always found an excuse to ring off quickly. It had taken her this long to accept that

Stephanie was only trying to help. Now she wanted to clear the air. Edward had wanted to intervene but she wouldn't let him. It was up to her to sort this out. Anyway, she wasn't ready for Steph to know how friendly she and Edward had become.

He'd been great. He often brought her out for coffee after she dropped Lucy off. Now she was disappointed if she didn't see his car outside the school. He was so easy to talk to and he never pried. He told her about his business, about his family, particularly his niece and because he was open with her, she relaxed with him. But she wouldn't talk about Chris. It was silly but she felt it would be disloyal to discuss her husband with another man. Especially when the man concerned was involved in her husband's business.

But time with Edward had helped her get a lot of things back into perspective. She took more care with her appearance and she spent less time lounging in front of the television and more time with Lucy.

Lucy was delighted with the change in her mummy. Most afternoons they went for a walk but if it was raining, they played Scrabble or Monopoly in front of the fire. Lucy especially liked it when Uncle Edward and Carol came around. Carol was fun to play with and Mummy always seemed to laugh when Uncle Edward was around.

* * *

Chris muttered to himself as he worked, barking occasional orders at his team. Pat and Marc exchanged nervous glances. Working with Chris was a bit like working with a time bomb. You never knew when he was going to go off.

Chris was oblivious to them. All he could think of was that slimy bastard, McDermott. It was bad enough having to put up with him in the restaurant, but now it seemed that he was seeing Liz.

Chris was fed up with Lucy saying "Uncle Edward says . . . Uncle Edward brought us to . . . Uncle Edward's so funny." Chris had a bellyful of "Uncle Edward". He'd tackled Liz about it but with no success. When he'd told Liz that it was disgusting to carry on an affair so openly in front of his daughter, she'd looked at him, her eyes full of contempt.

"Don't judge everyone by your own actions," she'd said. "Edward's a nice man, whose niece happens to be in Lucy's class. Nothing sordid is going on. I leave that kind of behaviour to you."

Chris tried to question his daughter once about the relationship. "So do you see a lot of Uncle Edward?" he'd asked casually.

Lucy just shrugged and concentrated on her milkshake.

"Carol's your best friend, isn't she? Does she come over to play?"

"Sometimes," Lucy said, uncharacteristically reticent.

"And does Uncle Edward bring her?"

"Sometimes," Lucy said again. "Daddy? Can we go to the playground now?"

Chris abandoned his interrogation. He lifted her up in his arms and carried her out of the restaurant. "Of course we can, princess," he said swinging her over his head till she shrieked with laughter. "We can do whatever you want."

Chris attacked the piece of meat in front of him with renewed vigour and wished it was McDermott's face. He didn't believe this relationship was as innocent as Liz made out. If nothing had happened yet, it wouldn't be long before it did. Chris knew Edward's sort. He was after something. Bloody cheek of him going after another man's wife. It wasn't on. Chris hardly recognised Liz these days. She was so hard and cold. He'd tried charm, flattery, money, but nothing worked. Eventually his temper got the better of him and he'd tried to bully her into a reconciliation, threatening all sorts of action concerning Lucy if she didn't come to her senses. He was giving up his restaurant for her. It was because of her that he was going to Galway. What more did the bloody woman want? McDermott was obviously influencing her. Turning her head. He'd have to get rid of him, one way or another.

CHAPTER EIGHTEEN

Stephanie flushed the loo, sat down on the side of the bath and wiped her mouth and face.

"Are you OK?" Seán asked from the other side of the bathroom door.

"Fine," Steph said before leaning over the loo once more. Ten minutes later she emerged, white-faced and trembling.

"You look awful," Seán said sympathetically. "Hop into bed, I'll make you a cup of tea and get you a hot-water bottle."

"But I have to go to work," she protested weakly.

"Conor would really appreciate that," Seán said laughing. "Just the image he needs to present to the press. The owner running to the loo every five minutes to throw up."

"I suppose you're right. But it's our first big night . . ."

"And they'll manage fine without you. You've done all you can, now it's up to Conor. Anyway, won't McDermott be there?"

Steph nodded as she pulled the covers up to her chin and reached for the phone. "I'll call him. Tell him who he should talk to, who he should chat up."

"I doubt if he needs any help there," Seán muttered.

"What's that?"

"Nothing. I'll go and make that tea. Would you like some toast?"

Steph's stomach lurched again. "God, no. I couldn't. I'll never eat anything from that Chinese takeaway again. I thought that chicken tasted funny."

"I'm going to call the doctor. If it's food poisoning you're going to need something to help you get over it."

"I'll be fine," Steph said half-heartedly.

"No arguments. You call Edward and leave everything else to me."

Seán put the kettle on and used his mobile to call the local GP. He was just handing Steph the tea when the doorbell went.

"That was fast," Steph said, taking a cautious sip.

The GP was a young and very friendly Scotsman who cheerfully informed Steph that he'd had to treat a lot of people who'd eaten in the local Chinese. "Take the antibiotics, plenty of fluids and stay in bed for a few days. You'll be fine."

Seán showed him out and then went off to the pharmacy. When he came back, Steph was back in the loo. He straightened the bed, fetched a clean nightie and knocked on the bathroom door. Steph groaned in reply. He went in, wiped her face gently with a face-cloth, helped her change into the nightdress and tucked her up in bed.

"You're so good to me," she said as her eyes closed. "What would I do without you?"

"Get yourself a toyboy, probably," he said cheerfully, but she was already asleep.

The phone rang and Seán leapt on it so it wouldn't wake Steph. "Hello?" he whispered.

"Seán? Is that you?"

"Yeah, who's that?"

"It's Liz. Sorry if I disturbed you, it's just I've being trying to reach Steph and all I ever get is her answering machine."

"Liz, hi. How are you? No, well you wouldn't get Steph, she's not there. That is, she's moved in here."

"Oh Seán, that's wonderful!"

Seán grinned. "It is, isn't it?"

"Yeah. How on earth did you manage it?"

"A combination of threats, charm and brute force. Anyway, how are you? I haven't seen you in ages."

"About four months," Liz confirmed. "I'm doing OK, considering."

"I was sorry to hear about you and Chris."

"Well, that's the way it goes. Maybe it's all for the best. Steph seems to think I should take him back, forgive and forget."

"She doesn't really, Liz. She just doesn't want you to rush into anything."

"I know, Seán. I overreacted. I'm very touchy these days. Is she there?"

"Yes and no," Seán replied glancing at the inert figure in the bed. "She's asleep."

"At this hour?" Liz said. Steph must be making excuses not to talk to her.

"She's sick. Food poisoning. The doctor's just left."

"Oh, poor Steph," Liz said, ashamed of her suspicions. "Can I do anything to help?"

Seán smiled. "You know, I think you can."

He quickly filled Liz in on the reception planned for that evening.

"I'll drop Lucy off with Annie," she said immediately, "and I'll go straight in. Will Chris be there?"

"No. It seemed more politic to pack him off to Galway for a few days. Steph didn't really trust him to show total support for Conor. And apparently he hates Edward McDermott."

"Then there's no problem. Get Steph to give me a call when she wakes up. I'll be her slave for the day."

"That'll really put her mind at rest," Seán said. "You're an angel. Why don't you drop over tomorrow night? I'm sure she'll be in better form and she'll be dying to hear all the news."

"I'd love that, Seán. And I'm delighted you two have finally got it together."

"Thanks, Liz. See you tomorrow."

Steph woke at five o'clock. Her mouth was dry and she felt weak but, thankfully, when she moved, her stomach remained calm.

"Hello, sleepyhead," Seán said from the armchair in the corner. "How are you feeling?"

"Not too bad," she said, sitting up gingerly.

"I'll get you a drink. You need to take your tablets."

"Did I hear the phone?"

"Yeah, it was Liz."

"How is she?"

"Fine. Feeling guilty about having a go at you. You're to call her at the restaurant."

Steph looked at him, confused. "At Chez Nous?"

"Yep. She's gone in to help out. She says you're to ring her with instructions."

"That's brilliant! She knows a lot of the journalists and she can represent Chris. It will look great! This is wonderful."

She was reaching for the telephone before Seán got to the door. After a brief but relaxed chat with Liz, Steph obediently took her tablets and promptly fell asleep again.

Seán went out and bought fresh bread and chicken soup. That's what you gave sick people, wasn't it? Surely she'd be able to eat that? When he got back he lit a fire. The days were warm, but Steph loved a real fire at any time of the year. It would cheer her up.

The living-room was quite large but comfortable nonetheless. The impressive bay window and high ceiling gave character to the room, but the decor – muted shades of cream and beige – was more suited to an office than a home. Seán was looking forward to Steph putting her mark on it. She had a natural flair when it came to colours and he wanted to see her style and personality reflected throughout his home. Their home.

It was almost nine o'clock before Stephanie appeared in the doorway. "Oh lovely. A fire." She shuffled over towards it and held out her hands.

"How are you feeling now?" He jumped up and led her

to the sofa, stacked pillows behind her and lifted her feet up.

She smiled weakly. "Not too bad."

"How about some soup?"

"Lovely," she said and sat contentedly gazing into the fire while he went out to the kitchen. She managed a few spoonfuls of soup and then settled back on the sofa in Seán's arms. They watched TV and talked about Liz and the restaurant. We might as well be married, Steph thought absently before she dozed off again, to be woken by the phone at eleven o'clock.

"It's Conor," Seán said, handing her the receiver.

"Conor? How did it go?"

"Brilliant, Steph. They loved my food. The *foie gras* dish turned out better than ever, I used brandy instead of champagne . . ."

Stephanie heard some shouts in the background. "What's happening?" she asked.

Conor laughed. "Edward and Liz want to talk to you. Liz says she'll strangle me if I tell anyone else about my *foie gras*. Here, you'd better talk to them. Sorry you weren't here, Steph. We missed you.

"Steph? It's Edward."

"Well, Edward, be honest. Did it really go well?"

"Like clockwork," he assured her. "Conor outdid himself. The food was amazing and Liz and I really worked the room. She sweet-talked the men and I chatted up the women. What a team!"

Steph felt a pang of jealousy.

"Steph? Oh Steph, it was wonderful. You should be so

proud of Conor. And of yourself. All your hard work paid off."

Steph smiled at the excitement in Liz's voice. "Hiya, Liz. Thanks for stepping into the breach. It sounds as if you did a great job. I'll get you back into this business if it's the last thing I do."

When Stephanie eventually hung up, Seán took her in his arms. "Well done, love."

"I did nothing," she said dismissively.

"You set it all up. You saw a talent in Conor and you gave him a chance. You organised this evening, you drew up the guest list, you did the PR. That's a lot of 'nothing'."

Steph hugged him gratefully. "Thanks, Seán. For everything."

Seán kissed her. A gentle, passionate, slow kiss. She felt her body stir in response. She was obviously over the worst of her tummy bug! She returned his kiss hungrily and made room for him as he pushed her back on to the sofa.

CHAPTER NINETEEN

"Can I have a word?" George stood in the doorway of the office.

Steph looked up. "Sure, George. Take a pew. What's the problem?"

George sat down on the edge of a chair and lit a cigarette. "I think it's time I moved on."

Stephanie was glad Conor wasn't present. He'd never have been able to suppress his delight. "Why's that, George? Is there a problem?"

"Ah no, but I'm too old for this caper. It's hard to teach an old dog new tricks. I don't think I'd fit into this new set-up."

"I'm sorry you feel that way, George. You're a damn good chef. You know how highly I think of you."

George warmed to the flattery. "Nice of you to say so, Steph, but I don't think the younger lads would agree with you. I'd prefer to go back to a more traditional kitchen."

"Have you something lined up?" Steph asked, hoping he wasn't planning to walk out immediately.

"No, no. I just wanted to let you know. Give you a bit of notice. Chris says I'm welcome in Galway, but I don't fancy leaving Dublin. What would I do in the middle of nowhere?"

Steph smiled. Only a die-hard Dub could think of a cosmopolitan city like Galway as the middle of nowhere. "Well, I'll be sorry to lose you, George. Thanks for the notice. I appreciate it. Let me know when you've found something. Have you mentioned this to anyone else?"

George looked surprised. "Of course not, Steph. I told you first. Aren't you the boss?"

Steph smiled and held out her hand. "Well, good luck, George. I hope you find something to suit you."

George shook her hand and left the office.

A few hours later, Steph grabbed a quiet moment to call Conor in Belfast. She closed the door of the office before dialling.

"You're kidding," Conor said. "The old bastard's leaving?"

Steph laughed. "Try to sound a *bit* disappointed when you talk to him, will you?"

"I'll even buy him a drink," Conor promised. "This is great news. I'll phone Kevin. Put him on notice. God, he'll be chuffed. Listen, I have to go, Steph. It's pretty busy here. I'll call you when I've talked to Kevin."

"Fair enough, Conor. See you next week. Bye." Steph hung up. Well, she'd made one person happy today anyway. It would help her through what she was about to do. She picked up the phone and dialled zero. Liam answered.

"Liam? Could you ask Sam to drop up, please?"

* * *

Steph sat down at the table in Annie's kitchen and pulled out her cigarettes.

Annie poured the tea and sat down. "So George is leaving and you've given Sam the push. What next?"

Steph exhaled a cloud of smoke. "Next, I get myself an assistant."

"How about Liz?"

Steph shook her head. "Oh God, no. I'm looking for someone at a very junior level to take over the routine office work. If I ever hire Liz, it'll be as a chef."

"Do you think she'd be interested?" Annie asked.

"Well, it doesn't look like she's going to Galway. She may well *need* a job. Still, I'm not sure how she'd feel about leaving Lucy. But we could do with an extra pair of hands part-time. That would probably suit her. Maybe I'll mention it casually. See how she reacts."

Annie nodded. "I think you should. She needs to be around other adults. I can't say I'll be sorry if she does finish with Chris. I never liked the man. She changed so much after she married him."

"I'm not sure about that. She really changed when Lucy came along."

"Yes, but it was Chris who insisted they start a family. I honestly think he wanted her out of the way. He couldn't handle the competition. I always thought Liz was the better chef."

Steph nodded. "Well, she was definitely more professional. So you think Chris wanted her out of the restaurant? Chained to the kitchen sink?"

"Well, maybe not consciously," Annie conceded.

"Interesting. I wonder will she ever meet anyone else?" Steph mused.

"Not if she doesn't get out more. If we can't talk her into going back to work, we're going to have to work on her social life. Speaking of which, I was thinking of having a bit of a get-together for Joe's birthday."

"Oh, great! It's ages since I've been to a party. Who are you going to invite?" Stephanie was only too happy to turn her thoughts away from business for a while.

"Well, that's one of the problems. All our friends are couples. How will that make Liz feel?"

"She won't come," Steph said glumly. "Could we fix her up?"

Annie raised an eyebrow. "Are you tired of living?"

"Well, then maybe we could invite a few single people. We must know some. What about Edward?"

"I thought you said he was seeing someone?" Annie said.

"I'm not so sure now. Any time I've talked about us getting together as a foursome, he's dodged it. But if he wants to keep the mystery woman to himself, let him. Invite him on his own."

Annie frowned. "But Liz would see that as a set-up. Though he's the last person I'd pair her off with. But if we invite a few others too . . . "

Stephanie clapped her hands. "I've got it! Conor! He's

between girlfriends and he gets on well with Liz. In fact we could kill two birds with one stone. He could talk Liz into going back to work. Leave us totally out of it."

"That's a great idea. But that leaves me with an odd number. We need another woman. What about Jean?"

Steph nearly choked on her tea. "You've got to be kidding! That lazy bitch? She's next on my hit list."

"Well then, it'll have to be Jacqui. She's a bit much after a few drinks but beggars can't be choosers."

"Who's she?"

"Oh, you know the one. Two doors down. Her husband ran off with the nanny."

"Great. You better keep her away from Liz, or it could turn into a wake."

"No, Jacqui's OK. She's living it up these days. Making up for lost time. She's good company as long as you don't mention *his* name. Now, another problem. What night can I have the party if Conor's coming?"

"As long as Chris is still with us, any night except Saturday will be fine."

"Well then, we'll go for a Friday. Joe's birthday's on a Sunday, so the Friday before. He won't be expecting it. I just hope I can keep the kids quiet." Annie knew there wasn't a chance of hiding the preparations from her children. The best thing was to get them involved. They loved that.

Steph rooted in her bag and pulled out her diary to check the date. As she did, a blister-pack of contraceptives fell out on to the table. She picked them up and stared at them, mesmerised.

Annie looked at her, concerned. "What's wrong, Steph? What is it?"

Steph's face was white. "I can't believe it. How could I be so bloody stupid?" she whispered.

Annie looked at her in alarm. "What?"

"I forgot to take the damn things. I had that bug and I was on antibiotics and, well, I forgot all about these."

"You're probably fine," Annie assured her. "When is your period due?"

Steph flipped through her diary until she found a calendar. She looked from the diary, to the packet and finally up at Annie. "Last week," she said, horrified.

"Well, maybe you're just late. Sometimes sickness can play havoc with your cycle . . . "

"I'm never late," Steph said frantically. "Never!"

"Go and buy a test, Stephanie. You may not be. There's no point in getting all worked up until you know for sure. And even then, well you and Seán *are* together . . . "

Stephanie looked at her as if she were mad. "I can't have a *baby*, Annie. Are you out of your mind? It's just not on."

Annie winced at Stephanie's ferocity – she was practically hysterical. "Stephanie, it wouldn't be the end of the world. Children can be very rewarding. Anyway, there's no point in even worrying about this until you take a test. There's a chemist on the corner. I'll go down and get one."

"No!" Steph barked. She took a deep breath and struggled to speak more calmly. "No, it's OK. I'll pick one up on my way in to work." She stood up and slung her bag over her shoulder. "Sorry, Annie. It's just a bit of a shock. I'd better go."

"Call me later and let me know," Annie said anxiously. She watched worriedly as Steph drove away.

Stephanie sat in the car trying to work up the courage to go into the chemist. She looked down at the pack of contraceptives still clutched in her hand. She'd always been so careful. How could this happen to her? She was almost sure that the test would prove positive. She was regular as clockwork. Her period was never late. Still, she shrunk from proving herself right. What a terrible mess. What lousy, rotten luck.

* * *

Ruth ran into the bathroom for the third time that morning. Luckily classes were in full swing and there was no one around to hear her retching. When the nausea passed she sat back against the toilet door and wiped her face with a bit of toilet paper. How had she got herself into this mess? Her dad would be so disappointed. He'd wanted a wonderful career for her, and that had looked more likely after the interview she'd had last week. Now it seemed that she was fated to become a housewife and mother. Tears welled up in her eyes. She'd always wanted to be a mother, but not quite so soon. She'd imagined a few years of good living and partying with Des. She'd planned to buy herself a car – nothing as flashy as his – just a banger that would get her from A to B. She'd imagined holidays in Spain, with Des rubbing oil into her tanned skin. She sniffed and blew her nose. No point in feeling sorry for yourself, Ruth. You got yourself into this mess, you're just going to have to deal with it. She made her way out of the loos and down to the telephones. She rummaged for coins and dialled Des's office number. She cursed the snobby receptionist as her money wasted away while she was left on hold listening to "Edelweiss". Eventually she was told that Des was in a meeting and couldn't be disturbed. She hung up, disappointed. She picked up the phone again and dialled Steph's office.

Steph agreed to lunch immediately she heard the panic in her friend's voice. That bastard Des must be the reason. He usually was. She wondered what he'd done this time. She pushed her way through the crowd in Bewleys to the table where Ruth sat staring into her coffee.

"Hiya, how's it going?" she said, dropping into the chair opposite her.

Ruth looked up at her friend and immediately burst into tears. "I'm pregnant, Steph," she managed eventually.

Steph sat back in her chair, her mouth open.

Ruth started to sob again. "I know I've been stupid, Steph. What are Mam and Dad going to say? They'll be so disappointed in me. They had such high hopes. I know they'd have wanted me to have a husband and family at some stage, but not yet. Not for a long time."

"You've talked to Des? He's going to marry you?"

Ruth smiled through her tears. "Of course he'll marry me, Steph. Don't be silly. He loves me. I haven't told him yet, but he'll be fine once he gets used to the idea."

Steph was amazed. How was it that such an intelligent girl was so dense when it came to men. "I hope you're right, Ruth. But maybe you should prepare yourself, in case . . . "

"In case what? Of course he's going to marry me. He's got to marry me." Ruth's voice rose in panic and Steph put an arm around her.

"It's going to be OK, Ruth. Don't worry. Everything's going to be OK," she said soothingly. Please God she was right.

CHAPTER TWENTY

Stephanie stared at the test-stick in her hand. How could two blue lines change her whole life? She tucked the evidence away in her bag, touched up her make-up and went back to her office. Calmly, she reached for the phone book and found the number she was looking for.

"Hello – Marie Stopes Clinic. Can I help you?"

Stephanie quickly wrote down some details and thanked the girl. Before she had time to think, she rang the number in London and booked an appointment for the following week. The sooner the better. She could only be a couple of weeks pregnant. Better to do it before she started to notice any changes. She'd have to stay over for a couple of days. She was to attend a counselling session and then go in for the procedure the following day. She would opt for the local anaesthetic. That way she'd be in and out in a couple of hours. Anyway, the thought of being conscious appealed to her Catholic mind. She knew that what she was doing was wrong. The least she could do was go through it consciously, acknowledge her sin.

She booked a British Midland flight. Now she had to think of an excuse for going to London. For the first time that day she thought of Seán. What was she going to tell him? She sighed heavily. She couldn't tell him she was pregnant. He'd expect her to keep it. She'd have to make sure Annie kept her mouth shut. She opened her diary. She'd have to rearrange a few things to fit around her trip to London. What bad timing. Maybe she could do a bit of business while she was in the UK. Kill two birds with one stone. God. What a lousy choice of words. Steph shrugged off the guilt. It was a pointless emotion. She was doing the right thing, that's all she had to remember.

Stephanie kept Seán at bay for a couple of days. She *was* busy but she left the house earlier in the mornings and arrived home later at night than was strictly necessary. When Seán wanted to make love, she pleaded tiredness. It wasn't really a lie. The combination of work and the burden of her secret left her exhausted. She couldn't face the thought of making love. It seemed wrong. She wasn't sure why. She avoided Annie's calls for three days. But Annie wasn't easily put off.

Steph looked up from her desk one day to see her sister-in-law in the doorway.

"We're going out," Annie said without preamble.

"I can't . . . " Steph began.

"Do you want to have the conversation that we're going to have *here*?" She looked pointedly at Liam who was rummaging through a filing cabinet in the corner.

Steph picked up her bag. "I'm going out for a while, Liam – I won't be long."

Ten minutes later they were settled with coffee in a quiet corner of a nearby pub.

"Well, was the test positive?"

Steph nodded.

"And what are you going to do?"

"I'm going to get rid of it, of course," she said abruptly.

Annie swallowed hard. She struggled to find the right words, the right tone. She had to tread carefully here. She couldn't risk Steph shutting her out. This was too important.

"Why?" she said eventually.

Steph looked at her in surprise. "What?"

"Why are you getting rid of it?" Annie stumbled over the last words. This was a new life they were talking about.

"I don't want children," Steph said flatly. "There's no place in my life for them."

"And what does Seán think?" Annie asked, knowing full well that Stephanie hadn't told him.

"It's nothing to do with him." Steph folded her arms in front of her, her mouth settling into a stubborn line.

"I'm not sure he'd agree with you. It takes two to make a baby. It isn't up to you to make this decision on your own. It's not your right."

Steph glared at her. "It's my body, for Christ's sake. I'm the one who'd have to carry it for nine months."

"True," Annie agreed as calmly as she could manage. "But we're not talking about some bastard who wouldn't stand by you. We're talking about Seán. The man you love, who loves you. You trust him, don't you? Even if you've made up your mind, you must see that you have to tell him. Don't you realise that there'd be no future

179

for you if he found out afterwards? It's just not fair, Steph."

Stephanie lit a cigarette and puffed on it silently.

"You love him, Steph. Don't hurt him," Annie persisted gently.

"What if he leaves me?" Steph said, her voice shaky.

"He might," Annie agreed. There was no point in beating around the bush. "But at least you'll be able to live with yourself." Stephanie seemed to have softened slightly, so Annie decided to probe further. "Do you really not want kids, Steph, or does all of this come back to Ruth?"

"I don't know, Annie. I don't know. I don't think I'm normal. I can't imagine being responsible for something so small and defenceless. I don't think I could handle it."

Annie laughed. "You're not abnormal. All prospective parents have doubts. It's perfectly natural. It's the biggest job you'll ever take on in your life."

"No, Annie. It's more than that. I just *know* it's not for me. I'm not in the least maternal. Maybe it is to do with Ruth. When she died, I died a little too. It's like I lived a lifetime over that weekend."

Annie put a hand out to her friend. All these years, drunk and sober, she'd tried to get Stephanie to talk. And now out of the blue . . . "You were only a kid, Steph. Of course it had a traumatic effect on you. And then you kept it all to yourself. You never talked, never told anyone her secret. You were a great friend, Steph."

Steph shook her head impatiently. "Not good enough."

"You did everything you could," Annie assured her. "Ruth made a mistake. Now you're in a similar position.

Don't make the mistake of shutting Seán out. Even if you're determined to do it, tell him first."

Steph nodded sadly. "You're right and I will, but I know it will be the end of us. It's hard enough that he doesn't see Billy. He'd never be able to forgive me for this." For the first time tears welled up in Steph's eyes and misery engulfed her. What was wrong with her? Why was she hell-bent on self-destruction? She wiped the tears away and patted Annie's hand. "Thanks, Annie. I'd be lost without you. I better go. I'll finish up early and I'll tell Seán tonight. No point in putting it off any longer."

"Have you, eh, made arrangements . . ." Annie shrank from the words.

"Next Wednesday. A clinic in London. I fly back Thursday evening."

"So fast," Annie said sadly. "Would you like me to go with you? I'm sure Joe would want me to . . ."

"Oh no, that's OK. And please, don't tell Joe." She paused when Annie looked away. "Too late, huh? Oh dear. He'll never understand this, will he? Try to explain for me, will you Annie? I couldn't stand it if he turned against me. And Mam and Dad must never know."

"I'll make him understand," Annie assured her, "and your folks will never hear it from us. I promise you."

Stephanie smiled, gave her a quick hug and left.

* * *

Seán was surprised to see Steph's car already in the driveway. It was supposed to be one of her late nights. He hoped she wasn't sick again. She'd been so tired lately and very withdrawn. He was getting quite worried about her. He wondered if he could persuade her to take a break. He was due to go back to the States at some stage. He'd been putting it off. Now that Steph had finally moved in, he hated the thought of leaving her. It would be wonderful if she came with him. She'd love the desert. He'd talk to her tonight. Loosen her up with a glass of wine first.

"Honey, I'm ho-*ome*," he sang out as he let himself in, dropped his briefcase in the hall and flung his jacket over the banisters.

Steph smiled despite herself. Oh, why couldn't she run to him and tell him there was good news? Why couldn't she rejoice in the new life growing within her? Eat too much ice cream, read baby books and let Seán spoil her? Stop it, Steph. Get a grip. This is no time for feeling sorry for yourself.

"Hello, love. You're home early. Everything OK?" Seán planted a kiss on her forehead and sat down beside her. She'd changed into a tracksuit and removed all her make-up and she was looking very young and very vulnerable.

"I need to talk to you," she said quietly.

"OK," he said, ignoring the sick feeling in the pit of his stomach. "Well, why don't we go out to dinner? Somewhere quiet."

"I don't really feel like it. Maybe we could get a takeaway later."

"Not Chinese," he quipped.

"No. Not Chinese," she agreed with a weak smile.

"Why don't I open a bottle of wine?" He was out of the room before Steph could reply. This wasn't going to be easy.

"I've had a lousy day," he said returning with the wine and two glasses. "You wouldn't believe how stupid . . . "

"Seán. I've something to tell you."

He refused to look at her, busying himself with the bottle. This was it. She was moving out. That's all it could be. He'd been so sure he could make her happy. She'd appeared to be settling in well although she had been tense in the last few days. What went wrong? He handed her a glass. "I'm all yours," he said lightly, taking the seat opposite her.

"There's no easy way to say this, no point in beating around the bush . . . "

He was right. She wanted to move out. Break up.

"I'm pregnant."

Seán looked at her blankly.

"Seán, did you hear me? I said I'm pregnant." Steph looked at him, wishing he'd say something.

Seán stared at her. She wasn't moving out. Thank God for that. But what was it – she was – she was . . . "You're *pregnant?*" he cried, jumping up and dragging her up into his arms. "Steph! I can't believe it. My God! When? How? Oh, that's a bloody stupid question. How do you feel? Are you OK?"

Stephanie quaked at the concern in his eyes. "I'm OK, no sickness, not yet anyway. But I – I . . . "

"What is it, love? Nervous? That's natural, believe me. You'll get used to the idea. You're going to be a fantastic mother, and a very sexy one." He trailed kisses across her face and down her neck.

Steph pulled away abruptly. "No. You don't understand, Seán. I can't do it."

His smile was sympathetic. "Of course you can, Steph. You'll be fine. I'll look after you."

"No, Seán!" She was shouting now. *"You're not listening!* It's not going to happen. I don't *want* it to happen. I'm flying to London next week for a termination."

Seán looked at her horrified. "No, you're bloody well not! What the hell are you talking about?"

Steph flinched at the cold fury in his eyes. "I'm sorry, but I've made up my mind."

Seán forced himself to calm down. It was natural that she was nervous. A first-time mother at thirty-two, with a career. Anyway, her hormones were all screwed up. Karen's moods had been very unpredictable when she was pregnant. "Look, love. I know this is a shock but give it a bit of time to sink in. Believe me, no one can make you as happy as your own child. You don't understand how much you'd be giving up. Please think about it."

Steph shrugged him off and turned her face away. She couldn't bear him like this. His fury was easier. "There's nothing to think about. I've made up my mind."

"And what about me? Don't I have a say? I am the father . . . or am I?"

Steph stared at him. "Of course you are. How could you even say such a thing? You know there's no one else. God, is that what you think of me?"

"I don't know what to bloody think," Seán said, pacing the floor and raking a hand through his hair. "I don't know how you could think of doing that!"

"I told you. I've thought about it. A termination's the only answer."

"Termination? Termination?" he shouted at her. "Call it

what it is, for God's sake. Abortion. Murder. This isn't just some neat little operation. You're not deciding on a 'termination'! You're deciding to kill our child."

Steph stared at him in horror and then ran up to their bedroom. She locked the door after her but Seán didn't follow. She lay on the bed, her body racked with sobs, listening for Seán's step. It didn't come. A short time later she heard the front door slam. This unleashed a new flood of tears.

Eventually she got up, undressed, and after a moment's hesitation unlocked the door. She climbed into bed and turned out the light. Finally she fell into an exhausted sleep but she was plagued by nightmares.

When she opened her eyes the next morning, she put out her hand but Seán wasn't there. It took a moment before she remembered. She groaned as it all came flooding back. She dragged herself out of bed and went down the stairs in search of Seán. Had he spent the night on the sofa? But she put her head around the living-room door and there was no sign of him. She padded into the kitchen, the pristine terracotta tiles cold underfoot. She'd make some tea and then call him on his mobile. But what would she say? She wasn't going to change her mind and that was the only thing he'd want to hear. She couldn't blame him for attacking her. She understood his horror, but was powerless to do anything about it. She crossed to the patio door and looked out on the large unkempt garden. She'd been nagging Seán for weeks to do something with it. He'd laughed at her and told her to call her father. She smiled sadly as she remembered their playful slagging. She made a mug of tea and carried it over to the table and for the first time noticed the note propped up against the sugar bowl. She picked it up and read it. Short and to the point.

I've gone to stay with my folks. I'm going to the States for a couple of weeks as soon as I can arrange it. Please move your things out before I get back.

Steph sat down at the kitchen table and cried like a baby. She'd prepared herself for his anger and for the possibility that he might not want anything more to do with her, but nothing had prepared her for the pain that was ripping her apart.

CHAPTER TWENTY-ONE

Stephanie leaned back, closed her eyes and ignored the flight attendant giving the safety routine. It had been the longest week of her life. She hadn't seen Seán again. He wouldn't take or return her calls. She wouldn't have got through the week without Annie. Even Joe had been great, despite his obvious discomfort. He'd moved all her stuff back out to Malahide. She felt sad as she closed the front door of Seán's lovely old house. In the few weeks she'd lived there, she'd come to look on it as home. By contrast, her apartment seemed cold and empty.

Joe had a quiet word with Edward, filled him in on the situation and asked him to look after things for a while. Edward didn't let on to Stephanie that he knew what was going on. He accepted her lame reason for going to London, and assured her he'd be available if any crisis arose in her absence.

Steph avoided Liz, afraid that in her emotional state she'd blurt everything out. She didn't know how Liz would react. She probably wouldn't be as sympathetic as Annie.

Anyway, she didn't want to tell anyone else. It was hard enough coping with Seán's rejection.

She turned as the hostess stopped beside her with the drinks trolley.

"Cognac, please," she said. She tossed back half the glass defiantly. *"I'm doing the right. I'm doing the right thing."* She repeated the words to herself like a mantra.

* * *

"Des, I'm pregnant," Ruth said before she lost her nerve. She was still breathless after their swift and intense lovemaking. She'd tried to talk to Des earlier, but he was hell-bent on making love and it was easier to go along with it.

"You're what?" Des rolled over in bed and stared at her.

"I'm pregnant, Des. It must have been that first time. I've been on the pill since."

Des stared at her. "Christ."

Ruth laughed nervously. "I know it's not what we wanted, but if we get married quickly, we can get away with it. My dad will probably go nuts, but he'll calm down eventually. I'm sure he'll give us his blessing in the end."

Des looked at her, panic-stricken. "I don't think we should rush into anything, Ruth," he said, struggling to keep his voice calm. "Marriage is a big step."

"But we love each other. We would have married sooner or later, this just means it has to be sooner."

Des pulled on his trousers and reached for his shirt.

Ruth looked at him nervously. "Des? You do love me, Des, don't you?"

He hesitated and then gave her a quick, awkward hug.

"Course I do, silly. But like I say, marriage is a big step. I think it would be better if you had an abortion. You have your whole life ahead of you, not to mention a very promising career. You don't want to throw it all away, do you?"

Ruth shook her head.

Relieved, he took her hand and continued more gently. "There you go then. There'll be plenty of time for babies. You're only nineteen, for God's sake. It would be very hard, Ruth. Too hard. Trying to bring up a child on my salary alone. And we'd have to get somewhere decent to live. It's really not a great idea."

Ruth looked at him solemnly. "So you want me to have an abortion?"

"Don't say it like that," he said angrily. "That's not what I said. I just want you to do what's best."

For who? Ruth wondered.

"So what do you think?" he asked anxiously.

She smiled weakly. "You're probably right."

The look of relief on his face was like a knife through her heart.

"Good girl!" He hugged her. "Why don't you get in touch with one of those clinics and I'll take care of your travel arrangements? I think you should fly. The boat might be a bit much if you're not feeling well."

"I can't afford it . . ."

"I'll pay. Don't you worry about a thing."

"Thanks, Des," she said quietly.

"You're doing the right thing, love. I promise you. You won't regret it."

Ruth stared into the distance. "No. No, I won't regret it."

* * *

Steph consulted her A to Z. The clinic was quite near the hotel so she set out on foot. Ten minutes later she was standing in front of the clinic. It looked exactly the same as all the other buildings on the street. Somehow that didn't seem right to Stephanie. The receptionist was kind but not over-familiar. She showed Stephanie into an office where a woman around her own age stood to greet her. She asked general questions about Stephanie's health and her family history.

With all the details out of the way, Eve Wilmot took off her glasses and looked at the young woman in front of her. Well-dressed, composed, but nervous. Still, who wasn't nervous in this situation?

"So, Miss West – Stephanie. Why have you decided to terminate your pregnancy?"

Stephanie was ready for this question. She'd no intention of telling the truth. It was too complicated. "It just wouldn't work. I've broken up with my partner and I'm in the throes of setting up a new business."

"Does your partner know you're pregnant?"

"Yes, but he's not interested," Steph lied, silently begging Seán's forgiveness.

"What about your family?"

"There's only my parents who are elderly and live in Co Wicklow. They wouldn't be able to help out." Steph lowered her eyes as she thought of the vibrant couple who lived life to the full.

"Could you afford a child-minder?" Eve Wilmot asked pleasantly.

Steph flushed. "Well, yes, I could, but I don't see much point in bringing a child into the world and then handing it over to someone else to raise. Do you?"

"I'm not judging you, Stephanie. But it's my job to make sure you've made the right decision."

"Well, I have," Steph said defiantly. "I don't want to be a single mother, not now, not ever. I've a business to run and that's my top priority."

Eve asked some more questions and then explained the procedure for the following day. "You'll see Doctor Knight, my colleague, first. Just in case you have any more questions or have second thoughts overnight."

"I won't," Steph said shortly. She felt guilty as the counsellor reassured her that she was probably making the right decision and she left the clinic feeling uneasy. She'd planned to go and do some shopping. Buy a present for Lucy and pick up something nice for Annie in Harrods, but she couldn't face it. She walked slowly back to the hotel where she ordered a bottle of wine from room service and ran herself a hot bath.

She undressed and slipped on a hotel robe while she waited for her wine. She lit a cigarette and then stubbed it out. You weren't supposed to smoke when you were pregnant. She laughed out loud. It was a bit pointless worrying about smoking now. The harsh, slightly hysterical sound took her by surprise. There was a knock on the door and she took the tray from the waiter. She poured herself a large glass of the Cote de Rhone and lit another cigarette, pulling deeply on it. Maybe she'd get drunk. It might make her feel better. Maybe she'd even miscarry naturally and she wouldn't have to go through with tomorrow. Wouldn't have to feel guilty. She pulled a clean blouse out of her overnight bag and hung it on the bathroom door to let the creases fall out. It would do for dinner.

Two hours later she walked into the dining-room and was led to a table near the window. She sat with her back to the room. She wasn't in the mood for company. The waiter handed her a menu and she scanned it quickly. "Consommé followed by the fish with a side salad," she said. She selected a wine and then settled back in her seat to wait. She'd never ordered a meal so fast – Seán would be in shock. Usually she pored over the menu for ages, examining the combinations and selecting the dish that she believed was the most challenging for the chef. But tonight she didn't care. She was just going through the motions. Killing time.

The waiter arrived back with the wine, and she waved at him to pour away. Another deviation from the norm, but she didn't much care what she drank as long as it knocked her out. She lit a cigarette and ignored the dirty look she got from a neighbouring table. She turned her thoughts to Chez Nous and the weeks of work ahead but she kept going back to the ordeal facing her, the look of disgust on Seán's face that night . . . She shivered and took a gulp of wine. When the starter arrived she pushed it around the plate. The main course got much the same treatment, but the wine got a quick death.

She signed for her meal and headed back to her room where she channel-hopped for an hour, paced for a while and then went back to the TV. Eventually she got into bed and turned off the light. It was only eleven and she was wide awake. The drink had neither dulled her senses or made her sleepy. It looked as if it was going to be a long and restless night.

* * *

Ruth picked up the phone and dialled Steph's number.

"Hello?"

"Steph? Hi, it's me."

"Ruth? Hi. What's happening?"

"Nothing much. Still pregnant." *Ruth gave a short humourless laugh.*

"Did you tell Des?"

"Yep."

"And?"

"He was . . . shocked."

"I'm sure he was. Is he going to stand by you?"

"Yes. Of course."

"Oh, Ruth. That's great. So when are you going to tell your folks? When are you getting married?"

"We're not. I've decided to get an abortion. I'm not going to tell Mam and Dad."

Steph stared at the receiver in her hand. How in God's name was Ruth able to talk so calmly? She was dead against abortion – always had been. This had to be Des Healy's idea, the bastard. "Are you sure that's what you want, Ruth?"

"Of course not," *Ruth said impatiently,* "but it's for the best. Listen, can you come over? Mary and Sinéad are still away and this place is like a bloody morgue."

"Oh, I'm sorry, Ruth. I can't. Seán's on his way over. We're

*meeting some of his friends. Look, I'll meet you for lunch
tomorrow. Bewleys at one, OK?"*

*"OK," Ruth said, her voice flat. She hung up the receiver,
wandered into the living-room and switched on the TV. An
image of a woman in labour with a concerned husband
bending over her swam onto the screen. Ruth groaned and
switched it off. She went back out to the phone.*

"Hi, Gary? It's Ruth, is Des there?"

*"Oh, hi Ruth. Eh . . . no . . . I think he's out at some
business do."*

*Ruth smiled grimly. "OK. Thanks, Gary. Bye." A work do
on a Sunday evening. Unlikely. She thought back over the last
few months and the number of strange and rather weak excuses
Des had given for his absence. No wonder Steph thought she
was dumb. It had had been obvious to everyone except her that
Des wasn't serious about her. But she'd only seen what she
wanted to see. She was in love and she desperately wanted him
to love her too. Oh, well.*

*She unplugged the phone from the wall and then locked the
front door. Sinéad and Mary had gone home to Tullamore for
the weekend. They weren't due back until Monday evening.
She went into the bathroom and opened the press. Mary's
medication for her migraine was neatly lined up. There was
also a bottle of aspirin and a half pack of paracetemol. Ruth
looked at them thoughtfully and then gathered them all up
with trembling hands. She went into the kitchen and set them
down on the table. She fetched a bowl, the bread-board and a
rolling-pin. She paused to turn on the radio. She needed some
kind of noise. "I'm Not in Love" by 10CC. That was
appropriate, she thought grimly. She emptied out each pack of
pills onto the board, crushed them and emptied them into the*

bowl. When she was finished, she went to the fridge. There was only one can of beer and a half bottle of cheap wine. That wouldn't do at all. She checked all the cupboards and found a vodka bottle with a drain in the bottom and half a bottle of whiskey. She'd never get that down her — she hated the stuff. She went in search of her purse. Twenty quid. That should be enough.

She put on her jacket, picked up her keys and went down to the off-licence.

"Howya," the owner said cheerfully.

"How's it going?" Ruth replied with a smile. "A bottle of brandy, please."

"Sure. Any particular brand?"

"Oh, whatever you recommend. It's a special occasion."

"It's well for you," he said, selecting a dark green bottle from the top shelf. "That's eleven-fifty, please."

Ruth handed over the money.

"Well, enjoy," he said and handed her the brown bag and her change,

"I will. Seeya," she said with a cheerful smile. She walked back to the flat, feeling calm and almost relaxed. After depositing the brandy on the counter in the kitchen she went into her bedroom and opened the wardrobe. She started flicking through the stuff on the shelf. Her red leather belt. Sinéad loved that. And then there was her new hairdryer. Sinéad could have that too. Mary wouldn't mind. Her new gypsy skirt — Steph loved that. It would fit her perfectly. Look better on her too.

She went through all her stuff adding selected items to different piles. All the shoes were Mary's to keep or discard. She was the only one who was the same size.

Ruth moved to the bedside table and flicked through her

small collection of books. The Jane Austen and the book of Irish poetry for Steph. The joke book for Sinéad, and the pristine good-as-new Pru Leith cookbook was added to Mary's bundle. It might actually get used now. She put all her trendiest stuff into another pile for her sisters and added her extensive collection of earrings. After the wardrobe was clear, she carefully labelled the piles and went back out to the kitchen. She poured some of the brandy into the bowl and mixed the concoction with a spoon. She emptied it into a tumbler and carried it and the bottle into the living-room. She settled down on the lumpy sofa and set her concoction on the coffee table in front of her. Now. Was there anything else to do? Should she leave a note for Des? No. He knew how she felt about him. There was nothing left to say. Should she ring her folks? No, too risky. They might come over. She'd have to leave them a note, but what would she say? Tell her parents that the daughter they'd been so proud of had got herself knocked up? It was so hard. How could she make them understand? Still, if she didn't leave a note, they'd always wonder. She found a pen and took a piece of Mary's pretty, scented notepaper from the drawer in the sideboard.

When she'd finished writing, she folded the page neatly and put it in the matching pink envelope. On the front she wrote "Mam and Dad".

She put down the pen, stirred her drink and took a deep breath before lifting the glass to her lips. She managed to swallow half of it without gagging. She winced at the bitter taste and took a slug from the brandy bottle before emptying the glass. Then she settled back and waited for the darkness to engulf her.

CHAPTER TWENTY-TWO

Stephanie walked into reception and the same girl welcomed her. "If you'd like to follow me, Ms West." She led the way towards the double doors. "Ms West?"

Stephanie tried, but she couldn't move. The simple act of putting one foot in front of the other seemed impossible. "I can't," she whispered.

The receptionist nodded, unfazed, and excused herself, returning moments later with the counsellor.

"Why don't we go into my office and have a nice cup of tea?" Eve Wilmot said kindly, taking Steph's arm.

"Feel better?" the counsellor asked, an hour and half a box of tissues later.

"Yes, thanks," Steph smiled shakily. "You've been very kind. I'm sorry for messing you about."

Eve dismissed her apologies with a wave of her hand. "Every time a woman decides to keep her baby, I go home happier."

"It happens a lot?"

"Oh my, yes. A lot of women can't go through with it. Some come back the following week, but others send me their baby pictures. I hope you will."

"Of course." Steph smiled shyly. It was still hard to come to terms with the idea of being a mother. It terrified her, but she knew she couldn't get rid of her baby. Seán's baby. Oh, he'd be so happy! She couldn't wait to tell him.

"Please consider counselling," Eve said seriously. "You had a terrible experience when you were very young, and it's being eating you up for a long time. You've taken the first step towards dealing with it, but you've still a long way to go."

"I'll have a word with my GP," Steph promised. She stood up and held out her hand. "Thank you so much, Eve. You've been very kind."

"My pleasure. Now why don't we get you checked out while you're here? Have you any idea of your due date?"

Stephanie floated down the steps of the clinic, one hand touching her stomach almost reverently. She was seven weeks pregnant! It was amazing! She couldn't quite believe it all. She'd been so sure that termination was the only way but, when it came to the crunch, she couldn't do it. Now it was as if an enormous weight had been lifted from her shoulders. The future suddenly seemed bright. She could manage work and motherhood, plenty of other women did. Women who weren't nearly as well-off as she was. She couldn't wait to tell her mother. She'd be thrilled. She'd be more thrilled if Stephanie was married of course, but that would happen soon enough. Steph hailed a taxi and directed him to Mothercare. It might be a bit early to buy, but there was no harm in looking.

Steph wandered through the shop with a silly smile on her face. She paused to touch a Moses basket, finger a lace quilt and linger over a tiny peach satin dress that was an outrageous sixty-five pounds. She went into the maternity section and looked in wonder at the smocks and dungarees, with their special pouches. Maybe she should buy some. It wouldn't be long after all . . . she forced herself to move on. It was too early to buy anything. She didn't want to tempt fate. She made her way to Hamleys and satisfied her sudden, surprising, maternal instincts by buying toys for Shane, Danielle and Lucy. Then she went to Harrods where she bought some pretty lingerie for Annie, perfume for Liz, table linen for her mother and a polo shirt for her dad. Her final stop was at the food hall, her favourite department. She spent an hour wandering around happily and finally headed for the restaurant laden down with goodies.

She ordered tea and a scone and resisted the temptation to light a cigarette. She had to be careful now. No more cigarettes, and only the occasional glass of wine. Now *that* was going to be hard. She'd only one purchase left to make. Something for Seán. What would make up for all the heartache she'd put him through? It came to her as she sipped her tea. A ring. Not a wedding ring, that would be presumptuous. No – a signet-ring. She gulped back her tea, gathered up her bags and made for the jewellers on Sloane Street.

It was an hour and two frustrated salesmen later before she emerged, satisfied with her gift. She hailed a taxi and sat back feeling happy and excited at the prospect of telling Seán her news and presenting him with her peace offering.

* * *

Seán stood up as his flight was announced and strode towards the gate. He was glad to be getting out of the country for a while. Thinking about Stephanie and what she'd done, or was about to do, tore him to pieces. He felt very depressed and suddenly he missed Billy more than ever. He phoned Karen and arranged to visit on his way back from Phoenix. At least that was something to look forward to.

Even Annie hadn't been able to take away the pain. He'd been surprised when she'd phoned him in work and asked him to come over. His first instinct was to say no. He didn't need to rake over the whole business again. He'd accepted Steph's phobia about marriage, but this was too much. He'd finally given in to Annie. She was insistent. And he *was* very fond of her.

Annie had opened the door as soon as he pulled up.

"Thanks for coming, Seán," she said, reaching up to kiss his cheek. She led the way into the kitchen. "Coffee?"

"Yeah, OK. Look I don't have much time, Annie. And I'm not too sure why I'm here." Seán leaned against the counter and watched Annie spoon instant into two mugs.

"It won't take long, Seán. But there's something I think you should know. I think it might help you understand why Steph . . ." She faltered.

"Why she's killing our child?" he said coldly. "I don't believe I'll ever understand or forgive that."

"I know it's hard, Seán. I'm a mother, remember. I'm finding it pretty hard to get my head around it too. But you must realise that no woman makes this decision lightly. There's always a reason." Annie looked at Seán and the sadness in his eyes mirrored her own.

She handed him a mug and waved him to a chair before taking the one opposite. "It all goes back to Ruth, Seán. You know how upset Steph was."

"Well, yes, we all were. She seemed to take it harder than most, but then they grew up together. I wanted her to talk to someone about it. You know, a professional. I mean, she wouldn't talk to me and her mother said she'd clammed up with her too. Did she talk to you?"

Annie nodded. "Oh not much, and certainly not willingly. I happened to be in the right place at the right time. You see, the thing was, Ruth was pregnant when she died."

"What?" Seán stared at her.

"Yes. She'd found out a few days earlier."

"Oh, Christ. Is that why she took the overdose?"

"It looks like it. Apparently Ruth had expected Des to rush her down the aisle and they'd all live happily ever after. Des wasn't so keen."

"The bastard. I never did like him. And you think this is why Steph wanted an abortion? Surely not?" Seán could understand Steph's horror at her friend's tragedy but he couldn't understand what it had to do with her pregnancy.

"Well you see, Steph was the only one Ruth confided in. She came to her for help and advice." Annie watched him steadily, took a deep breath and continued. "You see, the day that Ruth died she called Steph. She wanted her to come over. But Steph was, eh . . ."

"She was meeting me," Seán said staring into space.

Annie looked at his crestfallen expression and wondered if she'd been right to tell him. "Yes," she said gently. "And she told Ruth she'd meet her the next day instead."

"Oh, shit," Seán gasped, raking his hand through his hair.

"Yes. So, you see, Steph blames herself. Something else occurred to me."

"Yes?" Seán prompted.

"Well, I may sound like a reject from the Oprah show, but I sometimes wonder if she blames you too. She put you before Ruth. I think she's been punishing herself ever since."

Seán looked up as realisation dawned. "You think so?"

"It would make sense. Explain why she won't marry you. Why she went for the abortion."

"What do you mean?"

Annie shifted uncomfortably. "Oh, maybe I'm talking a load of bull, Seán. I just thought that maybe because Ruth couldn't have a family, Steph felt she didn't deserve one either. Does that sound ridiculous?"

"No, it actually makes a lot of sense," Seán said, thinking of Steph's recent behaviour.

Annie shrugged. "Maybe it's a bit Freudian. I don't think she's conscious of any of this and I could be completely wrong."

"I don't think so, Annie. I've tried so often to talk to her about Ruth but she always got annoyed. I wonder was that part of it. She felt she had to keep it a secret to punish herself."

"I don't know, Seán. I think a lot of that was just protecting her friend."

"How did her parents find out? Did Steph tell them?"

"No. Apparently Ruth left a note. But they didn't know about Des. She'd never mentioned him before."

"How come Steph told you all this, Annie. No offence. But why you?"

"Oh, it wasn't out of choice," Annie said with a sad smile. "I was with her when Ruth's dad phoned. He was in a terrible state. He wanted to know who the father was. He was sure Steph would know. She was in an awful way after that call and she just blurted it all out. But any time I've tried to talk to her about it since, she's cut me off."

"What about Des?" Seán thought of the man who'd caused all the heartache and wished he'd known so that he could have gone over and kicked the shit out of him. Poor little Ruth. She was such an innocent. Her only real sin had been loving that asshole.

"That was the curious thing," Annie said. "He left his job and went to England. Maybe he had a conscience after all."

"I find that hard to believe," Seán said grimly. "It's more likely that Ruth's dad caught up with him. I certainly hope so." He sat back in his chair, trying to take it all in. It was a terrible business and it couldn't have been easy for Steph. "What am I going to do, Annie?"

"That's your decision, Seán. All I can tell you is that Steph loves you, and that I really don't believe she's responsible for her actions."

Seán rubbed his eyes. He felt tired and sad. "I love her too, Annie. I always have. I'd like to spend the rest of my life with her but I'm just not sure I can get past this."

Annie squeezed his hand. "You need time, Seán. It's a lot to take in. You're grieving for your child. But just remember that whether she admits it or not, Stephanie is grieving too. She'll be home tomorrow night. Talk to her."

"I can't. I'll be on a plane to Arizona. Maybe it's just as well. I don't think I could face her just yet. I wouldn't trust myself. It's too soon."

Annie swallowed back her tears. "How long will you be away?"

"A few weeks. Do me a favour, Annie?"

"Anything," she promised.

"Look after her."

Annie raised an eyebrow. "Do you think you have to ask?"

Seán hugged her. "You're a good friend, Annie. To both of us. Thanks."

As the plane sped down the runway, Seán prayed that Steph was OK, and that one day they'd be able to put this terrible mess behind them.

* * *

Stephanie let herself into her apartment and immediately made for the phone. She got Seán's machine. No point in leaving a message. She knew he wouldn't call her back. She'd catch up with him in his office tomorrow. She took off her coat and picked up the post. The phone rang and she pounced on it.

"Hello?"

"Hi, Steph. It's me. How are you?"

"Oh hi, Annie. I'm great. How about you?"

"Eh, fine."

"Wait till you see what I got the kids. And I bought you a little something too."

"Oh, thanks," Annie said faintly. "You shouldn't have. And you're sure you're OK?"

"Yeah. Just tired."

"Of course you are. I'll let you go. By the way, Seán left for Phoenix today."

Steph's heart sank. "Already? How do you know?"

"He called me. Asked me to let you know," Annie fibbed.

"How long's he gone for?"

"A few weeks."

"Oh shit! OK so. Thanks, Annie. Bye."

"How is she?" Joe asked.

"Fine. Too fine. She sounded as if she were just back from a holiday. Until I told her Seán was gone. She wasn't too happy about that."

Joe frowned. "Maybe she's 'in denial', as the Americans say."

"Great. That's all we need."

Joe put an arm around his wife and hugged her. "Don't worry, love. She'll be all right."

Annie smiled at him, but she couldn't stop thinking about her sister-in-law. To go through what she'd just gone through was a terrible ordeal. Annie knew that Steph hadn't taken this step lightly. She had to be going through hell. She *couldn't* be happy.

* * *

Annie was right. Steph wasn't happy at all, but only because she couldn't talk to Seán and tell him the good news. He must be so miserable. She'd have to call his office and get a number where she could reach him in Phoenix. She'd burst if she didn't talk to him soon. She moved her hand protectively to her stomach. How was she going to manage to keep the wonderful news to herself? She'd have to. Seán had to be the first to know. She'd have to avoid Annie and Liz. She'd never be able to keep her mouth shut otherwise. Yes, that was the answer. Keep her head down and work hard until Seán got back. Annie wouldn't be that surprised. Between the abortion and breaking up with Seán she'd expect Steph to be miserable.

She smiled ruefully as she remembered her conversation with Annie. How dumb of her to chatter on about the presents when Annie thought she was just back from having an abortion! God, what must she think? Poor Annie. Still, she'd forgive her. When she knew the truth. Everyone would.

CHAPTER TWENTY-THREE

L<small>IZ</small> took Lucy by the hand and walked back towards the school gate.

"Hello, Lucy. Hi, you must be Liz."

Liz turned to the pretty woman smiling at her. "Yes, that's right. I'm sorry, I'm afraid I don't know . . ."

The other woman laughed, a merry, happy sound. "Oh, that's OK. We haven't met. Jennifer McDermott. Carol's mother, Edward's sister."

"Oh, I see. Nice to meet you," Liz stretched out a hand and received a firm handshake.

"I've heard so much about you. Edward's a different man since he met you."

Liz flushed. "I think you're mixing me up with someone else," she said stiffly. "Edward and I are just friends."

Jennifer smiled brightly. "Of course. Sorry. I must have got hold of the wrong end of the stick. Silly me. Ed's always saying I should put my brain in gear before I open my mouth."

Liz raised an eyebrow. "Ed? Is that what you call him?"

"Only when I want to annoy him. He hates it but it keeps him in his place."

Liz laughed.

"Do you fancy a coffee?" Jennifer asked.

Liz hesitated for only a moment. "Yes, OK. Why don't you come back to my place. I'm only down the road from you."

"Right so. I'll follow you. Just give me a minute to find Carol. She was here a minute ago."

Liz opened the car and helped Lucy in.

"Jenny's real nice, Mum. I like her."

"She seems lovely, pet," Liz agreed. She was amazed at herself. The invitation had been out before she realised it. She'd never asked any other mother home for coffee before. Still, Jennifer *was* Edward's sister, and he'd been very kind to her. She wondered what *exactly* he'd told his sister about her.

As soon as they got back to the house, Lucy dragged her friend up to play in her room and the two women were left alone.

While Liz made coffee, Jennifer wandered around the kitchen. Oak-panelled presses framed the room, a large oak workstation took centre stage and shining knives and utensils dangled from hooks above it. The kitchen table was in a corner by a large window that looked out on the small pretty garden. An oak dresser, with an alarming stack of cookery books and a row of shining copper pots and pans, stood in the corner.

"Wow! This is an amazing kitchen. But of course you're a chef. I forgot."

Liz smiled and poured steaming coffee into two mugs. "I do too sometimes. Looks impressive, doesn't it? But most of the time, baked beans and fish fingers are all that's on the menu. Especially since, well, since my husband moved out. I never entertain any more."

Jennifer ignored Liz's embarrassment. "Oh, you should. I'd crack up if it wasn't for friends coming over. I don't cook anything grand – a lasagne or chilli, but it's great fun."

Liz imagined that just being around this woman would be great fun. She was nothing like Edward. He was more conservative. Though the eyes and colouring were the same, Jennifer's eyes twinkled with fun and her mouth was turned up in a permanent smile. How sad that she was a widow.

"I used to be like you," Jennifer continued. "I didn't go outside the door after Finbarr died. I didn't want to see anyone. But eventually you have to pick yourself up, dust yourself off and start again. Sorry. Sermon over."

"That's OK. It's nice to meet someone who actually understands," Liz said. "Though of course it must have been much worse for you. Your husband died in terrible circumstances. I just lost a creep to his mid-life fantasies."

"Finbarr may have died, but he was no angel," Jennifer said drily.

Liz stared at her, slightly shocked. She'd been taught never to speak ill of the dead.

"Edward didn't tell you?" Jenny said when she saw Liz's face.

Liz shook her head.

"Finbarr died in a car crash on the Wicklow to Dublin road. He was supposed to be at a conference in Cork at the time. He was with someone. A woman. They were both killed instantly."

"Oh," Liz said inadequately. "I'm sorry. Maybe there was a simple explanation . . . "

"No. It was just as seedy as it appeared. We were able to trace them to a hotel in the area. I'm surprised Edward didn't tell you."

"I don't see why. It's your business, after all."

Jennifer looked at her curiously, but said nothing.

"It must have been awful for you. When did it happen?"

"Three years ago, now. Carol doesn't really remember Finbarr. I keep photos around the place and talk about him, but it's not the same. It's a pity. Whatever his faults, he was a great dad and he worshipped Carol."

Liz shook her head wearily. "Why the hell do they do it? Why are they ready to throw away so much for a quick fling?"

"Now *that* is the six-million-dollar question," Jennifer said as Liz refilled their cups. "I always thought we were blissfully happy. Oh, let's talk about something else before we start crying into our coffee. I'm having a bit of a get-together next week. Some of the neighbours are coming. None of the gossips, I promise. Why don't you come along?"

"Oh, I don't know . . . " Liz shifted uncomfortably.

"I'll ask Edward to. That way you'll have at least two people to talk to if you hate everyone else."

Liz brightened at the idea of seeing Edward. "Well, OK then. Why not? But let me help. I could cook something."

"Would you? God, that would be great. Some *real* food for a change. But look, I don't want you going to too much trouble," she warned. "Ed would kill me."

"I promise. I'll keep it simple. Please, I'd enjoy it." Liz went over to her cookery books and selected two. She quickly ran through a few menus, while Jenny sat gobsmacked. They finally decided on three dishes that they would serve buffet-style.

"We better leave it at that, Liz, or we'll never be invited back. You'll scare them all off with your talent. Have you ever thought about going back to work?"

"Well, not seriously. My friend Stephanie is always at me to go back to work, but I hate the idea of leaving Lucy."

"Stephanie West? Edward's partner?"

"Yes. She was with us from day one. We'd have been lost without her. Anyway, she's always telling me that I'm wasting my talents. I wouldn't mind doing something, but now it's going to be more difficult than ever. You see, Chris, my husband, is moving to Galway. Lucy's only going to have me. Well, full-time, that is."

"So you're definitely splitting up?"

"Yes, we are," Liz said and for the first time she knew she really meant it. "And it'll be hard enough on Lucy, without me going back to work."

"You're probably right," Jennifer agreed. "Kids can get really screwed up when parents separate. They start thinking they did something wrong. You probably have a tough time ahead of you."

"Thanks," Liz said drily. "You're really cheering me up."

Jennifer laughed loudly. "Oh, I'm sorry. Don't mind me. Subtlety was never my strong point. I better leave before you throw me out." She went out into the hall and banged on the staircase. "Carol? It's time to go home now."

211

Liz followed her out. "I'll give you a call next week, Jennifer, and we can go shopping for supplies."

"Great. Whenever suits you. I really appreciate this. Just do me one more favour? Call me Jenny or Jen. I've always thought Jennifer was such a mouthful. Jennifer and Edward. My parents have a lot to answer for."

Liz and Lucy waved as Jenny and Carol drove away. Liz was still smiling as she prepared Lucy's lunch. It was nice to have a new friend. One who understood exactly what she was going through. She was very glad she liked Edward's sister. He'd become an important person in her life. He'd be happy that they hit it off.

The phone rang and to Liz's delight it was Edward.

"You'll never guess who I just met," she said, settling herself on the bottom stair.

"My sister?"

"How did you know?"

"I just got a call from her. She couldn't wait to tell me how great you were."

"Well, she's very nice too," Liz said, gratified that Jenny had liked her.

"I think she's decided we're perfect for each other." There was a smile in Edward's voice.

"I don't know why," Liz said shortly. "We only talked about menus and lousy husbands."

"She told you about Finbarr?"

"Yes. It must have been awful for her. It's bad enough to find out your husband's been killed, but that he was with another woman at the time . . . "

"Yes," Edward agreed quietly. "It was a terrible time. So.

I believe she's bullied you into doing the cooking for one of her little soirées."

"Not at all. It was my idea. It's a good excuse to hide in the kitchen," she added with a grin.

"In that case, I'll be your waiter, I could do with a hiding-place. Some of Jen's female friends can be a bit overbearing."

Liz laughed. "That's because you're so eligible. If you were with someone you'd have some protection."

"Do you think so? Well, in that case I'll have to cast long loving glances in your direction and maybe they'll get the message."

"Don't be silly, Edward," Liz said brusquely. "I'm a married woman."

"Only on paper," he pointed out.

"I don't agree with that. Call me old-fashioned, but I happen to believe in the vows I took. Even if Chris doesn't."

"Well, of course. Quite right, too. But it doesn't mean you have to live like a nun, does it?"

"No," she agreed with a smile. "Not quite like a nun. But I'm not interested in a replacement for Chris . . ."

"Of course you're not," Edward agreed hurriedly. "Look, I'm just happy to be your friend, I promise. No strings. Is that OK?"

"Edward," Liz said softly. "I don't know how I'd have got through the last few months without you. You've been great. And it's done my ego the world of good to go out with a good-looking man."

"Umm. Good-looking huh?"

"Well, you're not bad."

"Too late. You said good-looking. Now I'm hanging up

before you say anything else. I'll see you in Jenny's next week."

"You will. Talk to you then. Bye."

"Bye, Liz. Love to Lucy."

Edward put down the phone and stared into space. Why, when he finally fell for another woman, did it have to be one as nice as Liz? He still wasn't convinced she wouldn't go back to Chris. He knew in Liz's mind it would be 'the right thing to do'. For Lucy's sake. He'd been delighted when Jenny had called to give her vote of approval. He was very close to his sister. More so since the crash. They'd looked out for each other. They'd concentrated their energies on Carol and tried to make up for the loss of her father.

Jenny had taken to Liz. She'd seen immediately the qualities that attracted her brother. Not least, her innate honesty. A virtue they'd both learned to value. He'd have to go gently, though. He knew Liz was fond of him, maybe even more than that, but if he came on too heavy, she'd run. No, he'd have to be patient. What she needed now was a friend, and that's what he'd be for as long as it took. He hadn't believed he'd ever feel this way about a woman again. He wasn't going to blow it. Liz was worth waiting for.

CHAPTER TWENTY-FOUR

Stephanie tucked her blue silk blouse into the cream linen trousers and studied her profile in the mirror. No sign of a bump, no matter how hard she looked. Her stomach was as flat as ever and she hadn't put on any weight. If it wasn't for the aching heaviness of her breasts she wouldn't believe she was pregnant at all! She couldn't wait to see some sign of the life within her, but it would probably be another few weeks yet. She couldn't wait for her eighteen-week scan. With a bit of luck Seán would be home by then and he could come with her.

If he wasn't she was going to have to disguise her condition until he was. He had to be the first to know. It would be a lot harder to explain why she continued to avoid alcohol and why she'd given up smoking. Conor was amazed that she'd given up – she'd always smoked more than he did! Steph told him she'd got a chest infection and it was doctor's orders. This was also her excuse for giving up the drink. She couldn't with the fictitious tablets she was taking. My God, but life was complicated!

She still hadn't talked to Seán and that was the only

cloud on her horizon. His secretary, Elaine, wouldn't give her an office number in Phoenix. It was against his express instructions, she said. He was also staying in a different hotel – Elaine conveniently forgot which one. She offered to relay messages, but Seán never returned them. Steph was getting embarrassed calling Elaine, and Elaine was definitely fed up being caught in the middle.

Stephanie was frustrated and annoyed that she was unable to give Seán the one bit of news that would make him happy. Damn it, she'd go barmy if she didn't talk to him soon. In the meantime, she avoided her family and friends.

Liz phoned a few times, but Steph usually managed to dodge the calls. When they did talk, Steph confined the conversation to Lucy, Chris and the restaurant and got off the phone as quickly as possible. Annie was easier to handle. She called once a week to see how Steph was, but she didn't ask any questions, or pry. Steph knew how uncomfortable Annie was with the whole situation and appreciated her discretion.

She slipped on the jacket of her suit, slung her Chanel bag over her shoulder and let herself out of the apartment. It was sunny, and the air was already warm. Steph was making an earlier start than usual. She was hoping to slip out this afternoon and do some shopping. She sang along to the radio as she turned the car onto the Malahide Road. All was well with the world. Well, it would be as soon as she talked to Seán.

"Steph? It's Dad. He's had an accident."

Steph clutched the phone tighter. "Joe? How is he? What happened?"

"Nothing serious, don't worry. He fell off the ladder. They think his arm's broken. The bloke next door drove him and Mam into the hospital. Can you get down there? I'd go myself but I'm due on a flight to London in a couple of hours . . ."

"It's OK, Joe. I'm on my way. What hospital?"

She scribbled down the details and, after assuring her brother that she'd call Annie as soon as there was any news, she went in search of Chris.

"I've got to go," she said brusquely. "Family crisis. I'll call in later."

Chris raised an eyebrow and muttered something about boyfriends.

Steph glared at him and left, slamming the door behind her. She cursed the traffic as she made her way out to the Merrion Road. It was only twelve, but already the lunch-time traffic was building.

Thirty minutes later she walked into Casualty and approached the desk.

"Stephanie? Over here."

Steph turned to see her mother approaching, smiling. Well, that was a good sign.

"Hiya, Mam. How is he?" she asked, kissing her cheek.

"He's fine, love. It's not broken. His wrist is just badly sprained, but you know him. With all the moaning, you'd think they were going to amputate!"

Steph laughed with relief. Her dad was great, but he wasn't the easiest patient in the world. She linked her arm through her mother's and they made their way to his cubicle.

"Oh, hello, love. You shouldn't have come. I'm fine. A lot of pain, you know, but I think they're going to give me an injection for that."

Stephanie kissed her dad and stepped back as a nurse arrived.

"All right, Mr West. Just take these and then we'll strap you up and you can go."

Tom West looked at the tablets, doubtfully. "Is that it, then?"

The nurse smiled brightly. "That's it."

"What are you giving him?" Steph asked.

"Ponstan," the nurse replied and disappeared behind the curtain.

"Are they any good, Steph?" her dad asked. "Are they strong?"

"Oh, yes, Dad. Very strong. They should make you feel a lot better," she assured him.

Tom West swallowed the tablets obediently, satisfied that his condition was being treated seriously.

Steph winked at her mother. "Why don't I go and get us some tea? We could be here for a while.

Her dad shook his head. "I've had enough bloody tea," he said grumpily. "And it's no fun trying to go to the gents' like this." He indicated his swollen arm.

"Poor you," his wife said sympathetically.

"Just two so," Steph said. "I'd better call Annie while I'm at it. Let her know you're OK. Joe was frantic when I talked to him."

"Well, I wouldn't say I'm OK, but you can tell them it's not too serious," her dad agreed reluctantly.

Steph made her way outside. After she'd called Annie

and reassured her, she went to the canteen and collected two plastic cups of grey tea. She was keeping clear of caffeine these days, but one cup wouldn't hurt. Mind you, looking at this stuff . . .

Her mother was leaning against the wall outside the ward when Steph came back.

"They're putting a bandage on," she explained. "What do you think, Steph? Will he be all right?"

"He'll be fine once the swelling goes down. It'll be uncomfortable for a while, but that's all."

"Those tablets . . . " Catherine West frowned.

"Just mild painkillers. Standard hospital issue, but don't tell him that. Anyway, tell me what happened."

"Oh the silly man was up the stepladder, trying to trim the top of the hedge. I told him to leave it, but you know what he's like."

Steph smiled. She knew. "Well, thank God he didn't do any real damage. We should be out of here soon enough. He'll be more comfortable when he's at home. At least it's his left hand, otherwise he might need help with his fly and you'd be on toilet duty."

Catherine West looked horrified. "I would not! He could wear track-suit bottoms."

Steph shook her head in mock disapproval. "There's true love for you!"

Her mother smiled. "Oh, thank God he's OK. He's not getting any younger, you know. I got an awful fright when I found him. He was very pale."

Steph silently agreed. Her dad had looked surprisingly vulnerable lying on the trolley. This little accident could

219

have been a lot worse. "He didn't have a dizzy spell, did he?" she asked tentatively.

Her mother frowned. "I don't think so. He said he was reaching over and lost his balance."

"That's good then. Still, maybe we should have a word with the doctor. Just to make sure."

Catherine West set down her tea. "Yes. Yes, you're right," she said and went over to the desk.

Steph called Liam while she was waiting and explained that she wouldn't be back.

"Nothing serious, is it?" he asked.

"No, Liam. But I've got to bring them back out to Greystones and I don't want to leave them alone. You can manage, can't you?"

"Yeah, sure. Want to talk to chef?"

"No," she said quickly. The last thing she wanted to do was talk to Chris. "He can call me on the mobile if he needs me. Talk to you later, bye." She rung off as her mother approached.

"He's fine," she said, smiling. "They checked him out and did a couple of X-rays and they're happy to let him go. He's got to check in with the GP next week and they've given me a prescription for those painkillers."

"Great. Let's get him home."

Two hours later, Stephanie sank down into a kitchen chair. Her GP, Maeve O'Farrell, had warned her she'd tire easily and she wasn't kidding. The journey down had been a nightmare. Tom West had groaned at every bump and complained that Steph pulled up too suddenly and took the corners too hard. She'd said nothing, but her grip had tightened on the wheel, and she was a nervous wreck by the time she pulled into the driveway. They'd finally settled her dad in front of the TV with his dinner chopped up into bite-sized pieces.

"You look tired," her mother commented. "Everything all right?"

Steph looked away from her mother's searching gaze. She knew her daughter well.

"I'm fine, Mam. Just not sleeping too well."

"You're very thin, Stephanie. I hope you're not neglecting yourself. You have to eat properly."

"I do, Mam," Steph assured her. She hadn't suffered from any morning sickness but she hadn't much of an appetite either. She pushed the food around her plate, half-heartedly. "Stop worrying about me, Mam. You could do with putting on some weight yourself." She looked worriedly at her mother. She looked tired and drawn, but then it had been a tough day. "Finish your dinner and then you can go and have a nice bath. I'll stay with Dad."

"That would be nice, love. I'll make a cup of tea first. I'm sure your dad would like a cup. He should be able to manage the loo now he's wearing pyjamas!" She chuckled as she went over to fill the kettle.

"Catherine? Stephanie?" Tom West's plaintive voice interrupted them.

"I'll go," Steph said, rising slowly.

"What is it, Dad?" she said wearily from the doorway of the living-room.

"Oh sorry, love. But I dropped the remote control."

"Oh, for God's sake, Dad! You only have a sprained wrist. There's nothing stopping you moving around. I don't want you letting Mam run after you all the time. She's not able for it."

Her father snorted indignantly. "Sorry I'm so much trouble. Don't worry about me."

Steph suppressed a sigh. "You're no trouble, Dad. I'm sorry." She bent and kissed his cheek and picked up his tray. As she walked back into the kitchen she slipped on the tiled floor and dropped the tray as she put out a hand to save herself. She let out a small yelp as her thigh collided with the kitchen table.

"Mother of God, what happened? Are you all right, love?" Her mother hurried over and started to clear up the mess, looking worriedly at her daughter's ashen face.

"Fine, Mam. I just got a bit of a fright that's all." Steph tried to smile but her face crumpled.

"Oh, love, what is it? What's the matter?"

"Nothing," Steph smiled shakily through her tears. "Everything's wonderful."

Catherine looked bemused. What on earth was . . . oh, goodness . . . "Steph?"

"I'm fine, Mam. Honestly. Blooming, in fact."

"Oh, Stephanie! You're pregnant?" Steph nodded and Catherine West gathered her daughter into her arms. "That's wonderful. I'm so happy for you. You're going to be so happy. Seán must be over the moon."

"He doesn't know yet," Steph said as she rummaged in her pockets for a tissue.

"What? Oh, you just found out?"

"No. It's a bit complicated." Steph's eyes filled up again. God, she hoped she wasn't going to be this emotional all the time.

Her mother settled her in a chair and then sat down beside her. "What is it, love?"

Stephanie hadn't meant to tell her everything, but somehow the words just tumbled out. About Seán, their split, Ruth's pregnancy and finally about her own aborted abortion. They both cried and Catherine West gripped her daughter's hand hard while she talked.

"Poor Ruth," she said. "Poor you. Why didn't you talk to me, Stephanie? I'm your mother. You know you can always come to me."

Stephanie sniffed and wiped tears from her cheeks with the back of her hand. "I don't know, Mam. As far as Ruth was concerned, well, it was all so long ago. A different time. I suppose I thought you might be shocked that she'd got herself pregnant. You were always so fond of her. I didn't want to tarnish her memory."

Her mother shook her head sadly. "It's terrible that she took her life over something like that. Of course there would have been trouble, scandal, but once the baby was born, everyone would soon have forgotten all that. Babies have a way of bringing people together. Peter and Joan McCann are good people. They'd never have turned their backs on their daughter."

"I know you're right, Mam. I can see that now, but then . . . " she shrugged.

"The poor girl. It's such a waste."

They sat in silence for a moment, Catherine drinking her tepid tea, Stephanie fiddling with a teaspoon and longing for a cigarette.

"Why?" her mother said eventually.

Steph frowned. "Why what?"

"Why were *you* going to get an – abortion?" Catherine West nearly choked on the words.

Steph was silent for a moment. How could she ever explain this to her mother? She wasn't sure she understood it herself.

"I was afraid."

"Afraid of what, love?" her mother asked, desperate to understand.

Steph stood up and went over to the window. She looked out on the neat rows of roses and hydrangeas that skirted the perfect green lawn. The colours blurred as her eyes filled again.

"I don't know, I just don't know, Mam." She buried her face in her hands.

Her mother jumped up and put her arms around her. "Shush, don't cry, love. It's not good to get upset in your condition."

Steph smiled through her tears. Her condition. Her wonderful condition. "I think I was guilty, Mam. About Ruth. I wasn't there for her. I should have been. I should have stopped her. I could have, you know? I could have gone over there, instead of going out with Seán. If I'd gone, if I'd said the right words, she might be here today. Her *and* her baby."

"If, if, if," her mother said dismissively. "You can't live in the past, Stephanie. You can't change things. You have to accept them and move on. And what about that new life growing inside of you? Doesn't it deserve all your attention now?"

Steph's hands went automatically to her stomach and she nodded.

"Right then. You nearly did something terrible. I'm sorry, but that's the way I feel about it. I would have stood by you, of course. Just as Ruth's mam would have stood by her. But you didn't do it, love. And I'm very happy that you didn't. Now you have to look to the future. Be happy that you've done the right thing. Made the right decision. Everything's going to be all right. Seán will be a wonderful father. And husband?" she added tentatively.

"Oh, I'll marry him, Mam, if he'll have me."

Catherine hugged her daughter tightly.

"Catherine? Stephanie?" Tom West's plaintive voice broke the mood.

"His Master's Voice," Catherine muttered. "*I'll* go. Dry those tears, now, and fix your make-up. Everything's going to be fine. And remember, Stephanie. I'm your mother. I'm always here for you, whatever happens. Always."

Stephanie kissed her mother and watched as she hurried off towards the living-room.

"Coming, Tom, coming."

CHAPTER TWENTY-FIVE

Annie made the children wipe their shoes on the mat, took off her coat and went into the kitchen. "Hi Liz? How's it going? Can I do anything?" She ran slender fingers through her auburn locks and leaned over to peer into a pot.

"Nope. It's all under control," Liz said as she tasted the sauce. "Hiya, kids." She smiled down at Shane and Danielle.

"Hiya, Auntie Liz," they chimed.

"Mummy, can we go out to play?" Lucy looked up hopefully at her mother.

"Just for a little while. Lunch will be ready soon."

Lucy pulled open the door and the three raced off.

"Have you seen Steph recently?" Liz asked Annie as she wiped her hands on her apron.

Annie busied herself with setting the table. "No, why?"

"Oh, I just haven't heard from her lately. Whenever I ring the house, I just get Seán's answering machine. They really should change the message. You'd never know Steph lives there."

Annie thought quickly. She didn't want to lie to Liz, but she didn't want to let Stephanie down either. "Yeah. Seán's back in the States again. I think Steph might be staying in Malahide while he's gone. She mentioned something about redecorating."

Liz brightened. "Oh, she should have said. I'd give her a hand. Surely she's enough on her hands with the restaurant. What a funny time to start decorating."

Annie cursed silently. God, she was no good at lying. "Maybe I got it wrong," she said lamely.

Liz frowned. She still didn't understand why Steph was so hard to get hold of. Maybe she hadn't *really* forgiven her for their run-in a few weeks back. Or maybe she knew that Liz was seeing Edward. Could she be interested in him herself? But no. She was living with Seán now. "Did she say anything about me?" she asked Annie.

"What do you mean? What about?" Annie asked, confused.

"Oh, I don't know. Anything," Liz said vaguely.

"No. Well, only that she was wondering whether you'd decided for definite about Galway. Oh, and if you'd consider going back to work." At least Annie was able to be honest about that! "Look, Liz. I'm sure there's nothing wrong. She's just very busy. I haven't talked to her myself in ages. Well, except when she rang about her dad."

"What about her dad?"

"He had an accident. Oh, it's OK, nothing serious," she added hurriedly as Liz's eyes widened in concern. "He fell off a ladder and sprained his wrist."

"Maybe Steph's down in Greystones. I'll phone the restaurant again later. See what the story is."

"Good idea," Annie agreed.

"So what are you buying Joe for his birthday? It's next week, isn't it?"

Annie nodded, only too glad to change the subject. Any idea of having a party had gone out the window after the events of the last few weeks. Annie had decided on a small family dinner instead. Just Mam, Dad and Steph, if she felt up to it. "I was going to buy him some new golf shoes. The only problem is he's so damn fussy. Maybe I'll ask Edward to get them for me. I could rely on him to get nothing but the best."

"What do you mean by that?" Liz said defensively.

Annie looked at her curiously. "Only that he's got expensive taste."

"Oh, right." Liz flushed. "You better call the kids. Lunch is ready."

Annie went to the back door. "Shane, Lucy, Dani. Lunch is ready."

"Mum, are we having sausages?" Lucy ran into the kitchen with her two pals hot on her heels.

"No, love," Liz said. "We're having pasta."

"Oh goody! I love pasta. So does Uncle Edward. Is he coming for lunch too?"

Liz bit her lip and looked away from Annie's open-mouthed stare. "Wash your hands, Lucy, and stop chattering," she said curtly, turning back to the oven.

Annie rolled up Dani's sleeves and then helped Lucy dry her hands. What was all that about, she wondered. Liz had been very embarrassed. "Uncle Edward" indeed. It had to be Edward McDermott. Who else? She'd get it out of Liz once the kids were out of the way. Annie hoped that

Edward wasn't moving in on Liz. She was much too vulnerable at the moment. But then why else would he be hanging around? Why couldn't he stick to single women? Or at least to women *she* hadn't introduced him to. Bloody Casanova.

"Uncle Edward, eh?" she said mildly when the children had gone back to their toys.

"What?" Liz said absently, playing for time.

"You heard." Annie watched Liz closely. She was looking an awful lot better these days. She'd got her hair trimmed again and it swung in a soft, silken sheen around her face. Her eyes were bright and her figure trim in white jeans and a tight red tee-shirt. "What's going on?" Annie asked curiously.

"For God's sake, Annie. You sound like my mother. Nothing's going on. Carol, Edward's niece, is in Lucy's class. They play together."

"Right. And Edward plays too?"

Liz scowled at her. "Don't be smart, it doesn't suit you. Edward happens to be a very good uncle. His sister Jenny's a widow. He helps out."

"Oh," Annie said, surprised. It didn't fit in with her image of him at all.

"Hah! That's taken the wind out of your sails, hasn't it?" Liz laughed triumphantly.

"Well, I didn't even know he *had* a sister," Annie defended herself. "God, men are useless. Joe's been his friend for years, and he doesn't know anything about him. So what's the sister like?"

"Very attractive and really nice. Like I said, she's a widow. Her husband was killed in a car crash."

"That's terrible," Annie said sympathetically.

"It gets worse," Liz said darkly. "He was with another woman at the time."

"Oh, the bastard!"

Liz nodded in agreement. "They're all the bloody same. Anyway, she and Edward seem very close and he dotes on Carol. He's like a father to her."

"That's nice," Annie said grudgingly. "So there's nothing going on then?"

"Nothing," Liz confirmed.

"But you do *see* him?"

"Only when he's on the school run," Liz said, not entirely honestly. "He comes in for coffee while the kids are playing."

"Very cosy," Annie said. "He has a lot of free time, then?"

"Annie, stop it! Look, Edward's very nice. I like him a lot. But there's nothing going on. I wouldn't *do* anything like that."

"Sorry," Annie said meekly. "So how are things with Chris?"

"Lousy. He's being very understanding and patient."

Annie frowned. "And that's lousy?"

"Yeah. It makes it harder for me to tell him it's over."

"Oh. You've made up your mind then?" Annie said.

"Yes, I have. I just can't have him back, Annie. It would never work. The more we're apart the more I realise how unhappy I was. And though I was a mess when I first threw him out, I'm a lot stronger now. I feel I can go on without him. In fact, sometimes I think I'm actually happier without him. Lucy was the only reason for taking him back, but I've decided that it's not a good enough one. She won't be happy if Chris and I are arguing all the time."

"How is she?" Annie asked.

"She's doing OK under the circumstances. She loves going out with Chris and she's stopped asking me when he's coming home. She probably sees more of him now than she did when he lived here!"

"So will you get a divorce?" Annie said, wide-eyed.

"No. Not unless he wants one. I'm not bothered. I certainly won't be getting married again."

"You're a bit young to make a statement like that, Liz."

"No, I'm not," Liz said firmly. "I may not be able to give Lucy a normal family life, but I'll never inflict a stepfather on her."

Annie decided not to argue. "Have you talked to Lucy about this? Does she understand?"

"I haven't actually spelled it out, but I've told her that Daddy is going to work in Galway. She was happy enough about that, once I told her she'd be able to go and visit him. I can't really say much more than that until I've talked to Chris." She sighed wearily. Getting through to her husband was the hard part.

"You'd better do it soon," Annie advised.

"I know, but it's almost impossible. He has this amazing knack of only hearing what he wants to hear. When I've hinted at it, he talks about giving me more time. Honestly, I could strangle him sometimes. He just can't accept that *I* would dump *him*. The vanity of the man!" Liz shook her head in frustration.

"When does he leave for Galway?"

"Next month, thank God."

"Why don't you go and see a solicitor? See what needs to be done in order to get a legal separation. I mean what about this house? You need to make sure that you're financially secure."

"I know. I was going to ask Edward. The only other solicitor I know is the one Chris uses, and I never liked him anyway. What do you think?"

"Good idea. Even if he can't help you, he'll put you in touch with someone who can." Whatever Annie thought about Edward's love life, she had complete faith in his business sense.

"There's also the money from the sale of the restaurant. Some of that should come to me. I put all my savings into it."

"Well, Chris wouldn't try and con you, would he?" Annie didn't like Chris Connolly, but she didn't think that he'd stoop *that* low.

"I suppose not," Liz said, not entirely sure. There was no knowing how Chris would react when he heard she wanted a separation. He wasn't likely to accept it calmly. He was possessive and jealous and unpredictable. She shivered involuntarily.

Annie looked at her, worried. "Do you want Joe to talk to him?"

"No, no. I must do this myself."

"Well, I'm not sure you should do it when you're on your own."

Liz laughed shortly. "He's not going to get violent, Annie."

"No, of course not," Annie said doubtfully, "but, well, moral support, you know?"

"Yeah, maybe. We'll see."

* * *

Joe agreed with his wife. From what she'd said and from what Steph had told him, he didn't entirely trust Connolly. He was full of hot wind most of the time, but there was no doubt he was a bit of a bully. It would be wise to keep an eye on Liz until Chris was safely out of the city. He promised Annie that he'd talk to Edward. "Have you heard from Steph?" he asked.

Annie shook her head. "Not this week. I don't want to keep ringing her. I'm sure she just wants to forget all about it. She knows where I am if she needs me."

"I suppose you're right. Mam seemed to think she was great." Joe set great store by his mam. She always seemed to know what was going on with Steph.

"Well, I suppose Steph was putting on an act for them," Annie said.

"True. What do you think will happen when Seán gets back?"

"Oh, I'd imagine they'll go on as before. Seán's pretty devastated but at least now he understands why . . ."

"Does he?" Joe said. "I wish I did." He couldn't get his head around what his sister had done. He looked at his two children and he simply couldn't understand any of it.

"You don't have to," Annie said firmly. They'd had this conversation many times. "You just have to be there for her. And don't judge her."

Joe nodded. He knew she was right, but still . . .

"Don't say anything either, Joe," she warned.

"I won't, I won't. What's for dinner?"

"Nothing. The kids were at a party so they're stuffed silly. I thought we might get a takeaway."

"Grand," Joe said. "Will I get us a video as well?"

"Why not. Let's live a little. Joe?"

"Yeah?"

"You don't think Chris would *do* anything, do you?"

"What do you mean?"

"Well, you know, hurt Liz."

"God, no. He's all talk."

"I suppose you're right," Annie agreed.

"Of course I am. Don't worry."

CHAPTER TWENTY-SIX

Stephanie ran through the flat, searching. Where was that awful crying coming from? It was dark, and she stumbled and knocked against things. The cries turned to screams and got louder. She reached the sitting-room and fell over something lying in the middle of the floor. She looked down to see Ruth, whose eyes stared at her unseeing. She screamed and jumped away, bumping against a cradle. She looked down into it and a tiny faceless baby screamed through an orifice that should have been a mouth.

"No!" Stephanie jumped up in the bed. Her face was wet with tears and she was bathed in sweat. She reached for the light-switch with a shaky hand and took a few deep breaths. It had been so long since she'd had the dream, she'd hoped it had gone away for good. Why had it come back now? Was Ruth coming back to haunt her? She cupped her hands protectively around the slight bulge in her stomach. No. Ruth had been her best friend. She wouldn't wish anything bad to happen to her or her child. She decided to make herself some hot milk. It might help her to get back to sleep. Getting upset like this couldn't be good for the baby. She padded out to the kitchen and turned on all the lights as she went to banish the ghosts. She nuked some milk in the microwave and carried the mug back to bed.

It was only ten o'clock in Phoenix. She wondered what Seán was doing. If only he'd call her. Oh well, at least now she had Mam. One person she could indulge in baby-talk with. She finished her milk and snuggled down once more. She said a prayer for Ruth, for Seán and for her baby, wrapped herself into a protective ball and fell into a dreamless sleep.

* * *

Seán closed the lid of his lap-top and looked out of the window. Lights twinkled on the pool below and a couple were relaxing in the bubbling jacuzzi. He wished he was the man in the tub, and Steph was by his side, carefree and happy. He wondered glumly if they could ever be really happy again. He still hadn't returned any of her calls. Elaine was getting really ratty with him. But then she didn't know . . . He called Annie once. She'd assured him that Steph was OK but was upset that he'd gone away. Oh well, he'd sort it all out when he got home.

He'd slowly come to terms with the loss of their child. In a way, it had been a blessing that he had to go on this trip. He wasn't sure he could have handled living with Steph, watching her go about her daily life as if nothing had happened. He knew there was no way he could be with her unless she admitted she had a problem and agreed to see someone. He couldn't take any more of this roller-coaster stuff. He sighed as the woman in the tub below leaned over and kissed her partner. He'd never felt quite as lonely as he did right now.

Billy had been on his mind a lot too. Seán was eaten up with guilt thinking how he'd let his son down. Just because his marriage had broken up, didn't mean he had to break up with Billy too. It seemed sensible at the time to leave him with his mother. Whatever her faults, Karen had been a good mother. Some of his happiest memories were of their family outings. Now he'd practically dropped Billy from his life. Sure he always remembered his birthday and Christmas and he picked up the odd toy when he was on his travels, but that wasn't enough. He was a lousy father. Here he was criticising Steph for getting rid of her baby, but was he any better?

Things would have to change. He'd go down to Cork more often, it wasn't that far. He could be down and back in one day. And he'd decorate the attic room for his son. He'd show him that he had a home in Dublin with him whenever he wanted to come and visit.

He wasn't quite sure what Steph would think of the idea but he was determined to go ahead with it regardless. If she loved him, she'd accept it. Maybe it would even unleash some maternal feelings in her. Billy was a great little kid. He couldn't imagine her being immune to his charms for very long. He couldn't wait now to get to Cork and talk to Karen. He was sure she'd be open to the idea. She wanted what was best for Billy and had always encouraged Seán to see him.

Seán jumped up and went down to the restaurant. He

normally ate in his room, but tonight he felt like a bit of company. It was a business hotel, so he was bound to run into a few guys in the bar. He ordered a steak and a beer and settled back, feeling slightly happier. He was going to take control of his life. Control of his family. Billy *and* Steph.

* * *

"Liz? Hi, it's Steph."

"Well, well, well. The Scarlet Pimpernel," Liz said drily.

"I'm sorry, Liz. It's been a bit hectic. What with the restaurant and Dad . . ."

"And the redecorating?"

"Redecorating?" Steph was confused.

"What's going on, Steph? You don't return my calls, Annie keeps giving me the run-around. Is everything OK? Have I done something?"

Steph sighed. How was she going to get out of this one? "I'm sorry, Liz. I had a row with Seán before he went away. It upset me. I knew if I got together with you or Annie you'd pull it all out of me and I just wasn't ready to talk about it."

"Oh, Steph. You know me better than that. All you ever have to do is say 'shut up, Liz'."

Stephanie laughed. "Sorry, Liz. Forgive me?"

"There's nothing to forgive, silly. Now do you want to talk or meet or will I leave you alone?"

Steph felt strong enough to meet Liz without spilling the beans. It was more difficult with Annie, who'd expect her to be depressed and sad. "I'd love to meet."

"Great! Well why not come over here later? I'm cooking some stuff for a party tomorrow. You can keep me company."

"What party?" Steph was surprised.

"I'll explain later. Come over about four."

"Right so. Seeya then." Steph hung up and sat smiling at the phone. Good old Liz. It would be nice to have a chat. She'd better call her mam first. Get a fix of baby-talk to ensure she kept quiet later. She was looking forward to seeing Liz. She sounded happy.

Annie had told her that she'd decided to split with Chris for good.

"Well, she can't have said anything to him yet," Steph assured her. "We'd have known all about it by now if she had."

"You think he'll take it badly?" Annie asked.

Steph laughed. "That's the understatement of the year. He'll blow a gasket."

Annie frowned. "I 'm not sure she should be on her own when she talks to him. Joe says I'm overreacting but who knows . . ."

"Well, he *has* a lousy temper, but I'm not sure he'd ever get violent. Like most bullies, he's just a coward behind all that ranting and raving. Still, losing his wife and child might be enough to tip him over the edge."

Steph chewed worriedly on her pen as she went back over the conversation. At least she didn't have to worry about the restaurant. Conor was back and she no longer needed to rely on Chris.

She jumped as the phone rang. Liam informed her that there was a double booking for that evening. Apparently a local businessman had booked a celebration dinner with Sam some weeks ago and Sam, God bless him, had failed to put it in the book. Steph wondered idly if Sam's lapse of memory had coincided with his dismissal. "I'm on my way, Liam." She put on her owner's hat and went down to deal with the latest crisis, family and friends momentarily forgotten.

* * *

Steph parked the car and walked up the driveway past the small garden with its border of roses and trim lawn. Liz certainly seemed to be managing fine without Chris. Mind you, Chris had never been a "New Man". He'd always left most of the household chores to Liz. She rang the doorbell and smiled as a flour-smudged Liz opened the door.

"Sorry I'm late, Liz."

"No problem." Liz wiped her hands on her apron. "To be honest I've been too busy to notice the time."

Steph followed her into the kitchen and gasped at the array of food on the kitchen table and the bubbling pots on the stove. "My God. Are you feeding the five thousand?"

Liz laughed. "Not quite. Only about thirty, actually."

Steph dipped a crab claw in the sauce boat and popped it in her mouth. "Uumm. Lucky them. This is gorgeous."

"That's a Moroccan lamb casserole," Liz said pointing to one pot, "and that's a Cajun chicken dish that I'm trying for the first time." Liz watched Steph's expression anxiously as she tasted the two dishes.

"They're great, Liz. You're wasted. You know that, don't you?"

"Don't start that again," Liz said but she was pleased with her friend's praise. Steph never lied about food.

"Anyway. Who's all this for?"

"Jennifer McDermott. Edward's sister. She's a neighbour. She invited me along to this party tomorrow and I agreed to come if she let me do the cooking."

Steph looked confused. "Let me get this straight. Edward's sister is your neighbour? God, it's a small world."

"Isn't it? Her daughter, Carol, is one of Lucy's best friends. I've known the child for ages, but I didn't know who she was. It all came out when I ran into Edward outside the school one day."

"So what's the sister like?"

"Really nice. Not at all like some of the nosy oul biddies around here. She's a widow, you know. It's a shame really. She's only about my age and she's really pretty."

"Oh, that's sad. What happened the husband?"

Liz rolled her eyes. "Oh, another asshole! You'll never believe it. He was in a car crash. His mistress was with him at the time. They were both killed instantly."

"Mother of God. Isn't it amazing what some people have to cope with? Poor woman. So you're getting well in with the family then?" she said with a sly grin. "Edward's sister, his niece, very cosy. When do you meet Mummy and Daddy?"

Liz looked cross. "You're as bad as Annie! It's not like that. It's all very innocent, I assure you. We meet when he's looking after Carol – oh and I've asked him for advice about my separation."

"Oh, right," Steph said happy to leave it at that for now, but not entirely convinced. "So when are you going to talk to Chris?"

"Friday," Liz said sinking into a chair. "I'm dreading it, Steph. I truly am. What am I going to say? What's he going to say?"

"He won't be happy," Steph said. "Where's Lucy going to be? In fact, where is she now?"

"Jenny's minding her while I organise the food. I was going to drop her in to my mother's on Friday. It would probably be better if she wasn't around, just in case . . ."

"Damn right. But I'm not sure you should be alone, Liz."

Liz tossed back her hair impatiently. "That's what Annie says, but I think you're both overreacting."

"Well, I hope you're right but why take the chance? You know what his temper's like."

Liz did, but for all Chris's ranting and raving, he'd never hit her. "No, Stephanie. I think I at least owe it to him to do this privately. I know what you think of him but he's not a bad man. He loves Lucy and in his own weird way, he probably still loves me. This is going to hit him hard. I want to make it as painless as possible. If there was anyone else here it would be a further humiliation. Nope, I've made up my mind. I'm going to handle this alone."

Stephanie hugged her. "You know best. Just keep a phone nearby in case you need to call in the cavalry."

* * *

Jenny McDermott pushed open the kitchen door with her hip and carried in a pile of dirty plates. "Liz, you're amazing! This stuff is going down a bomb. They're all asking for a recipe for the chicken."

"Can't tell them that," Liz said with a wink. "Professional secret. Tell them they'll have to hire me instead."

Edward turned from the sink where he was rinsing glasses. "That's not such a bad idea."

"What?" Liz asked

"Well, think about it. You're a great chef. You'd like to work but you don't want to leave Lucy."

"So?"

"So why not start up a private catering service? You could work from home, apart from the actual events, which will nearly always be in the evening . . ."

"After Lucy's in bed," Jenny finished. "That's a great idea! You could limit your availability to two or three times a week. All you need is a reliable baby-sitter."

Liz looked from one to the other, a bit flustered at how fast this conversation was moving. "Oh, I don't know . . . "

"What's the problem?" Edward asked. "Don't you think you're up to it?"

Liz threw a tea-towel at him. "Damn right I am!"

"Well, there you go," Edward said smugly.

"It's a great idea," Jenny said excitedly. "There's a lot of people around here that I'm sure would be interested."

"And I have business contacts. Single men who'd like to entertain at home but beans on toast doesn't really cut it."

Liz laughed, excited at the prospect. It *would* be perfect. She could do most of the preparation in her own well-equipped kitchen and not have to spend too much time away from Lucy. As Jenny pointed out, Lucy would be asleep for most of her working hours. It would bring in some regular money too and give her a chance to get out more. If there was one thing she'd found out tonight it was that she missed adult company. It was good to get out and have a laugh and she was enjoying the praise she was getting for her food. The limelight had been on Chris for so long, she'd forgotten how good a chef she really was.

"Do you really think it could work?" She looked anxiously at brother and sister.

"Yes!" Jenny said.

"Absolutely!" Edward said. "We could set up some nights to allow prospective clients to sample your cooking. I've been meaning to bring out some clients for a while. I could invite them to my house instead. They like the personal touch."

"That's a good idea," Jenny nodded approvingly. "And we could put the word around tonight that you do this professionally."

"Tonight? But I need to do some homework before I'm ready, I'd have to talk to an accountant, a lawyer . . . " Liz looked at her in panic.

"No problem." Jenny waved away her concerns. "If anyone asks, you're booked up for the next couple of months. They'll want you even more then! Now I better get back in and mingle. Come on, Liz. We need to introduce you to our more affluent neighbours!"

Jenny steered Liz back towards the living-room before she could protest. Edward followed with a tray of glasses, smiling broadly.

CHAPTER TWENTY-SEVEN

Liz paced the living-room, pausing occasionally to look out the window. Chris was due any minute and her heart raced at the thought of the ordeal ahead. The slight hangover didn't help matters. She was so high at the prospect of a new career last night that she had drunk more than usual. She'd enjoyed herself enormously, and was amused by the envious glances of some of Jenny's neighbours when Edward remained by her side for most of the evening. He seemed oblivious to the effect he had on women. His dark good looks, those startling grey eyes and his impeccable taste in clothes were guaranteed to draw every woman's eye from eighteen to eighty! The fact that he was also single and definitely not gay made him positively irresistible! And his slightly remote behaviour with strangers made him seem mysterious and made many women crave to be the one to break through that cool exterior.

"You could have a different woman every night," Liz had said, only half joking as he walked her back to her house.

"I do," he'd assured her, "but I rest on Sundays."

She started as Chris swung his Peugeot into the driveway. She felt a flash of irritation at his presumption. He didn't live here anymore.

She opened the door and watched him as he climbed out of the car. She noticed the thickened waist and the sagging flesh around his throat. He was letting himself go.

"Hello, love. How are you?" Chris shoved a bouquet into her hands and planted a wet kiss on her cheek.

"Fine," she said with a fixed smile. The flowers reminded her of churches and funerals. She left them on the hall table. "I'll arrange them later. Would you like some tea?"

Chris checked his watch. "Oh, the sun's over the yard-arm, I think a little drink would be nice."

He headed for the drinks cabinet and poured himself a large whiskey. Again, Liz suppressed her irritation at his familiarity.

"Can I get you one?" he asked.

What the hell. It might give her some courage. "A small brandy, thanks," she said settling herself in an armchair.

"Where's Lucy?" He handed her a glass and settled himself on the sofa.

"With Mam," she said.

"So it's just the two of us," he said with a leer. Things were looking up. It was about time she came to her senses. He looked her up and down appreciatively. She was looking really great. She'd lost weight, that was it, and her hair, it was shorter. His eyes dropped to the generous curve of her breasts. She hadn't lost weight from there, thank God!

Stupid bastard, Liz thought, reading his mind. "I

246

wanted to talk to you about the future, Chris. I've been doing a lot of thinking."

"Yes?" Chris downed his whiskey.

Liz fidgeted with her glass. "I've decided to stay in Dublin."

Chris looked confused. "What? You want me to pull out of the Galway deal? But it's a great package, Liz, and we could buy a wonderful house with the money we got from this place . . ."

"No," Liz interrupted. "That's not what I mean. Sorry, I'm not doing a very good job of this. The thing is, Chris, it's not Galway, it's us. I want a legal separation." There. She'd said it. She watched his face nervously.

Chris looked confused, then incredulous and then angry. "What the hell are you talking about?" he said finally.

"It's no use, Chris. It's over."

Chris crossed the room and refilled his glass. "Don't be bloody ridiculous. You're my wife. And what about Lucy? You're not thinking straight. What is it? Has McDermott screwed all the sense out of you?"

"Chris!" Liz flushed with rage and shock.

"Oh, come on. Do you think I'm stupid? You throw me out for having a drink with a woman and then you carry on an affair, in *my* house, in front of *my* kid."

Liz swallowed hard. She must remain calm. "Firstly, I'm not having an affair. I have never been unfaithful to you. Can you say the same thing? I very much doubt it. And secondly, this is *our* house. Don't you forget it. As for your 'kid'. Your beautiful daughter's name is Lucy. Edward McDermott is the uncle of her best friend. That's all." She swallowed a mouthful of brandy and watched Chris pace the room.

"She will always be your daughter, Chris," she continued more gently. "I would never try to come between you. But there's no future for you and me, and I'm afraid I couldn't play at happy families. It would be living a lie and it would make us all miserable in the end."

Chris sat down on the arm of her chair and took her hand. "But Liz we've been together so long. How can you just throw it all away?"

"I'm not. You did that all on your own," Liz said quietly, pulling her hand away.

"Oh, for God's sake! I tell you I did nothing!"

"You humiliated me. You led a double life. You left me at home with Lucy and you lived the life of a bachelor. Frankly it doesn't matter whether you slept with her or not. You left me behind. You left us behind."

"I don't know what you're talking about. I built up the business. I did it for you and Lucy. I worked my butt off, for God's sake."

"And what did you do when you weren't at the restaurant and you weren't here?" she asked.

Chris shifted uneasily. "I had to go out sometimes. Keep an eye on the competition. Socialise. It's expected."

"Really," Liz said drily. "How hard on you! Forcing yourself to go out on the town and drink with young girls. Tell me. How did *that* promote Chez Nous?"

"You're twisting everything," he said, annoyed. "Just because you've turned into a boring middle-aged housewife doesn't mean you have to drag me down with you."

Liz gasped. Her eyes filled with tears, but she struggled

to control them. She wasn't going to cry. At least not in front of him. "I think you should go now. My solicitor will be in touch. We need to work out our finances and there's the money from the restaurant."

Chris looked at her, scornfully. "You're not getting your hands on that."

Liz stared back in alarm. "I put money into it, I'm entitled to my share."

"Tough. I have to buy a place in Galway and if you're going to stay in this place . . ." He shrugged.

"You have to support us," she said, panicking.

Chris smiled, coldly. "No, I don't. You threw me out for no good reason. You needn't think I'm going to give you a penny. I'll support Lucy but that's it."

"There's no point in carrying on this conversation. I think we should let the solicitors sort this out."

"I suppose your precious McDermott is handling it."

"Not him personally, but his firm is," Liz agreed quietly.

"Very bloody cosy," Chris said bitterly. "Just keep that bastard away from Lucy, or I'll make you sorry you ever laid eyes on him."

"Don't threaten me, Chris. Don't bully me. It doesn't work any more. Look, I don't want this to turn into a bitter feud. We have to think of Lucy. I don't want her torn between us."

Chris snorted. "Really? I'm going to Galway and you're keeping her here in Dublin. You deliberately waited until I was committed to taking that job, didn't you? You wanted to make sure I'd be out of your hair."

"No, of course not!" Liz was utterly frustrated. "I didn't plan this, Chris. I hoped that I would be able to get through this. I wanted to go to Galway, you know that. But now . . . "

"But now you've found someone else. You're a stupid bitch, Liz. Look in the mirror, for Christ's sake. You're not getting any younger. McDermott will soon get tired of you and move on to a younger model."

"Like you did?" Liz challenged.

"Yes, dammit! You bored the hell out of me! All you could ever talk about was Lucy. You weren't interested in me or in what was going on in the real world. I had to keep the restaurant going on my own. And what support did I get from you?"

Liz looked at him in shock. "You never said anything."

"When did you ever listen?" he said bitterly.

"Dammit, Chris. Don't turn this around! Don't try to make me feel guilty. You broke this marriage up. I'm sorry I wasn't interesting or glamorous enough for you. Minding a child isn't a very glamorous occupation."

"Enough of all this, Liz. I'm angry and more than a little hurt. We've both said a lot of things. But there's too much to lose. Let's put this behind us. Come to Galway. Give it a go."

Liz couldn't believe her ears. He was incredible! He still thought she'd go back with him. "No, Chris."

"You'll never manage here on your own. I'm not going to support you. You'll have to move out of this house." He paced the room, red-faced, sweating.

"I'll manage," she said quietly. She was sorely tempted to tell him about her new business venture, but she held back. He'd only ridicule her. Tell her that she could never pull it off. "Please leave," she said instead.

Chris looked at her in alarm. This wasn't going the way it was supposed to. Liz wasn't strong enough to go on without him. She'd never done *anything* without him. But he looked into her eyes now and saw a determination that was new to him.

"You stupid bitch, you'll regret this," he said turning on his heel. He paused in the hall, threw the flowers on the floor and ground them into the carpet with his foot. "You'll never survive on your own. You'll turn into a sad old twisted cow!" He slammed the door after him and pulled out of the driveway with a screech of brakes.

Liz fell back in the chair and let the tears come. She grieved for the end of her marriage, for her lost youth and her lost love. She felt empty and old. Maybe Chris was right. Maybe there was nothing in her future but sadness and loneliness.

Edward watched Chris leave. It was obvious from the tyre marks on the road that he was not a happy man. He took out his mobile and dialled.

"I'm just outside if you want to talk about it," he said quietly, when Liz eventually answered.

"Yes, please," Liz said through her tears and went to open the door.

Chris drove to the nearest pub and ordered a double. He lifted the glass with a shaking hand and emptied half of it. He bought a pack of cigars and took his drink to the quiet end of the bar. He couldn't quite believe it. His quiet easygoing Liz. What had happened to her? No doubt Stephanie West had something to do with it. She was probably delighted that Liz had thrown him out. Encouraged Liz to take this step. Liz would never have had the strength to do it on her own. Yes, he was sure that interfering bitch had something to do with all this. And then there was Edward McDermott. What the hell was going on there? Despite what he'd said, he didn't believe that Liz was involved with him. She'd never do that. He was pretty sure, for all her protestations, that she still loved him. He threw back his drink and stood up. He'd go back there. Make her listen. Get her to see sense.

Chris drove around the corner in time to see Edward step out of the house, turn and take Liz in his arms. Chris fired up the engine and took off. The road blurred as tears of anger and self-pity filled his eyes. The bitch! He was only out the door and she had him in there. Christ! Maybe he'd been there all the time. Up in the bedroom just waiting for her to get rid of him. The tart. The lying bitch. Putting all the guilt on him. Well, she wouldn't get a penny out of him. No chance. Let her lover look after her. He wasn't going to finance her love life. He wiped the tears away angrily. How could she treat him like this? What had he ever done to deserve it?

CHAPTER TWENTY-EIGHT

Liam looked up uneasily as Chris called for another bottle of wine.

Jean looked at him beseechingly. "What do I do?" she hissed.

Chris had arrived an hour earlier and attached himself to a party of businessmen who were enjoying a late lunch. Judging by his high colour and loud voice he'd had quite a lot to drink already.

"Give it to him," Liam said. "There's not a lot else we *can* do."

Jean delivered the wine and Chris took it and waved her away. "I'll open it. If you want something done properly, gentlemen, do it yourself. Women are only good for one thing."

Two ladies, dining nearby, looked up in disgust. Liam shook his head, and headed for their table. "Can I get you a liqueur with our compliments, ladies?"

"No, thank you," one replied curtly. "We're leaving. Some of us have work to do. Tell me, isn't that Chris Connolly, the owner?"

Liam fidgeted uncomfortably. "It's Mr Connolly, all right, but he's no longer the owner," he said quietly, praying that Chris wouldn't hear him.

"I'm glad to hear it," she replied.

After they'd left, Liam hurried out to the kitchen in search of Conor. "Chef? We've got a bit of a problem."

"What is it, Liam?"

"It's Chris. He's out front and he's a bit worse for wear."

"Shit. Who's he with?" Conor wiped his hands and walked to the door.

"The Callaghan party."

Conor groaned. They were good customers. He couldn't really afford to upset them. "Has he upset anyone?"

Liam nodded. "Yeah. Two ladies left when he said that women were only good for one thing."

"Right, that's it," Conor said, angrily. "Get Stephanie."

"She's gone out."

"Well then," Conor said putting on a fresh apron, "it's up to me. Stay close by. I might need you."

Conor went into the restaurant and made his way to Chris's table. "Excuse me, gentlemen," he said, smiling broadly. "I need to borrow Mr Connolly for a moment."

"What is it?' Chris said irritably.

"Just need your advice on the dinner menu," Conor said, swallowing his pride.

Chris grinned and slapped him on the back. "Ah, what are you going to do without me?"

"I really don't know," Conor managed quietly.

"Carry on, gentlemen. Won't be long. Jean? Bring these gentlemen another bottle."

Chris wove his way out of the room. When he got

through the door, Conor grabbed him by his collar and pushed him back against the wall. "What the hell do you think you're doing?"

"What? What?" Chris tried to focus on him. "Take your hands off me. I'm going back to join my customers."

"Oh no, you're bloody not. You've already frightened off two customers. You're not going to ruin us. Go home and sober up, Chris. And don't ever come in here in this state again!"

"Don't you talk to me like that, you cheeky little bugger!" Chris said and took a swing at Conor.

Conor ducked to one side and Chris hit the floor.

Liam crouched down beside him. "He's out cold," he said looking up at Conor.

"Shit. We can't leave him here. Let's get him into the store-room. He can sleep it off. You take his legs." The two men tugged Chris into the back room and went back to work.

"Your blood pressure's fine, Stephanie," Maeve O'Farrell said, taking off the stethoscope. "Now, hop up on the scales."

"I don't think I've put on any weight," Steph said anxiously.

Maeve checked. "No, but it's not a problem. Women vary greatly in how the weight goes on. You'll be back here in a few weeks moaning because nothing will fit you!"

"No, I won't." Steph said fervently. "I can't wait. How long do you think it will be before I feel the baby move?"

"Probably two to three weeks."

Steph's face fell and Maeve laughed. "Don't worry. It will happen. When do you go for your scan?"

"Friday fortnight. And I see the obstetrician immediately afterwards."

"Great. You'll really enjoy the scan. It will make everything seem so much more real. Have you thought any more about seeing a counsellor?"

Steph had told her all about Ruth after she'd returned from London. "No," she admitted. She'd been so busy thinking about the baby she'd forgotten all about Eve Wilmot's advice.

"Well, I think we can leave it for the moment. I think pregnancy is probably a better cure than any counselling."

Steph beamed at her. "I *do* feel wonderful."

"Well, then. That's all that matters. Make an appointment to see me again in three weeks. Other than that, carry on as normal but don't work too hard."

Steph left the surgery and dropped into Mothercare on her way back to work. She couldn't resist it. It was late afternoon when she finally let herself into the now-empty restaurant. She went straight upstairs, tip-toeing past the kitchen. She didn't want to bump into anyone. Not with a Mothercare bag in her hand! She reached the sanctuary of the office and closed the door quietly. She emptied the contents of her bag onto the desk, smiling as she surveyed her purchases. She'd hesitated over the maternity trousers, but she was sure she'd need them soon and they'd be a lot more comfortable as the weeks progressed. She smiled ruefully as she examined the extra support bra. A real passion killer, but again, it was a necessary evil. Her breasts were very tender these days, and she'd already gone up a cup size. Seán wouldn't complain about that though!

The last purchase was a mobile of farmyard animals. She felt a bit guilty about that one. She'd promised herself that she wouldn't buy anything for the baby until she was at least six months pregnant. It was tempting fate. But she just couldn't resist the pretty little mobile with its bright colours and lovely melody. All she needed was for someone to walk in now. She tucked everything away in a drawer and turned her attention to the pile of CVs in front of her. She'd finally advertised for an assistant and was eager to find someone quickly. Once Chris left, there would be a lot more pressure on her and she'd need a backup. She also wanted someone to be trained in before she had to leave to have the baby. She didn't plan to take too much time off, but she wanted to be ready in case there were any complications.

Chris woke up and looked around him, disoriented. Where in hell was he? It took him a moment to get his bearings and another moment to remember the events from earlier in the day. He remembered the argument with Liz, the drinks in the restaurant and Conor having a go at him – cheeky bastard! He'd sort him out later! When his head cleared. He reached into his pocket and pulled out a cigar, lighting it with unsteady hands. McDermott! The memory of the bastard holding his wife came flooding back. The fucker. Chris stood up unsteadily and reached up to the top shelf for a bottle of whiskey, he opened it and took a swig. The bastard. He'd sort him out.

Chris had been pretty sure that Edward was screwing

Stephanie. Jesus, maybe he had both of them on the go. Poor old Seán. Another good bloke being taken for a ride. A ride. Hah! There was a Freudian slip for you! Chris puffed on his cigar and took another swig from the bottle.

Women. They were all the same. They were nice to you as long as you were giving them things. Liz had no appreciation of all he'd done for her. She'd never have had her fancy house in Stillorgan without him. And now she was demanding money from his business. Money-grabbing bitch. He was better off without her, he decided before he passed out again, the cigar slipping from his fingers.

"Marc? What the hell's burning?" Conor looked up irritably from the dinner menu he was preparing.

Marc looked at Pat who shrugged. "We're not cooking, chef. Nothing's burning here."

Pat sniffed. "You're right, though. Something's burning. Not in here, though." He followed the smell and saw smoke coming from the store-room. "Oh fuck! Chef! We've got a fire in the store-room!"

Conor jumped up. "Jesus! Chris is in there!"

Pat grabbed a fire extinguisher and moved cautiously towards the store-room door. He kicked it open, took a deep breath and sprayed in the general direction of Chris, who was surrounded by flames.

Back in the kitchen, Conor doused himself in cold water and soaked some cloths. "Dial 999, Marc! Get the fire brigade and an ambulance. Quick!" He made his way towards the store-room. The hallway was thick with smoke now and he couldn't even see Pat.

"Pat? Are you OK? Where are you?"

"Over here!" Pat shouted and then had a fit of coughing as the smoke hit his lungs.

Conor moved towards him and threw the cloths around his head and shoulders. "Can you see Chris?"

Pat nodded towards the corner, not willing to open his mouth again.

Conor followed his gaze and saw a large dark shape. Chris. The fire was behind him, but the smoke billowed around. Conor felt it tear at his throat and his eyes, mercilessly. "OK. You aim the extinguisher at him. I'm going in to get him." He made a lunge through the flames, grabbed Chris by the ankles and started to drag him from the room. He cursed Chris for his weight. It was like moving a beached whale. He persevered, trying to ignore the heat biting at his skin. Finally, when he'd got a safe distance from the room he stopped and took a breath, but all he got was another mouthful of smoke. "Come on, Pat," he gasped. "Give me a hand. Let's get out of here!"

When they got outside, Marc and Liam took over and dragged Chris out on to the pavement.

"Is everyone out," Conor said, taking in gulps of clean air and coughing uncontrollably.

"Yes, Chef. The fire people, they come soon."

Pat stumbled out onto the street, wheezing and coughing, the tears streaming down his face.

Chris seemed to be unconscious, his face and hands blistered, but he was breathing. Conor sent up a silent prayer of thanks that no one else had been hurt.

"Chef! Chef! Stephanie! She is upstairs! *Mon Dieu!* She cannot get out!" Marc was jumping up and down pointing at the upstairs window.

"Oh, my Christ!" Conor looked up in horror. Stephanie was standing at the barred office window. "I'm going in."

"Conor! No! The stairs are behind the store-room. You'll never get near her. It's too dangerous . . ." Pat was talking to thin air. Conor had gone.

When Conor opened the kitchen door, the smoke hit him like a brick wall. He took a last gulp of fresh air and went in. He felt as if he was drowning. The smoke was thick in his mouth and in his eyes and he had to feel his way through the room. After what seemed like an eternity, he found the door and made his way towards the stairs.

"Stephanie?" he called hoarsely.

"*Conor!*" she screamed and then broke down in a fit of coughing. "I can't get down," she managed finally. "The stairs are on fire!"

"It's your only hope, Steph. Don't worry – it's mostly smoke. It looks worse than it is," he lied, praying that he was doing the right thing. "You'll have to jump. I'll catch you. I promise." He broke off as the smoke ripped his throat apart. How in hell was he going to catch her? He couldn't even see her!

Steph moved gingerly across the landing. She could feel the heat of the floor right through her shoes. The old wooden floorboards cracked ominously. She hesitated for a moment and then started down the stairs. She screamed as she felt the second step give.

Conor caught her as she fell forward and dragged her down the rest of the way. "I've got you, Steph. I've got you."

He half-carried, half-dragged her back through the kitchen. At this stage he was just moving blindly in what he hoped was the right direction. When he got out into the yard Marc ran forward and lifted Steph out of his arms. He carried her out onto the road and laid her down gently on the pavement. She struggled to speak, her eyes wide and frightened, but her breathing was laboured and she didn't have the strength. Finally she gave up the struggle and closed her eyes.

"Chef! Chef! She has gone asleep!" Marc looked up at Conor.

Conor knelt down and shook Stephanie. "Steph? Steph? Oh, Jesus."

Pat pushed him out of the way. He checked for a heartbeat and loosened her clothes. "She's breathing. Where the fuck is that ambulance?" He looked anxiously at Chris who hadn't moved since they'd brought him out.

It seemed like hours, but within minutes the fire brigade and two ambulances arrived. Chris and Stephanie were whisked away in the first and Pat, Marc and Conor were loaded, under protest, into the second. A few of the kitchen staff had returned from their break in the middle of all the drama and were wandering around like headless chickens. Conor called George over before allowing them to close the ambulance doors. "Can you send everyone home, George? There's nothing they can do here. But would you hang on with the firemen and the police?"

"I'll take care of everything," George said gruffly. "Go on now. Don't worry about anything."

Conor grabbed his hand gratefully and then slumped back exhausted on to the seat.

George had a quick word with the staff, promising to get in touch if there was any news on the injured. When they'd wandered off, he went to the pub across the road and called Edward. It was probably better to let him get in touch with Chris and Steph's family. That done, he went back to find the fire chief to see what he could do to help.

As soon as he hung up on George, Edward phoned Joe and gave him the few details that he knew. After a moment's hesitation he called Liz and told her the news too. "If you like, I'll pick you up on my way in to the hospital," he offered.

Liz hesitated. "I'll have to call Chris's dad and I need someone to mind Lucy . . . "

"I'll call Jenny. We can drop Lucy on the way. It'll be OK, Liz."

"Will it?" she said dully before hanging up.

Joe and Annie were on the way to the hospital when he phoned his parents on the car-phone. Annie's fingers dug into her seat as she listened to Joe haltingly explain to his mother what had happened.

"She wasn't burned, Mam. It seems to be smoke inhalation. I'm sure she'll be OK."

"And the baby?" his mother asked anxiously.

Joe looked at Annie in confusion. "What baby, Mam? What are you talking about?"

Liz sat silently at Edward's side on the journey to the hospital. What had happened? Why was Chris the only one who was seriously hurt? What had he been doing in the restaurant anyway? He was off duty. And Stephanie. "Do they know if Steph will be all right?" she asked Edward quietly.

"I don't know, Liz. I'm sorry. George couldn't give me any real details about either of them."

"We should try to get in touch with Seán," she said.

"Joe may have already taken care of that. If not, I'll get on to his office. They should be able to get hold of him."

Catherine and Tom West sat silently in the back of the taxi. Suddenly, Greystones seemed an awful long way from Dublin. Joe had insisted on sending the taxi for them. He'd said it was because of Tom's wrist, but he was more afraid of his dad driving like a demon to get to his daughter's side.

"A baby, you say," Tom said quietly.

Catherine squeezed his hand and swallowed back the tears that threatened. "Yes, love."

"Oh, please God look after them both," he said.

"Amen," she said.

Jack Connolly poured himself a large whiskey and swallowed it back in one gulp. He didn't see that much of his son these days and they'd never had much to say to each other, but still . . .

He'd refused when Liz had offered to pick him up on her way to the hospital.

"No, love. I hate those places. Anyway, I'd only be in the way. You give me a call when you know how he is."

Selfishness runs in the family, Liz thought drily. Chris and his dad had never been close, but had stopped even making any effort when Chris's mam died three years ago. Liz tried to bring them together a number of times, but had given up when neither man had shown any interest. Now they only saw Jack Connolly a couple of times a year, and that was at Liz's insistence. She was determined that Lucy should see something of her grandfather.

She rung off, promising to call him later, and offered up a grateful prayer for her own tight-knit family.

Seán Adams was in JFK when he was paged and Joe's message was relayed. He ignored the call for his flight and went to the nearest phone. No answer at Joe's or at the restaurant. He cursed the fact that he didn't have Liz's number. He heard his name being called and he abandoned the phone, running for the gate. Shit! This flight only brought him to Cork. He doubled back to the Aer Lingus desk. There was a direct flight to Dublin in two hours. The thought of waiting frustrated him, but he knew it would be quicker in the long run. He headed for the bank of telephones.

Karen was very understanding. He promised to get in touch as soon as he knew what was happening. He talked to his son for a few minutes before making his way to the gate. He found a quiet corner and sat down wearily. He found himself praying. "Please let her be all right. Please God, let her be all right."

CHAPTER TWENTY-NINE

Marc stood at the door of Casualty, chain-smoking.

Edward went out join him. "Look, Why don't you go on home, Marc. Conor and Pat are going to be fine. There's nothing more you can do."

"*Non, merci, Monsieur* Mc Dermott, but I would like to see them before I go. Just to be sure . . ." He gave a Gallic shrug and smiled weakly.

Edward patted the pale young man on the shoulder and went back to the waiting-room. "Can I get anyone tea or coffee?"

"Tea, please." Catherine West smiled gratefully.

"I'll have a cup too," Annie said.

"I'll give you a hand," Joe said. "Liz?"

Liz looked at him blankly.

"Tea? Coffee?" he repeated gently.

Liz shook her head.

Catherine West leaned over and squeezed her hand. "He'll be all right, love. Don't worry."

Liz nodded dumbly.

Edward looked at her worriedly before heading for the canteen with Joe.

"I hate these bloody places," Joe said as he strode down the corridor.

"I think everyone does. My mother always wanted me to be a doctor. I said I'd consider it if I didn't have to meet any sick people."

Joe laughed and then felt guilty as the sound echoed around him. "It's not looking too good for Connolly, is it?"

"Fuck him," Edward said coldly. "If it wasn't for him, your sister wouldn't be in here."

Joe stopped. "What do you mean?"

Edward shifted uncomfortably. He'd walked himself right into this one. "Well, from what Marc says, it looks like Chris may have started the fire. Not intentionally of course . . . "

"The bastard! What happened?"

"Well, I'm not too sure. Marc's English isn't the best and my French is a little rusty. But from what I can gather, Chris got pissed with a couple of customers, passed out and they put him in the store-room to sleep it off. That's where the fire started."

"But how?"

"That we don't know, but he was probably smoking."

"The bloody fool," Joe muttered angrily.

"Well, it looks like he's going to pay a high price for it. I feel sorry for Liz. She told him this morning that she wanted a separation. I think she's blaming herself now for the whole thing."

"What a mess. I just hope Steph's going to be OK. And the baby."

"The baby?" Edward stared at him.

"Of course – you don't know, sorry. Mam told us that Steph decided not to go through with the abortion after all."

"Oh, that's great news, Joe – you must be delighted."

"Yes, I am. It's Seán I feel sorry for. He doesn't know about the baby and he probably hasn't heard about the accident yet either. I left a message for him, but it's unlikely he got it. I think he was already on a plane home. I talked to his office, though, and someone's going to meet his flight and bring him straight here."

They collected the drinks and brought them back to the waiting-room. Annie sipped the hot liquid but Catherine West just sat staring into her cup.

Tom West stood up suddenly. "I can't stand this place any longer. I'm going for a walk."

Annie looked pointedly at Joe who stood up, too.

"I'll come with you."

Edward sat down next to Liz. "You OK?"

"Not really. I keep thinking about how angry he was this morning."

"It wasn't your fault, Liz. He's a grown man, responsible for his own actions."

Liz glared at him. "He's my husband and he could be dying. And it *is* my fault."

"It's nobody's fault. No one said he was dying. In fact the doctor said he was stable."

"Edward's right, Liz. There's no point thinking like that. I'm sure he'll be fine," Catherine added, though she was finding it hard not to blame Chris. Her poor Stephanie. And the baby. Oh please God . . .

"Mrs West?"

She stood up as the nurse came into the room. "How is she?"

"She's going to be fine. If you'd like to come with me, the doctor would like to talk to you."

"I'll get Joe and Tom," Edward offered.

Catherine smiled her thanks and followed the nurse.

Tom and Joe were shown into the office where Catherine was already seated.

"I'm Stephanie's brother," Joe introduced himself to the impossibly young Asian doctor.

"How do you do?" The doctor shook hands with the two men. "I'm happy to say that Stephanie is going to be fine. She has some burns on her face, hands and legs, but they're not serious. It's unlikely there'll be any scars. The main problem was smoke inhalation. Her lungs are a bit raw and she'll feel sore for a couple of weeks, but there's no permanent damage."

"Thank God," Tom said.

"I'm afraid it's not all good news . . . "

"The baby?" Catherine said, her voice barely a whisper.

"Yes. I'm afraid she lost it."

"Oh, poor, poor Steph. Does she know? Can I see her? Tears streamed down Catherine's cheeks and she clung to her husband's hand.

The doctor shook his head. "I think you should leave it until tomorrow. She's sleeping now. She was unconscious when the miscarriage started so we went straight in and did a D & C. She's been given a strong sedative now so she should sleep until morning."

"I understand, but I'd like to be here when you talk to her."

"Of course, Mrs West. I think that's a good idea. I start my rounds at ten. Now I suggest you all go home and get some sleep. There's nothing more you can do tonight."

"Thank you, Doctor," Joe said gruffly, before guiding his parents out into the corridor.

"Why don't you stay with us tonight? It's closer."

Tom nodded. "Thanks, Joe. I think that would be a good idea."

"We should go to Malahide and get some of Stephanie's things . . . " Catherine struggled to concentrate.

"That's OK, Mam. Annie can lend her whatever she needs."

They returned to the waiting-room and collected Annie. Joe gave Edward a brief update on Stephanie's condition and Edward assured him he would stay with Liz. Marc decided to leave too. He'd been allowed in to see Conor and Pat. They were recovering quickly and would be let out the following morning. Marc was going to collect them and he'd also promised to call George and give him an update on everyone's condition.

"Stephanie's going to be OK," Edward said, sitting down beside Liz. He decided it was not the time to tell Liz about the miscarriage. She hadn't even known Stephanie was pregnant.

"Thank God for that," Liz said. "It doesn't look so good for Chris though."

"Why? Did you talk to someone?"

"No. But it's been such a long time."

Edward put his arm around her. "Don't jump to conclusions. I'm sure he'll be fine."

Liz shrugged off his arm. "Why don't you go on home, Edward?"

Edward watched her carefully. She hadn't looked him in the eye all day. "I'm fine here," he said.

"You don't understand. I don't *want* you here." Liz stood up and walked out of the room.

Edward stared after her. He went in search of a nurse. "I'm going down to the canteen. If there's any news on Mr Connolly, would you give me a shout?"

The nurse smiled warmly. God, he was gorgeous and he positively oozed class and money! She glanced hopefully at the ring finger on his left hand. "Of course, Mr McDermott. I'd be happy to."

Liz pushed open the door of the ward and looked in. There were three patients. An elderly woman in the bed nearest her lay still and white, with tubes attached to her nose, mouth and arms. Liz crept gingerly past and peered at the man in the second bed. Definitely not Chris. The form in the bed looked slight and frail. She moved on to the last bed. Chris lay on his back, very still. Half his face was covered with a bandage. The part that was exposed was an angry red. His right hand and arm were also bandaged. There were no tubes or machines, just a drip going into his left hand. That had to be a good sign.

"Mrs Connolly?"

Liz turned to look at the young girl in the white coat. "Yes? How is he? Is he going to be OK?"

The girl smiled. "He'll be fine. He's a very lucky man.

He has some minor burns and he inhaled a lot of smoke, but apart from that . . . "

Liz shook her head. "I don't understand. I've been waiting for ages. No one told me. No one explained."

The girl looked down at the chart in her hands. "I'm sorry about that, Mrs. Connolly. I was actually just coming to talk to you. You see, your husband had been drinking and we didn't know how much of his, eh, unconsciousness, was due to the smoke and how much to the effects of alcohol."

"You mean he's sleeping it off?" Liz exclaimed.

"Eh, yes. You could say that."

"I'd like to talk to a doctor," Liz said shortly.

"I am a doctor," the girl said gently. She was used to this.

Liz looked at her blankly. "Oh, right. Sorry."

"That's OK. Look, why don't you go home and get some sleep. I'm sorry for keeping you hanging around for so long, but we had to be sure."

Liz smiled weakly. "Of course. Thank you. Thank you very much."

When Liz left the ward, Edward was waiting in the corridor. "How is he?"

Liz took a deep breath and let it out slowly. "He was drunk," she said angrily. "The fucker was drunk! They thought he was unconscious, but the bastard's just been sleeping it off!"

Edward reached out and gripped her by the arms, trying to calm her. "Well, shouldn't you be grateful that it's not serious?" he said softly.

"Grateful?" She looked at him wildly. "He could have killed someone. He could have killed Stephanie."

"We don't *know* that he caused the fire," Edward pointed out more to calm her than anything else.

Liz gave a short laugh. "Oh, come on. The fire started in the store-room. He was the only one in the bloody store-room. You don't have to be Sherlock Holmes to figure it out."

Edward slipped an arm around her shoulders. "Come on. Let's get out of here."

* * *

"Her blood pressure's fine. I'll just check Mrs Molloy and then I'll go and make us a cuppa."

Stephanie stirred as the two nurses moved on to the next bed. It took a few moments for her to figure out where she was and why. She moved her arms and legs gingerly. They seemed to work, though her left hand was sore where a drip was attached. Her breath was short and rasping, despite the oxygen mask which made her feel slightly claustrophobic. She struggled to remember what had happened. The flames rising up from under the stairs had terrified her. She remembered Conor's voice, pleading with her to jump. It had taken all her courage. Her last memory was Conor's strong arms around her. *"I've got you, Steph. I've got you."*

Conor. God, was he OK? She looked around to ask a nurse. No one there. She noticed a call button on the wall. As she twisted to reach it, she became aware of bulky padding around her crotch. What the hell? She slipped a hand down under the covers.

The screaming went on and on. Nurses came running, lights were switched on, blinding her.

"Stephanie? Stephanie? You're OK. You're safe now."

Steph suddenly realised that the noise, that inhuman wailing, was coming from her. She became aware of a nurse bending over her and a doctor preparing a needle. "My baby," she gasped. "My baby. What have you done to my baby?"

"Calm down, love. Everything's going to be OK." The nurse stroked her cheek. "You poor pet. I know how terrible you must feel. It'll be OK. You're going to be OK."

The doctor stuck the needle in her arm. She looked up into his sad brown eyes. "My baby," she said reaching out to him.

He squeezed her hand. "Sleep now. Sleep."

She fell into an uneasy sleep, still holding his hand.

And then she was back on the burning staircase. Flames licking at her ankles.

"*Throw me the baby,*" Conor said.

She looked down at him and then at the bundle in her arms. She threw it to him. It flew up into the air, unravelling. There was no baby. She started to scream and then she felt herself fall into darkness. Nothingness.

CHAPTER THIRTY

Liz ran up the steps of the hospital and crashed straight into Annie. "Annie. How are you? How's Steph?"

Annie shook her head. "I don't know, Liz. Catherine and Tom are with her. I thought I better stay out of the way for the moment."

Liz looked at her strained, tired face. "Come on. Let's get some coffee."

"Aren't you going to see Chris?"

"Chris can wait," Liz said grimly.

Annie found a table in the crowded canteen while Liz queued at the counter. She carried two steaming mugs to the table and handed Annie a Kit-Kat. "Thought you might need a bit of sustenance."

Annie smiled and sipped her coffee appreciatively. "It tastes so much better when it's not in one of those awful plastic cups."

"Sure does. God, I wish I had a cigarette."

Annie nodded towards the no smoking signs. "They wouldn't be much good here. It's funny. I remember going to visit Jacqui, my neighbour, in St Patrick's."

"Isn't that a nut-house?"

Annie grinned. "Honestly, Liz! It's a psychiatric hospital. She had a bit of a break-down when her husband left. But, it's just so different from other hospitals. There was a haze of smoke throughout the whole building. You could hardly see through it in the canteen. Poor sods. I suppose they needed something to keep them going."

Liz shivered. "I've never been in a place like that. It must be very depressing."

"Oh I don't know," said Annie. "There must be comfort in the fact that you're not alone. We all lose the plot occasionally. Anyway. Tell me about Chris."

"Apparently he's fine," Liz said grimly. "Bugger doesn't deserve to be."

Annie didn't comment on this. Edward had filled them in on the part Chris had played in the fire. "Did you get to talk to him last night?"

"You're joking," Liz said harshly. "Sure he was comatose. Out cold. Drunk."

"You will go in to see him though, won't you?"

Liz nodded. "Yeah. I'll go. And I'll tell him exactly what I think of him. Then I'll go home and tell Lucy that poor Daddy is sick. And tomorrow I'll bring her in to see him. And we'll play happy families. And after that, the sooner I can pack him off to Galway the better!"

Annie grinned.

"It's not funny, Annie!" Liz glared at her.

Annie looked penitent. "Oh, I know it's not, Liz. It's awful. But it's done now. There's no point in going on about it."

"I wonder will Steph feel like that," Liz said.

Annie fidgeted with her spoon. She should really tell Liz about Steph's miscarriage. But if she told her now, Liz would probably kill Chris. It was so awkward. What would Stephanie want? No one had even *known* she was pregnant. Except for Catherine. Annie didn't envy Catherine now. Sitting up there with her daughter while she was told that she'd lost her baby. She sighed heavily.

"What?" Liz looked at her.

"Oh, nothing," Annie said with a forced smile. "It's just all such a mess. Things were going so well for Steph and Conor and now this."

"Is there much damage?" Liz asked.

Annie shrugged. "I don't know. Edward and Joe were going over this morning to have a look. The fire was in the store-room, so obviously that's gone. And apparently the stairs gave out completely just after Steph got out." She shuddered as she thought of what might have happened.

"The insurance will cover it all, though," Liz pointed out. "At least no one was seriously hurt."

Annie said nothing.

"They'll need to get an assessor in quickly and figure out how long it's going to take before they can open again," Liz continued. "They'll have to let the Michelin people know too."

Annie rubbed her eyes wearily. "God. What next? This is a bloody nightmare."

"Steph will sort it," Liz assured her. "She's a great organiser. Look, I better go and visit this man. Get it over with. Cheer up, Annie." Liz gave her friend a quick hug. "Give Steph my love. I'll drop in and see her later."

"Better not," Annie said quickly. "They said family only for now."

Liz frowned. "But I thought you said she was OK."

"She is, they just want her to get as much rest as possible."

"Oh, OK. In that case, give her my love. I'll call you later."

Annie watched her leave. Liz was going to be really pissed off when she eventually discovered the truth. But Steph had to come first for the moment and Annie didn't think she'd be up to a visit from the wife of the man who'd killed her child.

She finished her coffee and made her way up to the third floor. Stephanie had been moved into a private room. Tom West was standing outside staring into space.

"How is she?" Annie asked.

He shook his head, his eyes full of tears. "She's very upset. It's awful watching her. There's nothing you can do or say to make it better. I've left her with her mother. Catherine's better at this. She'll know what to say."

Catherine *didn't* know what to say. Her heart ached for her daughter. Steph looked beseechingly at her from distraught, red eyes. She wanted answers that Catherine couldn't give her. She wanted reasons, but there weren't any. She thought it was punishment because she'd considered abortion. Her mother assured her that God wasn't cruel. She cried because Seán had never known the joy of this pregnancy. Catherine had no words of comfort. She held Stephanie, rocked her in her arms, kissed her hair and wished that she could take the hurt away.

Steph felt like she was floating through some kind of nightmare. Everything seemed so unreal. One minute she was in this plain, clinical room and the next, she was reaching for Conor on the staircase. Then she was back in the London clinic, lying to the counsellor about her background and her circumstances. Then she was wandering through Mothercare.

Her hands constantly moved to her stomach, as if she could change things. Maybe they'd made a mistake. Maybe the baby was still there. Stupid, stupid, stupid. The doctor had explained about the D & C. He'd told her that they'd taken everything away. He'd told her that they'd done a scan and that there had been no heartbeat. He assured her that there was no reason why she shouldn't have a successful pregnancy in the future. She'd looked at him blankly. He thought she was going to *replace* her baby, just like that? But then it was just one of those things to him. It happened to a lot of women. What had he said? One in four pregnancies ended in a miscarriage. But why did she have to be the one in four? Anyway, there was nothing natural about what had happened to her. Her baby had died because of the fire. Because of the smoke.

A young girl banged open the door and shoved in a trolley. "Lunch," she announced, sliding a tray on to the table at the end of the bed. "It's fish. The woman who was here yesterday ordered it."

"I don't want it," Steph whispered, wincing at the pain that shot through her chest.

The girl ignored her and left the room, leaving the tray behind her.

Catherine inspected the meal. "It looks all right, Stephanie."

"I couldn't." It seemed wrong to eat, to drink, to live when her baby had died. Anyway, she thought she'd choke if she tried to get anything down her swollen, raw throat.

"Maybe some soup," her mother persisted.

"No! I don't want it, OK? I don't want it."

"Sorry, love."

Steph immediately regretted her outburst. She reached out and took her mother's hand. "Sorry, Mam."

"That's all right." Catherine patted her hand. "Everything's going to be all right. Seán should be here soon."

Steph looked surprised. "Seán?"

"Yes, he's on his way home. We left word with his office. They'll bring him straight here."

"Why?" Steph said sadly. "What for?"

"Don't be silly, love. He'll want to be here with you."

"I don't want to see him."

Catherine frowned. "But Stephanie, why? You need him now. You need each other. I know things seem very black now, but in time . . ."

"What? In time I'll forget?" Steph's eyes filled up and she snatched her hand away angrily.

"No. No you'll never forget," Catherine said firmly, "but you'll learn to live with it. Now you've driven Seán away enough times. Don't do it now. You need him. You know you do."

Steph nodded, tears streaming down her face.

Annie knocked on the door and put her head in. "Can I come in?"

"Come in, Annie," Catherine said standing up. "I'll just go out and stretch my legs. I'll bring you back some ice cream, Stephanie. That will soothe your throat."

Steph sniffed and accepted her mother's kiss with a weak smile. "Thanks, Mam," she croaked.

Annie exchanged looks with Catherine and then pulled up the chair she'd vacated. "How are you doing?"

"Lousy," Steph said, unable to stop the tears rolling again.

"Oh, come here to me," Annie said as she hopped up on the side of the bed and took Steph in her arms. "I'm so sorry, Steph. I'm so very sorry."

* * *

Edward and Joe stood in the restaurant and looked at the devastation around them. The fire hadn't reached the restaurant or the kitchen, but it had destroyed the side passage, the stairs and the landing. They'd no idea of the extent of the damage upstairs. The prompt arrival of the fire brigade had saved the day, but the resulting water damage was unbelievable.

"You won't be opening for a while," Joe said, wrinkling his nose at the stench of smoke and damp.

"No," Edward agreed, taking his jacket off. "Oh well. The sooner we start to clean up, the sooner we can sort things out. I'd better get on the phone."

"What do you want me to do?" Joe asked.

"Call Liam and George. Ask them to ring around the others. If we have enough people, we can get the worst of this muck cleaned up today. I'll call the broker and see if we can get an assessor out. We won't be able to start the clean-up until we get the all-clear from him."

They were both talking on their mobiles when Conor, Pat and Marc walked in.

"What the hell are you doing here?" Edward asked, putting his hand over the mouthpiece.

Marc shrugged. "I went to bring them home, but they insisted they come here first."

"Jaysus, this is a right mess," Pat said, picking his way through the hall.

Conor followed, silently. His dream had gone up in smoke. "How soon can we open, Mr McDermott?"

"I don't know, Conor. We have to see what the assessor says. I'm holding for him now."

Conor nodded and went out in to the kitchen. It was a mess. The firemen had dragged their hoses through it, knocking food and crockery from the work tops. The floor was a mishmash of dirty water, food and broken glass and delph.

"Merde," Marc swore softly. "We better get stuck up."

Conor laughed. "Stuck *in*, Marc. No, we can't clean up yet but you can throw open every window in the place. We need to get rid of this smell."

Edward had finished his call and followed them in. "Well, good old George is way ahead of us. The assessor was out last night. We can start cleaning up. But Conor, you and Pat should go home. You've been through a lot."

Conor shook his head. "I'm staying," he said obstinately. "This is my kitchen. You go, Pat."

"Not at all, Chef. I'm grand."

Edward smiled at them. "In that case, let's get too it!"

"Or as Marc would say," Pat said with a wink. "Let's get stuck up!"

They laughed at Marc's confused expression and got to work.

* * *

Seán strode through customs and out into arrivals. Michael Walsh, his General Manager was waiting for him.

"How is she?" Seán asked without preamble, not breaking his stride.

"She's fine," Michael assured him. "Joe called this morning. She has some superficial burns and she's suffering from smoke inhalation, but it's not serious."

"Thank God," Seán breathed. "Where's your car?"

Thirty minutes later, Seán walked into the hospital reception area.

"Seán?"

He swung around to see Tom and Catherine sitting in the corner. "Hello!" He bent down and kissed Catherine's cheek and shook Tom's hand. "She's OK, then?" he asked.

Tom looked away and Catherine's smile faded.

"What is it? What's wrong with her?"

"Nothing, nothing at all, Seán," Tom assured him.

"Why don't you sit down, Seán?" Catherine said quietly. "We do have something to tell you."

Seán pulled up a stool and waited.

"Stephanie didn't go through with the abortion." Catherine said simply. "She had a change of heart when she was in the clinic."

"Oh my God, that's wonderful." Seán's eyes lit up, but Catherine and Tom weren't smiling. His smile faded. "What's wrong?"

"She lost it, Seán. As a result of the fire." Catherine looked at him sadly. He was such a good, kind man. It really wasn't fair.

Seán raked his fingers through his hair. "Oh Jesus. Poor Steph." He looked at Catherine. "I didn't know you knew."

"She told me when she came home. Oh, Seán! She was so happy. She couldn't wait to tell you."

He nodded, his face stricken with grief.

"I'm so sorry, Seán. It's a terrible thing. But you have each other. You'll get through this," Catherine said, repeating the words she'd said to Stephanie.

"I'd better go up," he said finally. "Thanks for telling me. I'll see you later."

Catherine watched him walk away, his shoulders hunched. Dear God, would this day get any easier?

CHAPTER THIRTY-ONE

Seán pushed open the door and looked at Stephanie. Her hair hung limply on the pillow, and her pallor was emphasised by angry red patches on her cheek and forehead. She lay still, her eyes closed. He walked over and sat down in the chair at her side, moving as quietly as possible. His eyes fell to her right hand. It looked sore. She must have held it up to protect herself. He closed his eyes and sank back in the chair. It was all so hard to take in. When he'd found out that Steph hadn't got rid of the baby, his heart had jumped in his chest, with excitement and love. But when Catherine had told him that they'd lost the baby anyway, it was as if someone had punched him in the gut. He felt disoriented, tired and sad. What else could go wrong, for Christ's sake?

"I'm sorry."

Seán looked up to see Steph staring at him from sad tear-filled eyes. He jumped up and took her in his arms. "You've no need to be sorry, love. It's not your fault. You're not to blame."

She leant against him, letting the tears roll down her cheeks. "I was so happy, Seán." She struggled to speak, holding her throat in pain.

"Ssh, love. Don't try to speak."

Steph ignored him. She had to talk, no matter how much it hurt. "I was dying to tell you, but you wouldn't take my calls."

Seán groaned. "I'm sorry, love. I didn't know."

"I know that. I don't blame you. I wouldn't blame you if you never wanted to see me again."

Seán pushed her away so that he could look her in the eyes. "Listen to me, Steph. You are the most important thing in my life. The fact that you changed your mind about the abortion makes me very happy. Now I love you, and you're never going to get away from me again. I'm afraid you're stuck with me for life."

Steph hugged him to her tightly. "I hope you don't regret it," she said sadly.

"When are they going to let you home?" Seán stroked her hair.

"Probably tomorrow. The obstetrician wants to see me before I go."

Seán looked at her in concern. "There's nothing wrong, is there?"

"I don't think so. It's just routine." She coughed and winced as pain shot through her chest.

"Oh, you poor thing! I wish there was something I could do to make you feel better."

"You're here," she whispered.

He gathered her up in his arms. "I want you to concentrate on getting well. OK?"

285

Steph closed her eyes and hugged him tightly. "Promise."

* * *

Chris had also been moved to a private room. He sat up in bed, watching TV, and rang the nurse's bell on average every twenty minutes.

Liz approached the nurse's desk. "I was looking for Chris Connolly."

"Oh yes, Mr Connolly," the young nurse said grimly. "Room 225. Down the corridor on your left."

Liz smiled her thanks and moved down the corridor.

"Is that the wife?" The staff nurse stood up and looked after Liz. "Poor woman."

Liz took a deep breath and pushed open the door. When he saw her, Chris lay back and closed his eyes. Liz stood looking down at him. His eyelids fluttered and he looked up at her with a slight, pained smile.

"Oh hello, love. Didn't see you there." He turned off the TV and made a production out of sitting up, grimacing in pain.

"How are you, Chris?" Liz said calmly.

Chris winced again. "Oh, not too good, Liz. I'd a very bad night, a lot of pain. This is a terrible place. They wouldn't give me painkillers. Just left me to suffer."

Liz suppressed a smart retort. "I'm sure they didn't mean to."

Chris snorted. "They don't give a damn. God, they're always on strike saying they don't get paid enough.

Rubbish! This isn't hard work! They should come in to my kitchen. I'd show them hard work!"

"What happened, Chris?" Liz ignored his ranting. She wanted answers.

He looked puzzled. "What? What do you mean?"

"The fire, Chris. How did it happen?" Liz watched him steadily.

"I don't know, it's all a bit disjointed. God, I was damn lucky though."

"You were," Liz agreed. "The story goes that you were drunk, you passed out and Conor left you in the store-room to sleep it off."

Chris looked taken aback.

"And the fire started in the store-room," Liz continued.

Chris flushed. The combination of burned flesh and reddened skin made him look like a circus clown. "Well, I remember having one of my cigars," he said hesitantly.

Liz glared at him. "You stupid bastard! You could have killed someone. As it is, Stephanie's down the corridor in a bad way. Conor and Pat have only just been let home. You owe those two your life."

Chris glared at her. "If it wasn't for Conor I wouldn't have been in there in the first place!"

'You wouldn't have been in there if you hadn't got pissed!" Liz hissed angrily. "You've done a lot of dumb things in you life, Chris, but this . . . I just hope the place is properly insured."

"Of course it is." Chris was annoyed. This wasn't going the way it should. Liz should be fussing over him. Telling him how worried she'd been. Telling him she wouldn't leave him after all.

"I've got to go," she said. "I'll bring Lucy in to see you if you're still here tomorrow. Otherwise, give me a call and we'll set something up. By the way, your dad sends his best."

"Isn't he coming in?" Chris said petulantly.

"No," Liz said from the doorway. "He doesn't like hospitals. Seeya." She closed the door and leaned back against it. It had been hard to resist the urge to thump him. He was so caught up in himself. He didn't seem to feel any guilt. He hadn't even asked how Steph was and he showed no gratitude to Conor and Pat who'd risked their lives for him. She shook her head in disgust and, on impulse, made her way down the corridor to Steph's room. When she peered in she saw Seán draped across the bed, his head in Steph's lap. Steph gave her a shaky smile. Liz blew her a kiss and withdrew quietly. Thank God the two of them were OK.

* * *

Edward hung up after talking to the assessor and returned to the kitchen. The room had been restored to order and now the men sat around the preparation table, eating burgers and fries and drinking coffee.

"Well?" Conor looked up expectantly.

"Not good news, I'm afraid." Edward sat down. "Apart from the obvious damage to the store-room, there's a few other problems. The assessor thinks we need to replace all the floorboards of the landing and the ladies' loo."

"God, that'll mean tearing up all the floor tiles. They

288

were only put down last year and cost a fortune. Steph'll go spare." Conor looked at Edward mournfully.

Edward shrugged. "Well, that's not all. Apparently the whole place needs rewiring. The fuse box was destroyed in the fire. The store-room obviously has to be re-done from scratch. Still, it's an opportunity to get it exactly the way you want it, Conor. I'm sure it could be redesigned to make better use of the space."

Conor nodded, brightening a little. "How long before we can re-open?" he asked for probably the tenth time that day.

Edward frowned. "Hard to say. If I'm optimistic, two or three weeks. And that's only if we can get some reliable contractors."

"That's an oxymoron, isn't it?" Joe said drily.

"A what?" Pat asked.

"A contradiction in terms," Edward explained with a grin.

Pat shrugged and went back to his burger.

"I have my secretary ringing around some contractors," Edward continued. "I've told her to stress the time factor. Still, the insurance will cover us for our estimated earnings and expenses for the time we're closed." He glanced around at the crew. "Everyone will be paid."

A murmur of appreciation went around the room.

"Being closed that long isn't going to do us any good though," Conor said worriedly.

"No," agreed Edward.

"So your insurance is adequate?" Joe asked, ever the accountant.

"Well, I haven't seen the policy," Edward admitted.

"Presumably it's in the office. The broker wasn't much help either. He's going to get a copy of the policy and get back to me later."

"Steph would know," Pat said.

"I don't think we should bother her at the moment," Joe said quietly.

There was silence in the room. All the staff had heard about Stephanie's miscarriage.

"What about Chris, then?" Pat persisted.

"Maybe," Edward agreed. He wasn't entirely sure he could manage a civilised conversation with Connolly. He wondered how Liz was. He hadn't talked to her today.

"Joe? Can I have a word?" he said, and led the way out into the yard. "It's about Liz. She didn't know anything about Steph's pregnancy. It's only a matter of time before she finds out and I was wondering if it would be OK if I explained it to her?"

Joe frowned. "Shit, I didn't realise. Yes, yes of course. Please tell her. Steph's going to need her friends. Thanks, Edward. Well, I better get home. See how Mam and Dad are doing – unless there's anything else I can do?"

Edward clapped him on the back. "No. Thanks for all the hard work. I don't think there's much more we can do. It's over to the professionals now. Well, just one thing . . ."

"Yes?"

"I need to talk to Stephanie. Fill her in. I was going to drop in to the hospital later. I don't want to seem insensitive, though. What do you think?" Edward said worriedly.

Joe scratched his head. "I don't think there's going to be a good time. Drop in if you like. You can always back off if she's not up to it. Give it a go. If there's a problem, call me."

"Fair enough."

"I'll go so. I'm a bit worried about Mam and Dad. This whole business has taken a lot out of them. I might talk them into staying in town for another couple of nights." Joe bid the crew goodbye and left.

"We may as well call it a day, lads," Edward said. "Thanks for all the hard work."

Conor nodded his agreement. "Yeah, thanks lads. I'll give you a call in a couple of days and let you know what's happening. Remember, your wages are safe, so don't go looking for a new job. Relax and enjoy this unexpected holiday."

Pat grinned. "That's not a bad idea. Anyone for a pint?"

They made their way over to O'Neills, while Conor and Edward locked up. Conor looked up miserably at the blackened walls.

Edward saw his expression. "Don't worry, Conor. You'll have your restaurant. This is just a hiccup. Use the time to work on your recipes and menus."

Conor nodded vigorously. "I will, I will. Look, give Steph my best, will you? I'd go in but I don't want to intrude . . ."

"I'll pass on your message, Conor. Go and have a pint. I'll call you tomorrow."

Edward watched the lanky young man lope down the road. He hoped another restaurant didn't take this opportunity to make him an offer he couldn't resist. That was all they needed. He hated the idea of going up to the hospital and bothering Stephanie at a time like this, but he didn't know enough to sort everything out on his own. There was the whole business about the Michelin Star, for one thing. Then, despite his assurances to the staff, he was a little concerned about their insurance cover. The broker hadn't helped. He was a slimy character, full of platitudes, waffle and very few answers. Edward got into his car and started the engine. No point in putting it off any longer.

CHAPTER THIRTY-TWO

Liz tucked the duvet in around Lucy and tiptoed out of the room. The phone rang as she closed the door gently. She picked up the extension in her bedroom.

"Liz, it's Edward."

"Hi," she said softly.

"How are you doing?"

His voice echoed on the line. On the car phone, Liz surmised. "I'm fine."

"Could I come over later?" he asked. "I'm on my way up to the hospital to see Stephanie so it'll be late."

"That's OK. I don't feel much like sleeping. See you later."

Edward pulled into the hospital carpark. He wasn't looking forward to this meeting. He didn't know what to say to Stephanie. He didn't have any idea of what she must be going through at the moment. He sighed wearily. He was sure the last thing she wanted was to talk about Chez Nous. The prospect of seeing Liz afterwards didn't appeal to him either. He usually looked forward to seeing her. He liked to sit at her kitchen table and watch her throw an amazing meal together in half an hour. He liked the way she moved, the way she smiled. But tonight he would make her sad. He hated being the bearer of bad news, but he was afraid she'd find out accidentally. Too many people knew Steph's secret. He'd prefer Liz to hear the story from him. She'd probably be hurt that Steph hadn't told her about the pregnancy. He sighed again. It was proving to be a very long and tiring day.

Seán stood up and shook hands with Edward. "Steph's in the bathroom," he said.

"I'm very sorry, Seán," Edward said inadequately.

"Thanks." Seán said, raking his hand through his hair.

Edward looked at Seán. He looked terrible. His eyes were red and his face was drawn. Grief and jet-lag didn't go well together. "How is she?" he asked.

"Bearing up," Seán said. "She's coming home tomorrow."

"That's good. These places are very depressing." Edward cringed at his inane comments. Get to the point, man, he told himself. "I need to talk to her about the insurance, Seán. Do you think that would be all right?"

Seán shrugged. "Sure. She'll probably be glad of the distraction, though I'm not sure if she'll be much use to you. She's finding it hard to come to terms with . . ."

"Edward." Steph emerged from the bathroom and kissed his cheek before sitting up on the bed.

"How are you, Steph?" Edward perched on the arm of a chair, feeling awkward.

"Not so bad," she said. "How are the boys?"

"Grand. They were in today helping us clean up. Came straight from the hospital. You've got a good bunch there, Steph."

"I know," Steph agreed. "So what's the damage?"

Edward was relieved that she'd broached the subject. He gave her a quick summary of the situation.

"Sounds bad," she said glumly.

"Well, it won't be too bad if we're fully insured."

Steph frowned. "Chris used to take care of all that. I did get in touch with the broker when we took over, to check if the change of ownership affected anything."

"So whatever cover we have is what Chris put in place on day one?" Edward asked.

"I suppose so. You don't seem too happy about that." Steph looked at him curiously.

"I suppose Connolly doesn't instil me with confidence," he admitted. "That broker pissed me off, too."

Steph nodded. She'd never cared for Pat Mulvey and was quite happy to leave Chris to deal with him. "He's a bit of a sleaze-bag. What happens now?"

"He's getting a copy of the policy," Edward said.

"The policy's in the office, oh . . . "

Edward looked embarrassed. "Eh, yeah. We can't get up there. The other matter is the Michelin Guide. What do I need to do?"

"I'm not sure. They're going to want to pay a couple of visits once we're up and running again."

Edward frowned. "Well, that's not a problem, is it?"

"No but it doesn't give Conor much time to settle into the job." Steph chewed her bottom lip and felt a flicker of interest spark inside her. "We've got a lot to do."

"Don't you worry about anything," Edward said. "I'll take care of it. Just point me in the right direction."

"Don't be silly," Steph said brusquely. "I'm fine. I'll get on to the Michelin people and I want to sit in on your meeting with Mulvey."

Edward looked apologetically at Seán who shrugged. He wasn't pleased at the idea of Steph going back to work so soon, but on the other hand, it would probably be better if she didn't have too much time to think about the baby.

"Right," Edward said. "I'll call you tomorrow then. Oh, eh, where?"

"You'll get me on my mobile," Steph said, avoiding Seán's eyes.

Edward glanced from one to the other. "I'll be off so. Talk to you tomorrow. Take care. Bye, Seán."

"See you, Edward," Seán said distractedly. "Maybe I should get going too," he said.

"Yes," Steph replied.

"Right. I'll pick you up in the morning." He took a deep breath. "Then we can go out to Malahide and pick up some of your stuff."

Steph studied her fingernails. "I'd prefer to stay in Malahide for the moment," she said lightly.

"Why?"

"Well, it makes sense. With all my stuff there."

"Steph, I want you to move back in."

"Yes, and I will," she said impatiently. "Just not tomorrow. I'm going to have enough on my plate."

Seán bit his lip. "OK. You won't mind me staying too, though. Will you? I told you. You're never going to get rid of me."

Steph forced a smile. "I'm not trying to," she assured him.

Seán kissed her goodnight and left feeling slightly uneasy. It had been an awful day, yet he'd never felt closer to Steph. Until Edward arrived. Then she'd changed. Distanced herself from him. "You're imagining things," he told himself. "You're tired and you're over-reacting. Get a grip."

* * *

Liz opened the door and let Edward in. "You look terrible."

"You do wonders for my confidence," Edward said drily.

"Coffee? Drink?" she asked, hovering between the living-room and the kitchen.

"I could do with a drink," he admitted. He was going to need it. So was Liz.

"How's Lucy?" he asked, sniffing the cognac Liz handed him.

"Fine," she said, stretching out on the sofa. "I didn't tell her about the fire. I thought it might give her nightmares. I just told her that Chris had burned himself and that the doctors were looking after him. I told her he was dying for her to come in and kiss him better." She made a face. "It's terrible the crap you have to come up with when you have kids."

Edward laughed. "How's Chris?"

"Infuriating. Honestly, Edward, he never even asked how the others were!"

"So you're not having second thoughts then?" he asked watching her intently.

She looked confused. "What? About the separation? God, no! Now I'm *sure* I'm doing the right thing!"

Edward smiled, happy with her answer. He took another sip of his drink and wondered how to tell her.

"A penny for them?" Liz broke in on his thoughts.

He looked up and found her watching him intently.

"What is it, Edward? Something's wrong, isn't it?"

"Not really. Well yes, I suppose so. There's something I have to tell you, Liz. It's about Stephanie."

"Is she OK?" Liz looked at him in alarm.

"She's fine," he assured her. "Something happened a few weeks ago. She didn't tell you. She didn't tell me either," he added hastily when he saw her face.

"For God's sake, Edward. Spit it out." Liz leaned forward and looked at him expectantly.

"OK. Before Seán went to the States, Steph discovered she was pregnant."

"What?" Liz looked at him in astonishment.

"Yes. She decided not to keep it. Remember that time she went to London?"

"Well, yes. Oh my God . . ."

"That was pretty much Seán's reaction," Edward said drily. "When she told him, he told her to move out."

"Oh God. He must have been very upset."

"Yes, he was. Anyway. He went to America and Stephanie went to London. But it seems at the eleventh hour she had a change of heart."

"Oh, thank God." Liz's face lit up.

Edward lifted his hand. "I'm not finished."

Liz's smile faded.

"You see, she lost it. Last night. Because of the fire."

"Oh my God. Oh no. Oh God no."

Edward moved over on to the sofa beside her and put his arm around her.

"Does Seán know?" she asked.

"Yes. He got home today. He's with her now."

"This is awful. How many months was she gone?"

"I'm not sure." He thought for a moment. "At least three months I suppose."

Liz shook her head. Poor Steph. She'd lost her baby because of the fire. The bloody fire. Chris. "I'll kill him," she said bitterly.

Edward sighed. "You may have to get in line," he said, thinking of the pain in Seán's face.

"How is Steph? Did you see her?" Liz blew her nose.

"Yes. She's not bad, considering. Oh, Liz, I felt awful. I had to talk to her about work. It seemed terribly insensitive, but what could I do? We need to move quickly. Still, as soon as we started talking business, she was like her old self."

Liz smiled. "That's Steph for you. When is she getting out of hospital?"

"Tomorrow."

"Maybe Seán will take her away for a few days. A break would do them both good."

"I'm afraid not," Edward said. "She's straight back to work."

Liz shot him an accusing look. "Surely there's no need for that. Can't you handle things?"

Edward looked uncomfortable. "Most things, yes. But there are areas that I'm not familiar with. But Steph could take some time off once the work is underway."

Liz nodded, resignedly. "Is there anything I can do? Or what about Chris? It's the least he could do."

Edward thought for a moment. There was no doubt that Chris would be able to step in for Stephanie. His wounds seemed superficial and he should be up and about in no time. But Edward wasn't sure he could work with Connolly. And he certainly didn't like the idea of Chris negotiating with Michelin. He couldn't very well say that to Liz, though.

"I think it might be good for Steph to get back to work. Apart from which, I believe she's made up her mind. Have a chat with her, though. She might be happy to have you help out."

"But not Chris," she said quietly.

Edward looked down at his hands. "I don't think it's a good idea, no."

"Then I think my job should be to make sure Chris moves to Galway as soon as possible," she said grimly. "He'll probably be safer there. The further away from Seán the better."

Edward nodded. "You're probably right."

"So tell me. How come you knew everything that was going on and I didn't? Why didn't you tell me? Did Annie know?" Liz was a bit hurt that Steph hadn't confided in her.

"Yes, Annie knew. I think she was the only one Steph told. Annie told Joe and Joe told me. He wanted me to cut her some slack. Look after things at the restaurant. I didn't tell you, Liz, because it wasn't my secret to tell. Steph had intended to get an abortion. It would have been all over within a few days. She didn't want anyone to know."

"I understand," Liz whispered. God, Steph was her best

friend, and yet she hadn't known, hadn't noticed that there was anything wrong. "I feel so sorry for her, but I'm glad she didn't go through with the abortion. That must be a terrible thing to live with."

"I suppose," Edward agreed. "Though it probably depends on the circumstances."

"Is everything OK between her and Seán?"

"Well, they were together when I went in. A tragedy like this will either bring you closer together or drive you apart. Let's hope it's the former in their case." He stood up and stretched. Every bit of him ached. He felt closer to eighty than forty. "I'd better go home. I've an early start tomorrow. Do me a favour?"

Liz looked at him. "What?"

"Don't mention any of this to Chris."

Liz bit her lip. "Well, OK. I won't be able to anyway. I'll have Lucy with me. I wish I didn't have to go near the man at all."

"He's still Lucy's Dad," Edward reminded her gently. He leaned down and kissed her forehead. "I'll phone you tomorrow."

"All right. Edward? Look after Steph. She might put on a tough front, but she'll still be going through hell."

"I'll keep an eye on her," he promised.

* * *

Seán opened the door and watched Chris quietly for a moment. He was munching biscuits and watching a film, laughing at Steve Martin's antics. "Enjoying yourself?" Seán asked.

Chris jumped and then smiled uncertainly. "Seán! Good to see you. It's not a bad film. Distracts me a bit from the pain. How are you?"

"Not good, Chris. My girlfriend's struggling to breathe properly and she's just miscarried our child. So I'm not too good at all."

Chris opened and closed his mouth like a goldfish. "I didn't know . . . I never . . . nobody told me . . . "

"No. Well, there you go. When are you off to Galway, Chris?"

"Well I'm not sure . . . "

"As soon as possible, I think. That would be best. For everyone. Don't you agree?" His eyes were steely and there was a menacing note in his voice.

"Don't threaten me, Seán," Chris said nervously.

"It's no threat," Seán said grimly. "You've outstayed you're welcome, Chris. Time you moved on. The best thing for everybody."

CHAPTER THIRTY-THREE

Steph shut the hall door and breathed a sigh of relief. She thought she'd never get rid of Seán. His concern and solicitousness was beginning to suffocate her. He wanted to talk things through, analyse everything, but it was just too raw. All Steph wanted to do was forget. She walked across her living-room, enjoying the silence. She threw open the balcony doors and took a deep breath of sea air. It was a beautiful day and small boats were already heading out into the bay, taking advantage of the breeze that would probably abate before noon. It would be nice to have a day to herself, but it wasn't to be. Edward would pick her up in less than an hour. They had an appointment with Pat Mulvey at eleven-thirty. Seán was not impressed with her going back to work so soon. He'd finally left for work, slightly happier when she promised to go away with him once the restaurant was straightened out. Steph left her balcony and went into the bathroom. She started the shower and slipped out of her clothes. She wrinkled her nose. She smelled of hospitals and smoke. She got into the shower, turning up the heat until it was almost impossible to bear. She scrubbed her arms and legs, but her hands shook when she ran them over her stomach and abdomen. She felt the sadness well up inside of her. No. Get a grip. You've a job to do. She hopped out of the shower and dried her hair. She eyed it ruefully. Time she paid Jeanette a visit. She slicked it back with some gel. It would have to do. She applied her make-up carefully, using foundation and powder to camouflage the burns. She selected a cream Paul Costello suit. The high v-neck meant that she didn't have to wear a blouse. She added a chunky gold necklace and earrings and cream leather court shoes and felt ready to face the world. She studied her image. She was a far cry from the red-eyed wreck of yesterday. She jumped as the phone rang. She was tempted to let the answering machine pick it up, but it was probably her mother.

"Oh, you're home, love. Thank God. How's your throat?" Catherine's voice was full of concern.

Steph sighed. "I'm fine, Mam. Don't worry."

"Is Seán there with you?"

"No. He's gone to work."

"Well, we'll drop over, so."

"No, Mam. I'm going out. I have a meeting."

"A meeting? For God's sake, Stephanie! You're only out of hospital and you sound terrible."

"I'm fine, Mam," she lied. Talking was proving to be even more difficult today. "And there's a lot to sort out. It's only one meeting."

"Are you driving?" Catherine persisted, still not happy. Stephanie sounded hoarse and her breathing wasn't great.

"No. Edward McDermott's picking me up."

304

Catherine was slightly mollified by that. "Well don't stay out too long, love. It's only your first day. Don't push yourself."

"I won't, Mam. Don't worry. There's the doorbell. I have to go. Bye." Steph hung up, collected her bag and went out to meet Edward.

Edward glanced at her surreptitiously. She looked fantastic, if a little weary around the eyes. She'd said very little since she'd got into the car and the silence was uncomfortable.

"So how are you?" he said finally. He wasn't quite sure what he was supposed to say.

"Fine," she said staring out of the window.

"I'm very sorry, Stephanie. About – about the baby. "

"Thank you," she said and continued to study the scenery.

Edward gave up and they completed their journey in silence.

"Sit down, sit down," Pat Mulvey said, looking Steph up and down appreciatively. "Mr McDermott? Nice to meet you. Coffee?"

"No, thank you. Have you looked at our policy?" Edward asked without preamble.

The broker shifted in his chair and rummaged through the papers in front of him. "I have. There will be no problem in relation to damage cover. You need to submit quotes for approval, but there shouldn't be any problem there. Any hospital charges will be taken care of under you employer's liability cover. Again, just hang on to all the receipts. Will any of your staff be claiming against you?"

Steph looked at Edward who shook his head. "I don't believe so. Two suffered smoke inhalation but they were only kept in overnight. They were back working the following day."

"Good, good." The broker made a note.

"So what's the bad news?" Steph asked, her voice barely a whisper.

"Well, I'm afraid you've no consequential loss cover."

"What's that?" Steph looked at Edward.

"It covers your expenses and expected profit for the period the business is closed," Edward said wearily.

"Christ! Why the hell *aren't* we covered?" Steph eyed the broker angrily.

He shrugged. "Chris thought it was too expensive. He decided to take the risk."

Steph and Edward sat in stunned silence.

"You never mentioned this to me when I called to tell you I was taking over," Steph said finally.

"I assumed you knew," Mulvey said defensively.

"You're paid to advise your client," Edward said coldly. "Surely you should have advised Stephanie to increase her cover?"

"As I said. I assumed she knew. She's worked in the restaurant all along."

"I think, Stephanie, it's time we reviewed our insurance arrangements." Edward scowled at the broker.

"I think you're right." Steph stood up and walked to the door.

"That's up to you," Mulvey said smoothly. "But you won't get a better deal anywhere else."

"Maybe not, but we might get a proper service. Good

bye, Mr Mulvey." Edward resisted the temptation to bang the door.

"What the hell are we going to do?" Steph said when they got outside.

"Change brokers," Edward said grimly, starting the car. "Let's get some lunch."

Steph took a sip of her wine and looked around the bright, airy room appreciatively. "This is nice." They sat in Trastevere, an Italian restaurant in the heart of Temple Bar and Steph was feeling a bit better. The chilled Pinot Bianco was soothing on her throat and she'd ordered a creamy pasta dish that she should be able to swallow quite easily.

"I like it," agreed Edward. "We're lucky to get a table. It's always busy here. You and Seán should drop in some evening. There's always a great buzz. I like sitting at the window and watching the world go by."

Two girls passed. One had blue hair, elaborate eye make-up and a tanned midriff and the other had rings through her nose, lip and eyebrow. "I see what you mean," Steph said laughing. "So what do we do now?" Her smile faded as she thought about their predicament.

Edward tapped his nails against his glass. "Well, I think we have to pay the salaries. I've already promised them."

"Not the waiters. They can be easily replaced. Except for Liam Dunne. I want to keep him," she said. "We'll pay all the chefs except for George. I think we should let him go. How in hell are we going to finance it though? Every penny I have is in the restaurant."

Edward frowned. "I'm not much better. Most of my money is tied up. But . . ."

"Yes?" Steph prompted, wishing he'd stop tapping the damn glass. It set her teeth on edge.

"Well, Chris isn't due the second half of the payment until he leaves."

"That's in two weeks time," Steph pointed out. "We can't use that money. We won't be up and running by then. How would we pay him?"

"Maybe we could persuade him to wait," Edward mused.

Steph laughed harshly. "Yeah, right. And he'll do that out of the goodness of his heart."

Edward smiled. "Maybe not, but he might do it to protect his reputation. Or out of guilt and remorse."

"What do you mean?" Steph looked at him curiously.

"There's no doubt that he started the fire, Steph. It wouldn't be very good for his image, if that information got out."

Stephanie had paled. "Chris started the fire?" It was strange, but she hadn't asked anyone what had actually happened. She'd been so caught up in her miscarriage that she'd forgotten. "Tell me," she said quietly.

Edward cursed under his breath. He couldn't believe that no one had told her. Mind you, he couldn't blame them. "He was with Liz that day. She told him that she wanted a separation. He didn't take it well. No surprise there. He came into the restaurant later on. He'd been drinking. He joined some customers who were having a boozy lunch. They started to get a bit loud, and some other customers were getting upset. Conor got him into the back and he passed out. They put him in the store-room to sleep it off."

"Then what?" Steph's voice was husky.

"Well, it gets a bit hazy after that. Chris admits to waking up at some stage and lighting a cigar, and the remains of a whiskey bottle was found nearby. We assume that he fell asleep again and dropped the cigar. He'd been sitting beside the tablecloths and napkins and if the whiskey spilled . . . he could have been killed."

"Pity he wasn't," Steph said bitterly. "He should be charged for this. Can we sue him?"

Edward looked surprised. "We wouldn't have a hope, Steph."

"You'd prefer to blackmail him?"

"I wouldn't put it quite like that," Edward said with a small smile. "But we could appeal to his sense of decency."

Steph found it hard to believe that Chris had a decent bone in his body. But he would be concerned about his future employer finding out that Chez Nous had gone up in smoke as a result of his drunken antics. Not good CV material. "What have you got in mind?"

"I think we should look for a delay of three months before the final payment. I also think we should renegotiate the amount. Say a reduction of ten per cent?"

"Twenty," Steph said, her face hard.

Edward looked at her. "It's worth a try. I'll give him a call tomorrow. Is he still staying with his dad?"

"I don't think he's home yet. But don't worry about it. I'll take care of this." Stephanie's eyes were hard and determined.

"I don't think that's such a good idea," Edward said gently. For all her composure, he wasn't convinced she could handle a confrontation with Connolly.

Steph glared at him. "I said I'll handle it."

Edward wasn't happy but he decided to let it go. "OK. If that's what you want. You'll need to move quickly, though."

"I'll contact him tomorrow."

"Right. Next problem. The Michelin people." Edward topped up their wine and sat back.

"I'll call them and set up a meeting. They'll want reassurances that we're going to restore it to the same quality. Then they'll want to inspect it before we re-open." Steph made a note on the pad by her plate.

"I think we should see them together," Edward said.

"Agreed. I'll try and set something up for this week. It'll have to be in their offices."

Edward shook his head. "No, get them to come to my office. We can always walk over to the restaurant afterwards and show them what we're doing."

"Let's hope we *know* what we're doing. Any luck with contractors?"

"Yes. I'm meeting three this afternoon."

"Great. That suits me." Steph shivered involuntarily. She wasn't looking forward to going back, but it was better to get it over with as soon as possible.

Edward sighed as he remembered his promise to Liz. He wasn't very successful when it came to protecting Stephanie. Her first day out of hospital and she was determined to go back into the restaurant. "There's no need," he insisted. "It's only for preliminary quotes."

"Nevertheless. It's important I know the full extent of the damage when I talk to Chris. My argument will be more forceful."

Edward gave in again. "Fair enough. But you're going home after that. Seán will throttle me for keeping you out so long."

Steph made a face. "I'm not a child, Edward."

Edward called for the bill and they walked the short distance to Chez Nous. From the outside it looked all right, but as soon as Edward opened the door, a dank acrid smell enveloped them.

"We had every window in this place open yesterday, but that bloody smell is still here." He wrinkled his nose in disgust.

Steph had walked on through to the back. She stood looking at the remains of the staircase. Edward came up behind her and put a hand on her shoulder. "Are you OK?"

She nodded dumbly. It all looked so normal now. Ugly and dirty, but normal nevertheless. Not the terrifying inferno of two days ago. She shivered and moved into the area that had been the store-room. It had been cleaned up, but the walls were black. The timber wall that had faced out into the passage way was no more. The ceiling, a gaping hole. Steph's heart sank as she imagined the damage to the rooms upstairs. She forced herself to move on into the kitchen. It was a lot better. A good scrape and paint and it would be fine. "Does all the equipment still work?" she asked Edward, who'd followed her in.

"We've no electricity at the moment, so we don't know. We had to empty the freezers and fridges. I told Conor to divide the food out among the staff."

Steph smiled. "They must have thought all their birthdays had come together. Did you itemise the contents first?"

"All done," Edward assured. "And it is covered by the insurance."

There was a rap at the front door. Edward checked his watch. "That'll be the first builder."

Steph pasted a smile on her face. "Then let's get started."

CHAPTER THIRTY-FOUR

Seán watched Stephanie push her pasta around the plate. "My cooking's not that bad."

"What? Oh sorry," Steph gave him a weak smile. "I'm not very hungry."

"Tough day?" Seán asked.

"Not too bad. I feel exhausted though. There's such a lot to do. And then there's the insurance business." She sighed.

Seán frowned. "Do you honestly think Chris is going to agree to wait for his money?"

"I don't know," Steph admitted. "If he won't I may have to sell this place."

Seán managed to hide his delight. It would be great if Steph got rid of her bolthole. Maybe then they could settle into a normal family life. "Do you want me to come with you when you talk to him?"

"No, that's all right," Steph said firmly. "I can handle Chris."

"Are you sure? I don't want him upsetting you."

"If anyone's going to get upset it will be Chris."

Seán grinned. "I almost feel sorry for him."

Steph scowled at him.

"I said *almost*," he pointed out.

Steph stood up to clear the plates away.

"So we should move your stuff back to my place," Seán ventured.

"I suppose," Steph said doubtfully.

"There's no need to sound so happy about it," Seán snapped.

"Sorry, love. Sorry." Steph moved to the back of his chair and slipped her arms around his neck.

"Are you sure you're OK?" He twisted around so he could see her face.

She nodded.

"The hospital gave me some pamphlets," Seán said tentatively. "There's a miscarriage association. They have a helpline and group therapy sessions. Maybe you should contact them."

"I don't think so," Steph said. She couldn't see herself pouring out her heart to a therapist. Sharing her pain with other women who'd had a miscarriage.

"I think you should talk to someone, Steph," Seán persisted. "You've been through a lot."

"I'm fine, Seán," Steph said irritably. "Don't fuss."

Seán held up his hands. "I'm worried about you, Steph. Don't blame me for that."

Steph felt a pang of guilt. Why was she such a contrary bitch? "I'm sorry, love," she said again. "It's just I don't want to talk to anyone about anything. What's done is done. There's no point in dwelling on it."

Seán looked at her worriedly, but he decided to leave it

for the moment. He pulled her to him and kissed her. "Whatever you want, Steph. Just promise you'll talk to me if things are getting you down. You're not alone in this. I'm always here for you."

"I know, love," she murmured. "I know."

Steph lay still listening to Seán's steady breathing beside her. She hadn't really lied to him. She *was* all right. It was just night-time. During the day she could keep herself occupied. With so much to do to get the restaurant up and running again there wasn't time to think. But at night, when she was alone in the darkness, all the memories flooded back. All the pain resurfaced. She plumped her pillow and rolled over on to her side. She closed her eyes, willing herself to sleep. "Think nice thoughts," she instructed herself. She thought about her father's garden in Greystones. She imagined herself stretched out on a sun-lounger, the sun beating down on her face. She heard insects buzzing, the *clip clip* of her father cutting the hedge and the distant sound of the Gay Byrne Show coming from the radio in the kitchen – her mother loved to listen to him. She thought about her mother and the chats they enjoyed, sitting in the large airy kitchen, drinking copious amounts of tea. And then she thought about the day when she'd told her mother she was pregnant. She moaned softly as the memories flooded back. Her eyes filled up as misery engulfed her once more. Maybe she *should* go and talk to someone. Maybe she could do with some help. Still the thoughts of talking to some shrink didn't appeal to her. Anyway, what did women do fifty years ago? They got on with it, that's what. There were no helplines or therapists.

There was too much emphasis on therapy these days, Steph decided. If she needed to talk, she had Seán, she had her mother, she had Liz and Annie. Wasn't that what family and friends were for? OK, so she hadn't shared every waking thought with them. But to each his own. Everyone had their own way of dealing with things. She wasn't the sort to spill her guts. She just wanted to get on with her life. What was the point in dragging up the past? Going over it, regurgitating, analysing, examining. It was a waste of time and energy.

No, she didn't need to talk to anyone. She was bound to get upset occasionally. It was completely natural, but it would pass. Eventually. She flipped over onto her other side and shut her eyes tightly. She had to sleep. It was going to be a long day. And there was Chris to face. "Sleep," she urged herself. "Sleep."

"Come on, sleepy head." Seán prodded Steph's sleeping form. "It's almost eight o'clock."

Steph groaned. She felt as if she'd just closed her eyes. "Maybe I'll grab another couple of hours."

Seán frowned. "I thought you were seeing Chris at ten. It'll take you at least an hour to get out to Dun Laoghaire."

"Oh shit." Steph threw back the covers and padded out to the bathroom. "Put on the kettle, would you Seán?"

"Are you sure you'll be OK?" Seán asked through a mouthful of cornflakes.

Steph nibbled on a piece of toast. "What?"

"Chris. Are you sure you can handle seeing him?" Seán said patiently.

"Of course," she said carrying her dishes to the sink. "Will you be late tonight?"

"I don't think so. Why?"

"I thought we might move my gear back to your place."

Seán beamed at her. "In that case I'll make sure I'm early. No offence, love, but your bed's not very comfortable."

Steph thought of his comatose state last night while she lay wide awake beside him. "Poor you," she said drily. "I can't have your insomnia on my conscience, can I? Tonight it is then. It shouldn't take too long. I never really unpacked since, well since . . ." She flushed as she remembered the reason for her leaving.

Seán hugged her tightly. "Gotta go. Give me a call, let me know how you got on."

"I will. Bye."

An hour later, Steph was on the road to Dun Laoghaire. It was a horrible day. Rain lashed the windscreen and a strong wind buffeted the car on the coast road. "Lovely summer weather," Steph said to herself.

By the time she'd pulled up outside the Connolly home, the rain had passed off and the sun was trying to break through the clouds. Steph walked up the path, picking her way through the puddles. She rang the doorbell, noticing the chipped paint on the door frame and the tarnished brass fittings. Chris's dad was obviously as handy around the house as his son.

"Stephanie, how are you?" Chris opened the door and gave her a nervous smile.

Steph stared at him. "Chris," she said, brushing past him.

Chris closed the door, eyeing her warily. "Let's go into the lounge," he said indicating the door to her right. Steph went in and looked around her with distaste. She wondered idly when the place had last seen a duster. Poor Mrs Connolly would turn in her grave. She perched on the edge of a shabby wing-back chair beside the gas fire.

"So how are you?" Chris asked nervously. "I was sorry to hear about, your eh, miscarriage."

Steph looked at him coldly. A riot of emotions ran through her. He was sorry? He'd made her life hell for years, almost destroyed her livelihood and killed her child and all he could say was he was sorry? He didn't even mean it! It was just lip-service. He didn't *see* that it was all *his* fault.

She swallowed hard and closed her eyes as a wave of nausea engulfed her.

"Steph? Are you OK?"

She managed to nod and took a deep breath.

"So what can I do for you?"

"You've left us in a bit of a fix," she said faintly.

"How's that?"

"You didn't have full insurance cover."

"Of course I did."

"No," Steph assured him. "You didn't take out consequential loss cover. Apparently it was more than you wanted to pay."

Chris reddened as he remembered that particular "discussion" with Pat Mulvey. "Well, sure it's no big deal, is it? What is it anyway? It mustn't have been important or I'd have bought it."

Steph pursed her lips. "It covers the profits we would have made while the restaurant is closed for repairs."

"Oh?"

"Yes. And we're going to be shut for three or four weeks and we won't get a penny to cover our losses."

Chris looked away. "Oh."

"Yes 'oh'. So we need your help." Steph swallowed hard. It was tough having to ask this man for help.

"What can *I* do?" Chris looked at her suspiciously.

"We need to postpone your final payment."

Chris gave a short laugh. "Forget it! You owe me that money. We've a contract."

Steph glared at him. "Yes, we do," she said steadily. "But as our predicament is a consequence of your actions . . . "

"You've been running things for the last few months. The insurance was your responsibility," Chris said hotly.

"True," Stephanie said quietly, keeping a tight rein on her temper. "But I couldn't do anything to stop you getting drunk and setting fire to my restaurant!"

Chris glared at her. "It wasn't my fault."

Steph raised an eyebrow. "The evidence says otherwise. I'm sure your new partner would be interested in hearing about the incident."

Chris stared at her. "What are you saying? Are you threatening me?"

Steph's eyes widened. "Of course not. Just thinking aloud. It's such a small industry. Word travels fast."

Chris thought quickly. He didn't need the money in a hurry. And he certainly didn't want any bad press. There were rumours already. He didn't need them coming from Stephanie or McDermott. He'd be ruined. "I don't like your attitude, Stephanie. There's no need for it. I'd be glad to help out. What did you have in mind?"

Steph looked at him in disgust. Anything to cover his own ass. "We want an extension of six months."

Chris frowned. "That's a long time," he said cautiously.

"And we propose to reduce the payment by twenty per cent, to reflect the part you've played in this whole business."

"Now look here. That's not on. That's not on at all," he blustered.

"It's a small price to pay for the total support and backing of your colleagues," Steph said quietly.

"Ten per cent," Chris said abruptly.

"Fifteen." Stephanie watched him steadily.

"You'll make sure they say nothing? Conor? Pat?"

"I will," Steph assured him.

"OK," Chris said resignedly. "Draw up the papers and I'll sign them."

Steph opened her briefcase and handed him two sheets of paper.

Chris glared at her. "Presumptuous, weren't you?"

Steph shrugged. She'd actually printed out four versions of the contract, with five, ten, fifteen and twenty per cent. She signed her name to the documents and handed Chris his copy. "Nice doing business with you," she said coldly. "I'll see myself out."

* * *

"Well done, Stephanie," Edward smiled at her broadly. "I'm impressed."

Steph grimaced. "I can't say it was easy. I nearly hit him.

320

We better make sure we can keep to our side of the bargain now."

"Indeed. It's in all our interests to keep this under wraps."

They were interrupted by Edward's secretary arriving in with a tray.

"Thanks, Louise." Edward smiled at the older woman and poured steaming coffee into two delicate china cups. "Have you been in touch with Michelin yet?"

Steph helped herself to cream and sugar. "What do you think I am?"

Edward laughed. "Sorry. I'm just eager to get things moving."

"Me too. Actually I did contact them. They've to call me back."

Edward nodded. "Great. The builders are moving in tomorrow and they've promised to be out in ten days."

"That's not great, is it? The decorators won't be able to move in until they're finished."

"Probably not, but the builders are going to arrange the rewiring. They'll work with the electrician, so they should all be finished at the same time. At least then we can restock the freezers."

"That's true," Steph agreed.

"So what's next?" Edward asked.

Steph frowned. "I'm worried about the staff. We could replace any of the younger lads no problem, but if we lost John Quigly, or Pat Dunne, or Marc or, God forbid, Conor, we'd be in a right mess."

"I don't believe we'll lose Conor," Edward said. "He's very keen on running his own kitchen and it's unlikely that anyone else would offer him a better deal in the short time that we're going to be closed. I don't know about the others. What are the odds?"

Steph thought for a moment. "John might well be head-hunted. He's an excellent chef and a good worker and he's got a good reputation in the city. Pat, I'm not sure about. Him and Conor are good mates so he's probably happy enough. Kevin Nolan – you know, the lad that Conor was bringing in to replace George? I don't think he's given in his notice yet, so we're all rigat there. Marc is hot property. I'd hate to lose him. His mother's been ill though. Maybe I'll suggest he goes home for a while. I'm sure he'd love that."

"Good idea," Edward agreed.

Steph's phone rang. "Excuse me," she said to Edward. "Hello? Stephanie West . . . yes. *Michelin*," she whispered to Edward. "Three o'clock tomorrow?" she raised an eyebrow at Edward who nodded. "Three will be fine. You know where we are? Good. Thank you. See you then." She switched off the phone and smiled at Edward. "Well, that's another one to knock off the list. Now where were we?"

"Staff," Edward replied.

"Oh, yes." Steph frowned. "I think we need to sit down with each of the chefs and lay our cards on the table. Oh, and Liam too. I don't want to lose him."

"Agreed." Edward flicked open his diary. "Let's call them now and set up appointments for the next couple of days."

They worked steadily for two hours, and when Stephanie finally walked down the steps on to Merrion Square she was feeling tired but a lot more optimistic. If only she could be sure of a night's sleep. She dreaded the thoughts of another night lying wide awake in the darkness, with all her demons coming back to haunt her. Maybe she should talk to the GP about getting some sleeping pills. It was going to be a busy few weeks and she was going to need her rest. She checked her watch. If she hurried, she'd catch her GP before she went out on her calls. She quickened her pace, happier now that a night's sleep was a possibility after all.

CHAPTER THIRTY-FIVE

"Mummy, Mummy! Daddy's here." Lucy ran to the door and tugged it open.

"Great," Liz muttered drily. She checked on the lasagne and then joined Lucy in the hall.

"Hiya, Luce!" Chris waved at his daughter before ducking back into the car and pulling out some bags.

"Are they for me?" Lucy asked excitedly.

"Maybe," Chris teased.

"Come on in," Liz said. "I've made some lunch."

Chris smiled at her gratefully. "That's nice, Liz. Thanks."

Liz looked at him in surprise. "No problem," she said leading the way into the kitchen.

"The smell is great," he said appreciatively.

"It's only lasagne," she said dismissively. She deliberately hadn't gone to any trouble. Chris always found fault with her food. Either she hadn't added enough seasoning or the sauce was too thick or some other petty criticism. She eyed him suspiciously as he pulled Lucy onto his lap and allowed her to rummage in the bags.

"Barbie!" she cried delightedly.

"Another one?" Liz said and immediately hated herself for her bitchiness. "That's great, love," she added more gently.

Lucy pulled the other bags apart impatiently and squealed in delight as she found two outfits for Barbie and a miniature Barbie office, complete with computer.

"Thanks, Daddy. You're the best." Lucy planted a loud kiss on his cheek before dashing upstairs with her new toys.

"That was nice of you," Liz said.

Chris shrugged. "Well, it'll be a couple of weeks before I see her again. I'm leaving for Galway tomorrow."

Liz stared at him. "I thought you weren't going until the end of the month."

"There's no point in hanging around now the restaurant's closed." He didn't tell her about his little chat with Seán. "And sharing with Dad's driving me nuts. Besides, I'm not exactly popular at the moment."

"You can't really blame them," Liz said tightly. "You did a lot of damage. Not only to the business but to Steph . . ."

"I know, I know, Liz. And I'm sorry, believe me." He put his head in his hands.

Liz couldn't help feeling sorry for him. "Do you need some stuff for the flat?" Apart from some CDs and his trophies Chris hadn't taken anything with him when he left.

"Well, I wouldn't mind taking a few of the books." He eyed the stack of cookery books on the dresser greedily. "And I'd love the desk lamp from the study."

Liz smiled. "No problem. Take the nest of tables too."

"Oh, no. That's OK," Chris said.

"No, please. They were a present from your mother. It's only right that you should have them."

Chris smiled. "Thanks, Liz."

Liz looked away, embarrassed at this new, gentle, Chris. She opened the oven door. "This looks ready. Would you call Lucy for me?" Chris went upstairs to get his daughter and Liz set the lasagne on the table. She took a bowl of salad and a bottle of Chablis from the fridge. She was opening the wine when Chris returned, with Lucy chattering at his side.

"None for me," he said when Liz went to fill the glass in front of him. "I'll stick to water."

Liz stared at him and then smiled. She served the meal and sat down to eat. Chris asked Lucy about school and her friends and Liz relaxed and started to enjoy this precious, peaceful moment with her family. It had never been like this in the past, she realised sadly. On the few occasions that Chris ate with them, his head was usually buried in a newspaper. But today he was attentive and funny and Lucy was loving every minute of it. There was one dodgy moment when Lucy mentioned Edward, but Chris just smiled tightly and said nothing.

"Lucy, I'm going down to Galway tomorrow," he said when Liz was clearing away their plates.

Lucy's face clouded over and her bottom lip trembled. "But I thought you weren't going for weeks."

"Well, I have to go now," Chris said firmly.

"I don't want you to," Lucy said stubbornly.

"Don't be like that, Luce. We talked about this,

remember? I've got to get down there and decorate your room. It's going to be the nicest room in Ireland. Fit for a princess. I bet you'll be the only girl in school with her own holiday home."

Lucy brightened slightly at that. "What colour is my room?"

"Whatever colour you want it to be," Chris promised her.

"And can I bring my toys when I come and visit?"

"Of course. Though I think we should keep some toys down there too. What do you think of that?"

Lucy nodded happily and Chris thanked God that she was still at the age where bribes worked. He hugged her and winked at Liz over her head. "We'll have a great time together," he promised.

"Can Mummy come to Galway too?" Lucy asked.

"Of course she can," Chris said quietly, watching Liz. "If she wants to."

"Will you, Mum?" Lucy watched her mother solemnly.

"We'll see," Liz said, concentrating on the washing up. She fought back the tears and scrubbed the casserole dish furiously. God, this was hard. She felt guilty for breaking up her family. But it was for the best, wasn't it?

"Have you heard how long it'll be before Chez Nous's up and running again?" Chris asked, breaking in on her thoughts.

"The best part of a month I think," she said, repeating what Edward had told her.

"It'll never be the same again. Michelin will be keeping an eye on them. It will probably affect their rating in the guide."

Liz turned in time to see the smug look on his face and her heart hardened. "Why don't you decide what books you want," she said coldly. "I'll have a look around and see if there's anything else belonging to you."

Chris watched her leave the room, puzzled. What was wrong with her now? He shook his head. He'd never understand her. "Come on, princess," he said, sweeping Lucy up in his arms. "You can help Daddy."

Two hours later, Liz stood in the doorway, waving Chris off. Lucy ran down the road after the car, waving and shouting.

"What's all that about?"

Liz turned to see Jenny McDermott standing at the end of the driveway. "Hi, Jenny. Come on in."

Carol had run down the road after her friend, and now the two of them were skipping back towards them hand in hand.

"That was Chris," Liz explained leading the way back inside. "He's leaving for Galway in the morning."

"Oh," Jenny said, her eyes wide.

"Let's go and sit in the garden," Liz suggested, collecting the bottle of wine from the fridge. "Lucy. Why don't you show Carol what Daddy brought you?"

It was one of those unusually warm late summer days and the garden looked beautiful. Jenny settled herself in a large garden chair, adjusted her sunglasses on her nose and accepted the glass from Liz. "This is the life," she said contentedly.

Liz set the bottle down in the shade and sat down beside her. "I almost told him I'd go with him," she confided.

Jenny stared at her. "Really?"

Liz nodded. "Yep. But then he said something really nasty and I came to my senses."

Jenny laughed. "Thank God for that."

Liz frowned. "You don't even know him," she pointed out. "Why are you so sure that I'm doing the right thing?"

Jenny shifted uncomfortably. "Just from the things you've told me and from what Edward's said . . . "

Liz's eyes narrowed. "What has he said?"

"Very little," Jenny assured her. "But I know he was worried about you the day you told Chris about the separation. Edward isn't the sort to overreact. I figure if he was worried for your safety, then you're better off without the man."

"There was never any reason to worry about my safety," Liz said irritably. "Chris has never laid a finger on me."

Jenny sipped her wine and said nothing.

"I just feel sad about the way it's all turned out," Liz explained after a while. "Sitting having a meal together today. All three of us. Laughing and joking. It was nice. Why couldn't it have been like that when we were together? I'd thought that Lucy would have a little brother or sister by now. That we were a family for life. I can't help feeling guilty for not making it work."

"It takes two," Jenny said firmly. "Stop beating yourself up about it. It's a waste of time."

"I suppose you're right," Liz said sadly.

"Oh, come on. Cheer up! Have you done anything more about setting up your business?"

Liz flushed with pleasure. Her business. It sounded

wonderful. "There hasn't really been time," she said. "What with the fire and everything."

"That was terrible, wasn't it? How's Stephanie?"

Liz shook her head. "I wish I knew. I haven't really talked to her. Anyway, if I did get the chance, what would I say? Sorry my husband killed your baby?"

Jenny squeezed her hand. "It was nothing to do with you. You're her friend. Call her."

Liz nodded, swallowing back tears for the second time that day. "You're right. I will."

Jenny gave her hand another squeeze. "So what about the business? You are going to go ahead with it, aren't you?"

Liz gave her a watery smile. "I think so. I've been going over some recipes. It's not as straightforward as working in the restaurant. I have to consider how much preparation I can do at home, how long the food will keep for and how to cost the whole meal. That's really tricky."

"Well, you can't sell yourself too cheap," Jenny said. "You're providing an up-market service."

Liz nodded. "I agree, but if I go for expensive ingredients, the cost could be prohibitive. I think I'll need to come up with three menus. Standard, special and deluxe. Then I can tweak the recipes where necessary."

"What do you mean?"

"Cut costs by going for cheaper ingredients," Liz explained. "Use hake instead of turbot, lumpfish roe instead of caviar, that sort of thing."

"Oh, I see." Jenny looked at her admiringly.

"Once I've sorted out my menus I'll ask John Quigly to take a look at them. John is Chez Nous' pastry chef. He took over from me. He's a funny sort, but a great chef."

"What about a name?" Jenny asked.

"What?" Liz looked confused.

"You need a name. For the business. Something catchy, but classy."

"I suppose so. I hadn't thought about it."

"What about 'Dinner Service'?"

Liz wrinkled her nose. "I don't think so. How about 'Meals On Wheels'?"

Jenny laughed. "It hardly portrays a classy image, now does it?"

"Silver Service?" Liz offered.

"Mmmn. Not bad," Jenny agreed. "But maybe you should use your own name. After all, you were well known and certainly the Connolly name means something."

"Liz Connolly Catering?" Liz asked doubtfully.

"Maybe. Why don't you ask Steph what she thinks? She's the marketing guru, isn't she?"

Liz nodded. "That's an idea, and it's a good excuse to ring her."

"There you go then," Jenny said smugly. "I've earned my glass of wine."

Liz reached for the bottle and topped up their glasses. "You've earned two!"

Jenny raised her glass. "Well, for the moment, here's to Liz Connolly Catering."

Liz smiled broadly. "Cheers," she said. "Here's to the first million."

CHAPTER THIRTY-SIX

"Steph? Phone."

Steph stood up from the desk and went to the door. "Who is it?" she called down.

"It's Liz. Pick up the extension in the bedroom."

Steph went into their bedroom and lifted the phone. "Liz?"

"Hi, Steph. How are you?"

"Fine, Liz. How are you?"

"Grand. Listen. I need to talk to you. I want your advice."

Steph frowned. Liz wanted *her* advice. After the last time, Steph wasn't sure that was such a good idea. "What about?" she said cautiously.

"Business," Liz said.

Steph smiled. "You're going back to work?"

"Maybe. Well, probably. Look, I don't want to get into this over the phone. Will you meet me for a drink?"

Steph hesitated. She had so much to do. Still. She was the one that had been pestering Liz to do something. "Sure. When?"

"Well, I can get a baby-sitter for Wednesday night."

"Wednesday it is, so. Let's meet in town. Say The Bailey at eight?"

"Great. Seeya then." Liz smiled as she hung up.

Steph went down to Seán who was sitting in the kitchen, drinking coffee and reading the *Irish Times*.

"Liz wants to meet me on Wednesday. She wants to talk about work."

Seán looked at her over his paper. "Really? Does she want to come back to Chez Nous?"

Steph poured herself a cup of coffee and sat down opposite him. "I don't think so, but she's certainly got something up her sleeve."

"That's good," Seán said stretching lazily. "What will we do today?"

"I've got to work," Steph said.

"But it's Saturday! I was looking forward to having you all to myself. I never get the chance when the restaurant's open."

"Sorry. There's too much to do." Steph grinned at his woebegone expression. "I know what *you* can do, though."

"What?" Seán said suspiciously.

"The garden."

Seán groaned. "Oh, no! It's my day off, for God's sake! I've been working hard all week."

"Poor you," Steph said not at all sympathetically. "Oh, go on, Seán," she wheedled. "It's such a lovely garden. And you should get it sorted before the bad weather sets in. And it *would* be nice for Billy to have somewhere decent to play."

Seán scowled at her. "That's blackmail. Anyway, boys

prefer something wild. They can pretend they're in the jungle hunting wild animals."

Steph looked out at the overgrown garden. "They'd probably find some out there," she said drily.

Seán flicked her with his paper. "OK, OK. God, you're an awful nag."

"But you love me," Steph assured him.

Seán grunted and stood up. "I wonder if the lawnmower still works."

Steph grinned. "I'll leave you to it. God. Conor's due in half an hour. I'd better get moving."

"What wonderful things are you teaching him today?"

Steph poked him in the ribs. "I'm showing him the costing system on the computer."

"Sounds riveting. If he gets bored send him out to the garden."

Steph laughed and went back upstairs. She looked ruefully around the boxroom that Seán had turned into an office for himself. It had been so neat and tidy and now it looked like a bomb site. The builders had rescued all the files and filing cabinet from her office in the restaurant. The blackened cabinet stood next to Seán's pristine one. Some blackened, smelly files sat on his lovely mahogany desk and a bulky black sack full of files was propped up against the wall. Seán's sleek modern laptop was pushed to the back of the desk and Steph's old IBM sat in its place. At least it was working. All her computer files were intact and the packages were working.

She switched on the PC and started up the costing program. It was a great time-saver and it was a lot easier for Conor to learn than the manual version. Steph remembered the early days when Liz and Chris used to sit in the kitchen trying to cost a dish. They had to take everything from electricity, wages, rent into account down to the basic ingredients. It was a very cumbersome job. They'd been thrilled when Steph had discovered this computer program. It was a simple spreadsheet that prompted the user with all the possible factors, automatically added in the overheads and calculated the cost per portion. Conor should pick it up very quickly. He liked messing about with computers and he'd picked up the accounting system easily enough. He didn't really need to understand that one, but Steph figured they had the time and it wouldn't hurt. Anyway, she felt happier keeping an eye on Conor. As long as he was with her, he wasn't out getting himself another job.

Marc had gone home to his family, so she didn't have to worry about him. Unless of course he decided to stay there. She sighed. There was always something to worry about. Her thoughts were interrupted by the doorbell. There was no sign of Seán answering it. Good. Maybe that meant he was tackling the garden. She hurried downstairs and opened the door.

"Conor. Hi. You found us OK?"

"No problem. Nice place," he said, looking around the large bright hall. "One of these days, I'm going to buy myself a nice house. There's just no privacy in the flat."

Steph raised an eyebrow. "You're the first twenty-something I've heard complain about privacy."

Conor laughed. "It's the job. It's ageing me! So what are we doing today, boss?"

Steph made a face. "Costing, I'm afraid. Come on. I'll make you a cup of coffee before we get started."

"Great." Conor followed her into the kitchen. "Where's Seán?"

Steph nodded towards the garden and Conor walked over to the patio doors.

"Looks like he's got his hands full," he observed as he watched Seán wrestle with a large bush.

Steph joined him. "God. It looks like he's losing. Come on. We better get out of here before he ropes us in."

"It might be better than costing," Conor said gloomily.

Steph grinned. "Oh, shut up. If you're a good boy and you pay attention, I'll buy you a pint later."

Conor brightened. "Fair enough," he agreed. "Let's go."

Seán leaned on his spade, breathing heavily. He was knackered, but he looked around the garden with satisfaction. The lawn was in good condition. Luckily the previous owner had been a better gardener. Seán had cleared away all the overgrown shrubbery. Now the flower beds were clear. He'd be able to plant some flowers now. He chuckled at the thought. He didn't have a clue where to start. He'd cut back the hedges at the back of the garden, exposing the tree in the corner. It looked good and sturdy. He wondered idly what kind of tree it was. He could build Billy a tree-house. Seán had always wanted a tree-house when he was a kid. He and his brother had erected little houses out of tin and wood in the corner of their small backyard, but it wasn't the same. Yeah, a tree-house. It would be great.

Seán was thrilled when Steph had mentioned

somewhere to play for Billy. She obviously expected him to come and visit. He hadn't told her about his plans for the attic. Maybe he'd broach the subject tonight. He was planning to go down and see Billy next week. It would be nice if he could tell him about his special room. He wouldn't mention the tree-house though. That would be a surprise.

"Yo! Seán!"

Seán looked up to see Conor waving a can at him from the patio. "Nice one, Conor. I'll be right there." He picked up the shears and carried it and the spade back to the garage. Two black sacks of grass and shrubs stood waiting for the binmen. He wiped the sweat from his brow and went into the kitchen.

"Oh, Seán! Wipe your feet, for God's sake." Steph looked at the trail of muck from the door to the fridge.

"Stop nagging, woman. I'll clean it up," Seán swallowed half a can of lager. "So how did it go, Conor? Are you an expert now?"

"Of course." Conor grinned at him. "No problem."

"Good. Maybe you should be in the software industry."

Steph flicked him with a teacloth. "Don't you start poaching my staff, mate."

Seán winked at her. "It would be handy though. He could write a couple of programs in the morning and whip up a four-course meal for lunch!"

Conor laughed. "Ah, that sounds too much like hard work. I think I'll stick with Steph."

"Why don't you get cleaned up, Seán, and we'll go for a pint." Steph closed the patio doors and threw her empty can in the bin.

"Right so. I'm going to take a shower. Why don't you two go down to the Yacht? I'll follow you."

Conor stood up. "Sounds good to me."

Steph kissed Seán's cheek. "Ugh, you stink," she said, wrinkling her nose.

Seán swatted her on the bum. "There's love for you."

"Seeya later," she called over her shoulder.

Seán smiled after her. It was great to see her so light-hearted. Maybe she'd be able to give up those damn sleeping tablets soon.

"So, Conor. Do you think any of the lads are going to leave us?" Steph watched Conor over the rim of her glass.

"Nah. They're enjoying the time off. It's been a while since any of them have been able to enjoy Dublin nightlife."

"Good. I hope they party all night and sleep all day. That should keep them out of harm's way. It was a bit of luck that your friend Kevin hadn't given in his notice."

Conor nodded. "It was a close one. He was going to do it the day of the fire, but the boss took a half-day."

"Thank God for that. What are we going to do about a replacement for you, Conor?"

"*Sous-chef*? I'd like to use Pat. Marc's good too, but Pat has a bit more control over the lads."

"Yeah, I'm inclined to agree. I think Marc's going to be a force to be reckoned with some day, but I'm not sure he's ready yet."

"Good. So we'll give the job to Pat. He'll be delighted."

"Well, I'm glad you didn't want to bring anyone else in. I'm not sure we could have handled another salary."

Conor frowned. "You're not stuck for money, are you, Steph?"

"No, no," she said quickly. "The insurance company will cover all the repairs, but I thought I'd push the boat out on some of the decor. And that will come out of our pocket."

"What did you have in mind?" Conor drained his glass.

"Well, I thought we could clear out the back room upstairs and turn it into a private dining-room."

"That's an idea." Conor lit a cigarette. "But wouldn't that mean we'd need more loos?"

Steph frowned. "I don't think so. I'll check, but I think the number of loos isn't affected until the capacity goes over the hundred."

"Well, it's sixty-three at the moment and the back room would sit twenty tops, so we should be OK. That would be a nice little earner, Steph."

"That's what I thought," Steph said, happy that he liked the idea. "Is there anything you want for the kitchen?"

"We could do with a second fryer and what about putting a second door in?"

"You mean an 'In' and 'Out'?"

"Yeah. It's safer."

"Already agreed with the builders."

Conor grinned. "Nice one. Another drink?"

"I'll get that." Seán stood over him.

"That was good timing," Conor said. "Mine's a pint."

"What about the store-room?" Steph continued after Seán had gone to the bar.

Conor thought for a moment. "I think we just need a better shelving system and I think we should put the drink under lock and key from now on."

"Agreed," Steph said grimly. "Maybe they could build a lockable cupboard into the room. I'll talk to them on Monday."

Seán put the drinks down in front of them and pulled up a stool. "You should be sitting outside. It's too nice to be stuck indoors."

"My God, all this working outside must be getting to you," Conor said.

"Sun-stroke," Steph said solemnly. "There was nowhere to sit, Seán."

"There is now," he assured her. "Come on before someone else grabs it."

They carried their drinks out to the table at the front of the pub. Steph leaned back in her chair and slipped on her sunglasses. The sea was calm, and kids were skateboarding along the front.

Conor looked about him appreciatively. "This is nice. Maybe I'll move out of town."

Steph looked at him over the top of her glasses. "First you want to buy a house, now you want to move to the suburbs. Next you'll be telling me you want to get married."

Conor flushed.

Seán stared at him. "What's this? My God! The man's in love."

"Ah, leave me alone," Conor said, swallowing a mouthful of lager to hide his embarrassment.

"Who is she?" Steph persisted.

"No one you know," Conor mumbled.

"So when are we going to meet her?" Seán chipped in.

"Dunno. We'll see."

"God, you're a dark horse," Steph said smiling. "Why don't you give her a ring now? She could come and join us."

Conor shook his head. "She's in Kilkenny. She goes home at the weekends."

"A *country*-girl? You're going out with a *culchie*!" Seán exclaimed.

"Shut up, will ya?" Conor nudged him.

"What's her name?" Steph asked.

"If I tell you, will ya leave me alone?"

"Promise," she said.

"Anthea."

Seán burst out laughing. "Anthea! Anthea from Kilkenny!"

Conor glared at him.

"Stop it, Seán," Steph said suppressing a grin. "That's a lovely name. You'll have to introduce us, Conor. Bring her over some night for a drink."

"Oh, I will," Conor said. No bloody way, he said to himself. These pair would scare Anthea off for sure.

"Ah, young love!" Seán stretched in his chair. "Isn't it wonderful?"

Conor stood up. "I'll get the drinks in," he muttered.

Steph laughed. "Leave him alone, Seán. You were young and in love once."

Seán kissed her. "I still am. Well, in love, anyway," he

said becoming conscious of a dull ache in his back. "I'm not so sure about the young part. I think I've injured myself. That bloody garden."

"You did a great job," Steph assured him. "It looks great."

"Wait till you see it with a tree-house," Seán said.

Steph stared at him. "A tree-house?" Maybe he really did have sun-stroke.

CHAPTER THIRTY-SEVEN

Stephanie turned up the speed and the gradient on the treadmill and pounded on. She was still groggy from the sleeping tablets and the exercise helped to clear her head. Before the tablets, night-time had been the hardest. Now it was mornings. There was always those first few moments when she woke when she forgot what had happened. Then a feeling of unease would steal over her. She would know something was wrong. And then it would all come flooding back and the dull ache would return to her gut, to stay with her until the release of the sleeping tablets that night. Seán wasn't happy with her taking them. He hated any kind of medication. She usually agreed but right now she wasn't sure she'd be able to carry on without them. The thoughts of returning to those dark, sleepless nights terrified her. No, it was better this way. She hardly had time to think. Except when she was alone. She turned up the speed again, wiped her face with her sleeve and checked her watch. She had an hour to finish, shower and change, then a full day of meetings at Edward's office and then drinks with Liz. She grimaced at the thought. She wasn't looking forward to that. Liz said she wanted to talk business, but Steph knew they'd end up talking about the fire, about Chris and about the baby. She knew Liz knew. Edward had told her everything. Well, she would have heard it from somebody eventually. At least it saved her from having to explain. But she wasn't sure she could handle talking yet. It was too raw. She even avoided Seán's attempts to discuss it. "Running away as usual, Steph," she muttered to herself. She pushed the thoughts to the back of her mind and made her way back to the changing room. There was no time to feel sorry for herself. She had a business to run.

* * *

"This is really a brilliant idea, Liz." Steph stared at her friend in open admiration.

Liz glowed with pleasure. She'd explained her plans and was delighted when she'd been able to answer all of Steph's questions. All her hard work had paid off. She'd spent hours working out costs and overheads and she'd developed an impressive menu of dishes that would travel well.

Steph set the file down on the table in front of her. "I'm not sure why you need my advice. You seem to have everything covered."

"Not everything," Liz said. "I'm not sure how to market the business or where to advertise. And then there's the name. I think I should use my own name, but it's not exactly catchy."

Steph took a sip of her wine. "I see. Well, as far as

advertising is concerned, word of mouth will be your greatest earner. Mind you, that can work against you too!"

Liz rolled her eyes. "Don't I know it! I remember the early days in the restaurant. There was always someone important in the night the freezer broke down, or two staff didn't show. Murphy's Law!"

Steph laughed. "It hasn't changed." She thought for a moment and then looked intently at Liz. "What about linking yourself to Chez Nous?"

Liz stared at her. "Are you serious?"

Steph shrugged. "I've been trying to get you back to work long enough, haven't I? You're a damn good chef, Liz. We'd be proud to be associated with you."

Liz flushed. "Well, I certainly wouldn't object, but I think you should discuss it with Edward and Conor first."

"No problem there," Steph assured her. "Conor's heard all about you and Edward thinks you're perfect."

Liz tried to look annoyed but failed miserably. "So my card would say 'Liz Connolly of Chez Nous'?"

"Sounds impressive. We should really contribute to your costs, though." Steph frowned. They couldn't really afford to throw money around at the moment.

"Not at all." Liz shook her head. "Give me some good press occasionally and let me pinch some of Conor's ideas. That's more than enough."

"We'll see," Steph said. "We need to have a proper meeting about this. Work out all the details. When will you be ready to start up?"

"In the next few weeks," Liz said. "I've had a chat with Mary. You know the girl next door who baby-sits for me?

She's delighted at the idea of extra work. She's saving for a car."

"Great. I could layout the menus for you, if you like, and we could buy some fancy paper to print them on. Fifty copies should do you for the moment."

Liz made a note. "Good idea. I'll get the paper. I'll need some cards and some letterheads, but I suppose we should delay that until we talk to Conor and Edward."

"Yes. Well, let's arrange that soon. How are you fixed at the weekend?"

Liz frowned. "Well, a baby-sitter might be a problem. Mary needs a bit more notice at weekends. Tell you what. Why don't you all come to me? I'll cook something from my menu. After all, the proof of the pudding . . . "

Steph clapped her hands. "Brilliant! They'll agree to anything once they've tasted your food, though I suppose Edward already has."

Liz avoided Steph's teasing gaze. "Nothing fancy."

"OK. How about Saturday?"

"Fine," Liz agreed excitedly.

"Great." Steph took out her mobile and punched in Conor's number. Ten minutes later it was all agreed. Edward would pick up Conor and Steph and be in Stillorgan for eight.

"What about Seán?" Liz asked.

"He'll be in Cork. He'll be visiting Billy."

Liz watched Steph carefully. "Are you OK about that?"

Steph looked surprised. "Of course. He's his son, after all. I wish Seán saw more of him. We're hoping Karen will let him come and stay for a while. Seán's started clearing

346

out the attic and he's talked to a building contractor about converting it into a bedroom."

Liz looked at her. She seemed happy enough about it all but still, there was something wrong. She seemed edgy. She didn't look too good either. Very pale and she was so thin! Liz had often been envious of Steph's looks but not tonight. She was as elegant as ever in a beautifully cut, charcoal-grey suit. But the jacket hung loosely on her shoulders and her eyes seemed very large in her small face.

Liz reached out and took her hand. "Steph, we haven't had a chance to talk since the fire. I know about your miscarriage. I'm so sorry."

"Thanks." Steph managed a weak smile. "It was awful, Liz. I felt like someone had torn my heart out. It's so unfair."

Liz was surprised at Steph's openness. She'd expected to be stonewalled. She slipped an arm around Steph. "It's bloody unfair," she agreed. "You didn't deserve it. It's an awful thing to happen. And if it wasn't for Chris . . . "

Steph swallowed hard. "Well, the less said about him the better. Anyway, I think it's important Seán gets to know his son better. Billy's all he's got now."

"Seán's got you. And someday, who knows, maybe you'll try again."

Steph shook her head. "I don't think so, Liz. I couldn't go through that again. I'd always be scared. Terrified of losing it."

"That's natural, Steph. Every expectant mother feels like that. I panicked every time I had so much as a twinge. It was usually just indigestion. All the bloody doughnuts my mam kept feeding me, no doubt."

Steph giggled. "I got a real hankering for fruit gums. I hadn't eaten them since I was a kid. But in the last couple of weeks, I must have eaten five packets."

Liz looked at her slim figure. "It doesn't show."

"The gym," Steph explained. "I'm working out like a maniac. It helps me forget."

Liz frowned. "You don't have to forget, Steph. It's OK to grieve."

Steph sighed inwardly. Here we go. Lecture time. "I really don't want to talk about it anymore, Liz. Give me a look at those menus again. Let's see what you should cook on Saturday."

Liz took one look at Steph's face and obediently opened the file. There was no point in pushing her.

Steph pored over the menus, ignoring Liz's silence. Why couldn't they understand that she had to deal with this in her own way? Why did everyone want her to talk? What the hell was the point? Talk wouldn't bring her baby back. "What about the crab cakes to start?"

Liz shook her head. "Too simple. Conor wouldn't be impressed. What about the Globe Artichokes stuffed with prawns?"

Steph wrinkled her nose. "I don't like artichokes. What about a warm salad?"

Liz took the file and flicked over a couple of pages. "There. Chicken liver salad. It's difficult to get the livers just right. Too much cooking and they're chewy and tasteless. Conor would be impressed with my chicken livers. They're always great."

"Modesty becomes you," Steph said drily. "Right, now we've got that sorted what about a main course?"

"Lamb or beef," Liz said firmly.

"Is that not a bit boring?"

"Maybe but it's what most customers want and it's always a challenge to come up with a new or more interesting way of presenting the traditional dishes. How about shoulder of lamb with an apricot and walnut stuffing?"

"Mmmn. That sounds nice. And with your special gravy?"

Liz pulled a face. "Yes, with my special gravy. You're a terrible woman. You only like it because of the amount of booze in it!"

"Thas a malishus rumour," Steph slurred.

Liz laughed. "Onwards. What about afters? How about a coffee and orange soufflé?"

"No, no. It has to be a pastry or gateaux, Liz. Pastries are your trademark."

Liz flushed. "I suppose. Well, maybe I'll make my Baileys and chocolate gateau."

"I don't think I've tasted that, but it sounds perfect. I'll buy the wines to go with it."

"No, no, I'll take care of it, Steph. It's my show." Liz was looking forward to choosing the wines. Chris had always taken care of it in the past, and dismissed any of her suggestions. It had always irritated her. She had a good feeling for wines. She liked the prospect of choosing something to complement her food. Chefs rarely got the opportunity to choose their customers' wine. More's the pity. It was terrible to see someone wash down a delicate fish dish with a robust cabernet. Or team a strong game dish with a light burgundy. Sacrilege. No, this was one job that she was definitely going to enjoy. She was looking forward to impressing Edward.

Steph held up her hands. "Yes, Chef. Sorry, Chef."

Liz slapped her lightly. "Oh, Steph. This is so exciting. I can't believe I'm actually doing this."

Steph smiled. "Believe it. This time next year you'll be expanding."

"I don't know about that. I like the idea of staying small and select."

"It's not a bad ploy," Steph acknowledged. "People always want you if they think you might be unavailable. Daft, isn't it?"

"Suits me," Liz said happily.

"Hang on a minute. What about transport?" Steph didn't think that Liz's clapped-out little Fiat was up to the job. And it certainly wouldn't promote the right image.

"I'm buying a little van," Liz replied. "Dad's bringing me to see one on Friday. It's five years old but the mileage is low. It would be grand for carting around the food."

Steph looked at her in amazement. Liz had always left all the decision-making to Chris and now here she was, setting up in business, buying vans. Whatever next? "You're really on top of things, Liz. Fair play to you. I'm impressed."

"Thanks, Steph. It's gas but I feel ten years younger. It's like the early days in the restaurant. I feel in control and it's not a bad feeling at all."

"Good on you." Steph raised her glass. "To Liz Connolly of Chez Nous."

Liz lifted her glass. "To happier days," she said softly.

* * *

"How's Liz?" Seán asked sleepily.

"Unrecognisable," Steph replied, slipping out of her clothes.

"What do you mean?"

"She looks fantastic, is in great form and . . . "

"Yes?"

"She's setting up a home-catering business. She's even buying herself a van!"

Seán sat up in bed, wide awake now. "Do you think she's thought it through? It's a big step."

"She's got menus, costing sheets, projected profit and loss statements. Yes, I'd say she's thought it through." Steph patted some cleansing cream on and wiped it away with a tissue before slipping into bed beside him. "I'm telling you. She's a different woman."

"I'm glad. I like Liz and she's had a rough time with that asshole. What does he think of all this?"

"I don't know," Steph answered. "I never asked."

"I bet she hasn't told him," Seán said.

Steph felt the familiar knot in her stomach at the mention of Chris. She didn't want to talk about him anymore. "I want her to link her business to the restaurant. She's giving a dinner on Saturday for me, Edward and Conor to discuss it."

"God, I'm not gone yet and you're planning dates with other men," Seán complained.

Steph laughed and snuggled down beside him. "Poor baby."

He pulled the covers up over both of them and held her

close. "I think it's a good idea. It will add to her prestige and she certainly won't let you down."

Steph beamed at him. "That's what I thought. She's going to be an asset. You should see some of her recipes, Seán. She hasn't lost any of her creativity."

"I'm sorry I'm missing this dinner."

"No, you're not." Steph kissed his neck. "You're itching to get to Cork."

"That obvious, am I?" Seán grinned at her. "Yeah, you're right. It'll be good to see Billy again. I just hope he's OK with me. I haven't seen him since Christmas."

"He'll be fine," Steph assured him. "Especially when he sees the size of your goody bag."

Seán cringed. "Did I overdo it?"

Steph laughed. "No, of course not. Stop worrying. It's going to be fine."

Seán pulled her closer. "Thanks, Steph. You're the best."

Steph kissed him and turned to get her sleeping tablet.

Seán frowned. "Would you not try a night without them. I'm sure you'd be fine."

Steph's expression tightened. "Leave it, Seán."

"I just worry . . . "

"There's no need. They're only sleeping tablets, for God's sake! Not real drugs. Stop overreacting." She settled down as far away from him as possible.

"Sorry, love." Seán said and made to reach for her.

"Good night, Seán," she said coldly, closing her eyes.

Seán sighed and switched off the light. "Good night, love."

CHAPTER THIRTY-EIGHT

Seán caught a glimpse of red hair at the upstairs window as he walked up the driveway towards Karen. He bent down to kiss her cheek. "Hiya, Karen. You look great."

Karen tossed back her mane of red hair and smiled up at him. "How are you, Seán? It's good to see you. I'm afraid Billy's done one of his disappearing tricks."

Seán nodded towards the window above. "Has he? No point in bringing in the toys so," he said loudly.

Karen grinned. "No, probably not. You may as well come in now you're here. I'll make some tea." She led the way into the large sunny kitchen and put on the kettle. "How's Stephanie?"

Seán shrugged. "She seems fine but it's hard to know. She doesn't say too much."

"It's understandable. Give her time. How are you?"

"Sad," Seán admitted. "I think a baby would have settled us. Given us a more solid base."

Karen raised an eyebrow. "I think you've got that the wrong way around. You should have a solid base before you bring a child into the world. Surely you've learned something from our mistakes?"

Seán flushed. "We'd have done OK if . . . "

"If I wasn't such a flighty piece who wanted to enjoy life," Karen finished for him.

"I didn't say that," he said, dragging a hand through his hair.

"It's all right, Seán. I know I screwed up. I broke up this family, but I've made up for it. Billy's happy. We're doing all right."

"You're doing great," Seán said looking out at the pretty little garden, strewn with toys. "How's Mike?"

"He's fine." She sat down in the chair opposite him. "He's asked me to marry him."

Seán stared at her. "Congratulations," he said finally. Why was he surprised? Karen was a beautiful woman. She was only thirty and their divorce had finally come through. Why shouldn't she marry again? The only problem with their marriage was that she'd been too young. He'd rushed her into it. But she'd been seeing Mike Grogan for a good while now and he seemed like a nice bloke. Great with Billy. God, Billy. A new dad for Billy.

"You'll still be Billy's dad, Seán," Karen said reading his mind. "That will never change."

Seán smiled gratefully. Karen was a very understanding woman. He'd happily left Billy in her custody when they'd broken up, anxious to get back to Dublin and put his failed marriage behind him. It had taken him a couple of years to realise that he could never leave his son behind. Billy was a part of him.

"Can I have some lemonade?"

Seán looked up to see his son standing sullenly in the doorway.

"There's a word missing," Karen said, crossing to the fridge.

"Please," Billy mumbled.

Karen poured some lemonade into a Power Rangers mug and handed it to her son. "Aren't you going to say hello to your daddy?" she asked, tousling his hair.

Billy took a long, noisy drink and stared moodily at Seán over the rim.

Seán returned his stare, dumbstruck. This tall, skinny, boy with the fiery mop of curly red hair, was his son. Angry brown eyes, just like his own, stared accusingly at him. "Hiya Billy, how've you been?"

Billy said nothing and moved closer to his mother. Karen threw Seán an apologetic look.

"Why don't you show your dad your new football boots."

Seán grabbed the lifeline. "You play football, Billy? Good man. Who do you support? Liverpool?"

Billy looked at him in disgust. "Manchester United. They're the best."

Seán laughed. "Do you think so? Ah well, I suppose they're not bad. What about rugby. Do you like that?"

Billy shook his head.

"Gaelic, hurling?"

Billy shook his head again.

Karen laughed. "Soccer's his game. When he's not watching it he's playing it, or swapping cards. Football mad, aren't ya?" She grabbed her son and tickled him.

Billy giggled helplessly and Seán felt a lump in his

throat. "Why don't we all go for a walk?" he asked with a forced, nervous smile.

Billy watched him. "Can we go out to Kinsale?"

"Sure, wherever you like," Seán said, anxious to please.

"And go to McDonald's on the way home?"

"Don't push your luck, young man," Karen warned. "Go and put on your jacket."

"Ah Mum, I'm roasting."

"No arguments, Billy. Go." Karen pushed her son towards the door.

"It's gas to hear the accent," Seán said laughing.

"Oh, he's a right little Corkman," Karen agreed.

"He's got so tall. You'd think he was eight, not six."

"Almost seven," Karen reminded him.

"Time goes so quickly. He'll be a grown man before we know it."

"God, I hope not," Karen groaned.

Seán led the way out to the car and when Billy was safely belted into the back seat, he moved the car out of the narrow lane and on to the Bantry Road. "Will we open the roof?" he asked.

"Oh, yes!" Billy answered, delighted, his former moodiness forgotten.

Seán grinned at his son in the mirror and opened the sunroof. "Kinsale, here we come!"

Seán and Karen wandered along the waterfront while Billy skipped ahead of them.

"Daddy, can I have an ice cream?" Billy cried, stopping beside the Mr Whippy van.

Seán's heart lurched. "Daddy." It sounded great. "Sure,

son. We'll all have one." Seán bought three cones and obediently poured strawberry flavouring all over Billy's.

"He'll probably throw up later," Karen remarked.

"Oh, sorry," Seán said guiltily.

Karen laughed. "That's OK. It won't kill him. He's thrilled you're here, Seán. He's always talking about you."

"Really?" Seán found it hard to believe that his son had any time for him at all. Why should he? "He didn't seem too happy to see me."

"Oh, that's just an act. He's punishing you for staying away so long."

"I don't blame him. I haven't been much of a father."

Karen ignored him. "No, it's always, 'What team do you think Daddy supports?' and 'Do you think Daddy would teach me to play golf?'"

"I'd love to," Seán said fervently. "Karen, I know I've been a lousy dad, but I'd like to make up for it, see more of him."

Karen didn't answer for a moment and Seán watched her anxiously.

"I think that would be great," she said finally. "But only if you're going to keep it up. You can't drop him when the novelty wears off. I won't let you hurt him."

"I won't, I promise. I'm only sorry it's taken me so long to realise how precious he is to me. I just want to be a part of his life. I would never hurt him."

Karen smiled. "Good. I'm glad to hear it. Don't say anything to him yet, though. Let him get used to you again. He may be wary at first. He's only a little boy."

"I'll handle it whatever way you think best," Seán assured her. "I don't want to screw this up."

Karen squeezed his hand. "I'm sure you won't."

Billy ran up, breathless. "Dad? Can you make a stone hop across the water? Mike can."

Seán suppressed a wave of jealousy and crouched down beside his son. "Well, let's see." He selected a flat pebble and skimmed it across the water, making it skip three times.

"All right!" Billy squealed in delight. "Now it's my turn." He picked up a pebble and threw it, but it plopped in. "Aahh."

"Here, Billy. Hold it like this."

Karen sat down on a bench and watched father and son playing. Seán looked well. Older, but it suited him. She remembered her reaction when she'd first met him. He was gorgeous and she'd had to stretch her head back to look into those amazing brown eyes. His height and broad shoulders had always made her feel safe. He was wearing his hair much shorter these days, but the tight crop didn't disguise the strong natural wave. He was a good-looking man, but if she was honest with herself, she'd never been really in love with him and she shouldn't have married him. Still, if she hadn't, she wouldn't have Billy and that was unthinkable.

There'd been no bitterness or anger when they'd finally broken up. Just resignation and sadness. But it was different with Mike. Mike was definitely her type. Still, she was nervous of marriage and how it would affect Billy. Her son was the most important person in her life. Sometimes she thought she'd burst with love for him. It would be wonderful for him to see more of Seán. Whatever their differences, Karen was still very fond of Seán and knew he'd be a wonderful dad once he put his mind to it.

* * *

"Just one more story, Dad," Billy pleaded.

"No," Karen said before Seán caved in again. "You have to get some sleep. You've a big day tomorrow."

"OK," Billy agreed reluctantly. He didn't want to do anything to jeopardise his outing to Fota Wildlife Park. Maybe there'd be some lion cubs. It was going to be great. "Night Daddy, night Mum."

Karen kissed him and walked out of the room.

Seán bent down and hugged him. "Sleep well, champ. See you tomorrow." He turned off the light and closed the door quietly.

"Would you like a drink?" Karen asked when he joined her downstairs.

"No, I'd better get going. Are you sure you won't come with us tomorrow?"

Karen shook her head, laughing. "No, thank you. I'm going to have a lazy day. I'm going shopping and then I'm going to get my hair done and I might even meet my sister for lunch."

"Good for you. Why don't you arrange something with Mike for tomorrow evening? I'll baby-sit."

Karen stared at him. "Really?"

"Sure. I came down to spend time with him, didn't I?"

"Well, OK. If you're sure. Thanks. I'll give Mike a call, see if he's free."

"Great. That's settled then. I'll see you tomorrow. And Karen?"

"Yes?"

"Thanks for being so understanding. I'm not sure I deserve it."

"We've both had our moments, Seán. The important thing now is to put it all behind us and concentrate on Billy."

Seán kissed her cheek. "Agreed. Goodnight, Karen. And thanks again."

"Mum, you should have seen the baby tiger. It was *real* small but it'll probably grow to be bigger than me."

"Amazing," Karen said for the umpteenth time. Billy hadn't stopped chattering since he got home. He was always like this after a visit to the wildlife park. Maybe he was going to be a vet. "Why don't you get ready for your bath?"

Billy made a face. "Ah, Mum. *Gladiators* is coming on. Can't I have my bath after that?"

"No," Karen said firmly. "You know I'm going out, Billy."

"I'll look after him," Seán said from the armchair in the corner. "You go on and make yourself beautiful."

"Yeah! Great, Daddy!"

Karen frowned. "Are you sure, Seán?"

"Of course. I'll try not to drown him," Seán said, grabbing his son and tickling him.

Billy giggled. "I'll drown you!"

"Oh, will you now?"

Karen looked at them doubtfully. "I'm not sure I can trust either of you."

Seán winked at Billy. "Of course you can, can't she?"

Billy nodded, giggling again. "We'll be good, Mum."

"Mmnn. Maybe. OK. I'll trust you. But bed by nine, young man."

Billy started to complain but Seán nudged him. "Bed by nine," he promised Karen.

Karen left them in front of the TV, eating crisps and drinking lemonade. She looked back at the two heads close together. She hoped for Billy's sake that this was the beginning of a new relationship with his dad. She'd kill Seán if he messed this up.

When Karen left and *Gladiators* ended, Seán hauled Billy upstairs and ran a bath.

Billy, up to his neck in bubble bath, suddenly looked a lot younger and more vulnerable. "Daddy, why don't you live with us?"

Seán was taken aback at the question. Karen had probably answered it dozens of times already. It was important that he gave the right answer now. "Well, Billy. Mum and I weren't getting along too well. If we lived together we'd probably fight all the time. You wouldn't want that, would you?"

"No," Billy said reluctantly. "But why did you fight?"

Seán raked a hand through his hair. "I don't know, Billy. I suppose we're just very different."

"Was it because of me?" Billy's voice was barely audible.

"Oh no, son," Seán was horrified. He looked steadily into his son's eyes. "It was nothing to do with you. We tried to make a go of it because we loved you so much. But it didn't work."

"Is Mum going to marry Uncle Mike?"

"Maybe," Seán said hesitantly. "How would you feel about that?"

Billy shrugged. "Dunno. I like him. But I'd still be able to see you, wouldn't I?"

Seán felt a lump in his throat. "Of course. There's something you have to remember, Billy, no matter what happens. I'm your Dad. I always will be. I'll always be there if you need me. Mike isn't trying to take my place. He'd be your friend. A really good friend. And he'd look after you, just like me and Mum would."

Billy digested this for a moment. "Are you going to marry Stephanie?"

"I don't know," Seán said honestly. "Do you think I should?"

"Maybe. She's nice. Not as nice as Mum, of course," he said loyally.

"Of course," Seán agreed solemnly.

He told Karen of the conversation when she returned.

"I'm glad *you're* on the receiving end of the difficult questions for a change," she said smugly. "I get them on a regular basis."

"He seems to have accepted the situation. You've done a great job with him."

"He's a good kid," she said proudly.

"I'd like him to come and visit."

Karen shifted in her seat. "I know, but I'm not sure it's a good idea at the moment."

Seán frowned. Karen had been fine all along. "Why not?"

"Billy's at a very impressionable age, Seán. I've brought him up to appreciate family values. To understand the importance of marriage. I won't let Mike stay over at night.

I don't want to confuse Billy. I want him to understand the importance of love and commitment."

"So you object to Stephanie?" Seán said shortly.

"No, of course not. I just think it would confuse Billy to see you living together when you're not married. I'm sorry, Seán. I'm not trying to be difficult. I'm just doing my best for Billy."

Seán stood up. "Of course. Look, I'd better get going. I'll drop by in the morning to say goodbye."

Karen nodded. "I'm sorry, Seán. But I do feel strongly about this. You're welcome to visit *us* any time you want."

Seán tried to hide his disappointment. "Right. I'd better go. See you tomorrow." He sped away in his car, feeling angry and frustrated but he couldn't really blame Karen. She hadn't put a foot wrong with Billy so far. And having left her to bring up his son alone, he could hardly expect her to stand aside and let him take over now. So where did that leave him? Begging Steph to marry him so he could spend more time with his son? Or was he going to be forced to choose between Steph and Billy? He shook his head miserably. Why was life always so damned complicated?

CHAPTER THIRTY-NINE

Liz set down two bottles of 1982 Hermitage on the counter and went off to study the white wines. She'd decided on Pouilly Fuisse but now she wasn't so sure. Maybe a Riesling would be more suitable. She put off the decision, selecting a Sauterne to go with the desert. One bottle should be enough. She grabbed three bottles of Riesling before she changed her mind and carried them back to the counter. A bottle of cognac and vintage port completed her purchases. She blinked when the assistant told her the total figure. Oh well. It was an investment. She carried her bags carefully out to the car, where her dad sat waiting patiently.

"I thought you'd got lost," he said good-naturedly as she slipped in beside him.

"Sorry, Dad. At least this is your last chauffeuring job. I'll have the van next week." Liz had been delighted when her dad pronounced the little Peugeot van a good buy. He'd negotiated the price down another hundred pound and Liz had happily left a deposit and agreed to pick it up the following Tuesday. She could hardly contain her excitement. Things really seemed to be moving now.

"Where to now?" her dad asked cheerfully.

"The Merrion Centre, Dad. I've just a few things left to get."

"All right, love. No problem."

Two hours later, Liz waved her dad goodbye and went into her kitchen, eager to begin her preparations. Jenny had collected Lucy first thing and was keeping her overnight.

"Are you sure?" Liz had asked guiltily.

"Of course," Jenny said cheerfully. "I have to do my bit. After all, I was the one who pushed you into this."

"And I'm so glad you did," Liz said fervently.

"Good. Well, best of luck. I'll pick Lucy up at nine and you can collect her sometime on Sunday. In fact, come to lunch and tell me how it went."

Steph grinned. "I'd love to. Thanks, Jenny."

True to her word, Jenny turned up on the doorstep at exactly nine, and took an excited Lucy off for the day.

Liz consulted her list. Her first job was to prepare the salad and vegetables. She'd bought three types of lettuce that would be tossed in a simple French dressing and the lightly cooked chicken livers would be added at the last moment. She lightly rinsed the salad leaves, and left them to one side to dry.

For the main course vegetables, she was making carrot and courgette batons with baby corn. Boiled tiny new potatoes completed the meal. She'd considered doing a more complicated potato dish, but it would be too much with the stuffed lamb. She worked quickly, slicing and chopping the carrots and courgettes. They would be cooked lightly, about an hour before dinner and then refreshed just before serving. She checked her list. Next, the apricot and walnut stuffing and the crumb coating for the lamb.

When the initial food preparations were complete, Liz turned her attention to the table setting. She was considering offering clients a choice of themed evenings, extending the service to include special table arrangements. Steph had thought it was a great idea. Liz decided on a silver and midnight-blue colour scheme for tonight. It would go well with the Wedgwood blue of her dining-room walls. She'd bought silver and dark blue satin ribbon to tie around the white linen napkins and picked up some dark blue place cards, some silver paint and a tiny paint brush. After some practising, she'd done a reasonable job painting the names on to the cards, and now they sat drying on the kitchen window. Dark blue candles stood in her silver antique candelabra, a wedding present from a Chez Nous supplier. She'd spent an hour carefully pressing the white linen tablecloth yesterday and it now covered the large table, pristine and elegant. A variety of candles stood around the room. Different sizes and shapes, but all blue.

Liz opened the door of the dining-room cabinet and surveyed the glassware. Would she go for matching or individual? She decided on a more traditional look and selected four matching white-wine and red-wine goblets. To these she added four cognac balloons and some glasses for the port. She washed and polished them and set the wine glasses on the table and the others on the drinks cabinet in the sitting-room. She went back into the kitchen and checked her list. All that was left to do was to pop the lamb in the oven and then get herself organised. She'd slice up the breads just before the guests arrived and cook the chicken livers after she'd served them drinks. She took one last look at her table, poured herself a sherry and went upstairs to dress.

She'd chosen a formal navy blue velvet cocktail dress. She'd blend in with the decor, she thought smiling. The severe cut of the dress was relieved by a slit that revealed a generous amount of thigh when she walked. She'd splashed out on a pair of ultra-sheer tights and with the addition of a pair of very high suede shoes, she looked positively sexy. Her hair swung in shining waves around her face and her dark eyes shone with excitement. She put on gold earrings, sprayed herself with Chanel and ran downstairs. She had just finished lighting the candles when the doorbell rang.

"Liz! Hi! You look marvellous. The smell's gorgeous." Steph slipped a bottle into her hand and took off her jacket.

"Hi, Steph. Champers! Very nice!"

Edward stood in the doorway staring at Liz and then came forward to kiss her lightly on the cheek. "You look lovely, Liz," he said gruffly.

Liz blushed and took the bouquet of yellow roses. Her favourite.

Conor pushed pass his boss and waved a box of handmade chocolates at Liz. "Steph said these were the ones you liked."

"I love them. Thanks, Conor." Liz smiled and ushered them into the sitting-room. "Drinks?" she asked. "Sherry or something stronger."

"Sherry would be lovely," Steph said.

"G & T for me," Edward said.

"Me too. God, it's great to have someone else doing the cooking. A real novelty!" Conor stretched himself out in an armchair.

Steph sank down on the sofa. "It is, isn't it? And wait till you taste Liz's cooking, Conor."

Liz appeared with the drinks. "Please don't build me up, Steph. You'll only disappoint them."

"Not a chance," Edward said, his eyes warm.

Liz smiled back at him and sat on the edge of Steph's chair. "I bought the van."

Steph stared at her. "Crikey, that was quick."

Liz laughed. "Yeah, well Dad said it was a good buy, so I gave them a deposit and I pick it up on Tuesday."

"Brilliant. You're all set, so," Steph said happily.

"Well . . . " Liz looked at them.

"Unless you plan to poison us, Liz, we think it's a great idea." Conor raised his glass.

Edward nodded. "Absolutely. It adds a new dimension to Chez Nous. It's an exciting idea and I'm sure you'll do us proud."

Steph looked triumphantly at Liz, who was dumbstruck. "Right. Great. Well, I'll just go and check on things," she said finally and escaped to the kitchen. My God. They were going to back her. Just like that. Amazing. She put on the vegetables and melted some butter in the pan, adding a little olive oil. While it was warming, she sliced the breads she'd made that morning. White soda, brown and walnut. She arranged them in a long basket and carried it and the butter dish into the dining-room. Steph was in the kitchen when she returned.

"Everything OK? Can I do anything?"

"God, no. I'd never forgive myself if you got yourself dirty."

Steph laughed. "Do you like it?" She was wearing a richly embroidered golden knee-length cocktail dress with a mandarin collar. With her shining golden hair, she looked like an angel.

"You look stunning," Liz said without a trace of envy. She slipped on her oven gloves and lifted the lamb out of the oven.

"That smells fantastic," Steph said, "and it looks great."

"Well, that's a good start." Liz slipped some silver foil over the joint and left it to rest. Next she poured the dressing over the salad leaves and tossed them briskly. "You know I just can't believe this, Steph. Are they really serious? Are you sure you explained everything to them? They do know it's *just me* going into people's homes to cook some dinner, don't they?"

"They do," Steph assured her. "And not surprisingly it's *just you* that they're interested in. You're a damn good chef. Why wouldn't we want to be associated with you?"

"I just didn't expect it to be so straightforward, so quick. God, I could have got away with giving them steak and chips instead of going to all this trouble!"

"No chance! We're here for a super nosh-up and," Steph sniffed appreciatively, "it smells like we're going to get it."

Liz couldn't take any more of this praise. "Have you heard from Seán?"

"Yeah, he called this morning. He was taking Billy off to Fota Park for the day."

"That's a great place," Liz said, dividing the salad on to

four plates. "We brought Lucy there last year. She loved it, though she was a little afraid of the lions."

"Billy's favourites, apparently," Steph said with a grin. "Typical little boy."

"So they're getting on OK?"

"Seem to be. Seán's baby-sitting tonight. Letting Karen go out with the new man in her life."

"It all sounds very cosy," Liz remarked. "I can't imagine ever having that kind of a relationship with Chris."

Steph gave her a quick hug. "It's early days, Liz. Give it time."

Liz nodded. "Call the guys, will you? This is ready."

Steph went back to the sitting-room to call Conor and Edward and then led the way into the large dining-room. "Wow!" she paused at the door to take in the effect. "This is gorgeous, Liz."

Liz stood in the other doorway with the starters. "Do you like it?" she said.

Edward gave a low whistle. "Very elegant."

"Cool," Conor said.

Liz smiled. "Would you pour the wine, Edward?"

"Of course." Edward lifted a bottle from the ice bucket at his side and inspected the label. "Very nice," he said raising an eyebrow. "You're really looking after us tonight, Liz."

"Buttering you up, you mean. I'd have saved my money if I'd known you were going to be won over so easily."

"I'm glad you didn't," Conor said having sampled a mouthful of salad. "This is great. The chicken livers are melt-in-the-mouth."

"Try some of the walnut bread," Steph urged.

Liz beamed happily at them, but they didn't notice. They were too busy eating.

"How many psychiatrists does it take to change a light bulb?" Edward asked.

Steph shook her head.

"Only one, but the light bulb has to *want* to change."

Steph laughed. "That's a good one. Isn't it, Conor?"

"What?" Conor turned to her.

Steph rolled her eyes. "Never mind – when are you two going to stop talking about food?" She turned back to Edward. "This drunk and a giraffe walk into a pub . . ."

Liz groaned loudly. "Oh, no. Not that one. I'm going to get the cheese. Steph, make yourself useful and get the port and brandy."

"It's a good joke," Steph protested, winking at Edward before she went to get the drinks.

"Not for me," Edward said. "Unless Liz can put us up for the night."

Liz came back in and set the cheeseboard and basket of home-made crackers on the table. "No problem, as long as you don't mind sharing with Conor."

Edward shook his head. "He probably snores."

"I've never had any complaints," Conor told him. "I'll have a brandy, Steph."

"Port for me," Liz said.

"I think I'll stick with the wine," Steph said, helping herself to some brie. "That was a truly magnificent meal, Liz."

"Wonderful, Liz," Edward said. "That lamb was cooked to perfection. I just love it when it's still pink and moist."

"And the stuffing was great," Conor added. "I may add that dish to our lunch menu."

"What about the dessert?" Steph asked.

"Oh, that's definitely going on the menu. With your permission of course, Liz."

Liz stared at him. Now that was the best compliment of all. "Of course. I'd appreciate you looking through my menus, Conor."

"No problem. Let's do it now."

"Oh no you don't," Steph warned. "We've listened to you two talk food for long enough. Get together some other time. Let's relax and enjoy the rest of our evening."

Conor shrugged. "Fair enough. Give me a shout anytime, Liz. I'm sort of at a loose end these days."

"More's the pity," Edward grumbled.

"Any sign of the builders finishing?" Liz asked.

Steph frowned. "Not really. They seem to keep discovering more problems. Whether they're real or imaginary is anyone's guess."

"At least the stairs are finished and we can get back up to the office," Edward said, helping himself to a piece of Stilton. "And we should be able to get the decorators in on Monday to start work on the loos and the new dining-room."

"Well, that's not so bad," Liz said, looking at their glum faces. "Cheer up lads, for God's sake."

Edward smiled. "You're right of course, Liz. It could be worse. Let's talk about *your* business and cheer ourselves up."

"You know, I was thinking," Steph said thoughtfully. "There's one drawback to you associating yourself with Chez Nous."

Liz frowned. "What's that?"

"Publicity. Promoting your business is going to draw attention to your split with Chris."

Liz looked at her in dismay. "I never thought of that."

"Any ideas on how to deal with it, Stephanie?" Edward asked.

Steph chewed her bottom lip. "It's probably best to be up-front about it. There'll still be talk, of course, but it will be short-lived. If we say nothing, the press will have a field day."

"I couldn't handle that," Liz said, panicking slightly. "The last thing I need is journalists ringing the house, or worse, calling. What about Lucy?"

"Maybe a joint interview with you and Chris would be the best answer. If you're open about it, it takes away the mystery. The nineties couple who decide to go their separate ways, still good friends, that sort of thing." Steph twirled her glass thoughtfully. "Starting up your own business after a marriage break-up. Triumph over adversity. That'll go down really well with other women."

Liz looked at her, horrified. "That's a bit cold and calculating, isn't it?"

Steph shrugged. "If they're going to write about you anyway, you may as well turn things to your advantage."

"Steph's right, Liz," Edward said. "It'll be a storm in a teacup. Over before you know it."

"It's a good idea to do it with Chris," Conor joined in. "That will kill any gossip before it starts."

Liz looked around at her new business associates. "Right. OK. I'll talk to him. I'm sure he'll agree. It's important for him to get good press too."

"Good girl," Edward squeezed her hand.

"I think it's time we called it a night," Steph said with a yawn. "I've a load of work to do tomorrow."

"On a Sunday?" Liz stared at her.

Steph laughed. "It's all ahead of you, Liz. Weekends will be a thing of the past."

"True. Oh, what the hell, I'm looking forward to it."

"You're going to be a huge success," Conor assured her. "I'll give you a shout during the week and we'll go over those menus."

"Lovely. Thanks, Conor. And thanks to all of you for letting me use the name."

Steph waved away her thanks. "You helped make that name what it is today, Liz. Look on it as coming home."

Liz smiled. "Coming home. I like the sound of that."

Edward picked up his car keys. "OK folks, let's hit the road and let the lady get some well-earned rest. I'll call you tomorrow," he added quietly as he kissed Liz.

"OK," she whispered back. "But I'm having lunch with your sister."

"Are you, indeed? Maybe I'll invite myself along."

"Night, Liz. Thanks again." Conor wrapped Liz in a bear hug.

"Seeya, Liz. Call me." Steph blew her a kiss and followed Edward and Conor out to the car.

Liz waved as they drove away. She returned to the kitchen and surveyed the pile of washing-up. To hell with it. She closed the door on the kitchen, went into the living-room and poured herself a cognac. She curled up in an armchair and sipped her drink, thinking back on the evening and savouring every moment. The food had turned out perfectly. Conor was particularly complimentary about the lamb and Steph had loved the table decorations especially the place names. As she'd hoped, Edward had been very impressed with her choice of wines. All in all, it had been a great success. Liz felt quite pleased with herself. If she could please three such discerning and knowledgeable people, she could please anyone. "Liz Connolly of Chez Nous," she murmured. "Watch out catering world, here I come!"

CHAPTER FORTY

"Shane. Put on your jacket if you're going outside."

"Oh, *Mum*."

"You heard me." Annie ignored her son's dramatic moans.

Shane grabbed his jacket and tugged Tom West's hand. "Granddad! Come on!"

"Leave your granddad alone."

"It's OK, Annie. A bit of exercise won't kill me." Tom West went out into the garden with Shane. Joe and Seán were already kicking the ball around and Dani was running between them, shrieking with laughter. "I'll be the goalie," Tom announced.

Catherine West looked out the window. "My God, that man won't be happy until he breaks something. Sixty-six going on four!"

Stephanie laughed. "He looks fine, Mam."

"How are *you*, love?" Catherine West surveyed her only daughter. She looked lovely in a pale green trouser suit but she was as thin as a reed and very pale despite the expertly applied make-up.

"I'm fine, Mam. Can I do anything, Annie?" she asked her sister-in-law in an effort to avoid any more probing questions.

"No, thanks. Everything's done." Annie stirred the gravy and slipped the dish in beside the roast.

"It smells lovely, Annie. You shouldn't have gone to so much trouble." Catherine smiled at her daughter-in-law.

"No trouble, Catherine. So tell us about Liz's dinner party, Steph."

"It was amazing, Annie. She's going to be a huge success." Steph described the meal and the dining-room in minute detail.

"Oh, I wish I was there," Annie groaned. "It sounds wonderful."

"How's she managing without Chris?" Catherine asked.

"She's doing just fine without him," Stephanie assured her brusquely.

Catherine said nothing. Stephanie had no sympathy for Chris at all. And she couldn't really blame her. If it wasn't for him, she'd still be pregnant.

"What's she calling the business?" Annie asked as she poured them some wine.

"Liz Connolly of Chez Nous. We were only supposed to discuss it over dinner, but Edward and Conor had agreed it all in the car on the way over! It was great because then we were able to relax and really enjoy the night. Conor and Liz never stopped talking about food, and recipes." Steph rolled her eyes. "You'd think Liz had never left the business."

Annie laughed delightedly. "That's brilliant. The transformation in Liz is amazing, isn't it? Honestly,

Catherine. I know it's sad to see a marriage break up, but I honestly believe it will be the making of Liz. And Lucy's a very settled kid. I don't think she's going to have too many problems."

Steph nodded. "Yes, it's not like Chris was ever around that much. That was part of the problem."

"Well I hope you're both right," Catherine said doubtfully. "At least she's got you two and her mam and dad."

"They've been great," Steph agreed. "Her mam's done a lot of baby-sitting and her dad's been ferrying her everywhere she needs to go. Now she's got the van, he'll be able to take a well-earned rest!"

"Van?" Annie looked at her, wide-eyed.

Steph laughed at her expression. "Yeah, that was pretty much my reaction too. She wanted something sensible for carting the equipment and food about."

"So has she got rid of the car?"

"No, she's hanging on to that too. The van isn't suitable for ferrying Lucy about."

"Well, good luck to her, oh . . ." Catherine jumped as the football hit the window beside her.

"Sorry!" Seán grinned in at her. "Your grandson doesn't know his own strength."

Steph watched Seán throw the ball back to Shane and shout instructions to him. This was the happiest she'd seen him since he'd got back from Cork. He hadn't said much about his visit and he'd avoided any of Steph's questions. She wondered if Billy had rejected him. But that didn't make sense. When Seán had phoned on the Saturday, he'd been over the moon at how well he and Billy were getting on. She frowned. Something was definitely wrong and he wasn't telling her. She felt a bit hurt about that. She thought that they could talk about anything. That they had no secrets.

Annie took the roast out of the oven. "We'd better call them."

"Just as well," Catherine said drily. "Tom won't last much longer!"

Steph looked out at her father. "Oh, he's not doing so bad. How's his wrist?"

"Grand. It bothers him sometimes when it's cold or wet. Rheumatism, I suppose."

"Well, it's not bothering him today," Annie said as Tom leaped up and stopped the ball from going into the neighbour's garden. She started to carve the beef.

"Will I call them?" Steph asked.

"May as well. It will be five minutes before they hear you and another five before they heed you." Annie was well used to her family's selective hearing.

Steph laughed and let a roar out the back door. Annie was right. Adults and children alike ignored her. She put two fingers in her mouth and whistled. *"Dinner!"* she roared when she'd got their attention.

Minutes later the troop arrived in, red-faced and breathless.

"I'm starving!" Shane slipped in beside Annie and took a piece of meat.

"Hands!" Annie said, slapping him away.

Shane went off to the bathroom, chewing happily on his stolen beef.

"You OK, Dad?" Steph asked as he sat down heavily beside her.

He took a mouthful of wine. "I am now," he gasped.

Catherine shook her head. "Silly man. You're a bit old for running around like a maniac."

Tom looked affronted. "I saved two goals. And I could run rings around that pair any day." He nodded over at Seán and Joe, who were leaning against the fridge drinking cans of cold beer.

"No argument there," Seán agreed.

Annie served up the meal and everyone tucked in, the children talking excitedly between mouthfuls. Catherine looked around her. It was nice to see everyone together, happy and healthy. Her eyes fell on Stephanie and she frowned. She'd have to get her alone later. She balked at the thought. She wasn't sure how Stephanie was going to react to her news. It wasn't the best of timing. She was only just getting over losing the baby. She sighed.

"Are you all right, Mam?" Steph was looking at her.

"Fine," Catherine assured her. "Just full."

"Leave room for dessert," Annie warned. "It's Baked Alaska. Your favourite."

"Lovely." Catherine forced a smile.

When the meal was finished, the men disappeared to watch the football and the women started to clear up.

"Real nineties men," Steph said drily.

"Did you finish Shane's room, Annie?" Catherine asked as she dried the last plate.

"Yes. The carpet arrived yesterday. Go on up and have a look."

Catherine and Stephanie made their way up to Shane's room. Annie had painted the walls a warm mustard, and the door and skirting-boards a deep cream. The carpet was a tweed effect with brown and gold tones.

"Oh it's lovely," Steph said, studying the football posters over the bed. "A real boy's room."

"Isn't it?" Catherine agreed. "Ah well, he's nearly eight now. God, they grow up so fast."

Stephanie turned to leave the room.

"No wait, Stephanie. I have something to tell you."

Catherine sat down on the side of Shane's bed.

"What is it, Mam? Is there something wrong? Are you sick?" Steph looked worriedly at her mother.

"No, no, love. Nothing like that. I got a phone call during the week. From Joan McCann."

Stephanie sank down on the bed beside her. "Ruth's mother?"

Catherine nodded.

"But why? What did she want? Why call you? You hardly knew each other." The questions tumbled out of Steph as she tried to take in the news.

"She was trying to contact you but you weren't listed so she rang us."

"So what did she say? What did she want?" Steph wasn't sure why, but she felt very uneasy. Why was Mrs McCann looking for *her*? What would she want to talk about after all these years?

"She didn't say. She did tell me that Peter died last month."

"Oh. Did he? He wasn't that old." Steph had a very faint memory of Ruth's Dad. He'd never had a lot to say, retreating behind his newspaper most evenings, when he finally got home from the office. Joan McCann warned the children to leave their father in peace because he worked so hard.

"Cancer," her mother said. "Apparently he's been sick for some time."

"And she didn't say what she wanted to talk to me about?" Steph plucked nervously at the duvet.

"No. I didn't give her your number. I told her I'd get you to call her."

"Right," Steph said. "I suppose I should."

"I think you have to, love. Anyway, why not? She probably just wants to reminisce. Death has a way of reminding you of the past."

"I'm not sure I could handle it, Mam. What the hell can I say to her? 'Hiya, Mrs McCann. I went out with my boyfriend instead of going round and stopping your daughter from killing herself.' That should really console her."

Catherine patted her hand. "Don't be so melodramatic. Surely you talked about all that already?"

Steph shook her head. "No. We never really talked at all. The only time was when Mr McCann found out about Ruth's pregnancy. Even then, all he wanted was Des's name and address."

"Well, that's probably it, then. Maybe she wants to know all the details. I know I would."

"You think? But why now?"

"She's just lost her husband, Steph. She's quite young to have lost both a husband and a daughter. This is a very tough time for her."

"I suppose. How did she sound?"

"All right, but it was a very short call. Anyway, here's her number." Catherine rummaged in her pocket and produced a scrap of paper.

Steph took it and shoved it in the pocket of her jacket.

Catherine frowned. "You will call her, won't you, Stephanie?"

"Yeah. Sure. I'll do it during the week." Steph stood up. "We'd better go down."

"You're very quiet," Seán said, with a sidelong glance, on the drive home. "What's up?"

"Nothing. I'm just a bit tired."

Seán gritted his teeth. That was a load of crap. There was definitely something wrong. She'd been in a mood all afternoon. "Oh come on, Steph. I know there's something wrong. Did you have a row with your mother?"

"No, of course not. Look, I don't want to talk about it."

"You never do," he muttered.

"Well, you've been pretty secretive yourself lately," Steph retorted angrily.

"What's that supposed to mean?"

"You know damn well. You haven't told me anything about what went on in Cork and suddenly you've dropped any mention of converting the attic."

Seán said nothing. How could he tell Steph what Karen had said? She'd think he was trying to press-gang her into marriage. He was in a lose-lose situation whatever way he looked at it.

Steph took his silence as a rebuff. "Fine. If that's the way you want it." She couldn't believe his attitude. He'd never behaved like this before. He was the most open and honest man she knew. Well, next to her dad. What was he hiding from her? She sighed heavily. God, she couldn't handle this. Not on top of the bombshell her mother had just dropped. What the hell did Joan McCann want to talk to her about? Steph felt a shiver run down her back. Maybe she wanted to have it out with her. Tell her off for letting Ruth down. Well, she'd every right to. But it just seemed so weird after all this time. And for some reason, it seemed more sinister and terrifying than it would have fifteen years ago. Who was she kidding? She'd have been terrified of this confrontation at any time. In a way she'd always been waiting for the phone to ring. It was like unfinished business. She'd probably never rest until Mrs McCann screamed at her and told her what a lousy friend she'd been. She glanced over at Seán's grim expression. Now she'd even managed to alienate *him*. "No one can screw up life quite like you, kid," she thought.

CHAPTER FORTY-ONE

Edward picked his way through the workmen and went upstairs. There were two more working up here. One was painting the ladies' loos and the other was wallpapering the new dining-room. Things were looking a lot better and that God-awful stench was replaced by the smell of fresh paint. He joined Stephanie in the office. "Well? What do you think? It's not so bad up here, is it?"

"No. I'll get them to give the walls a lick of paint in here and it'll be as good as new." She flinched as Edward leaned against the blackened filing cabinet. "For God's sake, mind your suit, Edward. This place is filthy."

As usual he was impeccably and expensively dressed.

Edward carefully dusted off a chair and sat down. "Did you find the insurance policies?"

"I forgot to look," Steph admitted and pulled open the drawer of her desk. "Oh."

"What is it?" Edward watched as the colour drain from her face.

Steph took out the Mothercare bag and put it on the desk.

"*Oh*, Stephanie. I *am* sorry."

She gave a small shrug. "Don't worry about it. I knew it was bad luck buying things so soon." She drew the colourful mobile out and twirled it around.

"That's superstitious rubbish, Stephanie, and you know it."

"I suppose."

"Do you want me to go?"

She shoved the mobile back in the bag and threw it in the bin. "No, no. We've too much to do." She took out the policies and started to scan them. Edward watched her silently. She was an incredible woman for hiding her feelings. For a few seconds he'd seen raw pain in her eyes and then it was gone. Tucked away, replaced by a calm, businesslike front. He hoped she let the veil down with someone but it certainly wasn't with Liz. She'd complained about not seeing enough of Stephanie. Maybe she talked to Seán. He hoped so. It didn't do any good to bottle things up. He knew that from experience.

"Well, I'm afraid our esteemed broker was spot on," Steph said, sliding the policies across the desk.

"Not to worry. We're on top of the financial situation now. Thanks to Chris."

Steph frowned. "Let's not go overboard. I've nothing to thank that man for."

"Has Liz talked to him yet about a press interview?" Edward said, changing the subject. He knew the answer already, but Liz didn't want to broadcast their relationship, such as it was. And so he had to pretend he didn't know things when he did. It was all very confusing.

Steph shook her head. "No. She hasn't told him about

the catering business yet and she doesn't want to do it over the phone. He's due up at the weekend so she'll talk to him then."

"Good. The sooner the better. Now do you want to talk about the opening?"

"I'm afraid to," Steph admitted. "This place doesn't look as if it will ever be ready."

"They've promised us they'll be out by the end of the month."

"*If* there are no complications," Steph pointed out.

"Umm, true. Still, we have to be prepared. We need to talk to the staff and let them know when we'll need them back.

"OK. Did I tell you Jean got a job in the Italian place across the road?"

Edward raised an eyebrow. "You must be gutted."

"Devastated," Steph agreed with a grin.

"Have we lost anyone else?"

"No, amazingly enough. I think they're too busy enjoying the time off. I had a postcard from Marc. He's looking forward to coming back, thank God. I've a really good feeling about that guy."

"Great. Come on Steph, bite the bullet. Let's name a day for the opening." Edward reached up and pulled a dusty calendar off the wall. What about the end of the month?"

"But that's only three weeks away."

"Yes, and the builders will definitely be finished by then. If they finish early, we can open before then but keep the official opening as planned."

"I suppose. Well, we'd better start interviewing waiting staff and kitchen porters."

"Good. So what date, do you think?"

Steph chewed her pen and considered the calendar. "It needs to be mid-week. There's more chance of the press coming along."

"Early evening?"

"Yes. About six-thirty or seven. That way we catch the business people coming from work, who aren't willing to travel back into town."

"Right. So how about Wednesday, the twenty-fifth?"

"It's as good a date as any."

"Good. Well, why don't you call Conor and get him to organise a staff meeting?"

"OK. We can have it here, in the kitchen. What about Thursday evening? About seven?"

Edward stood up. "Fine. Right then, if there's nothing else, I'd better get back to my real job!"

Steph laughed. "They must think you've retired."

"They should be so lucky."

"Edward?"

He paused in the doorway.

"Thanks for everything. You've been great."

"Hey! It's my business too, you know. I believe in looking after my investments."

Steph ignored his flippancy. "I mean it, Edward. I'm very grateful."

Edward smiled, his grey eyes warm. "No problem, Steph. What are friends for?"

Steph smiled after him. It was hard to believe that she'd only met this man six months ago. He had turned out to be a good friend. Her thoughts were interrupted by the shrill of her mobile phone.

"Stephanie West," she answered.

"Stephanie? It's Mam."

"Hi, Mam. Are you OK? Is Dad all right?" It was very unusual for her mother to call her on the mobile.

"Yes, love, we're both fine. I just had another call from Joan McCann. She said you hadn't been in touch."

"Oh."

"She thought I'd forgotten to give you the message." Catherine West was a bit annoyed at this. As if she'd forget to pass on a message.

"I lost her number, Mam," Steph fibbed.

"Oh, I thought it must be something like that. Well, I've got it here. Have you got a pen?"

"Yeah, go ahead," Steph said and doodled while her mother called out the number.

"Have you got that?"

"Yes, Mam. Thanks."

"OK, love. You will call her now, won't you?"

"Yes, Mam."

"Right, love. See you at the weekend. Bye bye."

"Bye." Steph hung up the phone and sat staring at it. She'd thought about calling Mrs McCann every day, but she just couldn't bring herself to do it. What was she going to say to the woman? What did she want anyway? They'd never been exactly close. Not like Ruth and Catherine West. Joan McCann had had her hands full with a young family. She didn't have time to sit down for a gossip with the two girls. Not the way Catherine had – she'd poured over the Leaving Cert papers with them, advised Ruth on her Deb's dress and marked out suitable temporary jobs in the paper. Ruth spent a lot of time at the West's and so Steph had seen very little of the McCann's.

So why did Mrs McCann want to talk to her now? Steph bit her lip anxiously. Her mam must be right. It must be the death of her husband that had brought it all back. She took her wallet from her bag and extracted the crumpled piece of paper with Joan's phone number. She picked up her mobile and then put it down again. It rang, making her jump.

"Stephanie West."

"Steph, it's me."

"Hi, Seán," she said, relieved at the interruption.

"I'm in town and I was wondering if you wanted to meet for lunch?"

Steph smiled with relief. Things had been very frosty between them since the day at Joe and Annie's. It was time they put that behind them. She could barely remember what they'd argued about. "That would be nice. Where do you want to go?"

"Wait and see," Seán said and she could hear the smile in his voice. "Just don't bank on getting much work done this afternoon. I'll pick you up in an hour."

Seán rang off before she had a chance to protest. Oh, what the hell? She deserved a break. And it would be nice to share a tension-free meal for a change. It would do them both good. Feeling slightly happier she decided to bite the bullet and call Joan McCann. She dialled the number.

"Hello?" The voice was faint and tired.

"Mrs McCann? It's Stephanie West."

"Oh, hello, love. It's lovely to hear from you."

Joan's voice immediately sounded brighter and stronger.

"I was so sorry to hear about Mr McCann."

"Thanks, love. But he'd gone through a terrible time. It was a happy release, thank God."

Steph struggled for something to say. "And how are the family?"

"Grand, grand. John's working for a stockbrokers in London. He's getting on very well, and Celine just had twins. A boy and a girl."

"Celine!" Steph thought of Ruth's baby sister. But then she must be twenty-five now. "That's great news. Does she live in Dublin?"

"Oh yes. She's only around the corner. It's great. I get to see the children most days. I'm afraid I'm spoiling them, but then isn't that what grannies are for?"

Steph laughed. "It certainly is." She searched her memory for the names of the other children. "What about Brenda? Is she married?"

"God no! Brenda! I don't think any man is brave enough to take her on!"

Steph smiled, remembering the strong-willed child.

"Her career comes first. She's a senior manager in IBM. She spends most of her time in the States."

"Really! That's brilliant. Ruth always wanted to work for IBM . . . " Steph cursed silently. The words were out before she'd realised.

Joan was relaxed. "She did, didn't she? You know, Steph, she could have been anything she wanted."

"I know that. She always made me feel so brainless. She knew exactly where she was going, what she wanted to do. I never knew what I wanted."

"You've done all right," Joan remarked drily.

Steph laughed. "I have, but through accident rather than intention."

There was a small silence and Steph began to feel uncomfortable.

"I'd love to see you, Steph."

Steph swallowed hard. "Sure, yes. We must get together."

"Soon?"

Steph felt her throat go dry. "Of course, it's a bit difficult for me at the moment. I don't know if Mam told you, but we had a fire . . . "

"I'd really like to talk to you." Joan was insistent.

"Right. OK. Well, I'll call you next week and we'll arrange something."

Joan was silent.

"Mrs McCann?"

"Do you promise?" she said. She sounded like a small child.

"Of course," Steph said with a forced laugh. "It's just particularly difficult this week. I'll call you Monday or Tuesday and we'll set something up."

"OK, love. I'll look forward to it. We need to talk. Bye now. Take care of yourself."

"Bye Mrs McCann." Steph put down the phone with a trembling hand. *We need to talk.* What did that mean?

* * *

"The vegetable terrine sounds nice, doesn't it, Steph? Steph?"

Steph looked up at Seán. "Sorry?"

392

"What's wrong, Steph? You've hardly said two words since I met you. You're not still annoyed with me, are you?"

Steph shook her head. "No, no, of course not. Sorry. I'm just a bit preoccupied."

"I can see that. Talk to me."

"It's Ruth's mother," Steph said.

"What?" Seán looked confused.

"Ruth's mother," she repeated. "She wants to see me."

"Why?"

Steph shrugged. "I don't know why. I was talking to her this morning. She contacted Mam asking me to get in touch. I kept putting it off."

"Until today."

Steph nodded. "Her husband died. Mam says that's probably what started her thinking. Brought all the memories back."

"So when are you going to see her?"

"I don't know. I told her I'd call her next week and set something up, but I'm not sure I can do it."

He stared at. "You have to, Steph. You can't let the woman down."

Steph looked at him angrily. "And what the hell am I supposed to say?" she hissed.

Seán shrugged. "Whatever she wants you to say, whatever she needs to hear. It's her right, Steph. You have to do it."

Steph said nothing. How could she explain to him how terrified she was? How could she make him understand how she felt?

"You'll feel better once you get there, Steph. It may even help you. Exorcize some of those ghosts."

"Maybe," she said doubtfully.

"Definitely," he assured her, squeezing her hand. "Do it for Ruth, Steph. Do it for your best friend."

Steph stared at him for a moment and then nodded resignedly. "Yes. Yes, OK, I will."

CHAPTER FORTY-TWO

Chris looked out into the garden. The lawn was trim, the barbecue tucked in beside the shed for the winter in its all-weather cover. Everything in its place. He felt sad as he realised that he was now completely dispensable. Liz was moving on without him. There would be no reconciliation. He hadn't realised how much he'd loved his home until Liz had thrown him out. Now as he tried to make a life for himself in Galway, he understood the difference between a house and a home. No matter what he did to the flat, it still looked alien. He felt like a visitor. The only thing he'd really got enthusiastic over was Lucy's bedroom. Liz would have laughed if she'd seen his attempts at decorating. Still, after botching a couple of sheets of wallpaper he'd got the hang of it and the end result didn't look bad at all. He turned around as Liz walked into the kitchen. He couldn't get over how well she was looking. When she'd first open the door he'd been dumbstruck. She looked great! So vibrant and full of life and happy. Yes, that was it. She looked happy.

"Sorry about that. The phone never seems to stop these days. I should have left the answering machine on. I've put it on now, though, so no more interruptions. Would you like some coffee?"

"Yeah, great." Chris sat down in his usual seat at the kitchen table. "So how are things? Any news?"

"Yes, quite a lot actually." Liz busied herself with the mugs. She felt unaccountably nervous about telling Chris about the business. She was expecting him to ridicule the idea and she wasn't sure she'd be able to handle it. She made the coffee and carried the mugs to the table. "I'm starting a catering business, Chris. Catering for private dinner parties, that kind of thing."

Chris stared at her. "You're what?"

Liz bristled. "You heard," she said curtly, fidgeting with a spoon.

"That's great."

Liz blinked. "What?"

"I think that's a great idea. It would suit you to perfection. You never did want to work full-time while Lucy was small. This way you can do most of the work at home."

Liz stared at him. "That's right. I promise, Lucy won't be neglected."

Chris laughed. "God, I know that, Liz. You've always put Lucy first. You expected me to be against this, didn't you?"

"Well, yes I did," she admitted. "I thought you'd think I wasn't up to it."

Chris sighed. "Well, I suppose if I'm to be honest, I wouldn't have liked it if we were still together. It's your own fault, though. I liked coming home to find you here. I'd have hated coming home to a cold empty house."

"You sound like a schoolboy," Liz said with a grin.

Chris scowled. "Would you like me to take a look at your menus? I could give you a few pointers."

Liz grimaced. This was more like the Chris she remembered. "I think I'm on top of it."

"Well, I'd be happy to give you some advice . . . "

"I'll call you if I'm in trouble," she promised, thinking Chris was the last person she'd call.

"So when do you start? Where are you going to advertise?"

Liz explained her arrangement with Chez Nous and how the idea had started the evening in Jenny's. She didn't mention that Jenny was Edward's sister. No point in antagonizing him.

"That makes sense," Chris said grudgingly. "Using the name will give you a lot of prestige. So have you any bookings yet?"

"Three. The first is for Edward McDermott. He wants to entertain some of his business associates."

Chris grunted.

"Then there's a friend of Jenny's. A girl who was at the party that night and then I've a provisional booking from Madge McCarthy. You remember her? She owns the newsagent's in the village."

"Word of mouth. That's going to be your best advertisement."

"Yes, that's what I thought."

"You should talk to someone in the press too. When Steph reopens there's sure to be a few of them knocking around. Make sure you get a plug in for your business."

"Ah, yes. Well, I wanted to talk to you about that. Steph

thinks we may become the focus of some of the gossip columnists. When they know I'm starting my own business, they'll realise that we've broken up and that you've gone to Galway alone."

"Oh, shit. I hadn't thought about that."

"No, neither had I."

"Still, any publicity is better than none."

"Yes, but what about Lucy? I don't want journalists coming near the house. What if they tried to talk to *her*?"

"I'd bloody kill them."

"Steph thought we might avoid all of that if we gave a joint interview to one journalist. Someone we could trust. You know, take all of the mystery away."

Chris snorted. "Modern Ireland. The couple who support each other in separation."

Liz laughed. "It does sound a bit silly."

"No, it's a good idea. I'll give Adam Cullen a call. He could do it. He's fair. He won't print anything that we haven't agreed. I'll see if he can talk to us tomorrow."

Liz was taken aback. "So soon?"

"The sooner the better. We better get our stories straight. Decide what we want to discuss."

"He'll probably want to talk about the fire," Liz said nervously.

The press had spent a few days trying to get to the bottom of the Chez Nous fire. Stephanie had announced, following the re-negotiation of Chris's contract, that it had been an unfortunate accident and that no one was to blame. The press had reluctantly accepted this, but there were still some rumours flying around.

"I'll deal with that," Chris said firmly. "Adam's a mate.

He won't push it." He stood up. "Right then. I'll try and organise that and then I'll drop back later and we'll prepare our script."

"Thanks, Chris. And Chris?"

He paused in the doorway.

"When I get the business going, we'll talk about the maintenance again. I shouldn't need as much."

"That's OK, Liz," he said gruffly. "Lucy's my daughter. I want the best for her. Don't ever worry about money. It's not important." He patted her arm awkwardly and let himself out of the house.

Liz sank back into her chair. Who'd have thought a couple of months ago that they'd be able to have such a reasonable conversation? Chris had even been reasonable about her starting her own business. She'd been sure he'd laughed at her, tell her she'd fail. Support was the last thing she'd expected.

Maybe he'd changed. Liz was overcome with doubts. Maybe she should give him another chance. Maybe she'd acted hastily. She should seriously think about going to Galway. For Lucy's sake. Her heart sank at the thoughts of leaving behind her business. She didn't want to go back to just being somebody's wife. She wanted to be someone in her own right. She wanted to stand on her own two feet. Damn it. However much Chris changed, it would never change the way she felt. If she took him back, it would only be for Lucy's sake. Was that a good enough reason? Liz knew she'd end up resenting Chris. Anyway, leopards don't change their spots. It wouldn't take long before he reverted back to the old Chris. No, this was no time for doubts. She was doing what was best for her, what was best for Lucy. It would be great if she maintained a good relationship with Chris, but their life together was over. It was time Liz Connolly moved on and stood on her own two feet.

* * *

At three o'clock in the Shelbourne the following day, Chris stood and shook hands with Adam Cullen. "Thanks for coming, Adam. We appreciate it."

"Not at all." Adam bent and kissed Liz's cheek. "I'll fax you a copy of the article before I print it. Best of luck in Galway, Chris. And think about what I said, Liz. It would make a great article. See you both."

When he was gone, Chris signalled the waiter and ordered more drinks. "Well, I thought that went well."

"Great," Liz agreed. "I can't believe he wants to spend a whole evening following me around just to do an article."

"It would be even better on television," Chris mused.

"God, no. What if something went wrong. I'd be ruined."

Chris laughed. "Maybe. Still, it's worth thinking about. I told you he'd be OK, didn't I?"

"I'll reserve judgement until I see the article." Liz was nervous around journalists although Adam was obviously a very nice guy.

"God, you're awful suspicious, woman. Come on. Let's drink to success."

Liz smiled and raised her glass. "To success. For both of us."

CHAPTER FORTY-THREE

Jenny walked into the dining-room and gave a small gasp. Edward chuckled.

"Great, isn't it?"

She walked around the polished mahogany table, taking in the gleaming silver tableware, the crystal glasses and the rich crimson-coloured napkins. A crystal bowl of dark red tea roses completed the sophisticated picture. "It's marvellous," she breathed. She'd always felt this room was a little too austere, what with its dark wood, crimson walls and heavy cream drapes. But the candles around the room created a soft, warm effect. "Where's Liz?"

Edward raised an eyebrow. "Where do you think?"

Jenny went out to the kitchen. "How's it going?"

Liz jumped. "Oh! Jenny! Not too bad."

"The dining-room looks magnificent," Jenny said.

"Do you think so?" Liz asked anxiously. "It's a beautiful room. I hope I didn't overdo it."

"Not at all," Jenny assured her. "What are we eating? It smells gorgeous."

"Brill and crab terrine to start, followed by Confit of Duck, then cheese and orange liqueur soufflés."

Jenny licked her lips. "Sounds wonderful. Do you need any help?"

Liz looked around her. "I don't think so."

"Will you be joining us?"

Liz looked horrified. "God, no."

"For coffee," Edward said joining them.

"Oh, I don't think . . ."

"The point of the evening, Liz, is to introduce you. You can join us after you've served the dessert." Edward looked her straight in the eye.

Liz looked away from the intensity of his gaze. "OK," she said faintly.

"So who's coming?" Jenny asked. "Am I going to be bored out of my mind?"

"It shouldn't be too bad. Tim and Susan Wallace will be there."

"Oh, good." Jenny liked Edward's partner.

"John Moriarty and partner."

Liz gasped at the name of one of the largest property developers in the country.

"And a guy called Philippe Bacoux. He's a restaurateur from Antwerp," Edward continued calmly.

"Oh, Edward! How could you? Talk about throwing me in at the deep end!"

"I wouldn't do it if I didn't think you were up to it," he said smoothly.

The door bell rang and Liz jumped.

"Come on, hostess. Let's do it!"

Jenny winked at Liz and followed her brother out into the hall.

Liz closed the door after them and consulted her list once more. Her hands were shaking. "Calm down, woman. Everything's under control." She cut the bread and made butter curls and carried them into the dining-room. She took a quick look around, polished a knife, re-arranged a rose and went back into the kitchen. Edward wanted the starter served twenty minutes after the last guests arrived, and the duck needed another fifteen minutes so there was nothing to do but sit and wait. She wondered what it would be like to work for Edward. She'd seen a different side of him this week. He'd very fixed ideas about what he liked. He'd organised the wines himself, though he'd discussed them with her first. She was delighted when they'd agreed on the selection. Even now, she still suffered the odd crisis of confidence. Except when she was in the kitchen. Then she felt in control. The doorbell rang again.

Jenny's head appeared around the door. "Everyone's here, Liz."

Liz jumped up nervously. "Fine. I'll call you in twenty minutes."

When the starters were ready, Liz took a deep breath and opened the double doors between the dining-room and living-room.

Edward stood up. "Ah, Liz. People, I'd like you to meet our chef, Liz Connolly of Chez Nous."

Liz smiled shyly. "If you'd like to move inside . . . "

She stood aside as the guests entered the room, and went to collect the tray of starters.

There were murmurs of approval as she set the plates

403

down in front of them. "Enjoy your meal," she said quietly and withdrew.

The next hour went by in a whirl of activity for Liz, but the dining-room was calm and relaxed.

"Lovely meal, my dear," John Moriarty remarked as she took his plate.

"Excellent sauce," the restaurateur said with respect.

Edward beamed at her. "Why don't you bring in the cheese and desserts together, Liz, and join us?"

Liz looked doubtful but Tim smiled at her. "Please do."

Liz smiled back. "I'd love to."

She put on the coffee and took the soufflés out of the fridge. She added some grapes to the side of the cheese board and filled a silver basket with home-made biscuits. Edward's Denby china coffee service and a plate of petit fours stood on a silver tray in readiness. She carried in the tray of desserts first and went back for the cheese. Edward had already set the heavy crystal decanter of vintage port and the bottle of Beaume de Venise on the table. Decorum was forgotten as the guests eyed the dessert and Liz smiled as she served.

When he'd finished eating, Edward slipped out of the room and returned with the coffee tray.

Jenny put down her spoon and sank back in her chair. "I don't think I'll be able to eat for a week."

"It was a lovely meal," Mrs Bacoux agreed with a warm smile.

"You used to work for Chez Nous?" her husband asked.

"Liz started the business with her husband," Edward interjected quickly. "I firmly believe it was her desserts that secured them the Michelin Star!"

Everyone laughed and Liz felt her cheeks get hot. "I left

the restaurant some years ago to look after my daughter. Now I'm interested in a different challenge. Also, in the current economic environment, I believe there are a lot of people who want to entertain at home but just don't have the time."

"Amen to that," Susan Wallace said. "I'm long overdue to give a dinner party but with all the commuting to London I just don't have time. We must have a little chat later, Liz."

Liz nodded happily and Jenny smiled triumphantly.

Philippe asked her about the restaurant scene in Dublin and Liz talked knowledgeably, forgetting her shyness now they were on a topic that she loved.

Three hours later, tired but happy, she packed away the last of her equipment in the back of the van. Edward was at the door with Jenny when she returned.

Jenny gave Liz a quick hug. "Well done again. You were amazing. I'll call you during the week."

"Drive carefully, Jen," Edward said as he held the car door for her. "And thanks again."

"No problem," Jenny assured him. "I'll be your hostess any time if I get to eat food like that! Seeya."

They waved her off and returned to the kitchen.

"I'd better be off myself," Liz said regretfully, unwilling to let the evening come to an end.

Edward took her hand and led her into the living-room. "Not yet. Let's have a cognac first. I'm too wound up to sleep."

Liz curled up on the sofa while he poured the drinks. "Was it really OK, Edward?"

"Stop fishing for compliments. You know it was." He

handed her a drink and stretched out beside her. "You were a big hit with Philippe, that's for sure."

"He's an interesting man. Though a little overbearing."

Edward laughed. "A lot of people would agree with you. He's not an easy man to do business with. He thinks we're all philistines who don't understand the restaurant business."

Liz frowned. "He can't say that about you. You're part-owner of one of Dublin's most successful restaurants."

"Well, until tonight he thought that was merely a wise investment. Now he knows different. Thanks, Liz. It's all down to you."

"I think that might be an exaggeration, Edward, but thank you. I've really enjoyed myself." She looked around the living room appreciatively. The fire was nothing more than glowing embers now, but it cast a warm glow on the rich buttermilk walls and cream rug. "This is a lovely room. Did you decorate it yourself?"

There was a small silence.

Liz looked at the closed expression on Edward's face. "I'm sorry, I didn't mean to pry . . . "

"Not all, Liz. It was decorated by Christina, my fiancée."

Liz stared at him. "I didn't know you had one," she said, feeling slightly shocked. How come Annie or Jenny had never mentioned her?

"I don't. That is, I did." Edward passed a weary hand across his eyes. "She died."

"I'm sorry," Liz said, not knowing what else to say. "Was she ill?"

Edward looked at her over the rim of his glass. "No. She was killed in a car crash. She was with my brother-in-law."

It took Liz a moment to take in the significance of his words. "Jenny's husband? Oh, God, Edward. I'm so sorry." She put down her glass and took his hand.

Edward gave a short laugh. "Yeah, well. It's a long time ago."

"Had you any idea? Did you suspect anything?"

"No. No more than you, I thought we were perfectly happy. Don't get me wrong, it was a stormy relationship. We broke up more than a dozen times. Christina used to say it was what made us so great together. I kept asking her to marry me, to settle down, but she said life was too short. Then after one particularly angry bust-up, she came back, we made up yet again and she said she wanted to get married. In hindsight, I realised that her change of heart coincided with my becoming a partner."

Liz looked at the bitterness in his eyes. "Don't think like that, Edward. You were together a long time. I'm sure she must have loved you."

"Umm. Maybe. But the money and status helped. It was harder for Jen. She was crazy about Finbarr. Couldn't believe he'd been unfaithful. It took her a while to accept it. She came up with all sorts of excuses as to why they might have been together. Then she blamed Christina. Mind you, she's probably right there. Christina loved to live dangerously."

"When were you supposed to get married?"

"Two months after the accident. It was awful. The invitations had already gone out and there was no way of hiding the circumstances of the accident. A lot of people found it hard to look me in the eye. They were more embarrassed than I was."

Liz squeezed his hand. "I can't begin to imagine how you felt. I was devastated over Chris, and I don't even know he actually *did* anything."

Edward watched her steadily. "You do know, Liz. You knew that night."

Liz thought for a moment. "You're right. The bastard."

Edward laughed. "That's a good healthy attitude."

Liz laughed too. "Well, whatever else about Christina, she had good taste. But I'm surprised you wanted to stay in this house. It must have a lot of painful memories."

Edward shrugged. "It's been my home for fifteen years. I love it here. I was quite happy with the decor the way it was but Christina thought it was boring. It was easier to give in."

Liz looked at him with raised eyebrows. "I can't imagine you ever giving in to anyone!"

Edward pulled her close and smiled down into her eyes. "Oh, you'd be surprised."

Liz held her breath. His lips were very close and she had a sudden urge to pull his head down to hers. She pulled back, alarmed at the intensity of her feelings. "I'd better be going."

"Oh, no." Edward held her as she attempted to stand up. "Not like that, Liz. I played all my games with Christina. I want everything to be out in the open between us."

She watched him silently.

"I am very, very fond of you, Liz. I know you're not ready for a relationship yet, and I even accept that you may never want one again. I can understand that. That's why I wanted to tell you about Christina. I've been there. I've been hurt too and you have to understand that I will never do anything to hurt you or Lucy."

Liz's eyes filled up as she wondered what on earth she'd done to deserve this wonderful, kind man. She hugged him quickly. "I know that, Edward and I'm very grateful. I'm fond of you too. But I won't lie to you, I'm not ready to get involved. I feel so much better these days, and I'm thrilled that Lucy's adjusting so well. Right now I want to concentrate on her and the business. I need to feel in control again. Do you understand that?"

Edward took her hand and kissed the tips of her fingers. "Yes, Liz, I do. I really admire you. You're an amazing woman."

She flushed. "I don't know about that. But I'm certainly going to try and make a go of things and then, well, maybe . . . "

"Sssh. Don't. I'm not going anywhere. Let's agree to be best friends and just take things as they come."

Liz smiled. "Best friends. I'd like that."

CHAPTER FORTY-FOUR

Stephanie walked through the restaurant, tweaking the odd napkin and polishing a place setting. Except for the faint smell of paint, everything was back to normal and they would re-open their doors tomorrow. She moved into the passage that had been fully re-decorated and now boasted a new store-room. The mains box now had its own cupboard in the hallway, where it was easily accessible. The bannisters of the new mahogany staircase gleamed and a rich dark green carpet covered the stairs. The same carpet was used in the new private dining-room upstairs. Stephanie went into the kitchen and smiled in satisfaction at the hive of activity before her. Kitchen porters were running everywhere, and Conor was going through the vegetable order.

Steph picked her way through the madness. "Isn't Kevin here yet?" It was supposed to be the new *chef de partie*'s first day.

Conor grinned. "Been and gone. I've sent him out to get a few things from the Asian Market."

"I see. How's it going?"

"Not too bad. One of the freezers is on the blink, but there's a guy on his way over to take a look at it. The meat is due in half an hour and the fish will be in by ten in the morning."

"Right. Well, if you need me, I'll be in the office." She went upstairs and paused to check the ladies' toilets. The cleaners had got rid of all the dust and paint marks and polished everything until it shone. A pile of new fluffy lemon towels sat on a wicker shelf next to the washbasins, and tissues, hand-cream and perfume stood on the dressing-table. Several lemon satin cushions sat in the matching wicker chair. Stephanie looked around her, pleased with the overall effect. The three C's. Classy, cool and clean. She left the room and went into the new dining-room. She'd asked a friend in the antiques business to watch out for a suitable table and Terry had done her proud. The dark mahogany table was substantial and impressive. It had been expensive but Terry had picked up thirty chairs to complement it and got them at a bargain price. They were a cheaper wood, but stained to match the table and they were upholstered in a rich cream and green paisley brocade. The walls were also dark green and the skirting-boards and door were a pristine white. Stephanie had added bowls of flowers, six silver candelabras and some prints of Irish landscapes. The overall effect was of an old-fashioned sophisticated dining-room in a private house. She closed the door and went into her office.

A good clean and a lick of paint had restored the room to its former state. The darkened filing cabinet was the only physical reminder of the fire. Stephanie made a mental note to replace it. She sat down at her desk and reviewed her 'To Do' list. There was a Health and Safety official arriving in an hour. She wasn't expecting any problems there. The insurance company had already been through the place with a fine tooth comb. When he was gone, she would address the staff. There were a total of ten new people which made her nervous. There was a week to go before the opening but it was likely that some critics would pay a visit before then. Among them, representatives of the Michelin Guide. She made a note to remind staff of this. There was a sharp rap on the door and Liam Dunne stuck his head around it. "How's it going?"

"Liam! I wasn't expecting you yet."

He perched on the edge of her desk. "Ah, I wanted to have a look around and settle in before my troops arrived."

"I hope they're going to work out," Steph said anxiously.

"Well, all we were short of doing was inspecting their toenails," he said with a grin. "Don't worry. They're coming from good restaurants and we've personal references on all of them."

"True. I want to mention to them about the likelihood of visiting critics in the next couple of weeks."

"I've already mentioned it," Liam said. "But I told them that the service should be outstanding regardless."

Steph smiled at the earnest young man. What a difference to Sam! "Good man. That's what I like to hear!"

"Right. Well, I'll get to work."

He ran down the stairs whistling and Steph thought how nice it was to have things back to normal again. The phone rang beside her.

"Stephanie West?"

"It's Seán, boss," Liam's new assistant Brian put the call through.

"Seán?"

"Hiya, Steph. How's it going?"

"Not bad. We're fairly organised. But then that probably means I've forgotten something."

Seán laughed. "Murphy's Law. Listen, will you be in tonight?"

"Well, I've a meeting with Conor and Liam, but I should be home by about eight. I don't really want to go anywhere though, Seán. Tomorrow's going to be quite a day."

"Oh, that's OK. I was just checking. It's just that Karen and Billy are up for a few days and I was going to ask them over."

Steph groaned inwardly. All she wanted to do tonight was have a hot bath and then curl up in front of the TV with a glass of wine. "Oh, I don't know, Seán. I'm really knackered . . . "

"Fine," he said abruptly. "I'll take them out. See you."

"Seán? Seán?" Steph heard the dial tone and hung up. Shit! That's all she needed. God, his timing was incredible. Tonight of all nights. How could he be so inconsiderate? Oh, to hell with him! Let him play happy families. Her phone rang again but this time it was the wine merchant's. She turned her attention back to work and put Seán firmly to the back of her mind.

Stephanie looked around the room. "Any other questions? No? Conor, have you anything to add?"

"I'd just like to say a word of thanks to everyone for all

the hard work. The fire was a terrible business and now we can put it behind us and concentrate on putting Chez Nous firmly back on the map."

"Here, here!" John Quigly said in an uncharacteristic burst of enthusiasm. He flushed as Steph stared at him in surprise.

"I'd also like to wish Stephanie all the very best," Conor continued. "And to assure her that I will be working my butt off."

"You better," Steph retorted to cover her embarrassment and everyone laughed. "OK folks, let's call it a night. Go home and get some rest, and we'll see you tomorrow. Oh, by the way, for those of you on the early shift, we'll be having a small celebration tomorrow night after closing. You're welcome to come back in if you have the energy."

There was a small cheer and the staff started to gather their belongings.

"Conor? Liam? A word in my office?" Stephanie led the way upstairs. "Well, Conor. Are we ready?" she asked.

"I think so." Conor stretched out in a chair. "I don't foresee any problems in the kitchen." He glanced sideways at Liam. "It's the new waiters I'm more concerned about."

Liam reddened. "They know what they have to do and they're all very experienced."

Steph shot a warning glance at Conor. Why was there always this aggravation between kitchen and front-of-house staff? She sighed. "I'm sure everything will go smoothly."

An hour later, she locked up and headed for the car. She was tired but energised. Happy that things were back to normal. She wondered guiltily what Seán was doing. She should really have called him back. She looked at her watch. Seven-thirty. It wasn't too late. She punched Seán's number in on her mobile, but his phone was switched off. Damn. Oh, well, she'd make it up to him. Maybe he could bring Karen and Billy into the restaurant for lunch tomorrow. Yes, that would be brilliant! Billy would enjoy it and Seán would be thrilled she'd thought of it. She hummed happily to herself as she turned into the driveway but stopped abruptly when she saw Billy standing on the doorstop, his hand held by a beautiful red-head. Karen. Stephanie got out of the car and smiled nervously. "Hello, Billy. Karen?"

The girl nodded. "Yes. Hello, Stephanie. Sorry for turning up on your doorstep like this. I'm afraid we missed Seán."

"Not to worry. Come on inside and we'll try to get in touch with him." She opened the door and led the way into the hall. "Where were you supposed to meet?"

"Outside McDonald's in Grafton Street at six, but we got held up . . . "

"Mummy got lost," Billy said loudly.

Karen swatted his behind. "Yes, I got lost. I admit it. I always do when I come to Dublin," she admitted ruefully.

Steph laughed. "I'm the same in Cork. All those one-way systems. Where are you staying? Maybe Seán went there."

"Yeah, maybe. We're staying in Jurys. Can I use your phone?"

Steph waved her towards the phone in the living-room and took Billy into the kitchen for coke and biscuits. "So, Billy. What do you want to do while you're in Dublin?"

"Go to the zoo," he said without hesitation.

"It may disappoint you after Fota Park."

"Naw. They've got snakes and stuff like that. It'll be cool."

Steph laughed. It was uncanny the resemblance between Billy and his father. He had his mother's fiery mop, but apart from that he was his father's son. The same amazing brown eyes stared back at her and he ruffled his hair in the same impatient way.

Karen walked into the kitchen. "He was there all right. He left word for me to call his mobile. But I tried that and couldn't get through."

"Me neither. His battery must be flat. Did you leave word in case he called again?"

"Yes. I said we were here. But I don't want to hang around, Stephanie. I know you've a tough day tomorrow."

Steph flushed guiltily. "Not at all. It gives me an excuse to open a bottle of wine without feeling guilty. Billy, would you like to watch TV?" Steph led the little boy into the living-room and when he was happily engrossed in *Star Trek*, she returned to the kitchen and opened the wine.

"Well, it's nice to finally meet you." Karen took the glass from Stephanie. "Put a face to the voice. But again, I'm sorry for just landing on you like this. I'm sure it's the last thing you need tonight of all nights."

Steph smiled. Why couldn't Seán have thought of that? Why was it only women who considered these things? "Don't worry about it. I could do with the company. It stops me thinking about tomorrow and what might go wrong."

"You must be thrilled to be back in business again.

416

What with the fire and everything you've had a terrible time. I was so sorry to hear about your miscarriage.

For some reason the thought of Seán discussing her miscarriage with his former wife irritated Steph. "Thanks. It was awful, but now things are back to normal," she said with a forced smile.

"Tomorrow isn't the official opening, is it?"

"No. That's next week. I'll be on Prozac by then!"

Karen laughed. "I don't know how you do it. I'd never be able to handle that kind of responsibility and pressure. Billy causes me enough stress as it is!"

Steph's expression softened. "I'm not sure I really believe that. He's a great kid. Seán enjoyed his weekend in Cork. He's looking forward to spending a lot more time with him."

"He's very good with Billy," Karen admitted. "And I must say it makes it easier for me if he's going to play a more active part in Billy's life."

"How do you mean?" Steph said.

"Well, Mike, that's my boyfriend – God, that sounds so juvenile!" She laughed. "He's asked me to marry him. I wasn't sure what to do, how it would affect Billy. But if Seán plans to be around a bit more, I think it will be OK."

"In that case, congratulations." For some reason the idea of Karen safely married to someone else made Steph feel a lot happier. "We'll be happy to have Billy here any time. Seán's planning to convert the attic into a special room for him."

Karen looked at her curiously. Seán obviously hadn't told Stephanie her views on Billy staying in Dublin. "That's nice," she murmured.

"So when are you getting married?"

"Oh, as soon as we can get organised, I think. Now that the divorce is through there's no reason to wait."

Steph stared at her and then looked away quickly. "That's true. Well, I hope it all works out for you."

Karen saw the look of surprise on Stephanie's face and realised she'd put her foot in it. Why in God's name had Seán not told Stephanie about the divorce? What was he up to? Maybe everything wasn't rosy in the garden after all.

The awkward silence was interrupted by the phone. Steph picked up the extension in the kitchen. "Hi, Seán. Yes, I know. They're here. OK. Yeah. OK, see you then. Bye." Steph hung up. "He's on his way. Now, tell me. Does Billy still love fried chicken?"

"By the bucketful," Karen said with a grin.

"Right. Then that's what we're having for dinner."

"Oh no, Steph it's OK, we'll go out . . . "

"Nonsense," Steph said firmly. "It will do me good to keep busy. Anyway. I'm starving and I love fried chicken too."

"You're not really nervous about tomorrow, are you?" Karen was surprised. This beautiful and sophisticated woman looked like very little would rattle her.

"A bit. And it's silly, really. I know it will be a total anti-climax. Listen, I was wondering. Why don't you and Billy come to lunch tomorrow? Seán could bring you. It would give you a chance to catch up."

Karen looked surprised. "Well, I don't know . . . "

"You'd be doing me a favour. I could do with filling another table. And I can promise Billy a kid's special."

Karen smiled. "Well, what the hell? Why not? I've never ate in a restaurant with a Michelin Star before."

"Well, I'll make sure we live up to your expectations. Let me know what time suits you and I'll set it up."

By the time Seán arrived the smell of fried chicken filled the house and the two women were working together and chatting comfortably.

"Hi, Seán," Steph said with forced casualness. "Grab your son and sit down. Dinner's ready."

After a fairly relaxed meal, Seán waved Karen and Billy off, having agreed to pick them up for lunch at one the next day. "Thanks, Steph," he said as he climbed into bed beside her. He reached for her but she slipped out of his reach.

"No problem. Night, Seán."

He looked at her back, puzzled. What had he done now? "Good night, love."

CHAPTER FORTY-FIVE

"Stephanie? Can I bring in a party of six for lunch, at say, twelve-thirty?"

"Edward? Absolutely. I'll be happy to fill another table."

Edward frowned at his end of the phone. "Is there a problem? You put the advertisement in *The Times* didn't you?"

"For the full week, but it's very slow. Still, it's only Tuesday."

"True. Right, well I'll see you later."

Steph hung up, but before she lost the nerve she picked up the phone again. "Hello? Mrs McCann? It's Stephanie West."

"Oh hello, dear. How are you?"

"Fine thanks. Sorry I didn't call sooner but it's been really busy."

"That's OK, Stephanie. So when are you coming to see me?"

Right down to business, Steph thought grimly. "I thought one afternoon next week."

"Good. What about Wednesday?" Joan McCann wasn't letting her get away this time.

Steph opened her mouth to protest. Wednesday was the opening. Still, that would be an excuse to get away early. "That's fine. Say about three?"

"I'll have the kettle on. See you then, dear."

Steph hung up. Well, she'd finally done it. She was very nervous at the thought of the visit, but it was only one hour out of one afternoon. It wouldn't kill her. The phone rang again, making her jump.

"Hi, Steph. Are you all set?"

"Hi, Liz. Yeah, I think so. It's very quiet though. Only five tables for lunch and two of them are Edward and Seán."

"Six," Liz said. "Me and Liz are coming in. Is one-thirty OK?"

"Great! A few more relatives and friends and I might actually fill the place."

Liz heard the nervousness in Steph's voice. "Don't worry, Steph. It's only the first day."

"Yeah, you're right."

"Listen, did you see yesterday's *Independent*?"

"I'd a quick look," Steph said vaguely. "Why, was there something important?"

"Adam Cullen's piece on me and Chris."

"Oh, Liz. Was it OK?"

"It was great, Steph. I'll bring it with me at lunch-time and let you have a look at it."

"Oh, do! I'm delighted for you. That will really take the pressure off."

"Hopefully. Listen, I'd better go. I'll see you later."

As Steph hung up Liam walked in and slumped into a chair. "It's going to be a very quiet lunch," he said glumly.

"It won't be too bad, Liam. I've just booked in two more parties. One of six and one of two."

"Great stuff. And things are looking good for tonight. A crowd of Americans just stuck their heads in and made a booking. A party of ten, no less."

"That's brilliant! Well, I'm going down to talk to Conor. Tell him the good news."

"Good luck," Liam said darkly.

Steph frowned. "Problems?"

Liam shrugged. "Let's say things are a little fraught in the kitchen."

She grinned. "I'd be worried if they weren't. Chefs work best when the adrenaline's pumping. Anyway, this is Conor's first big day."

"But he's been practically running the place for the last year," Liam pointed out.

"True, but it wasn't his name on the menu. I'll go and have a word. You better get back downstairs. It's your first day too, you know!"

Liam looked at her nervously and ran down the stairs ahead of her. Steph smiled. He was a good lad, but there was no harm keeping him on his toes. She made her way down to the kitchen. It was ominously quiet. "Everything OK?" she said brightly.

There were a few mumbles and Conor just looked at her. Oh dear. "Conor?"

"I'm not happy with the turbot and the avocados aren't ripe enough."

Steph swallowed hard. Conor was in the driving-seat

now. She wasn't going to bail him out. "You checked the vegetables yourself," she reminded him.

"I know that," Conor said through gritted teeth.

"So what are you going to do?" she asked quietly.

He looked surprised.

"It's your kitchen, Conor."

He nodded and thought for a minute. "The turbot is too small. I'll add some prawns and caviar to the dish to make up for it. And I suppose the avocados aren't *too* bad," he admitted. "We'll put them in the microwave for a few minutes and see if that helps. If not, I'll puree them with some cream and lemon."

Steph smiled. "Good. Well, I'll leave you to it. Good luck everyone."

There was a more cheerful response this time and she left the kitchen with a grin on her face. In the dining-room a waiter was putting out vases on each table, a single yellow rose in each. Winter sunshine flooded the room making it look warm and welcoming. "Liam? I think a welcoming aperitif on the house for our customers today. What do you think?"

"Nice idea," Liam agreed. "I'll take care of it."

Steph checked her watch. Thirty minutes to go before opening. She picked up glasses and forks, ignoring Liam's hurt expression. He grinned triumphantly when she found no faults.

"Good luck, everyone," she said and went upstairs feeling slightly dispensable.

She was back down at the door to greet Edward when he arrived. He was accompanied by his partner and four customers. Stephanie guided them to a circular table towards the back of the room and Liam arrived to offer them drinks.

"Everything OK?" Edward asked quietly, taking in the table for two nearby. The only other occupants.

"Fine," Steph assured him, trying to look confident. "We've twenty-five covers booked."

"Is that good?" he asked.

Steph grinned. "It's all right. Enjoy your lunch." She smiled at his guests and left them to their drinks and menus.

Brian moved quietly to her side as she moved in behind the front desk. "Stephanie? I think that man over there may be a journalist or something." He nodded towards the table of two.

"Oh?" Steph took a discreet look.

"Yeah. He looks vaguely familiar, and he asked a lot of detailed questions about the menu."

"Right. Good. Well you know what to do, Brian. Make sure he leaves with a smile on his face. And Brian? Well spotted."

Brian beamed at her. "Thanks, boss."

* * *

Karen helped Billy into the back of the car and then turned back to Seán. "Seán, I just wanted to let you know. I'm afraid I may have dropped you in it with Stephanie."

"Oh," Seán looked at her.

"Yes. I mentioned that the divorce had come through."

"Oh," Seán said again.

"Why didn't you tell her?" Karen looked at her ex-husband in frustration. It was obvious that he was crazy about Steph. She even felt a bit jealous. He'd never cared about her like that.

"I don't know," Seán started. "No, I *do* know," he contradicted himself, suddenly angry. "I didn't tell her because she wouldn't be interested. It wouldn't make any difference. Just like I didn't tell her why Billy wasn't coming to stay. She'd think I was trying to pressure her into marriage. Well, I'm not. If she marries me it has to be because she wants to, and I don't think she does."

"I'm sure you're wrong," Karen said, looking in at Billy's face staring curiously out at them.

"You don't know her," Seán said shortly. "Don't try and sort out my whole life on the basis of one evening's conversation, Karen."

"Sorry I spoke." She went round to the passenger door.

Seán dragged a hand through his hair. "No, I'm sorry, Karen. It's not your fault."

"Just talk to her, Seán. Tell her how you feel. What harm can it do?"

What harm indeed? Seán smiled at her and got into the car. "Right. Let's go eat. I'm starving. What about you, Champ?"

"Yeah, Dad, but I'd prefer to go to McDonald's."

"Don't be rude, Billy," Karen admonished.

"Sorry," Billy muttered but grinned when Seán winked at him.

"I tell you what, Champ. If you don't like your lunch, we'll go to McDonald's later."

"Cool!"

Karen gave Seán a dirty look.

"But I *know* he'll like his lunch," he assured her. "Trust me."

* * *

The restaurant was humming by the time Annie and Liz walked in. They paused briefly to say hello to Edward on the way to their table and then settled down to take in everything.

"It's very busy," Annie commented.

"They must have had some people drop in on spec," Liz said. "They'd only five bookings when I talked to Steph earlier."

Annie did a quick count. "Well, I count ten tables now, oh and here comes Seán, that's eleven. Is that Billy with him? Gosh, he's got so big and who's that . . . ?"

Liz looked up. "It must be Karen. Pretty, isn't she?"

"Mmmnn. They look very good together." Annie frowned.

"Naw. She's involved with someone else, and you know Seán's nuts about Steph."

Annie nodded. "Let's have a look at the menus. I'm starving."

"Good afternoon, ladies. Can I get you a drink on the house?"

"Steph! How's it going? The place looks great." Annie grabbed Steph's hand.

Steph smiled down at her. "So far, so good. Listen, let me get your drinks organised and then I'll come back and talk to you when things calm down a bit. Wine?"

"Fine. Seán's here," Liz said.

"Yes, I know. I'd better go and say hello." Steph made her way down to Seán's table. "Hi folks," she said with a bright smile. "Are you being looked after OK? Can I get you a drink?"

"Liam's getting them," Seán said searching her face.

Steph avoided his eyes and turned her attention to his son. "How are you doing, Billy?"

"OK. Do they do burgers here, Steph?" He looked around doubtfully.

"Billy! Don't be rude! Sorry, Steph. You know kids." Karen shrugged apologetically.

"No problem, Karen." She crouched down beside the child. "Well, as it happens, Billy, I know the Chef pretty well, so you leave it to me. I'll see what I can do." She winked at the little boy and went straight into the kitchen.

Conor was moving between his chefs, inspecting dishes and barking orders. "Marc! That sauce needs more seasoning. George! Surely that duck is done by now. Jim! Get a move on with those vegetables, for Christ's sake! My granny moves quicker than you."

The young commis blushed profusely as Conor stood over him.

Steph approached her chef nervously. "Conor?"

"Steph? Yes?" Conor looked at her vaguely and then back at the vegetables.

"That very special young customer I was telling you about is here."

Conor grinned. "Is he now? Well, we'll make him a Conor O'Brien special. Pat? I've got a special order I want you to look after." He winked at Steph. "Don't worry. We'll look after him." Now that he was in the middle of the lunch rush, Conor was suddenly relaxed. This is what he was good at. This is what he loved.

Steph left the kitchen shaking her head. It was strange the way different people reacted to pressure. Thankfully Conor seemed to thrive on it. Lucky for Billy! There weren't many head chefs that would stoop to making burger, fries and baked beans!

Seán was waiting for her in the hallway. "It seems to be going well."

"Yes," she said absently. "So far, so good. Did you want something?"

"Eh, no. I just wanted to talk to you."

"This is hardly the time, Seán. I'll see you tonight."

"What time?" he persisted.

"First night, I'll probably be home by twelve."

Seán sighed. "Right. I'll wait up."

"You don't have to," she said moodily.

"I want to." He looked at her intently.

"Right. Well, I'd better get back." She brushed past him and went back to her post at the front desk. The man that Brian thought was a journalist was just leaving. "Was everything OK for you?" She smiled at him.

"Fine, thank you. Glad you're open again. My compliments to your new chef."

"Well, thank you very much. I'll pass that on. He isn't new, actually. Conor O'Brien has been with us for nearly three years. He's recently taken over as head chef, though."

He nodded. "Yes. From Chris Connolly. Tell me. Isn't that his wife over there?"

Steph looked at him curiously. "Yes, it is. You're very

observant. Liz has actually just started a new business herself. A home catering silver service, associated to Chez Nous."

"And what's her husband doing now?"

Steph frowned. Was that what this guy was really after? Gossip. "Chris has moved to pastures new. He's running The Yellow House in Galway. You seem very well informed, sir. Are you in the business?"

He smiled. "No, no. Just interested. Well, I'd better be going. See you again." He collected his companion and left.

"So what do you think?" Liam was at her side.

Steph frowned. "He has to be from the press. He certainly asked enough questions and he knew Liz. What was his name?"

"Well, the booking was in the name of Jones, and he paid by cash so I'm afraid that's all we've got."

"Well, make a note of it anyway. Anyone else of interest in?"

"The party of four over there all ordered different dishes and they seem to have spent a long time discussing them."

"Right. Well, make sure someone is watching them all the time. Don't wait until they ask for service . . . "

"I know. Pre-empt the request. Will do."

Steph smiled at him and went over to join Annie and Liz who were just starting their main course.

"This is wonderful, Steph," Liz said through a mouthful of turbot. "I love the addition of the prawns and the caviar."

Steph grinned as she thought of Conor's minor crisis. "Yes, Conor's adding a few of his own touches here and there. How's the venison, Annie?"

"Lovely, Steph. Though I hate to think of the number of calories in the sauce."

"Then don't," Liz retorted. "We're here to enjoy ourselves. I got another booking, Steph. A dinner for twelve. You'll never guess who."

"I give up," Steph said pouring herself a glass of water.

"None other than our Minister for Finance."

"Well, at least he should be able to pay you. Ah no, Liz. Sorry. That's brilliant. You'll get a lot of custom out of that one. So let's have a look at this article, then."

Liz rummaged in her bag and produced a piece of paper that she handed reverently to Steph.

Steph read the article carefully and smiled contentedly as she handed it back. "That's great, Liz. He gives you a great plug, doesn't he?"

Liz grinned. "Yeah. I don't think Chris was too impressed."

"He doesn't come out of it too bad either," Annie remarked, not looking up from her plate.

"You don't know Chris," Liz remarked drily. "He'll count the words of praise each of us got, and be rightly pissed if I come out on top."

"Sod him," Steph said cheerfully.

Liz laughed. "Tell me – that guy who just left, who was he? He looked familiar."

"He knew you too. I don't know who he was. The booking was in the name of Jones but he paid in cash so that could have been fake. We suspect he's a critic."

Liz frowned. "Could be. He's definitely familiar."

Steph stood up. "If you remember his name, let me know. Better circulate. Talk to you later."

Edward's table were rising to leave when Steph approached. "Was everything all right?" she asked Edward anxiously.

"Wonderful," he whispered, smiling broadly. "Tell Conor. They all think it's even better than before."

"Maybe that's because they were sitting with one of the owners," Steph said cynically.

Edward raised an eyebrow. "You mean you don't agree?"

Steph flushed. *"Touché."*

He patted her shoulder. "I'll call you tomorrow. Good luck tonight."

"Thanks, Edward."

Steph walked him to the door and then went to check on Seán's table. She didn't really want to but she knew it would look odd if she didn't. "So, Billy. How's lunch?"

"Better than McDonald's," he said through a mouthful of fries.

"High praise indeed," she said, sitting down beside him. Karen and Seán were just finishing their starters. Liam had brought Billy's main course at the same time so the child wouldn't get bored. Steph made a mental note to thank him.

"This is all so wonderful, Steph," Karen said, her eyes wide. "The roulade was great and the bread is melt-in-the-mouth."

"John Quigly, our pastry chef. A very strange man but bloody marvellous with bread and pastries. Wait till you taste the desserts!" She turned to leave.

"Will you join us for coffee?" Seán said hopefully.

"If I can," Steph said, not meeting his eye. The place would probably be empty by then, but she'd find something to occupy her. She couldn't stand looking at Seán with Karen and his son. They looked like a family and she felt like the outsider. every time she looked at Billy, she felt a knot in her stomach. He reminded her of the child she'd lost. She wondered if the baby would have had Seán's eyes. She shot a sidelong glance at him. Why hadn't he told her his divorce had come through? Why hadn't he asked her to marry him? She forced the thoughts to the back of her mind. There was no point in dwelling on it. Her efforts were better employed in the restaurant. At least she seemed to be making a success of that.

CHAPTER FORTY-SIX

Seán stood in the foyer of Jurys with Billy.

"When will you come to see me again, Dad?" Billy was subdued now that it was time to go home.

Seán squatted down beside him. "Soon. Before Christmas, I promise."

Billy's eyes lit up. "Will you bring me in to town to see the Christmas lights?"

"Sure. And we should go and have a word with Santa Claus, make sure he knows where you live."

Billy looked at him scornfully. "Of *course* he does, Dad. He's been coming to our house for years now."

Seán grinned at him. "So what are you going to ask him for?"

Billy considered the question seriously. "A mountain bike, I think."

"Good choice," Seán said. "And what would you like me to buy you?"

Billy hesitated only a moment. He looked up at his father hopefully. "A Sony Playstation?"

Seán pretended to look horrified. "A Playstation? Have you any idea how much those things cost? Your poor Dad could never afford one of them."

Billy's head drooped. "Sorry," he mumbled.

Karen thanked the receptionist and walked over to join them. "Well, I'm ready to go. Billy, go to the toilet before we leave."

"Don't want to."

"Billy," she said, a warning in her voice.

Billy slouched off towards the gents'.

"Thanks, Seán. It's been a nice couple of days. He really enjoyed himself."

"No problem. I told Billy I'd be down before Christmas. I'll give you a call and let you know when. By the way, we were just talking about Christmas presents."

"Oh yes?"

"He wants a mountain bike off Santa."

"Thank God for that. I was afraid he'd changed his mind again."

"I'll organise it if you like."

Karen looked a bit uncomfortable. "Oh, sorry, Seán. I've already bought it. Mike helped me."

Seán tried to hide his disappointment and his irrational envy of Mike. He'd quite liked the idea of going in search of the best bike for his son. "No problem. He wants me to get him a Sony Playstation."

"He asked me too but I told him it was too expensive," Karen said shaking her head.

Seán grinned. "That's what I said, but I'll get it anyway."

"Are you sure?"

"Yeah. It will save me trying to think of something. I'll take the lazy way out. You don't mind, do you?"

"No, no. I'm sure you can afford it and he will be chuffed. Why don't you bring Stephanie when you're coming down the next time?"

Seán studied his shoes. "We'll see."

"Talk to her, Seán. Straighten things out." Karen looked at his bent head. Silly sod. He was mad about the woman. It was funny, really. Here she was, his ex-wife, giving him advice on how to handle his girlfriend. She laughed.

He looked at her. "What?"

"Oh, I was just thinking that I'm probably the last person who should be advising you on your love life."

Seán laughed too. "I suppose."

Billy ran up. "Ready."

"Right, well let's go."

Seán carried their bags to the car, kissed Karen and hugged his son. After he'd made sure that Billy was securely strapped into the back seat, he walked around to the driver's door. "Drive carefully."

"I will – and Seán? Talk to her."

He laughed. "OK, OK, I'll talk to her."

He stood waving until they disappeared into the afternoon traffic and then made his way to his own car. Talk to Stephanie. It sounded so easy, so straightforward. Easier said than done, though.

He'd hoped to talk to her the night that Chez Nous had re-opened. But when she finally got home, she said she was too tired to talk. He'd tried to explain about the divorce but she said it was no problem, that it was his business anyway. His business! Christ, they were living together. Almost had

435

a child together! He drummed the steering wheel angrily. He couldn't take much more of this. When Steph had moved back in after the miscarriage things had been a lot better between them. He hadn't agreed with her taking all those sleeping pills but she'd come through that. Now the restaurant was open again and things should be looking up for them. So what was going wrong? Was it the miscarriage? Was it him? Or did it all come back to her obsession with Ruth's death. That was probably it. Mrs McCann getting in touch after all this time had unnerved her and she was fairly rattled after talking to her. He'd asked her when she was going to go and see the woman, but Steph just made excuses and got quite ratty with him. He hadn't asked again. It wasn't worth the aggravation.

He dragged a hand through his hair. How were they ever going to be a proper couple if she didn't trust him enough to confide in him? He started as the car behind blasted the horn. The light was green. He waved an apology, and on a sudden impulse he indicated, switched lanes and turned in the opposite direction. Talk to Steph? Well, there was no time like the present.

* * *

"Steph? Steph, I've just realised where I know that guy from."

Steph tore her mind away from the invoices in front of her and tried to concentrate on the voice at the other end of the phone. "Liz? Is that you? Slow down. What are you on about?"

"The mystery guy in the restaurant – Mr Jones?"

"Yes?"

"It was Mr *Godfrey* Jones, no less. Affectionately known as God? You must know him, Steph. He's been on all the UK cookery shows. He used to write a column for one of the tabloids."

"Oh. He did have an English accent, now that you mention it. Still, he's not much good to me." Steph wasn't interested in ex-journalists. Especially ones based in a different country.

"No, you don't understand. He's moved to Wicklow, for tax reasons I think. Anyway, he's been hired to write a food column for one of the Sunday papers."

"One of the Irish papers?" Steph perked up.

"Yep. I'm not sure which one."

"So Chez Nous is going to be his first victim."

"Don't be so pessimistic. Everything went like clockwork on Tuesday. I'm sure you'll get a great write-up."

"I hope so."

"It doesn't really matter what he says," Liz said matter-of-factly. "If he raves about you, everyone will come along just to find fault. And if he criticises you, they'll get all patriotic and try to prove him wrong."

Steph laughed. "That's true."

"And any publicity . . . "

"Is good publicity," Steph finished. "You're right."

"Of course I'm right. Well, I must dash. I've work to do. I'll call you on Sunday. Good luck."

"Thanks, Liz. Bye." Steph hung up. She racked her brains for any possible faults the illustrious Mr Jones might have found, but could think of none. She shook her head. This was pointless. She couldn't change things. He'd write what he would write and she was going to have to get used to seeing things in print that upset her. There was no point in taking it personally. It came with the job. She turned her attention back to the accounts and forgot all about Godfrey Jones.

* * *

Conor cursed and emptied the contents of the pan into the bin. He pulled out a cigarette and lit it. That was the third attempt at that dish and he still wasn't happy with it. It had to be perfect for the opening. It was his big chance to show off his new ideas.

Steph wouldn't let him make too many changes to the standard lunch and dinner menus. It was those menus that had won them the Star. He'd have to introduce his own dishes gradually. Establish himself, Steph said. He knew she was right but it was a bit frustrating. He'd hoped that once he was head chef he'd be able to do as he liked. It was a pain to have to continue to turn out Chris's dishes. He ground out the cigarette and started again. The rest of the crew would be back soon. He cursed when he heard the banging on the front door. He ignored it, but the knock came again. He strode out front, cursing the interruption.

"Hi, Conor. Is Steph here?"

"Howya, Seán," Conor said gruffly. "She might be upstairs. Can you find your own way? I'm in the middle of something."

Seán looked curiously at the normally good-humoured young chef. "Sure. Thanks." He took the stairs two at a time and pushed open the door. He studied Stephanie, who was completely unaware of him. She'd discarded the jacket of her black business suit and opened the top button of the grey silk shirt. Her hair was pushed back behind her ears and she was chewing distractedly on the top of her pen.

"Hi."

Steph jumped, her blue eyes large, startled. "Seán! Hi, what are you doing here? Is everything OK?"

"Fine," he said lowering himself into the chair in front of her. "I just wanted to talk to you."

Steph looked away. "Can't we do that at home, Seán. I'm very busy." Her voice was cool, distant.

"Well, we could but then you keep avoiding me at home. So we'll talk here."

Steph looked at the determined look on his face and put down her pen. "So what shall we talk about?"

Seán looked at her. Well, she wasn't exactly enthusiastic, but at least she hadn't thrown him out. "Well then, I'll start, shall I? My divorce came through a week after you told me you were going to get an abortion. It somehow didn't seem the right time to bring it up."

Steph cringed at the sarcasm in his voice.

"After the, eh, the miscarriage, I meant to tell you, but it didn't seem so important in the scheme of things. We were back together, there was plenty of time."

"That was two months ago," Steph pointed out.

"Yes, well, to be honest, I didn't think you were interested. Any time I mention marriage or the future, you get all hot and bothered or run a mile."

Steph flushed. "But we're not talking about marriage, we're talking about your divorce. The two aren't linked."

Seán shook his head, incredulous. "Oh come on, Steph. You've always linked the two."

"I still think you should have mentioned it," she said stubbornly.

"Yes, I should have and I'm sorry."

"OK," she said grudgingly.

"Now what about you?"

She looked down at her crimson nails. "What about me?"

"I'm not the only one who's been hiding things. You haven't talked to me about the miscarriage, or about the sleeping pills, or about Joan McCann."

Steph's expression was closed. "There's nothing to say."

"I think there is," he persisted. "It was my baby too, Steph. I'd like to talk about him."

She smiled weakly. "It's 'him', is it?"

He grinned back. "Just an expression. I wouldn't mind a little girl."

"You'd spoil her."

"Probably."

She softened a little. "I don't know what you want me to say. Once I decided to keep the baby, I felt really happy. I couldn't wait to tell you. You would have laughed at me. I kept studying myself in the mirror. Willing my bump to get bigger! I was *sure* everything would work out. You and me. The restaurant. And then when I lost it . . . " Her eyes filled up. She wiped them away angrily. "Well, are you happy now?"

"No. I'm not happy, Steph. Not at all." He leaned over and brushed her hair back out of her eyes tenderly.

She took his hand and clutched it tightly. "I can't believe

how much it hurt," she said shakily. "Not physically. That might have made it easier. But there was hardly any pain at all. I just woke up and my baby was gone. It was like someone had played a horrible trick on me. I couldn't believe it. I don't think I realised how much I wanted it until that moment. It probably seems silly to you. After all, I was only a few months pregnant."

Seán looked at her, his eyes full of tears. "Don't, Steph. Don't do that to yourself. Don't play down the importance of it. It was our baby. Our baby died. Of course you were devastated, of course you grieved."

Steph swallowed back the tears. "I thought it might be a punishment."

"For what?"

She looked at him, her eyes dark with grief. "For letting Ruth and her baby die."

Seán remembered Annie's words and realised just how accurate she'd been. "Oh, love. You didn't. That wasn't your fault. And I'm not the most religious of men, but I certainly don't believe in a God that punishes."

Steph sniffed. "I'm not sure what I believe anymore."

"Do you believe I love you?" his eyes searched her face.

She touched his cheek, tenderly. "Yes. Yes, I do. I just think I forgot for a while."

He smiled at her, his dark eyes gentle. "Then that's a start."

"You were wrong though, Seán."

"I should have known. What was I wrong about?"

"The pills. I wasn't hooked. But I was cracking up lying awake at night thinking. I needed them. But I haven't taken any in about two weeks."

"I noticed. I'm sorry if I over-reacted. I just worry about you."

She dried her eyes. "Well, don't. I'm a lot tougher than I look."

"No, Steph. That's just it. You're not, and don't try to be. No one expects it. You're allowed to be sad. Now what about Joan McCann?"

"I see her next Wednesday."

"Would you like me to come with you?"

She shook her head. "I'll be OK."

"Well, if you change your mind . . . "

"Thanks. So was there anything else we had to talk about?" Steph's gaze was challenging.

Seán looked at her innocently. "I don't think so."

She scowled at him. "Are you sure?"

He pretended to think for a minute. "Yep. But if you've something to say to me or to *ask* me . . . "

She leaned over and gave him a long lingering kiss. "Just one thing," she murmured.

Seán's eyes lit up. "Yes?"

"Well, I was wondering if – if . . . "

"Yes?'

"If you'd like to stay for dinner."

Seán dropped her hand in disgust. "Oh, very funny! Well, yes, I will stay to dinner but I warn you, I'm an expensive date!"

She smiled. "That's OK. I get staff discount!"

His smile faded for a moment and his eyes searched her face. "Steph? Are we OK?"

She moved around the desk and into his arms. "I think so."

"I'm glad," he said and bent his head to kiss her.

She returned his kiss ardently, and shivered as his hands move down to her hips, pulling her close against him. "Oh stop, I've work to do," She protested weakly. She reached for her jacket and her bag. "I'm going to the ladies' to try and make myself look respectable."

"You look gorgeous," he said looking at her flushed face and sparkling eyes. He grabbed her again as she tried to leave the room.

She pulled away eventually, laughing. "Go downstairs, man, before you lead me astray. Liam should be in by now. He'll get you a drink."

Seán looked after her longingly. "I could do with one. Don't be long. I want to spend some time with you before the place fills up. Is there any chance of you getting away early this evening?"

"I think that can be arranged." She blew him a kiss and disappeared into the ladies'.

Seán grinned and ran down the stairs whistling. Things were definitely looking up.

CHAPTER FORTY-SEVEN

Steph turned off the tap and ran for the phone, wiping her hands in the towel she'd tied around her. "Hello?"

"Steph? It's Liz."

"Hi, Liz," Steph secured the towel around her and sat down on the bed.

"Well, what do you think?"

Steph thought she must have missed something. "What about?"

"The article, idiot. Haven't you seen it?"

"No. What article?"

"Oh, *Steph*. Godfrey Jones, remember? It's Sunday, or hadn't you noticed."

"Oh, right. Sorry, Liz. It was a late night last night and I'm not really awake yet. Seán's just gone out for the papers. So let's have it. Does he slate us or praise us?"

"You sound remarkably calm considering this is your first review."

"So much has gone wrong already, I've decided that I'll

go nuts if I worry about everything. So don't keep me in suspense. What does he say?"

"He's very complimentary. You've nothing to worry about."

"Oh, good." Steph sank back against the pillows.

"The only thing he didn't like was the wine list."

Steph shot back up again. "What? What's wrong with it, for God's sake?"

"He says: *The wine list is a little uneven with very little choice under £20.*"

"Bullshit! We've a great selection! What else does he say?"

"Well, he's very complimentary about your treatment of younger customers."

"What?" Steph frowned in confusion.

"He says: *It's nice to see that in a restaurant of this calibre they still look after the little things – or in this case, the little ones! While most of the customers were tucking into quail's eggs, breast of guinea fowl and turbot dressed with caviar – the real thing, folks! – one young man was happily munching his way through a burger and fries!*"

"Oh dear." Steph sighed.

"What? That's good, isn't it?"

"Not if it means we start getting a lot of kids in, all demanding burgers, it isn't. Conor will go berserk!"

Liz laughed. "I don't think too many people can afford to bring their kids to Chez Nous for a burger."

"I suppose. What does he say about the service?"

"Hang on." Liz scanned the page. "Here we are: *Service was unobtrusive and efficient. The staff, while friendly, were happy to stay in the background. This restaurant has changed hands recently, but as it was my first time to visit Chez Nous I'm not in a position to tell you whether it's improved or not. Suffice to say, I will definitely be coming back."*

"Well, <u>that's</u> good, I suppose," Steph said, slightly mollified.

Liz laughed. "Oh, Steph, if you're not happy with that review, you've got a lot of heartache ahead of you."

"I know, I know. I suppose I'll get used to it. Does he give Conor a mention?"

"No." Liz checked again. "No, and he doesn't mention you either."

"Oh well. I suppose we were lucky that our first review wasn't by one of Chris's fans."

"You were. Really, Steph. It's very positive. Oh, and he does say right at the beginning that it was your first day open after the accident and that the official opening isn't until Wednesday."

"That's good. I'd better send him an invite."

"You'd better. Listen, I've got to go. I'll see you on Wednesday."

"OK, Liz. Thanks. Bye." Steph wandered back into the bathroom to wash her teeth. It was a pretty good review, she had to admit. But she was a bit peeved over the criticism of her wine list. She'd taken great pains in making changes to Chris Connolly's selection. She'd forced herself to be objective and had consulted Edward whenever she doubted her own motives. If anything, she'd *improved* the list in the lower price range. But then, she reasoned, Godfrey Jones wasn't familiar with the old list. As he'd admitted, he wasn't in a position to make comparisons.

The hall door banged and Seán ran up the stairs. "You'll

never guess," he said coming into the bathroom, waving the newspaper.

"There's a review of the restaurant?" Steph said calmly.

"Yes! How did you know, you witch? Were you expecting it? You never said."

"I wasn't sure. Liz thought she recognised Godfrey Jones. To be honest I'd forgotten all about it. Liz was just on. She read out some of the main hits. I believe Billy gets a special mention."

"He does." Seán handed her the paper.

She read the article slowly, looking for criticisms. "It's not bad," she said finally.

"Not bad? God, you're hard to please, woman! It's positively glowing. Especially from Godfrey Jones."

"You know him?"

"You'd want to be living under a stone not to know him. He's always on the box."

"Oh. Well, I better send him an invite for Wednesday."

"Are you going in to work today?"

"No. Conor's experimenting today. I think it's better if I keep out of his way. I thought I'd do a bit of work here."

Seán moved closer and slipped his arms around her waist. "Why don't you take some time off?" he murmured in her ear and tugged gently on the towel.

Steph smiled. "Mmnn. I suppose I could. I tell you what. Give me two hours, and then I'm all yours."

"Promise?" He kissed the nape of her neck.

"Promise," she said, resisting the temptation to drag him back to bed there and then. She had to get *some* work done.

He took the paper and headed for the stairs. "OK. I'll make some coffee."

"I won't be long," Steph called after him. She went into the bedroom humming happily to herself. She took a faded pair of Levis from her wardrobe and a navy check shirt from Seán's. With her face bare, her hair brushed back and the voluminous shirt hanging loosely over her tight jeans, she looked about fourteen.

Seán eyed her appreciatively when she padded into the kitchen ten minutes later in stocking feet. He loved her when she was decked out in one of her dark business suits or in a sexy little evening dress. But he liked it even more when she was like this. She looked so young and vulnerable. And she seemed more relaxed when there was just the two of them. "Are you sure you want to work?" He reached for her and pulled her down onto his knee.

Steph planted a kiss on his mouth and stood up. "Yes, I do. Stop trying to distract me. Why don't you make a start on clearing out the attic?"

Seán picked up the newspaper. "Oh, I don't know."

Steph frowned. "You haven't changed your mind about seeing more of Billy, have you?"

"No, of course not."

Steph shrugged. "OK. Well, I'd better get to work. I'll be up in the office if you want me."

"OK," Seán said from behind the paper.

* * *

"Joe, take a look at this." Annie shoved the newspaper in front of him.

Joe opened one eye. "What?"

Annie poked him in the ribs. "Wake up. It's an article about Chez Nous."

Joe grunted and sat up in bed. "Where are the kids?"

"Playing in Jessica's."

"Any chance of a cuppa?"

Annie shook her head and went downstairs. She should have brought it up in the first place. He was impossible to talk to until he'd had his first mug of tea. She carried the large *World's Best Dad* mug upstairs and handed it to him, before climbing up on the bed beside him. "So what do you think?"

Joe took a cautious sip of the hot liquid. "*Aah.* That's better. He's quite complimentary. A bit of a celebrity, isn't he? A good review from him must count for something."

"Godfrey Jones. Yes, he's fairly well known. I don't know why he gets at the wine list, though. I think it's fine."

"I thought it was the same as it always was," Joe remarked. He'd brought a client to dinner during the week and been very impressed. Joe had told him, with no small amount of pride, that the restaurant was now owned and run by his sister. He'd watched with some amusement the effect his sister had on the man when he introduced them. He'd always enjoyed introducing Steph to his colleagues. She always managed to turn even the most sophisticated of men into drooling teenagers.

"Steph made some changes," Annie replied. "She added more New World wines and, funnily enough, more to the ten to twenty pound range."

"Well, to be fair, he *does* say that he's never been there before," Joe pointed out.

449

"True," Annie agreed. "Are you going to come home and pick me up on Wednesday?"

Joe pulled her down beside him. "What's in it for me?" he murmured.

Annie raised an eyebrow. "You get to spend more time with your beautiful wife."

"That sounds OK. Speaking of spending some time together, why don't you come back to bed for a while?"

Annie pretended to look shocked. "Joe! What about the children?"

"They're next door, aren't they. They'll be fine for a while."

Annie slid down beside him. "I was going to ring Stephanie."

Joe started to open her shirt. "You can do that later."

"I suppose."

* * *

"Catherine, listen to this." Tom West walked into the kitchen with the newspaper.

"Chez Nous is a bright airy restaurant. The large room is spacious and cool, but the atmosphere is warm and inviting. Tables are set with immaculate white cloths and napkins, polished silver cutlery and sparkling good-sized glasses. Tables are large and chairs comfortable making the idea of going back to work seem ludicrous. The menu makes interesting reading . . ."

"Let me read it myself," Catherine said impatiently, wiping her hands in her apron. She took the paper from him and put on her glasses.

"Look at the bit about the service," her husband prompted. "Though I'm not sure I like what he says about the wine list."

Catherine glared at him before turning her attention to the article. "That's wonderful," she said happily when she'd finished.

"It is, isn't it? But what about the wine list?"

Catherine brushed that aside. "What about it? The kind of people who can afford to eat in Chez Nous aren't too worried about the prices now, are they?"

Tom laughed. "That's true. Let's ring Stephanie. Do you think she's seen it?"

"I'm sure she has, but let's ring her anyway. Congratulate her."

* * *

"Edward. Hi." Liz stood back and let him in. She could hardly take her eyes off him. The faded denims, trainers and white shirt took years off him and he looked gorgeous.

"Hi, Liz. I hope you don't mind me just dropping in. I'm on my way up to Jen's."

"No problem as long as you ignore the mess. I'm trying to catch up on the ironing."

"Did you see this?" He held out the newspaper folded over on the page of the review.

"I certainly did. I was just on to Steph. Would you believe, she hadn't seen it!"

"Pretty good, isn't it? Was she happy? What did you

451

think?" It had seemed like a very good review to him, but then he was only an amateur.

"It was great," Liz assured him. "Though Steph wasn't too impressed with the barb about the wine list."

Edward grinned. "I'm not surprised. She takes her wines very seriously indeed. And she's actually made very few changes to Chris's original selection."

"Yes, I know that, but Godfrey Jones didn't."

"True. Where's Lucy?" He stretched out in a kitchen chair and watched her iron a pair of miniature dungarees.

"She's at a party. Carol's there too. Is Jen expecting you?"

"No, I just thought I'd drop in on the off-chance. Take them out for lunch and a drive. Why don't I take you out instead?"

Liz looked at the pile of clothes still to be ironed and thought about the bathroom that needed cleaning. "I don't think so, Edward. I've so much to do."

"Oh, leave it," Edward said carelessly. "You should get someone in to take care of the housework now you're working."

Liz raised an eyebrow, amused at how simple it all was to him. "Should I? And by the time I've paid a housekeeper and a baby-sitter, what would be left of my wages?"

"If there's nothing left, you're not charging enough," he said matter-of-factly.

Liz smiled. There was plenty of money left. Sometimes she thought maybe she was charging *too* much but Conor assured her that she wasn't. She'd been amazed at how much she'd made already, and bookings were flooding in for the Christmas period. She'd refused any bookings for Christmas week, determined that Lucy wasn't going to miss out. She'd even invited Chris to dinner on Christmas day. She wasn't thrilled at the idea but she knew it would make Lucy happy. Besides her parents would be there too and that would make it easier. Her mother wasn't impressed. She wasn't ready to forgive Chris just yet, but she'd agreed to behave herself for her granddaughter's sake.

"So what about it?"

Liz started.

"Lunch?" Edward asked patiently.

"Yeah, why not? But I have to be back by five to pick up Lucy."

Edward stood up. "Fine, let's go."

"Not yet," Liz looked at him in dismay. "I have to change. Where are we going?"

Edward sat down again with a sigh. "Well, I'm not exactly dressed for anywhere too formal. Let's go to Morel's Bistro. That way we'll have plenty of time." The little bistro was less than fifteen minutes' drive.

"Lovely." Liz smiled and ran upstairs. It was a very cold day, but sunny. Maybe they'd have time for a walk along the pier. She chose a bright red polo-neck, black pants and high black ankle boots. She renewed her lipstick – since Edward had taken to calling unexpectedly she'd always applied some make-up in the mornings – ran a brush through her hair and went back down to join him.

He looked up approvingly. "Good enough to eat," he said.

Liz flushed and busied herself with the zip of her jacket.

Edward smiled at her discomfort. She couldn't take a compliment, but it didn't stop him doling them out. He loved the way she blushed. She was so different from

Christina. Christina expected compliments, acknowledging them with a slightly imperious nod. She saw them as her due. It had both amused and irritated Edward.

"Let's go. I'm starving." Liz pushed him out into the hall.

"Me too," Edward said leaning down and kissing her lightly on the lips.

Liz pushed him away but she was smiling. "Enough of that. You promised me lunch."

"So I did." Edward opened the door and led the way out to the car.

CHAPTER FORTY-EIGHT

"Jesus! Why the hell did I agree to do lunch today? It's going to be a bloody disaster. Isn't table fourteen ready to order yet?"

"No, Chef," Brian muttered nervously. "And a man at table five wants to change his main course from monkfish to beef."

"For Christ's sake!" Conor banged the work-top with his fist, making a nearby trainee jump nervously.

"Chef, the potatoes are burned." Alan, a young commis looked at his boss nervously.

"I'll look after that, Chef." Marc took Alan by the arm and steered him back down the kitchen.

Kevin looked at Conor's flushed face. "Why don't you concentrate on this evening, Conor, and let me finish lunch?"

Conor nodded gratefully and went out into the yard to have a smoke. Not for the first time, he thanked God for bringing Kevin Nolan to his kitchen. The guy was proving to be a valuable addition to the team and was twice the man George was.

He checked his watch. Only five hours to go to the opening. How were they going to be ready on time?

"Haven't they even *started* their meal yet? How are we going to be ready on time?"

Steph looked around the restaurant and cursed herself for staying open for lunch.

"They wanted to take some time before ordering. I can hardly force them now, can I?" Liam said irritably. It was a crazy bloody day. What on earth had possessed Steph to stay open for lunch? They were going to have to work their butts off this afternoon. And Jane had gone home sick, though he thought it was a phobia to hard work that she suffered from. God, they'd got rid of surly Jean and replaced her with sickly Jane!

Things weren't any better in the kitchen. Conor was like an Antichrist. He almost made Chris seem reasonable! The chefs were tip-toeing around him, afraid to speak. Apart from old Quigly, that is. He just carried on in his own little corner, oblivious.

Steph shot Liam a conciliatory smile. "Sorry, Liam. What time does the place need to be cleared if you're to set up on time for tonight?"

"Three at the latest," he said firmly. Three-thirty would probably be time enough but there was no harm in asking for more.

"OK. I'll drop down later and see how we're doing. Then I have to go out for a couple of hours, but you'll be able to reach me on my mobile."

Liam stared after her. God, she was going to swan off for the afternoon and leave him to get everything ready *and* deal with Conor. He shook his head. It was about time he asked for a bloody raise.

Steph went back up to the office and sat staring at her checklist without seeing it. She checked her watch nervously. The phone rang, making her jump.

"Hello?"

"Steph?"

"Hi, Seán."

"Are you OK?"

"Of course."

"I just rang to wish you good luck."

"But I'll see you later, won't I?" Steph frowned. Seán had promised to be at the opening.

"Of course you will. I meant good luck with Mrs McCann."

"Oh. Right."

"You are going, aren't you Steph?"

Steph thought for a moment. She could always ring and say she was too busy. It was a bit crazy going AWOL today of all days.

"Steph?"

"Yes. Yes, of course I'm going."

"Good girl. Well, I'm sure it will be fine. She probably just wants to chat about old times."

"Yeah. Listen, I have to go, Seán. Conor's looking for me. See you later." Steph banged down the phone and tucked a lock of hair nervously behind her ear. For the first time in months, she longed for a cigarette. She checked her watch. It was nearly two-thirty. She stood up, slipped on her jacket, grabbed her bag and went downstairs.

There were two parties left in the restaurant, one eating

dessert and the other on coffees. After a quick word with Liam, she went to each table, introduced herself and explained that they were closing at three to prepare for the opening. She apologised for rushing them and invited them to come back later that evening to join in the celebrations. Both parties were delighted with the invitation and wished her luck. Steph winked at Liam and left the restaurant. If only personal situations were as easy to handle, she thought as she climbed into her car. She drove across town and out through Fairview. Traffic was heavy and she checked her watch again. Five to three. She shouldn't be too late. The traffic started to move again and she turned up the Howth Road. Not far now. She took a few deep breaths and tried to ignore the butterflies in her stomach. In an hour it would all be over. She reached Killester and turned into the small street of terraced houses. She sat in the car for a moment, tempted to drive away again, but she looked up to see Joan McCann standing on the doorstep.

Steph took a deep breath, planted a smile on her face and started up the path.

"Hello, Stephanie, How are you?"

"Fine Mrs McCann," Steph said, kissing the proffered cheek. She was slightly taken aback at this frail woman. She could only be in her early sixties, but she looked so much older. "How are you keeping?"

"Can't complain, love. I've just made some tea. I hope it won't be too strong for you."

"I love it strong," Steph lied, following her into the room that Ruth had always referred to as the parlour. Steph had only been inside it a couple of times before. It was the good room reserved for important visitors and kept locked most of the time. Steph looked around the small room full of china ornaments. The red chesterfield suite, now faded, had crocheted covers on the arms and little doilies stood on the small table in front of the sofa, in wait for the teacups. Steph sat down and accepted the tiny china cup and saucer that Mrs McCann handed her. She held it carefully, terrified that the slightest pressure would break it and eventually set it down on the table, not trusting her trembling hands.

"I'm sorry if I bullied you into coming to see me, Stephanie, but I really needed to talk to you."

Steph was startled by her directness. "That's OK, Mrs McCann. I was just a bit surprised to hear from you after all this time. I wasn't sure . . . "

"I understand, dear. You were probably terrified to come here."

Steph gave a small embarrassed laugh. "Just a little," she admitted.

"I'm not going to interrogate you, Stephanie, or ask you anything awkward. I'm just trying to put some pieces of a puzzle together. I've already talked to Mary, but I can't track Sinéad down. Mary thinks she's in Australia."

Steph frowned. "Ruth's flatmates. I don't understand."

"No, of course you don't, dear. I'm sorry. I should start at the beginning. But I'm forgetting my manners. Have a piece of cake."

"No, thanks." Steph knew there was little or no chance of her getting the fruit cake down her throat without choking.

Joan put the plate down and took a sip of her tea. "It all started when Peter died. I put off going through his things for a few weeks. Oh, I let the girls get rid of his clothes and all that, but I wanted to go through his papers myself. Peter was very sentimental, you see. He kept every card I ever sent him. I didn't want anyone else to go through all of that. His finances were all in order. He'd known for a few months that he was going to die and he used to closet himself in here with the accountant and the lawyer making sure that everything was in order. He transferred everything into my name before he died so we wouldn't have to worry about wills or probate or any of that nonsense. He was a very thoughtful, kind man."

She stared into the distance, a half smile on her face and tears in her eyes. Steph patted her hand awkwardly.

Joan McCann smiled at her. "Sorry, dear. Where was I? Oh yes. Peter's papers. Well, you see, he kept them in a box at the top of the wardrobe in our bedroom. I never went near it before. Well, I knew what was in it. Peter was a sentimental old fool, I wasn't expecting any surprises. I put off opening it. I knew it would upset me and bring back a lot of memories. But one day, the day before I called your mother, I felt strong enough to open it."

Steph looked at her expectantly. She'd obviously found something. Something belonging to Ruth? "Yes?" she prompted. Joan McCann had that faraway look in her eye again.

"Yes." Joan pulled herself back to the present. "Just a moment, dear." She went to the sideboard and pulled a large, thick envelope out of the top drawer. "Here we are." She opened the envelope and carefully extracted the contents. The first was a pale pink envelope, slightly faded and this she carefully put to one side. She rifled through the others and took out three more standard, white, business envelopes. "Did you know Des?" She asked.

Steph put down her cup with a clatter. "Des Healy?"

Joan nodded.

"Well, yes. I knew him."

"What did you think of him?"

Steph swallowed hard. How honest was she supposed to be, here? "Well, we didn't see too much of him. He liked to keep Ruth to himself. He wasn't really into going out in a crowd."

"But what did you *think* of him?" Joan repeated, impatiently.

"He was a bit flash for my liking," Steph replied honestly. "He seemed to think he was better than us. He had a job, a fancy car and we were just poor students."

"Yes, I see. Do you think Ruth loved him?"

Steph had no problem answering this one. "Oh, yes. No doubt about that. She was crazy about him. She couldn't see any of his faults. That's real love, isn't it?"

Joan smiled. "It is when you're very young."

Steph laughed. "True. We get less tolerant as we get older." She thought of how hard she made life for Seán sometimes, when he'd done nothing to deserve it. In comparison to Des, he was an absolute saint!

"He wrote to us," Joan said quietly.

"What?" Steph stared at her.

"I didn't know. Peter hid the letters, you see. I suppose he thought they'd upset me."

"I see," Steph said, afraid she was drifting back into the past again.

"I'm sorry, Steffi."

Steph flinched at the nickname Ruth had given her. "These letters. They're from Des. He sent them after he went to England." She handed one over and Steph took it gingerly, reluctant to touch anything tainted by Des Healy.

"Read it, Steffi."

Steph looked at her and then down at the letter in her hand. It was dated June 20th. Two months after Ruth died. She started to read.

Dear Mr & Mrs McCann,

I know I am probably the last person you want to hear from at the moment, but I had to write. It may seem to you that I didn't care about your daughter, but that's not true. I did love her in my own way. She was always so full of life, it's very hard to believe that I will never see her again.

Here, the writing was smeared as if Des was crying as he wrote.

I told her I'd stand by her. I wouldn't have left her to cope on her own. Please believe that. It's not my fault she's dead. I don't understand why she did it. There was no need. Everything would have worked out.

Please believe that I did care very much for Ruth, and would do anything to undo this terrible tragedy.

I would love to come and see you. It would mean such a lot to me. I understand, though, if you don't feel ready to talk. I'll be here whenever, if ever, you do want to see me.

Yours, very sincerely,

Des Healy.

Steph folded the letter and put it back in its envelope. "What a nerve," she said.

Joan said nothing and just handed her the next letter.

Steph took it reluctantly. She didn't want to know about Des's feelings. She'd never forgive him. Why hadn't Mrs McCann just thrown this garbage in the bin? Mr McCann had been right not to show it to his wife. How dare Des write to them?

Joan watched her expectantly and she obediently opened the second letter and read. It was dated August 4th.

Dear Mr & Mrs McCann,

I hope you are both keeping well, I think of you a lot. I understand why you have not been in touch – this must be such a dreadful time for you.

Steph snorted in disbelief.

I've got myself a job in an insurance company. The pay isn't as good, but it's a start.

"I don't believe this guy," Steph said shaking her head. "Did he honestly think you'd care?"

Joan watched her steadily but said nothing.

I'm trying to start again, but it's hard. I can't stop thinking about Ruth and when I go to sleep I dream of her. It's all such a waste.

I hope that some day you'll forgive me and understand that it wasn't my fault.

Kindest regards,

Des Healy.

Steph's inclination was to crunch the page up into a ball, but she forced herself to fold it neatly and hand it back to Joan. "My God, he doesn't even take any responsibility for his part in it. It's sick."

"Maybe. Maybe he was the one that was sick," Joan said cryptically, putting the letters away.

Steph looked at her, confused. How could she take all of this so calmly? How could she forgive him – this man who'd been the cause of her daughter's suicide? Especially given the tone of his letters. They weren't filled with guilt, just a kind of distant sadness. It was as if he'd disassociated himself from the whole thing. But then why had he written in the first place?

"That was the last we heard from him," Joan said quietly, almost sadly.

"Well, that doesn't surprise me," Steph retorted. "He probably was too involved in the good life in London."

"Manchester," Joan said absently.

"What?"

"He lived in Manchester."

Steph looked at her, puzzled. She was behaving very strangely.

"This letter came a couple of months later." Joan handed her yet another envelope. It was different notepaper, this time, and it was typed.

Dear Mr & Mrs McCann,

I regret to inform you that my brother, Des Healy, died on the 15th of September. He took his own life, and in the note he left my parents, he asked them to inform you of his death. I am afraid that his suicide may in some way be related to the death of your daughter, Ruth. My parents know nothing of their relationship, or it's unhappy outcome. I would ask you, humbly, not to tell them of it now. It can only cause more hurt and pain and I'm not sure they can take much more.

I would like to take this opportunity to sympathise with you on the loss of your daughter. I only met her a couple of times, but I liked her a lot.

I know it must be hard for you to feel any real sorrow over Des's death, but I ask you to try and forgive him, and say a prayer for him.

Yours sincerely,

Cathy Jackson (nee Healy).

Steph put down the letter. Her hand was shaking. All these years, she'd been hating a dead man. He hadn't been the hard bastard that she'd believed him to be. He obviously *had* felt guilty.

"Stephanie? Are you all right?"

She nodded dumbly.

Joan McCann took a bottle of brandy from the sideboard and poured her a large glass. "Drink this."

Steph took a large gulp of the drink. The glass shook in her hands – she put it down. Joan knelt in front of her and covered her hands with her own. "I'm sorry, dear. I've shocked you. I should have prepared you – oh, I'm so sorry . . . "

"No." Steph looked down at the distraught woman trying to comfort her. Surely it should be the other way around? "I'm all right, really. It's just a bit of a shock."

"Yes. Yes it is. The poor boy. He must have gone through a terrible time."

Steph glanced at her watch. "I'm really sorry, Mrs McCann, I'm going to have to go. Could I come back tomorrow, though?"

"You must. We're not finished yet."

Steph stared at her. What else was to come? She checked her watch again and cursed herself for arranging this meeting for today. She stood up reluctantly. "I'm really sorry I can't stay now, I'd love to but . . . "

"Go and do what you have to do. I'll still be here tomorrow." Joan McCann smiled serenely and walked her to the door.

Steph looked at her, nodded vaguely and stumbled out to her car.

CHAPTER FORTY-NINE

It was five-fifteen when Steph let herself back into Chez Nous. "How's it going?" she said timidly, coming up behind Liam.

Liam turned to look at her, with raised brows. "Very well."

"I'm sorry for running out on you, Liam. I didn't expect to be so long. It was important."

"You're the boss," Liam said, dismissing her apologies. "Conor's looking for you."

"Right." Steph went back to the kitchen. The noise was deafening. Cold dishes were already laid out on tables near the door and the chefs were working at a frenetic pace. Brendan, one of the kitchen porters, was frantically trying to clear any debris away from the floor around their feet. He was shouted at to work faster or to get out of the bloody way in equal measures. He carried on regardless. Steph saw Conor at the other end of the room, gesticulating wildly at Pat. Pat stood looking at him, nodding occasionally. Steph smiled and wondered if Pat was actually even listening. She walked up to the two of them.

"Steph! God, where were you?"

"Out. Is something wrong?"

"Well, no. It's sorted now."

Steph smiled at her head chef. "Well, there you are then. So everything's under control?"

Conor looked surprised. "Yeah, I think so. The cold dishes are almost finished, four of the hot dishes have been started and we'll do the monkfish and scallop kebabs, the wild mushroom soufflés and the mini steak-and-kidney pies as they're needed. And John's desserts are all ready, of course."

"We'll stagger the food over two hours?" Steph asked.

"Yes, as agreed, we'll start with two of the cold dishes, the melon and Parma ham sticks and the chilli tiger prawns and then we'll serve a mixture of the hot and cold dishes, say two at a time."

Steph nodded in approval. "Well, if there's nothing else, I'd better go and get ready. Try and plan, Conor, to be ready to mingle by about seven."

"Will do," Conor said, managing a nervous smile.

After checking with Brian that the white wine and champagne were sufficiently cold and that there was a plentiful supply of ice, Steph ran upstairs to change. While she still planned to wear a suit, she was swapping her dark tones for a rich cream brocade Paul Costello creation. A gold chunky neck chain, bracelet and earrings and very high, beige Bruno Magli court shoes completed her outfit. She'd only time to touch up her make-up, and she noticed her hand trembling as she tried to apply mascara in front of the mirror in her office. She studied her reflection. She looked strained and upset. She smiled widely, willing herself to look and feel calmer. A cigarette would be very welcome right now. She blended some bronze tones in around her eyelids, added some rich coral lipstick and fluffed up her hair. A spray of Chanel and she was ready.

"Steph?"

She jumped as Seán walked up behind her.

"Sorry, I didn't mean to startle you. How did it go?"

Steph returned his kiss. "I wouldn't know where to begin, Seán, and there's no time now. We'll have to talk later."

"I'll die of suspense," Seán complained. He looked at her strained expression. "Are you OK?"

"Yes. No. Oh, I'll live." she smiled wanly.

"You look fantastic," he said and she did, despite the slight air of sadness.

"Thanks." Steph looked him up and down, taking in the beautifully cut, charcoal-grey suit, the pale cream shirt and the dark red, paisley silk tie. "You don't look too bad yourself."

"Thank you, ma'am. Shall we?" He held his arm out to link her.

She took it and they descended together just as Edward put his foot on the first step.

"Oh, there you are. I was just coming to get you. Liam wants you to have a final look around before he opens the doors. Hi, Seán." Edward turned and led the way into the dining-room.

The waiting-staff were lined up along the back wall. They wore snow-white shirts, black trousers and long dark green aprons. Liam stood beside them, impeccable in a black suit, white shirt and dark green bow-tie.

Steph smiled at them. "Well, is everybody ready?"

Liam smiled back. "As ready as we'll ever be."

"Great. Well, good luck everyone and thanks." She turned to Edward. "Have you seen Conor?"

"I put my head around the door but I didn't interrupt him."

"Come on then, we've time for a quick chat before we open the doors."

The kitchen was a lot calmer when they walked in. Some of the chefs were out in the yard having a smoke and Conor was going through some last minute details with Pat and Kevin.

"Steph, Edward, is everything ready out front?"

"It certainly is," Edward said, "and it looks like everything's ready in here too."

Conor grinned. "Yeah, we're on top of things. No major catastrophes so far."

Steph checked her watch. "Then I think we better open up. Remember, Conor. Try and be out by seven."

"Will do. What about the photo call?"

Steph looked at him blankly. God, she'd forgotten all about that! She'd have to pull herself together. "Oh, right. I think we'll do that now. How about a couple of shots with some of the fish dishes? They're nice and colourful."

"Fine."

"Right, I'll go and get the photographer."

When she left them, Edward moved nearer the food. "Some of your new creations, Conor?"

"Yeah. I thought I'd try them out."

"Well if they taste as good as they look, they'll be a huge success. Best of luck, Conor."

Conor took the hand Edward held out to him and shook it firmly. "Thanks, Edward."

Steph appeared back with the photographer and the three of them posed in different positions. Steph insisted on a few of Conor on his own and Edward pointed out that there should be some of her on her own too. After all, she was the boss. Steph posed, thinking this should be one of the happiest moments of her life – so why was smiling such an effort?

Seán put his head around the door. "Liam's opened up."

"Right. Good luck everybody," Steph shouted and followed Edward out to the front door to greet their guests.

The evening flew by in a flurry of activity. A photographer from one of the social pages wandered around snapping anyone who looked vaguely familiar. Lavinia Reynolds was holding court in the centre of the room and drinking copious amounts of champagne.

"It's worth it if the old bitch gives us a good write-up," Steph said when Liam remarked on it.

Adam Cullen and Conor were in deep conversation in a corner. From the look on Conor's face and the way he was gesticulating they had to be talking food. He looked wonderful in his chef's hat and whites and was wearing the dark-green silk neckerchief that Steph had bought him to match in with the other staff.

Seán moved quietly around the room, listening in on conversations and watching the reactions to the food. He joined Joe, Annie and Liz. "What do you think?"

"It's going brilliantly," Liz said, her eyes sparkling. "Everyone's raving about the food."

"I don't see this Godfrey chap." Joe looked around.

"I'm sure he'll be here. He probably likes to make an entrance," Annie said.

"Well, there won't be much point if the food is all gone," Joe remarked.

Steph caught the comment as she joined them. "Don't worry. Conor has a couple of surprises left up his sleeve."

Seán nudged her. "I think the entrance is being made." He nodded towards the door, where Godfrey Jones stood looking around.

Steph moved towards him. "Mr Jones. I'm glad you could join us." Brian appeared at her elbow with some champagne and she smiled at him gratefully.

"Miss West?" Godfrey Jones looked her up and down appreciatively.

"That's right, but please call me Stephanie," she said with a warm smile.

"Godfrey," he replied with a small bow.

"Let me introduce you to my partner." She led him over to Edward. "Edward McDermott, this is Godfrey Jones."

The two men shook hands. Steph looked around for Conor and saw him slip out of the room. She suppressed a smile and turned her full attention back to Edward, who was explaining the background of the restaurant. Lavinia Reynolds had signalled her photographer and Steph, Edward and Jones posed obediently.

"I see that dreadful woman is here," Godfrey remarked drily. "She wouldn't know good food if it jumped up and bit her."

"That's very harsh," Steph said reprovingly.

"But true," Edward said and they all laughed. He watched Godfrey take a small sip of his drink. "Would you like something stronger? I can't stand champagne myself."

"I'd love a gin and tonic," Godfrey admitted.

Steph could have kicked Edward. "Leave it to me." She said grimly and left them. She made a bee-line for the kitchen. "Conor? Are you ready to serve the food. Godfrey Jones is about to start in on the G & T's."

"Two minutes."

Steph left him, asked Jane to get the drinks and returned to the two men. They were chatting comfortably now and Godfrey had deliberately turned his back on Lavinia who was trying to edge nearer.

A waiter arrived with the scallop and monkfish kebabs, moments before Jane delivered the drinks.

"I'll hold your drink," Steph offered casually, and carried on chatting while Edward and Godfrey tucked into the food. As she'd expected, Godfrey drank some champagne after eating the fish and she watched in delight as the explosion of flavours hit the gourmet's taste buds. She saw Conor approaching and winked at him. "Godfrey, let me introduce our head chef, Conor O'Brien."

"Pleased to meet you." Conor shook the older man's hand.

"The pleasure is all mine, Chef," Godfrey replied, helping himself to another kebab.

Conor beamed happily and Edward raised his glass to him in a silent toast. Steph sighed and took a gulp of champagne. It wouldn't get much better than this.

At twelve midnight, she sat exhausted, listening to her friends dissect the evening.

"Did you see Lavinia's face when Godfrey Jones turned his back on her?" Liz shook her head laughing.

"She looked like she'd swallowed a wasp," Annie agreed.

"The woman was drunk," Joe remarked trying hard to focus.

"I'm not surprised," Liam replied. "Every time I looked, Brian was filling her glass. I think she fancied you, Brian."

"Oh don't," Brian said in disgust and they all laughed.

"A toast," Seán stood up, slightly unsteadily. "To the new crew of Chez Nous – hey, that rhymes – well done, guys. It was a great night."

"Here, here," Annie said.

"Cheers," Liz said.

"Up yours!" Conor grinned happily.

"I've got to go home," Steph said sleepily.

"We should be going too," Annie agreed. "The baby-sitter will go nuts. Shall we share a taxi?"

"Grand. I'll go and call one." Steph went up to the office, rang for a taxi and collected her bag. The day had taken on a slightly surreal quality. Her conversation with Joan McCann seemed days ago. She hadn't allowed herself to dwell on any of it all evening. She didn't trust herself, and anyway, she'd a job to do. She'd think about it tomorrow. She was too tired tonight. She met Conor at the bottom of the stairs. "Conor, I need to take tomorrow off."

"No problem, boss. We'll manage."

"And Conor. Well done. You were great." She reached up to kiss him and he wrapped her in a bear hug, lifting her off the ground.

"Thanks, Steph. Thanks for giving me the chance. You won't be sorry."

"I know that."

"Come on, you two. No canoodling in the hallway. I'm a very jealous man."

Conor clapped him drunkenly on the back. "That's OK, Seán. She's wonderful but I'm in love with someone else."

"Well, thank God for that. Come on, Steph. Looks like you're stuck with me."

"Damn. And I thought I was finally going to be able to trade you in for a younger model."

Seán smacked her bum and pushed her into the dining-room. "Move, wench. Wait until I get you home."

"Promises, promises," Steph said giggling. "How are *you* getting home, Liz?"

"Oh, Edward said he'd drop me," she said casually.

Steph rounded on her partner. "Did he now? You better look after my friend," she said, wagging her finger at him.

"I will," he promised. "I'll call you tomorrow, Steph. Congratulations."

"Congratulations yourself," she said returning his kiss. "But I won't be here tomorrow. I'm taking a day off."

Seán pretended to faint. "A day off? Are you OK?"

"I'll live," she said, smiling faintly.

Through a haze of alcohol, Seán realised that something important was happening tomorrow. He slipped an around her and hugged her tight to his side. "Let's go home," he said softly.

Steph kissed Liam, Brian, Pat and John. She told Liam she'd call him in the morning and as the only sober one left, he promised to lock up.

"Check all the ashtrays and bins," she said.

"I will," Liam promised. They'd all got a bit paranoid in their safety measures and it wasn't unusual for Liam to walk the restaurant twice checking for fire hazards.

"Goodnight then, Liam and thanks for doing such a great job." She hugged him again and got into the taxi.

CHAPTER FIFTY

Stephanie was sound asleep when Seán left for work the next morning. He was dying to talk to her about her session with Joan McCann but he didn't have the heart to waken her. He'd got no sense out of her the night before. She'd fallen asleep in the taxi and he had to almost carry her up to bed. Maybe he'd come home and take her out to lunch. The thought of food made him groan. Still, after some coffee he'd probably feel a bit more human.

Steph heard the front door close and hopped out of bed. After a quick shower, she dried her hair, put on a pair of faded levis, a heavy cotton shirt and leather ankle boots. She applied her make-up quickly and carelessly and ran downstairs. After dumping her mobile phone into her large brown leather shoulder-bag, she grabbed her suede jacket and ran out the door.

Joan McCann only lived five minutes away but Steph

headed in the opposite direction. She made two stops. The first to collect scones and soda bread, still warm from the baker's oven and the second, to pick up a bouquet of pink roses. She checked her watch. Almost ten o'clock. That wasn't too early. Fifteen minutes later she stood on the small doorstep and rang the doorbell.

"Stephanie!"

"I'm sorry, Mrs McCann. Is it too early?"

"Not at all, love. I've been up for hours. I've no reason to now, but I can't seem to get out of the habit. Come along in."

Steph smiled as she followed her into the small kitchen. This was much more familiar territory. The number of times she'd sat in here, drinking milky coffee, fantasising about the future, moaning about teachers and homework, or wondering what to wear to the dance on Saturday night. "I brought you these." She put the scones and bread on the table and handed the flowers to the older woman.

"Oh, thank you, dear. I do love roses." She looked in the bag. "And scones! Lovely! I haven't baked in ages. I suppose it's because I had to do so much of it over the years. I'll make a cup of tea and we'll have some."

A few minutes later, Steph, biting hungrily into a thick slice of bread smothered in butter, looked up to see Joan McCann smiling at her.

"This takes me back. In that outfit you look like a schoolgirl."

Steph rolled her eyes. "I don't feel like one, but sitting in this kitchen does bring back a lot of good memories."

"Was she happy then?"

Steph was surprised by the question. "Yes, yes she was," she said. "She was so sure of what she wanted to do, where she was going. She had so many plans."

"She couldn't wait to move out," Joan said sadly.

"Only because she needed some privacy from the other kids," Steph assured her. "It was nothing to do with you. She loved you. She loved you all."

"She was a good girl and I know that I didn't give her enough time, but it was so hard . . . "

"And she knew that." Steph squeezed her hand. "She was so grateful that you were prepared to put her through university. She knew how difficult that was for you both and it meant an awful lot to her. She was always talking about the things she'd buy you when she got her first pay cheque." She thought for a moment. "I think it was going to be a fur coat for you and a remote-control colour television for her dad."

"I don't think she'd have been able to afford all that on one salary cheque!" Joan McCann laughed, but her eyes were bright with tears.

"Oh, she would. With the job she was planning to get it would have been no problem. She'd have done it too," she added quietly.

"Yes, I do believe she would. How long had she been seeing Des?"

Steph considered the question. She'd met Seán just before Des arrived on the scene. "They would have been going out for eight or ten months, I think."

Joan shook her head. Even after all this time, it was hard

for her to accept that her daughter had been sleeping with her boyfriend. They'd hardly known each other. Eight months! It was nothing! Ruth had never told them about Des, never mind brought him home. The first time they'd heard of Des Healy was after Ruth died. "I wish I'd met him," she said with a heavy sigh.

"Really?" Steph was surprised. She'd only seen Des once since Ruth died and she could hardly bear to look at him.

"Yes. Peter shouldn't have kept those letters from me, it wasn't right."

"I'm sure he was just trying to protect you."

"He couldn't protect me from lying awake at night wondering where I'd gone wrong," Joan said bitterly. "Why my brilliant, beautiful daughter couldn't face the thought of living. Why she couldn't turn to me, her mother."

"Don't think like that, Mrs McCann, please." Steph looked at the distraught woman, her own eyes filling up. "If anyone should feel guilty it should be me. I'm the one that let her down."

"What do you mean?" Joan wiped her eyes and looked at Stephanie curiously.

Steph took a deep breath. Finally the time had arrived. Finally she had to admit to Ruth's mother how she'd let her down. "She called me that day. The day she died," she said playing nervously with a teaspoon. "She wanted me to come over, but I wouldn't. I told her I had a date. That I'd meet her for lunch the next day." Her voice broke.

"Oh, is that all?" Joan said, almost cheerfully.

Steph looked at her in surprise. "But I let her

down. If I'd gone around to the flat she'd be alive today."

"Now you're just being silly," Joan said briskly. "You might have stopped her doing it that night, but she would have done it eventually."

"That's what Mam said," Steph said faintly.

"Then you should listen to your mother, Stephanie. She's a sensible woman. I've talked to a lot of people about this. The hospital sent a counsellor out to see me. She was a very kind lady. She explained that Ruth had probably been planning the suicide for some time. And Mary says that she'd been very calm and controlled on the Saturday."

"But I talked to her on the Sunday and she was very down." Steph protested. Why the hell had she said that? She was supposed to be comforting Ruth's mother, not adding fuel to the fire.

"I understand that, Steph," Joan said patiently. "All I'm saying is that it's unlikely it was a sudden decision. She may not have intended to do it that actual night, but it was probably on her mind for awhile."

"I still wish I'd been there," Steph said stubbornly.

"Of course you do. That's only natural. I wish she'd felt she could come and talk to me. But we can't wish our lives away, Stephanie. It happened a long time ago. I've got the rest of my family and my grandchildren to think of and you've got your whole life ahead of you. Ruth would want you to live it."

A sudden realisation hit Stephanie. She'd thought Ruth was planning an abortion. But that hadn't made sense, even then. Ruth was dead against abortion. It was never a consideration. Steph couldn't believe her own stupidity in swallowing the line Ruth had fed her. She'd known, that night as they talked on the phone, what she was going to do. Like Mrs McCann said. She probably just hadn't decided when.

Steph felt all her control slip away and great, racking sobs engulfed her.

Joan patted her hand and left the room.

Steph gave in to the tears and it was several minutes before she got her feelings under control. She was dabbing helplessly at her eyes with a sodden tissue when Joan McCann returned.

Joan smiled tenderly at her. "You'll be all right now, love. Sometimes it's good to cry. Now I hope this won't upset you even more, but I thought you should see it."

She put a pale pink envelope on the table in front of Stephanie.

"What is it?" Steph looked nervously at the envelope.

Joan looked at her expectantly. "I think you should read it. It might help."

Steph picked up the envelope and slipped out the sheet of pale pink notepaper. She gasped as she unfolded it, immediately recognising the distinctive slanting style of Ruth's handwriting.

Dear Mam, Dad,

Please forgive me for doing this. It seems the only answer — I can't explain why. I'm pregnant and life as an unmarried mother is not the future I'd planned for myself. I can't do what he wants me to do. I know that he doesn't really love me. Not the way I want him to. It's not his fault. It's not really anyone's fault. It's just the way it is.

I'm sorry I've disappointed you and I'm sorry the money you invested in me has been wasted – I wish there was another way.

I love you both. You're the best parents in the world – please forgive me. Tell everyone I'm sorry.

Ruth.

"He wanted her to have an abortion, didn't he?" Joan said quietly.

"Yes," Steph admitted. "Ruth said she wanted it too but obviously that was a lie."

"The poor lad. No wonder he couldn't live with himself. His only fault was that he was a young man who didn't love his girlfriend as much as she loved him. I can't say I approve of him making love to Ruth, but then I suppose all young men are the same. I've written to his sister. Asked her to come and visit me. She must have gone through a terrible time. And his poor parents."

Steph looked at her. "You're so kind, thinking of everyone else."

Joan shrugged. "I just want to fill in the blanks. I want a full picture of Ruth's life. I want to know as much as possible. Somehow, the more I learn, the closer I feel to her. That's really why I wanted to talk to you. You seemed to know her better than anyone. I want you to talk to me about her. Tell me everything. Does that sound silly?"

Steph shook her head. "No, it sounds very sensible. I've

spent the last fifteen years trying to push her out of mind. I didn't want to talk about her or think about her, and when I did, I just felt guilty for letting her down and hated Des Healy for letting her down too." Steph put her head in her hands and started to cry again.

Joan moved closer and put an arm around her shoulders. Steph cried harder. She cried for Ruth, for Des for Joan and for herself. And then she thought of her baby and Ruth's and cried even harder.

Joan rocked her, smoothed her hair and made comforting noises, and Steph cried on. When the sobs finally abated, to be replaced by hiccups and sniffs, Joan left her and returned a moment later with a bottle of brandy and two glasses.

"It's a bit early," Steph protested half-heartedly.

"Nonsense. It will do us both good." Joan poured two large measures and put one glass into Steph's hands. "Let's drink to Ruth."

Steph looked at her. "To Ruth," she agreed solemnly and took a gulp of the fiery liquid.

"Good girl," Joan said and tossed down half of her drink. "Now I think you should tell me about you. I don't believe all of those tears were for Ruth."

Steph sighed and told her everything.

"You poor pet," Joan said when she'd finished. "You're too young to have such heartache. But you *will* be a mother someday. And you'll be a good one."

Steph laughed shakily. "I'm not so sure."

"Well, I am," Joan said firmly. "And it sounds like you have a wonderful man too."

Steph smiled. "He is. I don't know why he's put up with me."

"He loves you. But it's time you sorted things out with him."

"You're right I . . . " She was interrupted by her mobile phone. "Sorry," she said, rooting in her bag for the offending instrument. "Hello? Oh, Seán."

Joan beamed at her.

"Lunch? Oh well . . . "

"Go," Joan commanded.

Steph smiled. "OK. What time? Right. I'll meet you there. Bye, love." She put down the phone and smiled. "He must be psychic."

"You go and meet him. Tell him what we've talked about."

"But I haven't told you anything yet . . . " Steph started to protest.

"We'll talk another day. I think you've enough to think about for the moment and I can wait. We have all the time in the world."

"Well, is it OK if I come back tomorrow?"

"Drop in anytime. But only on one condition. Call me Joan."

Steph laughed. "OK. Joan." On impulse she leaned over and hugged her. "Thank you."

"For what?"

"Listening, understanding. I feel better than I have done in a very long time."

"I'm glad to hear it, love. Now go and meet Seán and bring him to meet me sometime."

"I will. You'll like him."

"I'm sure I will." Joan waved as Steph pulled away from the kerb and disappeared out of view. She went back inside and took up the pink envelope, stroked it gently and kissed it. "Rest in peace, my love. Rest in peace."

CHAPTER FIFTY-ONE

Liz put down the phone after calling both Chez Nous and the house and wondered where Steph was. Her mobile was off or out of range, so God only knew where she'd got to. Liz looked at the papers in front of her, frustrated that she couldn't reach her friend and congratulate her. There were two write-ups and a wonderful photograph of Conor, Steph and Edward and they hadn't been expecting anything until the Sunday supplements. She picked up the phone again and dialled Edward's office. She'd never called him there before, but today was different, she decided. She just had to talk to him! She felt herself blushing as his secretary asked her name. Dammit, this was ridiculous!

"Hello, Liz. How are you this morning?"

"A little fragile," Liz admitted. "How about you?"

"Once I had four Alka-Seltzer and three cups of coffee, not bad. Have you seen the papers?"

"Yes. That's why I called. Wonderful, isn't it?"

"It seems to have gone well."

Liz laughed. "God, you're the master of understatement, do you know that?"

"I'm a lawyer," Edward pointed out. "Listen, I was going to try and get hold of Stephanie, meet for a drink or something to celebrate. Will you come?"

"I've been trying to get hold of her, but she seems to have vanished off the face of the earth. When and where did you want to meet?"

"I thought between five and six at the Merrion. Don't worry about Steph. I'll get hold of her."

"Fair enough. You can count me in."

"When's Lucy coming home?" The little girl had been spending her mid-term break with her dad. In a rare moment of consideration, Chris had offered to take her so that Liz could enjoy the opening.

"She'll be back on Saturday."

"Mmnn, and have you any jobs on between now and then?" Edward asked thoughtfully.

"No, as it happens, I don't."

"Then I think we'll have to get Cinders out to enjoy herself. Why don't you put on your glad rags this evening and we'll have dinner in Guilbaud's?"

"You're pushing the boat out, aren't you?"

"Well, we're celebrating, remember?"

"OK. You've talked me into it. I'll see you in The Merrion."

"Great, I'll be there from five. Bye, Liz." Edward put down the phone and buzzed his secretary. "Louise? See if you can pull a few strings and get me a table in Guilbaud's for two people at eight, will you?"

Louise smiled. "No problem. I'll take care of it."

* * *

Seán poured more sake into Steph's cup.

"Don't," she protested. "I'm half drunk as it is."

He topped up his own cup. "So what? We've a lot to celebrate."

"We're meeting Edward and Liz to celebrate," Steph reminded him. "But at this rate, I'll be ready for bed by seven."

Seán grinned wickedly. "All part of my plan. Don't worry. We'll go for a walk to sober up."

"But it's freezing!"

"All the better. You'll be ready for a hot whiskey by the time we get to the hotel."

Steph looked down at her jeans and shirt. "I have to go home first. I can't go out looking like this. Not to the Merrion."

"You look fine."

"No, I don't. You're just saying that."

"OK, well how about we go into the Blackrock shopping centre and I'll buy you something more suitable."

Steph raised an eyebrow. "Now that's very generous of you. What are you after?"

"I've already told you that."

She laughed. "Well, thanks, but I'd really prefer to go home and grab a shower."

"In that case, woman, drink up."

"OK, but first, a toast."

"To Ruth?" he asked gently.

"No, not this time." They'd toasted Ruth and, unbelievably, Des Healy a number of times already. "This time I'd like to drink to us and to our future."

"I can think of nothing I'd rather drink to. To us and the future."

"*Our* future," Steph corrected and emptied her cup.

* * *

Three hours later, looking very chic in a black wool dress with a high neckline and a short skirt, Steph walked into the bar of the Merrion. Edward and Liz were already there.

"Steph! Congratulations! Isn't it wonderful?" Liz hugged her friend.

Steph smiled and returned the hug. "It's great," she agreed. "Oh, champagne, lovely. How are you, Edward?" She kissed his cheek and sat down beside Liz.

"Feeling a lot better than I was this morning."

"You and me both," Seán sat down in the armchair beside him.

Edward poured them some champagne and lifted his glass. "To Chez Nous."

"To Chez Nous," they chorused.

"You look wonderful, Steph." Liz studied her friend closely. Steph always looked great, but tonight she was almost glowing.

"Thanks very much. You don't look too bad yourself. I thought we were only meeting for a drink?"

Steph was studying her friend. She looked stunning in a red velvet dress that was quite simple in style but had a daringly low neckline.

"We're going on to dinner in Guilbaud's," Edward said casually.

"Very nice. We'll come too," Seán announced.

Steph kicked him. "Maybe they don't want company."

Liz flushed. "Of course we do. Edward?"

"Certainly." He stood up. "I'll go and see if I can arrange it."

"You've spoiled everything, Seán! I'm sure Edward wanted to have Liz all to himself."

"Stephanie," Liz said warningly.

"Sorry." Steph smiled brightly at her.

"Have you just found out you've won the lottery or something?" Liz hadn't seen her friend this relaxed and happy in quite a while.

Steph glanced at Seán. "Well, let's say I've laid some ghosts to rest today. I went to see Ruth's mother," she explained.

"Oh," Liz said, at a loss for words.

"It seems I got a few things wrong. I got Des all wrong."

Liz frowned. "What do you mean?"

"Well, it looks like he had a conscience after all. He's dead, Liz. He committed suicide too. It seems he couldn't handle Ruth's death."

"Oh, God. Two lives. What a waste."

Seán nodded. "It *is* terrible. I was never one of Des's biggest fans, but I can't help feeling for the guy. He must have been in an awful way."

Edward arrived back to a brooding silence. "Did I miss something?" he asked lightly, sitting down.

"We were just remembering some old friends. They're dead now."

"Oh, I'm sorry. But come on, folks. This is a celebration."

Seán held out his glass to be topped up. "You're right. So did you manage to squeeze us in for dinner?"

"I certainly did."

"I haven't stopped eating and drinking all day," Steph complained. "If we continue this my liver will be shot by Christmas."

"No, no. Champagne has healing properties. It's really very good for you."

"I'd like to believe that, Edward, but I'd say that's a rumour started by Moet & Chandon's PR man."

Seán shook his head. "You're a terrible cynic, woman."

"Well, it's certainly making *me* feel a lot better," Liz said happily.

"Until tomorrow," Steph said darkly.

"Oh, I don't care. I don't have to get up and get Lucy off to school and I don't have another job for a week."

"Good woman," Edward said and ordered another bottle of champagne.

After a wonderful dinner and several more drinks, Steph and Seán fell into a taxi and headed for home.

"You all right, love?"

Steph struggled to keep her eyes open. "Yes, wonderful," she said sleepily.

"You're a different person tonight, do you know that?"

"Am I?"

"Yes, you are. You're very relaxed. I think that chat with Ruth's mam has done you the world of good. I know it made you sad, but even so . . . "

"You're right. I do feel better. I'm not sure why. I

suppose it's the fact that Des must have cared after all. And as for Ruth. Well, I wouldn't have been able to change her mind, would I?"

Seán hugged her close to him and kissed her forehead. "No, love. You wouldn't."

She looked up at him. "I really love you. You know that, don't you?"

"I know that," he said softly. "And I love you too."

Steph woke at six the following morning. She lay quietly for a moment, listening to Seán's breathing and reliving the day before. Seán's arm was draped across her and she moved it gingerly before slipping out of bed as quietly as possible. She picked up her handbag and padded down to the kitchen in her bare feet.

After putting on a large pot of coffee – they were both going to need it – she inspected the contents of the fridge. Excellent. Eggs, bacon and some white pudding. That would do. She switched on the radio and the grill and hummed along to Boyzone as she worked. While the food sizzled on the grill, she made a pile of toast and broke two eggs into the frying pan. She served up the food onto two warmed plates and set a tray. Then she took the small box out of the pocket in her handbag. It had been sitting in there for quite a while now. It was about time it saw the light of day. Steph opened the box and smiled down at the contents. Yes, this was definitely the right time. She'd never been so sure of anything in her life.

She carried the heavily laden tray upstairs, set it down on the dressing-table and opened the curtains.

Seán groaned. "Oh, God. What time is it?"

"Seven."

"Oh hell. Ring the teacher and tell him that Seán is too sick to go to school today, will you?"

Steph laughed. "I certainly will not. There'll be no skiving off in this house. What a bad example to set for your son. Now sit up. Breakfast will sort you out."

Seán sat up and brightened as Steph put the tray down in front of him. "Mmnn. What did I do to deserve this?"

Steph sat up on the bed beside him. "Well, quite simply. You're the most wonderful man in the world and I love you."

Seán stared at her, his eyes tender. "I am?"

"You are. Now, there's something I'd like to ask you."

"Yes?" He looked at her curiously.

She handed him the box.

Seán looked at the box in his hand and then back at her face.

Steph looked at him nervously. "Well, open it," she urged.

Seán opened the box and stared down at the platinum signet-ring.

Steph took a deep breath. "Seán? Will you marry me?"

Seán stared silently at the ring.

"Say something, for God's sake," she whispered desperately.

He dragged his eyes away from the ring and looked up into her face with such love that she almost gasped.

"Yes."

"What?" she said.

"I said yes. Yes, I'll marry you. Yes, I love you. Yes, I want to spend the rest of my life with you."

He reached for her, almost toppling the tray and all its contents.

Steph saved it, laughing shakily. "Careful."

Seán moved the tray on to the bedside table and took her in his arms. "Are you sure, Steph?" His eyes searched her face, and he smoothed back the blonde tendrils tenderly.

She looked into his eyes and nodded. "I'm very sure, Seán. Now, don't waste all my hard work. Eat your breakfast."

"It seems a bit unromantic to eat after a proposal."

Steph gave him a lingering kiss. "Rubbish. You're going to need your strength. Why do you think I woke you early?"

"I see," Seán piled bacon and egg on to a slice of toast. "So this is the shape of things to come."

"Are you complaining?"

"No, no. Not at all." He finished his toast and slid the ring on to the third finger of his right hand.

"Not on your left?" Steph asked frowning.

"No. That's where my wedding ring will go."

"Oh. Will you wear one?"

He looked surprised. "Of course I will. I have to make it clear to the legions of women that chase me that I am no longer available."

Steph raised an eyebrow. "Legions, eh?"

"Certainly. This will break a lot of hearts."

"Tragic," Steph said drily. "How do you think Billy will take it?"

"I think he'll be delighted. At least now he'll be able to come and visit."

"What?"

"Oh, shit. That just slipped out."

"Tell me." Steph ordered, pushing the tray away.

Seán sighed. "Karen wasn't too keen on Billy visiting while we were just living together. She thought it would be sending the wrong message, contradicting everything she'd taught him."

"That's a bit narrow-minded in this day and age," Steph retorted.

"Steph. She was only doing her best for Billy."

Steph nodded. She knew he was right. She might have suspected Karen's motives if it wasn't for Mike, but now that *he* was on the scene she was pretty sure Karen didn't have a hidden agenda. She smiled up into his worried face. "Then we better get married soon, hadn't we? And you better get started on the attic."

Seán pulled her into his arms and kissed her soundly. "You are the most amazing woman, do you know that?" he said when he came up for air.

"No. But I do know I am a very lucky woman. You've been very patient with me, Seán. I've led you a merry dance for quite a while now. Thanks for not giving up on me."

"I didn't have a choice," he said simply. "There's no other woman for me, Stephanie. You're my life."

Her eyes filled up and she hugged him fiercely. They cuddled and talked for a while until Steph caught sight of the time. "I suppose you should go and shower. You'll be late."

"But I'm the boss."

"The boss with a lot of responsibilities. A wife and one son – so far."

Seán's eyes lit up. "I'd love us to have a family, Steph."

"So would I," she admitted.

"Really? I wasn't sure you'd want to after . . . "

"The miscarriage? I didn't, Seán. I'll never forget my baby, but it's time to move on, now."

He kissed her, a long, warm, sweet kiss and then he pulled her down in the bed with a grin. "Let's start trying now."

"Seán, *don't!*"

"Don't what? Do this?' He kissed her neck. "And this," he kissed her throat. "And this." His head moved down to her breast and she gave a small groan.

"Well, *maybe . . .* "

EPILOGUE

"She'll murder us," Liz said for the umpteenth time as she surveyed the buffet with a critical eye.

She stood with Annie in the kitchen doorway, where she could keep an eye on her little sister, Cathy, who was acting as lookout.

"Of course she won't," Annie said cheerfully. "Every bride secretly wants a hen party."

"Not Steph."

"Oh, as soon as we get a couple of glasses of champers down her throat, she'll be fine. Is everyone here?"

Liz looked into the other room. "Think so." She'd opened the doors between the living-room and the dining-room and the doors to the garden so that there was plenty of room, and air. It was a beautiful balmy June evening and several women were sitting in the garden enjoying the evening sunshine.

Annie helped herself to a smoked salmon sandwich. "I never thought this day would come."

Liz grinned. "Yeah, hard to believe she's finally going to take the plunge, isn't it? I'd almost given up on her."

"You *and* Seán. These sandwiches are lovely, Liz. My God, it's great having a mate in the catering business."

"Thanks – I think. It was so funny yesterday. Steph dropped in and I was right in the middle of getting everything ready. I had to pretend I was catering for a party *last* night. But you know Steph. She wanted to know who, where, when. I was sure she was going to twig what we were up to."

"She's here!" Cathy squealed excitedly.

Liz ran to the front window. "OK, everyone keep quiet." She closed the door on them as the doorbell went. She waited a moment and then opened the door. "Hi, Steph."

"Hiya, Liz. How are you?" Steph hugged her friend and stood back to look at her. "You look very flushed. I hope you haven't gone to any trouble."

"No, no. Annie's inside. You go on in and I'll just check on things in the kitchen."

Steph eyed her suspiciously. "OK." She pushed open the living-room door and then took a step back in surprise at the throng of women standing smiling at her.

"*Surprise!*"

"Oh my God," she muttered, but no one heard her as they broke into a chorus of *I'm Getting Married In The Morning*.

Annie kissed her and shoved a glass of champagne into her hand. "Try and look like you're enjoying yourself."

Steph pasted a smile on her face. "I suppose this was all *your* idea."

"Me?" Annie's green eyes twinkled.

Steph was about to say more but she was dragged off into the middle of the room and was immediately surrounded.

"Hello, Stephanie. Congratulations."

"Joan!" Steph's eyes widened when she saw Ruth's mother standing in front of her.

"I hope you're going to be very happy. I'm sure you will. Seán's a lovely man."

Steph and Seán had visited her a few times and attended a memorial service for Ruth. Steph had cried her heart out but felt remarkably better after it. "You're coming to the wedding?"

"Oh, I wouldn't miss it, love. And Celine thinks all of her birthdays have come together. She says it's going to be the wedding of the year. She has me driven mad talking about hats."

Steph laughed. She'd told Joan to bring a partner and Joan had decided to give her daughter a break from her two boisterous babies.

"I don't think she's too impressed." Liz watched Steph nervously.

"She's having a ball," Annie assured her. "You take care of the food and I'll take care of her glass. She'll have the night of her life."

Steph moved from one group to another, glad that at least Liz had only invited family and close friends. "Hi,

Mam." She plonked down on the sofa beside her mother. "You could have warned me."

Her mother looked at her, her eyes twinkling. "And spoil the lovely surprise?"

Steph glared at her. "Are you sure you're not *Annie's* mother?" She took a sip of champagne. "Well, at least I know things won't get out of hand if you're here. No more funny surprises."

"Oh dear. And I only came because I wanted to see the stripper." She burst out laughing at the expression on her daughter's face. "Enjoy yourself, love," she added gently. "You deserve it. You're going to be so happy."

Steph hugged her. "Yes. I think I am."

It had been a wonderful few months. She'd gone to Cork with Seán for a few days before Christmas and they'd spoiled Billy rotten while they were there. They'd even had a meal out with Karen and Mike and it had been surprisingly enjoyable.

Chez Nous had got two more reviews, and both were complimentary. And the icing on the cake had been the publication of the Michelin guide in February. Not only had they held on to their star, but their general rating had gone up a notch too. Conor had been over the moon. The only sad point had been when Marc had decided to go home to France. He'd been offered a *sous-chef* position in an outstanding restaurant in Lyons and Steph had wished him well. She knew that she'd hear his name in the future. He was going to be a fine chef. Conor had brought in Gerry Lynch – another old mate – to take over and he was settling in nicely.

* * *

The party was in full swing when Steph slipped upstairs with Liz for a natter. Steph sat, trying to focus on her reflection in the mirror of Liz's dressing-table while Liz stretched out on the bed.

"You're not annoyed with us, Steph, are you?"

Steph glared at her. "I bloody well am. But, I'm enjoying myself anyway," she added with a grin.

"Oh, good." Liz was relieved. Edward had thought they were mad planning a surprise party.

"She'll hate it," he'd warned her. "She may even walk out."

Liz told Steph.

Steph looked horrified. "I'd never do that on you, Liz. Don't mind him. He was just winding you up."

"Probably. It won't be the first time."

"You two are getting on really well, aren't you?"

"We're doing OK," Liz said loftily.

Annie put her head around the door. "What are you two doing up here? You're supposed to be circulating."

"I'm not *supposed* to do anything I don't want to," Steph said, pickling up a bottle and topping up her glass. "It's my party, isn't it?"

"And you'll cry if you want to? Fair enough." Annie grinned and hoisted herself up onto the bed beside Liz. "So any second thoughts yet?"

"Annie!" Liz looked shocked.

Steph smiled. "None."

"That's not natural," Annie insisted. "I had second, third and fourth thoughts."

"My poor brother."

"He's done all right." Annie grinned smugly.

Steph climbed over her and sat down between the two of them, carefully filling up the glasses. "Well, *I've* no doubts. None at all. Mind you, we've known each other fifteen years. If I don't know what I'm getting into by now, I never will."

Liz put an arm around her and gave her a sloppy kiss. "I think it's brilliant. Seán's always been nuts about you." She lifted her glass. "To a wonderful day and a wonderful life."

"Here, here," Annie said, downing her champagne and hiccuping.

Steph giggled. "You're drunk."

"I'm not. Just happy."

"I've seen you happy before," Liz remarked. "It's usually just before you pass out."

"Rubbish."

"Listen, you two. Seriously. I just want to say thanks. For everything. You're very good friends."

Annie waved her hand magnanimously. "No problem. We love you. Don't we, Liz?"

"We do, we do," Liz agreed, smiling vaguely.

"Thas nice," Steph said, struggling to focus on them.

"We'd better go down." Annie curled up more comfortably on the bed.

"Umm." Steph slid down beside her, slopping some champage. "We'll go in a minute.

"Right."

"After I tell you my joke. Is a great joke. A man and a giraffe walk into a bar . . . "

Liz snorted into a pillow and Annie groaned.

"And he said to the barman. A pint for me and a pint for the giraffe . . . "